# ASSIGNMENT—SLAVERY!

Terril, one of the most powerful empaths known to humankind, had faithfully served the human Confederation government on mission after dangerous mission. And each time, the cost of serving had proved higher than the last. Now, without her consent and for reasons unknown to her, she had been stolen from the one world where she had actually begun to make a life of her own with a man she could love

And suddenly Terril was faced with the most desperate encounter of her career. For she and many of her fellow Primes had fallen into the hands of a group of fanatics out to betray all that the Confederation and its Prime Agents stood for—a group determined to use Terril and her comrades to create an unbeatable weapon with which to conquer the galaxy!

**SHARON GREEN**
**has written:**

THE REBEL PRINCE

THE FAR SIDE OF FOREVER

LADY BLADE, LORD FIGHTER

*The Terrilian Series*

THE WARRIOR WITHIN
THE WARRIOR ENCHAINED
THE WARRIOR REARMED
THE WARRIOR CHALLENGED
THE WARRIOR VICTORIOUS

*The Jalav: Amazon Warrior Series*

THE CRYSTALS OF MIDA
AN OATH TO MIDA
CHOSEN OF MIDA
THE WILL OF THE GODS
TO BATTLE THE GODS

*The Diana Santee Series*

MIND GUEST
GATEWAY TO XANADU

# THE WARRIOR VICTORIOUS

SHARON GREEN

DAW BOOKS, INC.
DONALD A. WOLLHEIM, PUBLISHER
1633 Broadway, New York, NY 10019

Cover art by Ken Kelly

DAW Book Collectors No. 737.

**FOR: MARIAN STENSGARD**
**LONI LITT**
**CATHY PALEY**

**In thanks for their warm, supportive comments on Terry V.**

First Printing, March 1988

1 2 3 4 5 6 7 8 9

Printed in the U.S.A.

# 1

The room was extremely clean, but also suffered from other sorts of extremes. For one thing, it was small and very bare and had no windows or closets or furniture except for the narrow bed—

For one thing. I stopped pacing and sat on the edge of the high bed, putting a hand to my head. Ever since I'd awakened in that tiny cell of a room my mind had been acting strangely, flying in all directions trying to get a grip on the reality I'd been dropped into from somewhere. At least I thought it was reality, but I wouldn't have bet anything valuable on the possibility. I'd never seen a room like that before, with nothing in it but a bed, stark white ceiling and walls, and a warmly resilient matching white floor. Even the bed frame was rounded and very soft, made of something other than metal, and there had to be a door somewhere even if I couldn't find it. The light was artificial and came from nowhere and everywhere, letting me see the thin white—garment—I'd awakened in. The thing had a round neck and sleeves that almost reached my elbows, but didn't go down any farther than the middle of my thighs. It closed with a full-length frontal tab and didn't *quite* show my otherwise naked body through its thin fabric, but I didn't feel cold in it. The room was more than warm enough, no drafts and not stuffy and—

"Okay, enough of that," I told myself aloud, the faintest touch of annoyance easing the terrible fear that had gripped me as soon as I'd opened my eyes. "You don't know where you are or what's happening, but you should remember what went on before you reached this point. Start with that, and see if you can work your way up to the present."

I took a deep breath, realizing I'd given myself good advice, but bringing back the past might not prove to be done as easily as said. It somehow didn't feel as clear to me as it should have, and until then I'd been afraid to touch the fabric of it, half anticipating an immediate crumbling if I did. Right then I understood I really had no other choice than to try, so I lay down across the narrow bed and made the effort.

I had no trouble remembering I was Terrilian Reya, a Prime of the Centran Amalgamation who usually lived on Central. It had been quite some time since I'd been on Central, I knew that as well, which meant I must have been elsewhere Mediating for the Amalgamation. Being a Prime Xenomediator meant I traveled a lot, and I'd been doing it for a fair amount of years. Since the assignment was obviously over I must have been returned to Central, and that meant I was also turned off—

Turned off. I lay very still as that thought came to me, a thought I couldn't remember ever having had before, but one I knew beyond doubt was true. I was—turned off—from the way I was supposed to be, all my abilities taken away, but once I'd been returned to Central without that having been done. I knew I had, could almost remember the time, could almost feel how unhappy I'd been even though almost no one else had known. It had been a special reward, a reward for having done particularly well, a reward for having accomplished—

I strained to remember, my body stiff as though the effort were a physical one, but I couldn't reach through. My hand closed on a fold of the very clean bed linen that refused to come free of the bed, the resulting fist trying to act as an anchor, but it was simply no good. The memory I was after seemed locked behind a door, and scratching frantically at the door with my fingernails wasn't doing anything to open it. I needed the key, and that was one thing I didn't have.

"One thing," I muttered with a snort, finding that the faint trace of annoyance was growing toward a better supply. I was missing a hell of a lot more than one thing, and I had the sudden conviction that my memory lapse wasn't anything other than induced. I could also remember having thoughts about conditioning, and who I'd been conditioned by. Those who ran Central and the Amalgamation wanted to make sure they had a tight grip on the empaths who worked for them, so they'd—

Empaths. This time I sat up slowly, knowing that that was what *I* was. An empath. Someone who could read the emotions of others and also soothe or intensify those emotions, and even pass them on from one person to the next. I was very important to the people of the Amalgamation, I'd worked long and hard for them, and now I was about to be given the highest reward possible. I didn't yet know what that would be, but I would know soon and would be extremely grateful and delighted.

I was so shocked I couldn't even curse, and without my wanting it to the fear flared again all along my backbone. The memory I'd just found was crystal clear, no effort of any sort needed to reach it, and that could mean only one thing: I was *supposed* to reach it, and also to believe it. It had been put in my mind with the same conditioning that had covered what someone didn't want me to remember, a body of knowledge that would conceivably do him or them harm. But who could I possibly be a danger to, that they would go to such lengths to confuse and restrain me?

"They did a really good job on you, didn't they?" I muttered to myself, the annoyance beginning to return in the company of disgust. If it was the wonderful Amalgamation I was going to be all that grateful to, who else could possibly be responsible? I still didn't know why they considered me dangerous, but that was really a very minor point. A much more major one was that I shouldn't have known what they were up to, but somehow I did. Maybe that's why I was dangerous to them, because their conditioning was beginning not to work on me, and I was able to see behind the imposed facade to get a hint of the truth. Once I got all of it, the game would be over.

But that couldn't be it. I folded my legs under me and leaned my forearms on my knees, immediately seeing how wrong that was. If they'd known their conditioning wasn't working properly they wouldn't have tried using it again, not with any hope of success. And they did expect it to be a success, the very simplicity of my brand-new conviction told me that. There was nothing in it that suggested any possibility of resistance or nonacceptance, nothing that commanded obedience which might not be forthcoming. I was supposed to believe without question everything I'd been told, even the part that wasn't completely accurate. I was an empath, all right, but empaths were able to do much more than the few trifling things listed in the suggestion. Or, at least, *I* could. . . .

I straightened as another thought came to me, one that went quite a distance toward clearing up some of the confusion. I'd noticed in the first place that my memories weren't complete because of the half-memories remaining, ones that dangled without support. I'd also become aware of the conviction because it wasn't entirely true, just the way you'd notice on a chilly night a blanket that covered you only from the knees down. It was there but not complete, present but not right. It wasn't enough to keep you warm, not enough to make you believe nothing was missing. If the entire blanket had been taken you might not have known anything was gone, but with the small bit you still had—as though whoever had taken the rest of the blanket wasn't aware of the lower part—

Didn't know it was there, and therefore hadn't taken it! The realization wasn't anything like triumph, but it was enough to give me more than a dash of hope. The ones in charge of conditioning me hadn't known I wasn't turned off on my last visit home, so they hadn't suppressed the memory of the time. They also obviously didn't know I was able to do more than they thought I could, or the conviction/suggestion would have been complete enough for me to be able to accept it. All I had to do was figure out what I *could* remember, make a list of the blanks, and try to use the list to batter down the door to memory.

"Oh, is that all you have to do?" I muttered, unfolding my legs so that I could let myself fall back flat onto the bed. Since I knew I hadn't been turned off on my last visit back to Central as a reward but couldn't remember what the reward was for, that and where I'd been since were two heavy candidates for the list. With those for starters I should have been nicely on the way to remembering it all, but all I could find in my path was the thick frustration of a dead end. The memories hadn't simply slipped my mind, they'd been conditioned away, and it was going to take more than finding empty spaces to bring them back.

"So you *are* finally back among the living," a voice said suddenly, a female voice that sounded more arrogant than interested, more imposed upon than concerned. "I don't want a thousand questions from you, and I certainly won't allow any crying fits. You'll be told why you're here in due course, and until then you're to behave yourself. And don't bother putting on any airs, either. You'll find I couldn't possibly be less impressed with you."

I sat up and turned my head toward the spot the voice was coming from, finally discovering where the door to that room was hidden. Part of the righthand wall had slid back to show something of a corridor beyond, and the woman who had spoken to me stood directly in the middle of what was now a doorway. She was my height or possibly a bit smaller, had dark hair tinted with orange, and wore an expensive Alderanean day suit and short boots of a matching orange. The makeup on her face was impeccably done, a thick peach with orangy highlights and black emphasis lines, but I found myself almost as repelled by that as by her attitude. It was hate at first sight between us, but somehow that didn't bother me as much as it once would have.

"Of course you could be less impressed with me," I answered, swinging my legs over the side of the bed and getting to my bare feet. "You could be as impressed with me as I am with you. If a thousand questions are too many for you to handle, how about just one: where am I?"

"I told you your questions would be answered later," she came back, a graceful frown denting her makeup, something like faintly outraged shock in her dark eyes. "And don't you dare try taking that tone with me, not unless you want to find yourself in more trouble than you can imagine. I happen to be very important around here, and no one talks to me that way."

"If you don't even know where we are, how important can you be?" I countered, moving closer to where she stood. She *was* shorter than I, by two or three inches, and for some reason that felt very, very strange.

"Of course I know where we are," she retorted with a snort, raising her head in a superior sort of way. "We're on New Dawn, and—"

Her mouth closed again with a snap, furious annoyance twisting her face, the darkening of her skin obvious even under all that makeup. By trying to show how important she was she'd told me something she wasn't supposed to have, not that it did me any particular good. I'd never heard of a planet named New Dawn, and had no idea what it had to do with Central or the Amalgamation.

"So, we have one who thinks she's really smart," the woman said with a good deal of fury in her sneer, her right hand closed into a fist, her eyes smoldering. "We'll see how much good being smart does you once you're transferred out of here to the main complex. I know all about you, you—*Prime,* and once you're with the others you'll spend most of your time trying to attract the attention you'll need. If you don't attract it you'll spend your time crying, just the way the other oh-so-smart ones do. Just wait, you'll get yours."

"Others?" I said, beginning to get really confused again. "What others are you talking about? What is going on here?"

"I thought I told you not to bother me with questions," she replied with a smug, vindictive look, then took a step back, out into the corridor partially visible behind her. "The director has time for you now, and maybe *he'll* feel like telling you things. If you behave yourself and ask him nicely. Or maybe not, after I tell him how *I* feel about it. Probably not, since he usually listens to me, but you'll see that for yourself. Come along right now, you've wasted enough of my time."

She took her self-satisfied smirk up the corridor to the left, apparently not caring whether I followed or not. I had the oddest feeling I'd been treated that way before, by another woman in another place who had expected me to follow just because she told me to, and the memory wasn't one I enjoyed. I looked down at myself and the—*thing*—I was wearing, compared it to what the woman had on, and the odd feeling hadn't changed. The situations weren't the same, only somewhat alike, but were enough like one another that I walked out into the corridor filled with a very unusual, unexpected anger.

My new surroundings weren't much like the room I'd awakened in; the corridor was a very pale green instead of white, and there were no beds in sight. Aside from those things, however, there was a distinct similarity in that there were still no windows and artificial light lit our way. The woman led me past quite a few closed and silent doors, her pace rather slow where she walked about ten or fifteen feet ahead of me, but she wasn't taking it easy for my benefit. Someone seemed to have taught her that one must undulate when one walked, even though undulation doubled the time it took you to get somewhere. Due to that I was able to close the lead she'd started with, so that I was only just behind her when she got to a blank wall at the end of the corridor. She paused to touch her fingers to the wall on her right at about mid-body height, the movement indicating a combination of sorts rather than print identification, and then, when the wall slid aside to make a doorway, walked on through. She knew well enough that I was behind her, but still couldn't be bothered with acknowledging the fact.

The other side of the doorway brought a considerable change in my surroundings, all of it plush and luxurious. The resilient floor changed to thick carpeting, the walls now shimmered with tasteful, shifting color, works of art hung in the midst of the shimmering, and starbursts lit the tessellated ceiling with purely decorative light. True daylight came in from the window wall on the right that was designed to match the ceiling, but most of its squares were closed to top-of-head height. I would have enjoyed opening one of the large squares and looking out, but my guide was moving off to the left, toward a door of gently glowing red. To the right of that door and about thirty feet away was a second door of pink, but the glow of that one had been turned off. In common usage that meant the red door was closed on someone who was in and available to visitors, but whoever belonged to the pink door was gone off somewhere. It would have taken a lot of really deep thought to figure out who belonged to the door, but the woman I followed didn't give me the two or three seconds necessary for consideration of the matter. She walked to the red door, stroked her hand through the air in front of it, then stepped forward to enter the room beyond.

"Director Gearing, I have the newest one," she began with a sniff of distaste, standing a few steps into the room with her hand on the oblong extrusion of the door dial. "She's really quite impossible, and should be sent to the main complex immediately for strict reorientation. She actually had the nerve to insult me!"

"Now, now, Resson, you know our guests are upset when they first get here," a man's voice came, and I stepped past the woman to see him where he was just rising from behind a large, ornate desk that held nothing whatsoever. Even the woman I'd followed was taller than he, and she and I together might have made up most of his weight. He wore a conservative, well-tailored leisure suit of red with hints of gray, and despite the air conditioning of the room his round, pudgy face was sweating. It was also wearing a look of upper-class condescension, the superiority in his dark eyes turning his smooth smile into an outright lie. His brown hair was thinning quite a bit, but that didn't stop him from brushing at it with a swollen hand as he came to a stop beside the desk to stare at me.

"She wasn't upset, Director Gearing, she was rude!" the woman insisted with sullen belligerence, sending a glare of hatred in my direction. "She tried to treat me like an Eject, and I want her punished for it!"

"Calm yourself, Resson, I'll see to the matter personally," the man Gearing assured her in firm tones of authority, his tongue wetting his lips as he looked at me. "I have the situation well in hand, so you may leave us now."

The woman Resson couldn't have missed his reaction

to the sight of me, and she didn't miss it. What she did more than that, however, was resent it, and her frustrated anger quickly found the outlet it wanted so badly. Without realizing it I'd stopped in a place that kept her from closing the door and leaving the way she'd been ordered to do, and rather than asking me to move she chose a more satisfying method of accomplishing the same end. Her hand hit the middle of my back, shoving me forward, the blow so hard that I nearly went down on my face. I caught my balance with a couple of quick running steps then turned furiously to face her, the anger I'd been feeling suddenly boiling up and over. If the woman had been smart she would have left as soon as she'd accomplished her revenge, but she'd already proven that smart wasn't a word in her vocabulary. She was standing there smirking when I first turned toward her, but the smirk lasted only until I reached her. Without thinking about it I put my own hands to her shoulders and pushed, hard enough to send her flying backward and down to that plush carpeting we'd crossed so recently. She screamed in shock and fear until she hit the floor, then sat there making appalled noises of utter disbelief.

"Here now, here now, we'll have no more of that!" the man Gearing said with outraged sternness, waddling forward to break up a confrontation that was already done. "Young woman, you take yourself over to my desk right now, and Resson, you get off that floor. As soon as I'm through with the Prime, we'll have a long talk about your inexcusable behavior. I don't intend seeing anything like this ever again."

With that he closed the door on the woman who was still sprawled on the carpeting, and waddled back behind his desk to sit again. I'd been looking around in the moment or two I had until then, and had noticed that despite the richness of the furnishings and decorations in the office, the only chair it held was the one that now held the director. I was just coming to the conclusion that their hospitality toward their "guests" was the least bit on the lean side, when Gearing cleared his throat.

"Now then, young woman, I believe a word or two with *you* is in order," he said, his voice and eyes still deliberately stern. "I have seldom seen such disgraceful behavior, and I certainly have no intentions of seeing it again. When you and I are through here you will apologize to Resson, asking her to excuse your barbaric behavior. Is that clearly understood?"

"If I apologize to her, she'll only do the same thing to someone else at another time," I answered, wondering why the man was so dense that he couldn't see that. "Since I was *able* to stop her it was my job to do it, to protect others who might not be able to do the same thing. She doesn't deserve an apology, so she won't be getting one."

"My dear Prime, it happens to be *my* place to remonstrate with and discipline my underlings," he came back with a rumble of incensed anger, a heavy air of territorial protection about him. "If one of them offers you affront you report it to me, and then *I* take care of the matter. *I* am in charge here, and no one else has the authority to do the same."

"But that just means that anyone who enjoys tormenting people has only to stay out of *your* way in order to continue with the practice," I pointed out, trying to be reasonable and show him how wrong he was. "On the other hand, if they try it with someone who bounces them on their head for their trouble, they'll probably hesitate the next time before doing the same thing. They won't know, you see, if they'll be bounced again, so that will make them cautious—not to mention help to keep innocent people safe. Don't you want your—guests—here to be safe?"

He opened and closed his mouth a few times, looking like a fish trying to learn how to breathe air, and then he ended the fumbling by snapping his lips closed with a frown.

"Where in the world could you have picked up such outlandish ideas?" he demanded, close to total outrage. "I've never heard such barbaric nonsense, and I'll listen to no more of it. All you need remember is that *I* am in charge, and our future association will be an extremely pleasant one. Now then, let's get on to the reason you were summoned to my office."

"Is our conversation going to be so short that it isn't worth sitting down for?" I interrupted to ask, giving up on trying to teach him anything. He was obviously too concerned with privilege to understand right and responsibility, but I wondered fleetingly just where I *had* gotten such ideas. As soon as I had a moment, I would have to think about that. "What I mean, Director, is that if it *is* going to be that short, why are *you* sitting?"

"I am sitting, my dear, because I am director," he answered in very careful and overly sweet tones, back to giving me that condescending smile. "If you consider the matter carefully, you'll find it's quite proper for you to be standing there before me, waiting for great honor to be bestowed on you. Honor must be balanced with humility, you know, and so it shall be. The arrogance of a Prime must be left behind as you travel the road to meaningful immortality."

By the time he was through speaking, the words were echoing in my head rather than simply being picked up by my ears, and I was definitely feeling dizzy. I put a hand up to the echo, having no understanding as to why it was happening, having no idea how to make it stop. What he'd said—leaving arrogance behind and being suitably humble—humble and grateful—yes, that was the way it had to be. It was so obvious I was surprised I hadn't seen it sooner, and I suddenly couldn't wait to be given my honor.

"Yes, of course you're right," I answered, looking up at him with a smile that felt as shy as I did. "I'm sorry, Director Gearing, I must have forgotten that for a moment. Did you say—immortality?"

"I most certainly did," he agreed with a broader, warmer smile, the expansiveness of his generosity coming through clearly as he sat back in his chair. "What lesser thing might be given to one who has served the Amalgamation so well, a Prime of your quality and caliber? You've earned immortality, my dear, and that is what you will have."

"Oh, I can't possibly be worthy of that great an honor," I protested, needing to speak the truth I felt, feeling the blush in my cheeks as my fingers twisted together. "Really, Director Gearing, it's too much . . ."

"Nonsense, my dear, and do call me Johnston for the moment," he came back, a sleek smoothness coating his assurance, his eyes heavy-lidded. "I have the pleasure to inform you that you've been chosen as one of those few who are permitted to pass on your qualities and abilities to those who will come after you, those who will attempt to equal your service to the Amalgamation. We bestow this honor with glad pleasure, but also ask that you accept it as another of the many indications you've given of loyalty and dedication and selflessness. Will you accept the honor in such a way, with eagerness and gladness?"

"Eagerness and gladness, yes," I breathed, my hand to my head again as the words echoed a second time, the privilege so great that it made me dizzy. "I can't believe that *I've* been chosen for this, Johnston, I just can't, but I'll do everything in my power to be worthy of it. What must I do?"

"Quite simply, Terrilian, you must be a woman," he said, his expression now sober as he rose again and came around the desk to take my hand. "In the main complex we have quite a large number of male Primes, and it will be *your* duty to interest as many of them as possible in you. Without them you won't be able to fulfill your destiny, you know, but there are other female Primes already there, already attempting to fulfill their own destinies. You must be more attractive than they are, more beautiful and desirable to the only men who can help you achieve immortality. You must do everything and anything to attract and please them, but then, you don't have to be told that, do you? You already know that and mean to succeed, don't you?"

My head swam for a third time, but although I agreed with just about everything that had been said to me, some parts of it confused me more than others. People had always been told that there *weren't* many male Primes, so how could that complex have quite a large number of them? I wanted to ask where they could have come from, but the director was stroking my hand and then he raised it to his lips.

"It's my personal opinion that you'll have very little trouble being attractive, my dear," he said in a husky voice, my hand still held in both of his. "I know you're somewhat unsure of yourself, however, so I'm prepared to assist you even further. Although I have almost no spare time in my very busy schedule, I'm going to take some anyway just to find out how pleased the men will be with you. No, no, you needn't thank me, it can easily be considered part of my job, and you do deserve help with the honor you've been given. Just come this way."

He led me by the hand he held to the wall to the left of his desk, where he pressed a small recess which caused the wall to slide noiselessly back. Behind it was an area with low lighting, soft music, faintly perfumed air—and a very wide square of a couch draped with silk. The couch had no back to it, only seat flanked by armrests, and the man's left arm went around my waist as he urged me forward toward it. At first everything felt as right and proper as it had all along, nothing out of the ordinary except that I was about to be done a rather large favor, but then we crossed the threshold into the small, cozy room—and the director's right hand came to squeeze my breast through the thin material that covered it—and something inside me screamed that he had no *right*—that I couldn't let him—that I damned well *wouldn't* let him—and then I was pulling away and shoving at him, slapping and scratching—

When the dizziness and confusion finally receded to a point where I could look around me with some measure of sanity again, I was sitting on the carpeting of the director's office, my back against a wall that was staying solidly closed. Low, moaning sounds were coming from the desk to my left, and I turned my head to see Gearing in his chair, what must have been a mirror raised up from the side of the desk. He was staring into the mirror as he dabbed at long, bleeding scratches on his cheek with a wet cloth, and the eye toward me was blackened and almost closed. I could see that the battle in my mind hadn't been the only one I'd fought, and for a moment I was confused all over again. The struggle I'd put up didn't seem all that strange, but the results of my efforts didn't feel in any way familiar.

"Oh, I should have known you'd be one of those, I should have known," Gearing moaned, talking to me without taking his eyes from the mirror. "After what you did to Resson I should have called security immediately, but instead I relied on the conditioning holding. Now that you've broken out of it you think you've won something, but what you've really done is lost. You'll still serve the program just as you're meant to, but without the comfort of believing you're being honored. And I'm glad you'll be suffering, do you hear me? I'll come and visit where they have you, and I'll laugh!"

He ended his outburst with another moan instead of a laugh, but it didn't make that much of a difference. I put my hand up to my head as I leaned back against the wall, shivering on the inside at how close I'd come to doing and believing exactly what they'd wanted. Even after I'd found part of the conditioning myself, I'd still fallen prey to the rest of it without a murmur. I'd been so terribly eager to accept that "honor," so willing to do everything I could! The second time I shivered on the outside, but not only at what had almost been done to me. They were still going to try doing things to me, and when they did I'd have no fantasies to hide behind. I'd have to face it knowing exactly what was happening, and that was the part that made me tremble. I'd have to find the courage to be strong, and I didn't know if I could.

A moment later the door to the office opened, but instead of it being the woman Resson, two big men walked in. They both had dark hair and eyes and were dressed in identical white uniforms, but the part that made me wish I could get closer to the wall was the expression on their faces. Or, more accurately, the lack of expression. Totally uncaring is too weak a descriptive phrase, but when they saw the director they actually smiled.

"You called for security men, Director Gearing?" one of them said, his tone showing very little in the way of respect for a superior. He and the other were silently laughing at Gearing, and the way the fat man stiffened showed he knew it.

"Get her out of here," he said, still looking at nothing but the mirror, briefly waving one pudgy hand in my general direction. "Tell them she's broken through the conditioning, but that isn't to exempt her from the program. Take her to the main complex, and don't bring her back until she has to be here. By then there won't be any fight left in her."

The eyes of the two men came to me, still filled with faint amusement, and then it was they who came to me, reaching down to pull me to my feet. I tried to resist but they weren't Gearing, and then I was going through the door, on my way to what was called the main complex.

# 2

The wooden bench I sat on got harder and harder as the time passed, but no one seemed overly concerned about my comfort. I'd been pulled out of the building that housed the director's office and the room I'd awakened in, thrust into a ground vehicle, then taken for a short ride. At the end of the ride I'd been pulled from the vehicle through the same bright but chilly sunshine I'd seen a few moments earlier, thrust through a door into a building, and walked up a corridor to a particular door. The door led to an anteroom with nothing in it but a wooden bench and another closed door, and I'd been offered a seat by being pushed down onto the bench. The two men in white uniforms stood to either end of the bench, saying nothing to me and not even to each other.

Between the confusion still rattling around in my head and the dull tan and gray of the room I sat in—not to mention the presence of my two silent companions—I was beginning to feel depressed. No, what I really felt was all alone, with no one there to help me or be on my side. All of those people were from the Amalgamation, some probably even from Central, but to them I was nothing but an animal to be experimented with, a prize animal to be sure, but still nothing but a beast. I didn't want to think about what they were going to do to me, and had been helped in fulfilling that desire by the presence of other thoughts crowding my mind and demanding attention. There were so many things I couldn't explain or understand or make any sense out of at all—

"All right, go on in there," the man to my right said suddenly, and I looked up to see that the gray door the room held was now glowing with the message that visitors were welcome—or at least currently permitted. I hesitated only a moment before getting to my feet, but was abruptly aware of the thin garment I wore. The two men who had brought me there were staring at me, I knew that even without looking at them, and to say the idea disturbed me was like saying I didn't much want to fall off the roof of a twenty-story building. Once standing, I resisted the urge to try tugging the thin covering lower and went instead to the softly glowing gray door, opening it as if I really belonged there.

Inside there were a larger number of amenities to be found, like thick carpeting, stylish drapes on wide windows, chairs and couches, artwork on the walls, and a desk that actually had papers and folders on it. It was basically the same tan and gray as the anteroom, but enhanced by faint touches of other colors and softened by richer fabrics and mediums. Like the first office I'd seen the desk had a man behind it, but unlike the portly Director Gearing this man really seemed to be working. He wore a uniform rather than a suit, in a gray to match his door, and his tanned, unlined face didn't seem to go with his very white hair. He glanced up at me as I came in, his light eyes touching me in a distracted sort of way, and then he waved his hand toward the chairs in front of his desk.

"Close the door and sit down," he said, his voice as distracted as his glance had been. "I'll be with you as soon as I finish this."

For something I'd expected to be dramatic and terrorizing, his few words had been a crazy sort of letdown, as though a ravening beast had paused in its bloodthirsty attack to hastily check its pockets. I closed the door as directed and went to the chairs indicated, and actually found myself annoyed that the chair I chose was comfortable. When you're braced to resist horror, running into the humdrum instead can totally ruin your mood. I began to cross my legs, remembered what I was wearing and decided against it, then simply sat back until the man finished with the folder he was working on and raised his eyes to really look at me for the first time.

"So you're the Prime Terrilian Reya," he said, tossing

his stylus away before leaning back in his chair. "You caused us trouble when we went to pick you up, and now you're causing even more. Why couldn't you have been a good girl and behaved yourself?"

"If the choice had been mine, I still would have done it exactly this way," I answered, the annoyance I'd been feeling beginning to grow to true anger. "And if you persist in talking to me as though I were a backward child, you're suddenly going to find all those pieces of paper in the air, most of them flying at your head. You haven't the right to treat me the way you've been doing, and I demand to be released."

"If you're not a backward child, you should know you're wasting your time demanding to be released," he answered, a faint smile turning his lips. "And if you throw any of these papers at me, you'll waste a lot more time picking them up again. You're not the first Prime to break through the conditioning, Terrilian, but usually it doesn't happen quite this fast. That fool Gearing must have caused it with the itch he wanted scratched, and if he wasn't so useful I would have had him shipped back to Central a long time ago. It would have been easier for you if you'd gotten used to the routine before the conditioning went, but you're still going to have to go through with it. All of it. Do you understand what I'm saying?"

"No, as a matter of fact I don't," I said, suddenly finding his calm, patient attitude more chilling than threats would have been. "I don't understand anything of what's going on, and if you'd like the truth I don't particularly want to know. All I want is out of here, and a chance to go back to things as they were. I've worked for the Amalgamation most of my life; is that too much to ask in return?"

"It's not precisely a matter of too much," he answered, something of a shrug in his tone. "The simple fact is that the Amalgamation needs to make use of you, and has no choice in that need. They can't take someone else in your place because it's a Prime they need, not just anyone off a city street or out of a Neighborhood. And if you stop to look at this reasonably instead of emotionally, you'll find that you're getting excited over very, very little. The Amalgamation isn't asking you to have your arms and legs cut off, Terrilian, all it's asking you to do is have babies."

All. I put my hands to the chair arms as he continued to stare at me calmly and reasonably, his own hands unconcernedly crossed on the desk in front of him. I'd expected having it put that baldly to be enough to make me feel any number of things, like disgusted or vastly reluctant or even very much afraid. Surprisingly enough none of those feelings surfaced, but what I did feel quite a bit of was embarassment.

"You see?" he asked, still the most reasonable of beings. "It isn't anything vile, or obscene, or even outrageous. It's simply something that women do, and you're inarguably a woman. I'll admit we had you conditioned against wanting children while you were still a working Prime, but that was only to keep you from being contaminated by someone whose blood wasn't worthy of yours. Here we have many men worthy of you, men like yourself, the best of the breed. I'm afraid that initially the choice of who will have access to you will be theirs and ours rather than yours, but intelligent cooperation will earn you what should be a pleasant and satisfying bonus. Would you like to hear about that?"

He held the question out in front of me as though offering a special sweet, the sort that small children will do just about anything for. I think I would have been really angry if I hadn't been busy digesting that piece of information about having been conditioned in regard to reproducing, and he took my lack of open hostility for unvoiced and reluctant but active interest.

"You, of course, won't be carrying a fetus yourself for very long, only until it can be safely transferred to a host mother," he said, the explanation so matter-of-fact it could have been about accounting procedures. "Your time and genes are much too valuable to be wasted with one-at-a-time offspring, so you'll actually produce quite a number of babies in the time it normally takes to produce only one. Each child will have a different father, and the results of each pairing will be carefully kept track of for the statistics we need almost as badly as the babies themselves. The chance of a bonus comes in when you realize that after a given number of interrupted pregnancies, the exact number varying with the individual woman involved, your body will need to carry one child to term. If you've cooperated with us, when you reach that point you'll be allowed the choice of who the father of the child will be, even if it's someone who has already sired a child on you. It will be our gift to you for having helped us so much, and from past experience we know how valuable a gift it will be. Believe me when I say you'll need and appreciate something like that.''

''Oh, I do believe you,'' I said, almost disbelieving, instead, that anything that bizarre could be real. ''What I don't understand is why you're not using test tubes instead of people, or at the very least artifical insemination. If mass production is what you're after, that's the way to get it.''

''I can't deny that we tried it,'' he said, this time smiling wryly. ''It would have saved us an enormous amount of trouble if it had worked, but by the second generation we discovered we weren't getting any Primes at all. There are few enough Primes produced under normal circumstances, but *in vitro* matings seem to eliminate them completely. We haven't any idea why that should be, only that it is. That's the reason all of you is here now, not just your ova.''

''And the reason why you don't use artificial insemination?'' I asked, having my own suspicions as to the reason for their failure. ''Did that prove to be just as unproductive?''

''It proved to be undesirable,'' he answered, the faint amusement back again. ''If the female Primes have to be here in their entirety, so to speak, and the only usable sperm donors are also here in training, why deny them the pleasure of delivering that sperm to its destination themselves? It would be a waste of a good reward opportunity, and would save us very little in the way of time. In other words, there's no true reason to deny the men their fun.''

''Whether or not it turns out to be fun for the women,'' I said with a nod, finding myself completely unsurprised.

"The only thing you haven't mentioned yet is why you need that many Primes. What are they being trained *for?*"

"Only the male Primes are being trained, and the reason for that is none of your business," he said, still as friendly and pleasant as he'd been all along. "Being handed around among the fathers of your future children will be the hardest thing for you to get used to, that and the fact that their wants and desires are far more important than your own. You'll find that if you don't defer to them in every way possible they'll make your life here very unpleasant, but once you learn how to behave you shouldn't have any trouble. Your records tell me you'll have time to adjust to the system before you're ready for your first impregnation, so take advantage of the fact and work hard toward fitting in. You'll do much better for us if you're happy here, and we'll do everything we can to help you."

"Such thoughtfulness is positively awe-inspiring," I commented, this time acceding to the urge to cross my legs and not giving a damn about the length of my covering. "Of course, you've left out or glossed over a number of rather important points, such as the fact that I'll probably never be allowed to see the children I produce, or the details on what's done with the babies who aren't born as the Primes you're so eager for. I'm probably supposed to be too anxious to become one of the team to worry about things like that, but I do have what might be considered a pertinent question. What happens if I decide I want nothing to do with your team, and also decide to give as good as I get in the way of misery and unpleasantness? In other words, what if I decide *not* to be one of your brood mares, and refuse to change my mind?"

"I would seriously recommend against a decision like that," he said, a faint frown replacing the amusement he'd been enjoying. "Your file shows a penchant for troublemaking, but it also shows a definite aversion to discomfort and pain. Our trainee Primes aren't the only ones who can make life unpleasant for you here, and you'd do well to remember that. If you try to judge us all by Director Gearing, you'll find yourself making a very bad mistake. The rest of us are neither incompetent nor helpless.''

''But you're going to persist in treating *me* as though I were both,'' I said, glad we'd finally gotten to the threats even though my hands were beginning to tremble. ''You expect me to start cooperating because you've given me no choice, and then expect me to continue because I'll have gotten used to doing it your way. I can imagine the various things you're able to do to me and very frankly they frighten me, but not half as much as the thought of waking up one day to find that I'm *accepting* this—this—travesty you're perpetrating. I can vaguely remember going along with something similar to this once to keep from being terribly hurt, but I can remember even more strongly how shamed I felt. The pain is more intense but the memory of shame lasts longer, and I really don't need any more memories like that.''

By that time my voice was almost unsteady enough to match the tremor in my hands, but I'd still managed to say what I had to. The memory I'd spoken of was very distant and hard to touch, but although I couldn't reach all the details of what had happened where, my reactions had been so strong that *they* were more than clear. I waited for the man behind the desk to understand I was serious and begin to make arrangements for hurting me the way only civilized people can accomplish, but all he did was make a sound of annoyance and shake his head.

''I can see you're still too theatrically interested in saving what you consider your virtue to discuss anything rationally,'' he said, and there *was* more annoyance than anger in his voice and eyes. ''We'll get you checked over and settled in, and once you've learned our routines we'll talk again. By then you'll have learned how undramatic this all is, and that there really is nothing else for you to do but cooperate. We're not villains here, just practical people doing a practical job, one that you'll eventually be helping us with. My name is Serdin. If you need to talk to me before I send for you, apply to your sector head for a pass.''

He flicked his finger over a small, lit circle on his desk, and I knew even before the door to his office was opened from outside that I'd been dismissed. One of the two men in white uniforms was waiting calmly for me to get up and go with him, and the man Serdin had already picked up another folder and had begun losing himself in it. I got to my feet slowly, expecting to be confused over what was happening or relieved that I wasn't about to be hurt, but what I did feel was even more frightened than I'd been a moment earlier. When people mistreat you it isn't difficult to resist them and their desires, to fight them with all your strength to the very end of it, but what do you do when you throw out your most direct challenge and all they do in return is pat you on the head and send you on your way? You can grit your teeth and swear not to budge an inch, but after a while you find teeth-gritting tiring and not really necessary, and you notice how hard they're trying to help you, and they really are being very understanding, and they're not asking for anything all *that* terrible—

The shudder that ran through me was covered by my movement as I left the office, but it chilled my mind enough to keep it awake and alert, which was what I needed. If I let myself forget, even for a moment, what those people were trying to do to me, their brand of "helpful assistance" would infect me and I'd be through. I would *not* give them what they wanted, no matter how many times they patted me on the head, and that was something I would not be changing my mind about.

I was able to feel brave and dedicated while the two men in white uniforms led me through even more corridors, but when I was deposited in yet another bare anteroom, this one all pale brown, my emotions began fraying around the edges. Rather than staying with me the men had closed the door and left, and once closed in I could no longer see a way of returning to the corridor. This second anteroom had two remaining doors leading out of it, both in the wall I'd faced when I'd first come in, but both stayed closed and quietly unglowing. There were a few pale brown, plain metal chairs standing around the walls, and after five minutes of hovering and waiting for something to happen, I gave up and walked to one of them.

In which I sat and waited. After another year or so had passed, it came to me that waiting rooms had to be even more fiendishly clever in the way of torture devices than a rack, on which at least you had something to do and occupy you. After being left long enough in a waiting room, you find yourself willing to do anything to be allowed to leave it, anything at all. Tell every secret you have? Certainly! Agree to accept physical pain without struggles? No problem! Ask for immediate execution? Of course, of course, only please be sure that it isn't *boring!* I can't take any more of being *bored*. . . .

I shifted in the hard metal chair for the ten thousandth time, convinced that the wait was all part of their master plan. Why waste time and effort on trying to force people into doing things your way, when you can slide them into it once they're half asleep from boredom and no longer paying attention? In between shifting I'd been trying to understand why their careful conditioning had broken down, but I'd been too distracted by the waiting to get anywhere. When you're waiting for something to happen, you can't really concentrate on anything else; your inner mind is too afraid you'll miss an opportunity to end the wait, thereby making you wait even longer. And with some waits, you *really* can't wait for them to end.

I sat straighter in the chair, realizing I'd just touched something, the very outline of a buried memory. Once, not long ago, I'd been waiting for something to happen, something I'd needed very badly. It was also something I'd been afraid of, but I'd needed it so badly that I hadn't cared how frightened it made me. I'd lost something, something I couldn't bear to go on without, and the wait was going to end the pain of the loss for me. I could remember the trembling eagerness with which I'd waited for a particular thing to happen, willed it closer and closer, greeted it as the end to agony—but I couldn't remember what it was I'd lost. There was a large, square tear in the fabric of memory at that point, which told me with absolute certainty that the information had been conditioned away. You don't casually forget something like that on your own, not when even the softened memory is able to bring aching . . .

"I said, you can come in now," a voice broke into my thoughts, a female voice filled with annoyance. I looked up to see that the lefthand door of the two had been opened, and the woman stood in the doorway. She wore a light brown uniform and had brown hair and eyes, and seemed to have spoken to me once before without my having heard her. She was slender and fairly tall, and without the frown she might have been pretty.

"I suppose you were too busy thinking about the honor you've been given to pay attention to anything else," she added, stepping back to give me room when I rose and walked over to her. "I've noticed that that's usually the case."

"Well, it doesn't happen to be the case with me," I answered, wondering why she seemed so—distantly angry and accusing. "I told them what to do with their honor, and they smiled and told me to run along and play. If you're about to add your own excellent advice and assistance, do us both a favor and save it for someone else."

I was annoyed that she'd interrupted me when I'd been on the track of something important relating to my stolen memories, but she didn't come back at me the way I thought she would. I could almost see her blinking in surprise, and then she looked at me with more interest and a good deal more concern.

"You're not being held by the conditioning," she said in a tone of near-revelation, but not what might be called a happy tone. "I've never seen one like you coming through here, and although I thought I'd find a meeting like this satisfying, I'm afraid I'm suddenly more deeply into feeling sorry for you. Why didn't the conditioning work?"

"We're all still trying to figure that out," I responded, moving into the small office she'd come out of. "That man Serdin thinks it was because of the way Director Gearing tried to welcome me to this place, and that might even be true. When he put his hand on me I was really repelled, so much so that I fought back. Before I knew what was happening I had won the fight, and the world had suddenly changed from gilded to brassy."

"I'm not surprised to hear you were repelled by Gearing," she said, making a face as she moved past me to get back to her small desk. "He—welcomes—every non-fertile Prime brought to the facility, and they do nothing to stop him because they need his stupid arrogance as a protective facade. Maybe this time they'll at least give him a few regrets."

Her office was really tiny, with nothing but the desk and a chair for her, and one chair in front of the desk. There were a few plaques scattered around on the walls in place of artwork, but one thing she did have was a full square yard of dot storage, the largest private library I could ever remember seeing. She'd closed the door behind me so, thinking I'd be there at least as long as I'd been in the other two offices, I moved to take her guest chair. She herself had stopped beside the desk instead of sitting down behind it, and when she saw what I was doing she shook her head.

"Don't bother sitting down," she said, picking up a folder set into a clipboard. "I usually spend a few minutes adding my congratulations to everyone else's just to keep the pretense balanced, but this time it's obviously not necessary. We'll go straight to the examination and skip the small talk."

"Examination?" I echoed, not understanding the sudden flash of heavy annoyance I felt at the suggestion. "Why do I have to be examined? And why do they need Gearing as a front for them? I'd like to know what's really going on here, and why you're working for them if you're all that disapproving. If it was me, I'd leave."

"Really?" she said, raising brows with no true surprise behind the gesture. "Just the way you're leaving now because you're unhappy about being here? I didn't volunteer for this any more than you did, I was assigned to the post by my superiors. Once I learned what was going on I tried telling them I wanted no part of it, but all they did was smile and tell me to get back to work. Does that sound at all familiar to you?"

"Too familiar," I agreed with a sigh, wondering if there were more than three people on that planet who were free to come and go as they pleased. I was tempted to say she was only being forced to stay, not to cooperate, but I wanted to see first how *I* did against them before I accused anyone else of improper resistance. "They seem to have a lot of experience ignoring protests. And all that learning you did about what was really going on—It explained everything and answered all your questions?"

"Yes, it certainly did," she said, a dryness having entered her voice as she stared at me. "Unfortunately, though, it won't be doing the same for you. I don't know what they'd do to me if I started spreading around the little details of their plans, but it would undoubtedly be something to teach me the attractions of discretion. Don't underestimate them at any time, my friend. Their plans are more important to them than you or I as individuals could ever be, and they won't let anyone stand in their way. My examination room is through here."

"Here" was a door leading into another, larger room, and the woman entered it without giving me a chance to argue with her. The new room had lots of very modern equipment designed for the most thorough of diagnoses and examinations, and even if I hadn't been feeling frustrated from all the stone walls I'd been running into I wouldn't have liked it. It was the sort of place that made me feel as though I'd just come off an assembly line, one of ten thousand others just like me, nothing but a unit to be run through the next process and then sent on my way. There was nothing of the personal in that very clean, light brown room, and once again I felt the ghost of being absolutely and completely alone.

"I'm sure you know that none of this is here to do you harm," the woman said, and her voice had suddenly become kinder and more compassionate. "Let's start with a general check, shall we? It will only take a couple of minutes."

She was looking at me as though she thought I needed comforting, as though she thought I couldn't take care of myself. Other people I couldn't quite remember had thought that about me, but I'd proved to them and everyone how wrong they were. I didn't need *anyone* to take care of me, and walking over without a fuss to the table the woman had patted simply proved the point another time.

I had to take off that thin cloth smock before lying on the table, but that didn't make me any more uncomfortable than I already was. I started wondering if I were already beginning to do what they wanted by not refusing to be examined, but by the time I decided I certainly was, the top of the machine had already been closed over me. As the lights came on I thought I understood just how alert I'd have to be in the future to keep something like that from happening again, but the entire truth of that thought hadn't yet been brought home to me. The machine began to hum as the examination started, and then I was taught the lesson a bit more thoroughly.

Most physicals aren't "physical" in the least, in the sense that you aren't touched during them, not even by sensors. You're completely scoped and scanned by the machinery all around you, measured and weighed and checked for blockages and stoppages and irregularities and anything that deviates from your particular norm. If something is found the doctor in charge is alerted, and more specific testing is then done. As the woman had said, the general check doesn't usually take more than a couple of minutes, during which time you just lie there watching the pretty-colored lights blink. Most people know the lights have nothing to do with the exam; they're there to give you something to look at while you're waiting.

For me, the lights turned out to be a distraction. They drew my attention when the rate of blinking changed in a way that seemed to be *trying* to draw my attention, and as soon as I looked up at them the machine took advantage of the fact. It actually required the sound of multiple small clicks before I understood I'd been distracted for a reason, and by then, of course, it was far too late. My wrists were held firmly to the table where they lay to either side of me, my ankles were snugly looped, and a thin strand of the same material loosely circled my throat. I cried out and pulled at the bindings, unable to tell whether I was more frightened or more furious, but the material holding me was designed to resist efforts like mine. It was too soft to cut or cause any other damage, and much too strong to be parted by anything I was likely to be able to do.

Once the mechanism had me the way it wanted me, it went on with what it had obviously been instructed to do. Its very first act was to draw some of my blood, and then, even before the sting of the needle was gone, it began to check my reactions to certain stimuli. Considering what I had been brought there for I shouldn't have been surprised that my ankles first had to be separated, and I wasn't surprised. Ravening outrage was more like what I felt, but that didn't entirely negate the machine's efforts. I lay there on my back, struggling uselessly against what held me, but could still feel myself reacting faintly to what was being done to me. The sensors or probes or whatever they were felt like fingers, and seemed to have been programmed by someone who knew what he was doing. I hated being touched like that with everything in me, but for some reason that didn't keep me from reacting to it.

The testing went on for a number of minutes before stopping abruptly, a needle put something into my veins instead of taking something out, and then the bindings withdrew to wherever they had come from. Right after that the colored lights went out, which meant the hood could be raised from the table I lay on. I was about to do it myself when it was done for me, and the woman in the light brown uniform looked down at me with a plastic smile pasted on her face.

"See, I told you it would be easy," she said, offering my thin cloth smock as though it were a lounging robe being given to someone just stepping out of a bath. "Now it's behind you, and you don't have to think about it again."

I sat up and got off the table without saying anything, then took the smock without looking at anything else. I preferred the smock to being naked so I put it on, but without the help that had been offered. I'd had enough help from that woman, but at least I'd learned my lesson. From that moment on it wouldn't matter *how* compassionate anyone was; trust would be the last thing I gave them.

"Terrilian, I had no choice about doing that to you," the woman said from behind me, helpless regret heavy in her voice. "It's part of the processing every female Prime goes through here, and if you'd tried refusing they would have forced you. This way it's over and done with without the trouble refusing would bring, and without the anxiety you would have suffered. Isn't it better this way?"

I smoothed the smock closed with a single firm stroke of my hand, but didn't make any attempt to answer the woman's question. Lying to me might have made things easier for *her,* but in my opinion I should have been entitled to choose for myself. If I preferred trouble and anxiety to letting myself be taken advantage of, that was my business.

"Well, you're certainly healthy enough," the woman went on when the silence grew too thick for her, the heartiness her voice now carried an excellent match to the smile she'd worn. "You'll find participating in the program no strain at all, and it won't be long now before you can begin. Part of the injection you were given was a neutralizer meant to shorten the life span of your protection against pregnancy."

"And what was the rest of it, *friend?*" I asked in a growl, turning finally to look directly at the woman. She and I were almost the same size, so our eyes should have had no trouble meeting levelly. "Judging by everything else around here, it should have been the chemical equivalent of that happiness conditioning. What's the matter, didn't it work? —Or is it just that it hasn't worked *yet?*"

If she flinched at the harsh accusation I threw at her, I couldn't tell from looking in her eyes. The gaze that should have been level with mine wasn't, and then she was the one turned away, her shoulders rounded with whatever burdens were hers. Her hand rose to her face, probably covering her mouth for a moment or two, and then it went higher to touch her hair as she straightened.

"The main problem is that you really don't understand what you're facing," she said without turning, her voice slow and very reasonable but also audibly trembling.

"You still believe you can refuse to do what these people want, that you can be stubborn and make trouble for them and do anything you please to obstruct them, and the worst that can happen is that they eliminate you. What you *must* make yourself believe and understand is that they *won't* eliminate you, not under any circumstances, no matter what you do. They *will* keep you for and in the program, and if I let you believe anything else I'd be hurting you worse than you know. I'm supposed to be here to help people, and I want to help *you.* You're the first to come through here like an actual, living being instead of a programmed doll. If helping you means I also have to hurt you— What choice do I have— What else can I do—?"

Her words seemed to die rather than end, and her hand reached out slowly to move over a glowing circle on the wall near her. Her body had the same tremor that her voice had had, but she straightened even more and gained some control of it.

"Once you see more of this place and think about what I've told you, you'll come to understand," she said, the reassurance she groped toward more for herself than for me. "You'll know then that I really am your friend, and if you need me you won't hesitate to come. Ask for Cataran Olden in Medical, and they'll bring you to me. Don't forget, Cataran Olden."

Once again I knew when I was being dismissed, so having the door in the far wall open came as no great surprise. The white uniform was familiar enough, but this time it was being worn by a woman rather than a man. She wasn't quite the size the men had been, but she wasn't small and she wore the same nonexpression they had, making her clearly one of the breed. Her blond, untinted hair was very short, and for some reason that struck me as being wrong.

"Please take the Prime to her assigned sector," Cataran Olden said to the woman in white, handing over some sheets of paper from the folder she held. "She isn't like the others are when they first come in here, so do please try being patient with her. You will—won't you?"

The bigger woman smiled very faintly as she took the

papers, then crooked a finger in my direction. As I passed Cataran Olden I could see she was still waiting for an answer to her question, not realizing she already had her answer. I walked out of the examination room without looking back, and door was quietly closed behind me.

# 3

I was expecting another corridor outside of the examining room, but that wasn't what was there—or at least not like the previous corridors I'd seen. This one was three or more times as wide as the others, and there weren't simply doors to either side of it. There were also desks here and there along the walls, and some of them had women in smocks like mine seated in chairs beside them, talking to the people behind the desks. There were more women in smocks standing in lines farther back, and most of those looked distracted but very pleased with themselves. Four men in the white uniforms of security watched the large area casually, clearly expecting nothing to happen but nevertheless appearing fairly alert.

My own security-guide led me in the direction of the end of the lines and beyond them to a set of guarded doors, then through the doors and past what looked like another guard post. This one was at the end of a normal-type corridor, but one without any doors or desks or anything. We walked the thirty feet to the end of it, stopped in front of yet another door, and after a moment were allowed in through it to the inner sanctum. There seemed to be an awful lot of guards for a bunch of women who mostly appeared to want to be where they were, but maybe the Amalgamation simply wasn't in the mood to take chances. The far side of the door had its own set of white uniforms, and also a fork in the road. The corridors to either side curved away out of sight, and we took the one to the left.

When we rounded the curve I was able to see another widened area, one that had three desks to the right and a single door of glowing yellow to the left. The door was what I was led up to, and when my guide opened it I saw an older woman seated at a large desk in an office decorated almost as well as Director Gearing's had been. At first I thought her desk was also almost as empty, but moving closer showed me it was neat rather than unused. She had a number of folders in precise stacks in front of her, and when my guide gave her the papers she was carrying they were placed carefully on top of one of the folders.

"Ah, the Prime Terrilian Reya," she said, looking up at me with a smile that could have used something to warm it. "I'm pleased to welcome you to our facility, dear, and will do everything possible to make your stay with us a pleasant one. I'm sure you already know how unusual your condition is, and frankly I'm looking forward to having you as a guest. We so rarely get the benefit of an outside opinion regarding our efforts."

"So I'm a guest," I said, moving to one of the chairs in front of her desk and sitting in it. "I seem to have noticed an awful lot of guards in this vacation facility. Do you have that many guests trying to refuse your hospitality?"

"Of course not," she said, and her smile widened just a little, to show she was properly amused at the joke I'd made. "The guards aren't for the ladies of our facility, they're for another purpose entirely. The young men are too often visitors to our areas, and it's on their account that the guards are stationed where they are. Some of them consider it amusing to attempt leaving the complex in ways other than the ones permitted to them, and we really can't allow that. They're—too high-spirited—to be allowed out on their own, but boys will be boys and they continue to try."

"They must be absolutely adorable," I commented, a mutter the woman didn't seem to hear. She was too busy reading the papers she'd been given by my guide, and didn't even look up when another woman wearing a uniform in the same yellow as hers came in and put a cup of something on the desk in front of me. The second woman left as quietly as she'd entered, and a minute or so later the older woman looked up again.

"Your medical preparations are complete, so we can get right to seeing you settled in," she said, sounding as though there had been no lag in our conversation. "It's nearly lunchtime, so you'll soon be having your first introduction to the young men. The thing you must keep in mind at all times is that they know exactly how special and important they are, and you are to do nothing that will seem as though you're challenging them. They challenge each other on a regular basis, you see, as part of their training, so you must be sure not to involve yourself in that. It would be very unwise, and we certainly don't want their instructors lodging protests, do we?"

Once again I was given that small, cool smile meant to be so companionable and approving, the smile that went so well with the woman's lean face. Her eyes were dark and her hair a reddish brown worn very short, and her hands were long-fingered and fairly graceful. She hadn't done a single thing to offend or harm me, but it was all I could do to bear her presence without screaming.

"As a newcomer, you'll almost certainly find yourself the center of attention, at least for a short time," the woman went on, folding her hands on the desk as she looked at me. "The fact that you're also quite attractive will no doubt add to that, and you mustn't be upset if the men become somewhat—boisterous. It's simply the way they show approval, and they won't cause you any true harm. All you need do is go along with whatever they ask of you, and everything will be fine. You'll find that we've helped you out as far as your own interest is concerned, so you needn't worry that you won't find an eagerness to match theirs. You . . ."

"Just a minute," I interrupted, finally finding a reason to resume my end of the conversation. "What do you mean, you've 'helped me out'? What sort of help are you talking about?"

"My dear girl, you don't think we'd throw you into a situation like this *without* help, do you?" she asked in turn, just as unbearably patient as that man Serdin had been. "You've been given a stimulant to match your body chemistry, one that will cause arousal in you when the men are present. You'll find yourself *wanting* their attention, which is, after all, preferable to being frightened and unsure. As I'm sure you've already been told, we're here to assist you in every way we can. We want you to be happy while you're with us."

Happy. In the way that herd animals are kept happy. I sat back in the chair without saying anything, one hand rubbing at my forehead, trying to remember the time I'd been given the same sort of selfless help once before. There *had* been a time, I was as certain as I could be of that, but I couldn't quite recall the circumstances. All I could remember was a sense of terror and shame, mixed well with the sure knowledge that I was completely alone with no hope of rescue. Just like right then, trapped on a world I'd never even heard of.

"Now, despite the fact that you'll be distracted, you'll be expected to eat everything given to you at every meal," the woman went on, apparently taking my silence for agreement. "In your position you'll require a carefully balanced diet, and that's what you'll be given. That, combined with proper exercise, will bring you to full health and keep you there. I learned from your file that you were fed this morning before being allowed to awaken, but you haven't yet had anything for midmorning. That broth in front of you should do for now, and as soon as you've finished it I'll have you shown to your assigned place."

The woman ended her little speech and gave me another of those smiles, her expression showing she was waiting patiently for me to comply. Since there was no real reason for me to refuse, there was no reason for her to expect that I would. Reason was the key, with everyone being as reasonable as possible, and it didn't matter to anyone how completely and totally unreal it all was to me.

"I don't want any broth right now," I said, trying to push back narrowing, invisible walls. "I haven't done anything to make me hungry or thirsty."

"You don't need to be hungry or thirsty, dear," the woman came back, all ready with her smile and her patience and her reasonable explanation. "What you need is proper nourishment, and we're here to be sure that you get it. Drink the broth, and then you may go."

"And then I may go," I echoed, suddenly remembering very vividly that same attitude in the woman who had run the crèche I'd been raised in. I hadn't particularly cared for the attitude then, and I certainly didn't like it now. Most especially didn't like it now.

"I may be your prisoner, but I haven't been a child in quite a few years," I said, looking directly at the woman who continued to stare at me. "You will at the very least do me the courtesy of treating me as something other than a mental deficient, or this whole thing will be a lot more unpleasant than it's naturally destined to be. You have my word on that."

"Do I indeed?" she said, the smile and the patience still completely untroubled. "So you mean to persist in seeing us all as your enemies, at least for a short while. If you feel that clinging to such an outlook will help you in your adjustment, dear, by all means continue to cling to it. What helps you helps us—as long as you remember the lessons you were taught in childhood. You're free to rebel as much as you like, as long as you obey all of the really important rules. We don't want to punish you, but if you give us no choice in the matter we won't hesitate. Take the broth and drink it."

Still that same patience and calm, only now I remembered why I disliked them so. Those were the primary emotions I'd been accorded as a child by those in authority around me, the two emotions I'd never quite been able to master and accomplish for myself. I'd been able to force a sort of calm and pretend to patience, but had never really reached through to the real thing. Now that I looked back on it, it almost seemed that I was *supposed* to fail where those emotions were concerned, to fall short of the place others, better than myself, had reached with ease. I could see the conditioning went back a lot farther than I'd first thought it did, but these—"better people"—were in for a surprise.

"I'm really not much in the mood to play the game of rebellion," I said, leaning back in my chair as I regarded the older woman with the true calm I'd learned—somewhere. "As far as your rules go, you can take them and cut paper dolls out of them if you like. No matter how unreasonable you try to make me believe I'm being, I will *not* cooperate with my own officially proclaimed ravishment. If you need any other point-blank statements, feel free to ask me for them."

"I think I've had quite enough for now, thank you," she responded, the new smile measurably cooler but no less sure of itself. "It seems you *have* forgotten a good deal of your childhood, but the memories are certain to come back rather quickly. Right now you'll be shown where your place is, and you and I will speak again later."

Of all the dismissals I'd had that morning, hers was the most unimpressive—if you discounted the look in her dark eyes. The meeting she'd promised for later was one she was looking forward to, and that fact was supposed to make me uneasy. That I refused to *let* it make me uneasy was not quite the same as being unaffected, and I didn't really mind when the woman in the white uniform tapped me on the shoulder. The thought of being elsewhere was an attractive one, if any place on that planet could be thought of as attractive.

Once out of the office we continued on up the corridor to its end, no more than ten feet away from the desk area. My guide pushed through a swinging door and held it for me, then led the way left along a circular balcony area that surrounded a very large, round room. At intervals along the four-foot-high balcony were white-uniformed guards, all keeping a casual eye on the very large room, and the same on the people it contained. More than twenty feet of tall windows let in bright sunshine from behind one section of the balcony, the only illumination the women in the room had. The women were seated on plain, narrow beds, little more than cots, and the cots were arranged so that they covered the entire floor, one practically on top of the next. Even the cots at the outer edge of the big room were standing away from any wall, which meant not one of those women had the least feeling of privacy. I stopped with my hand on the railing to look down at them, wondering where they all could have come from. If they were all Primes there were a lot more than fifty of them, and that was a number out of all proportion to everything I thought I knew.

"Come on, girly, let's wake up here," a voice said from behind me and to my left, a female voice despite its being on the gruff and gravelly side. "You can do all the sightseeing you like later, once I have you where you're supposed to be."

I turned to look at the speaker over my shoulder, and found I'd been given away again to someone new. My original guide was gone, and in her place was a tall, burly woman in white, her uniform doing nothing to hide the bulge in her middle. Her hair was a dark, dirty blond and her eyes a very light gray, and her face was somehow more open than the faces of others in the same uniform. She stood beside a small desk that wasn't far from a ramp leading downward, and in her hand she held a thin rectangle of wood. When she gestured to me I walked over to where she waited, and as a reward had the wooden rectangle pressed to my thin smock on the left side of my chest. There were letters left behind when the rectangle was taken away, but I didn't have to bother trying to read them upside down.

"Now you're officially Terry, and your bed number is sixty-five," the woman said with a grin, obviously amused by my expression. "Stop looking so sour, it's better than having it branded on your backside. We haven't had one starting out wide awake for years now, but I can still remember the trouble she tried giving us. Take my advice and behave yourself, or you won't find anything but the grief she did. She yelled and screamed and cried and threw tantrums until they finally had to punish her, and then she tried so hard to be good that she looked like a fool. You don't strike me as someone who wants to look like a fool. Am I wrong?"

"About the fool part, no," I answered, wondering why this woman, out of all the others, was bothering. "As far as the rest of it goes, I've already told everyone in sight, so I might as well let you in on it. I won't cooperate with the sickness that goes on here, and nothing they can do will change my mind. No screaming and no tantrums—but no cooperation either.''

''Girly, I admire your guts,'' the woman said quietly, sitting down on the edge of her desk to look straight at me. ''I don't think much of your intelligence, but I do admire your guts. Look, I know how you feel about this, because I know how *I'd* feel if it was me they were trying to turn into a dolly-sow. I'd hate everything and everyone around here, and I'd swear to fight them with the last ounce of strength I had. Since it wouldn't take me long to find out that they never use drugs on their sows, I'd start to believe I really had a chance of doing it my way. The only thing is—I'd be wrong.''

She was keeping her voice down and the sober tone she'd adopted was very impressive, but after hearing the same thing so many times I wasn't feeling particularly impressed. She'd been searching my face to see how I was taking her advice, but didn't have to look hard or far for the answer.

''You're hearing me, but you aren't listening or believing,'' she said, without any anger behind the observation. ''They bring you here and tell you you'll be opening your legs for a bunch of strangers so they can knock you up for the good of the Amalgamation, and that gets you so mad you tell them to try it first on themselves. You might be feeling a little nervous about saying it, but you say it anyway and to hell with them all. You say it and say it to everyone you meet, but maybe you don't notice that no one gets mad or bothered or starts throwing threats at you. If you do notice you don't let yourself pay attention, because that's enough to make you start worrying. If *they* aren't worried, it's a good enough reason for you to be.''

''I don't happen to see it that way,'' I said, finding that her conversation was beginning to make me uncomfortable. ''If they haven't failed yet to get their way, that doesn't mean they're invincible, only that no one has discovered the right way to fight them. Since I have nothing more important on my calendar right now, I've decided to try *my* hand at it.''

''And you're not interested in anyone else's opinions,''

she said with a nod. "You're the type who has to see for herself if the paint really is still wet, or if it's raining out the way everyone says it is. That's not a bad way to be, I'm that way myself more often than not, but— Did it ever occur to you that all they have to do is tie you down to a bed, and then send the parade in your direction? I'm not saying it *is* what they do, because I've never seen it or heard about it happening. The question I want you to think about is *why* they don't do that, why they never find it necessary to be that crude. We've had more girls through here than I know the number of, but they've never once had to do that. If you come up with an answer, I'd be interested in hearing it. I'm Finner, and I'm here on most day shifts. Right now, you go in that direction."

She gestured toward the ramp, then got off the desk to lead the way, asking nothing more from me in the way of response. I followed without feeling an urge to respond, but not because she had convinced me of anything. They were all really good at talking people out of intentions they didn't approve of, which might be the reason no one had won against them. It was like having two equal forces of Kabrans facing each other in the field. Everyone knew neither side could win against the other, so most often they didn't even bother to fight. It would have been a waste of good fighting men to have them go at it anyway, or at least so most people believed. I knew one Kabran who didn't agree with that, Colonel Garth R'Hem Solohr, and I also knew Garth had tried doing something about it. I knew he had—I'd been there when he had—but what he'd done I couldn't quite reach—

"The sanitary facilities are through those double doors," the woman Finner said, pointing to a short downramp that led to an access point for the area under the circling balcony. "Nothing but the bare necessities, plus shower stalls. If you want anything better, you have to make your own arrangements."

"Who do you make arrangements with?" I asked, wondering how long I'd be able to hold out if they tried trading me a bath for my cooperation. For some reason, it seemed so long . . . "Is that woman in yellow I met in charge of that, too?"

"Quatry?" Finner asked, for some reason amused again. "No, Quatry is your section leader, and deals with other sorts of arrangements. The ones you have to talk to about a softer life are the men you'll be meeting, the Prime trainees you're here to—get together with. Every one of them has his own apartment, and unless he's officially paired with one of the girls during her fertile period, he can choose any girl he pleases to spend the night with him. Or, possibly I should say, 'any girl who pleases *him.*' I would have put that a little more delicately, but you're strong enough to take the facts of life as they come, aren't you?"

She glanced at me where I walked to her left and a little behind, following through the maze of cots, but I didn't give her anything to add to her amusement, at least not voluntarily. She seemed to notice and enjoy the faint flush I could feel in my cheeks, but didn't press the point any harder than she already had.

"And here we are," she announced after another couple of minutes of walking, stopping beside a cot no different from any of the others in the room. "The number is on a disk hanging at the foot, so you shouldn't have much trouble finding your way back. If you do happen to get lost, just ask one of the guards around the wall to guide you. If you turn out to be one of those here at lights out, remember that you have to be *in* bed, not next to it or on your way to it, or in the sanfax thinking about it. Your night-duty guards won't listen to reasons or excuses about why you aren't, they'll just ask the assistant section leader for punishment permission. From what I hear they usually get it, so don't let the point slip your mind. There's a box under your bed with a comb and brush in it, and you have just enough time before lunch to make use of them. And maybe even enough time to do a little thinking."

The look she gave me didn't have much amusement left in it and then she was gone, threading her way back through the cots toward the balcony ramp we'd come down. I turned away before she reached the ramp, looked around at what I'd been brought to, then sank down on the cot with one leg folded under me. There were occasional, very soft conversations going on in different parts of the big room, but the women nearest me were too busy seeing to their hair to be distracted by talk. They looked deliriously happy and eager to be on about their business, and the empty cot next to mine seemed more real than they did. Didn't they know what was being done to them, and didn't they care even a little? How could they just sit there, prettying themselves up for sanctioned rape. . . ?

I gave it up and lay back on the cot, draping one arm over my eyes to blot out a world I could no longer bear to look at. Of course the rest of them knew what was being done to them, and of course they cared. They knew they were being honored, and they cared so much they would do whatever they had to in order to continue being honored. And out of gratitude as well, let's not forget about gratitude. I felt so ill it was all I could do to keep from throwing up, but I couldn't give them the satisfaction of that, I just couldn't. It would be the first step toward letting them win, and that was one thing I refused to do.

Again one thing. If I hadn't felt so terrible I would have laughed at myself, constantly listing a dozen different items and then calling them one thing. Maybe it was the first sign that I was going crazy, that I was about to lose *all* touch with reality and the world around me, and if that was so then I wished it would hurry up. It was just me against what felt like an entire world, and they were all so sure they would win, that I didn't have the least chance against them. If I went insane I would no longer know what they were doing to me, no longer need to fight a battle that even I was beginning to believe I'd lose. I was so tired, as though I'd already fought a battle like that, and had learned that there were things a good deal worse than losing. What I wanted—what I wanted was—

What I wanted was an end to everything, not just the end to struggle that madness would bring, but the absolute end of everything. I took my arm down from my eyes but kept them closed, making no effort to chase myself out of the warm, embracing darkness I'd found. The cot I lay on was more comfortable than I'd thought it would be, but it was too narrow and only just long enough. Less privacy than an exotic animal on public display, the bare minimum in sanitary facilities, no personal possessions other than a comb and brush in a box, strict rules and guaranteed punishment for breaking them—everything necessary for encouraging me to find a man whose private apartment I could share, even for a single night at a time. It might have gone quite a way toward working, but instead it had backfired on them and had helped me to find what I really wanted. I had no idea why the conviction was so strong and steady, but what I wanted more than anything was to die.

I stirred just a little on the cot, wondering why that thought didn't frighten me. It should be frightening to discover that you want nothing more than to die, but I couldn't find fear anywhere inside me. It was as though I had more of a reason than simply being at that facility, that I had considered the question calmly and objectively and had come to the only conclusion possible. I had no urge to change my mind, not even a mild preference covering a desire to think about it a little longer. All decided, all bottom line, no indication of the least amount of hesitation.

What the hell could possibly have done that?

I stirred on the cot again, annoyance and frustration filling up the spaces left vacant by the absence of fear. It was the stupidest situation I'd come across in a long while, and it was really beginning to make me angry. Those miserable people whose prisoner I was had taken away so much of my memory that I couldn't remember why I wanted to die! Since I still knew I wanted to die that meant *they* didn't know it, otherwise they would have taken it away with the rest. If you stretched a point you could say they were working toward saving my life, but I didn't seem to *want* my life saved. And how could I know one way or the other, when I couldn't remember why I wanted to die in the first place? What right did they have, interfering in things that were none of their business? How did they dare to—

"Hi there, you must be the new one they said was due," a voice interrupted, coming from somewhere on my right. "I'm Merador Sanglin, but you can call me Mera the way everyone else does."

I opened my eyes to frown at the voice, and found myself looking at a small, dark, very pretty girl. She was kneeling on the cot that had been empty when I'd gotten there, and she paused in the middle of brushing her hair in order to smile at me. I suppose I must have looked surprised; her smile widened as she raised the brush again.

"That's right, I'm not any more—'honored'—than you are," she said, her dark, lovely eyes twinkling. "I went one day for my weekly physical, floating along as usual, but when the doctor congratulated me on being pregnant, something—twisted loose. They tell me it was the shock of hearing about my first pregnancy, but whatever it was it brought me all the way back down. From then on I've been as you see me now."

"Which is how long?" I couldn't keep from asking, making no effort to return her smile. It was one thing to be conditioned into cooperating, but to do it voluntarily—!

"About three more pregnancies worth of time," she answered evenly and calmly, not even insulted enough to stop brushing her hair. "Right now that sounds terrible to you, really low and awful, but you'll find out it isn't anything like that. I had a lot of time to think after I broke out, with no one to bother me and no schedule to keep to. Once you're confirmed pregnant they transfer you back to the outer part of the complex, and they give you your own apartment with entertainment centers and servos and anything else within reason that you ask for. I wasn't confused any longer and knew I could make a fuss about going along with them again, but the plain truth is I couldn't think of a reason why I *should* make a fuss. Once you understand the routine it isn't difficult being comfortable, so why make trouble when there's no point to it?"

"If you don't mind being a brood mare, I suppose there isn't a point to it," I agreed, not in the least interested in arguing. "Now, if you don't mind, I think I'll take a little nap."

"You don't have the time," she said before I could turn away and close my eyes again, still friendly and outgoing. "It's too close to lunch. And just what exactly is that supposed to mean, if you don't mind being a brood mare? Didn't they teach any history in whatever crèche you grew up in? Didn't you ever get to look around at everyday life on whatever world you happened to be? Since when have women ever been anything *but* brood mares? If we're the only ones physiologically able to carry and give birth to babies, who else are they going to get for the job?"

"Being able to do something isn't the same as being required to do it," I countered, sitting up as I was drawn into the argument against my will. "I never asked to be brought here, and I never volunteered to give my all to the Amalgamation. They decided to take it and me, and I have every right to give them all the hell I can in return. They want to force me into something I want no part of, and that they have *no* right to do!"

"Oh, come off it," she said with a snort, finally putting the brush aside. "Societies have been doing that to women ever since there have been societies, and before that it was the men doing it on their own. Are you silly enough to believe a woman has to give her permission before she can get pregnant? Do you think every woman married off to a man was married by her own consent? It's nice to have a man you're madly in love with to give you children, but how many women have that kind of luck? And have you forgotten what we are? We're *Primes,* special women with a special talent. How long do you think it would have been before someone in the government came along to tell us it was our duty to preserve and pass along our genes? That it was time we married and did something to pay for those expensive educations and soft lives we were given for almost nothing? You and I seem to be about the same age. How much longer do you think we would have had?"

Her question was a demand, straightforward and unashamed, but I had no equally straightforward answer. I *had* occasionally found myself wondering when the Amalgamation would ask something more of me than

Mediating, something along the lines of what other empaths had been asked to do. I'd never heard of a Prime being approached, but normal empaths were constantly being urged to pair off, with all sorts of extras thrown their way if they did. But it wasn't the same thing, not the same at all.

"If someone had come by and asked, I would at least have had a choice as to who I was going to be involved with," I pointed out, feeling familiar sourness flowing back in my direction. "I would have had some freedom of say in the matter—and I wouldn't have produced babies I'd never even get a chance to see, let alone hold. I'm not a machine, I'm a woman, and I won't let anyone turn me *into* a machine."

"No, you're not a machine, but you're not a woman either," she came back, still looking determined. "You're a *Prime*, which makes you something else entirely. If you'd paired off with a single man, even one of your choice, what would have happened if you'd suddenly discovered you didn't like him after all? Nothing, that's what would have happened, because you'd be stuck with him. And after having the baby of someone you didn't like grow inside you, how long do you think you would have gotten to keep it? How long do other empaths get to keep their children? How long do normals producing talented children get to keep them? At least here you don't have to go through the hurt of giving up a part of yourself, and you don't have to worry if you don't like the partner you're assigned to. After he's done his job you don't have to look at him again, there are enough others around who are pleasant to look at. You have fun during your off-times, fun during most of your fertile periods, the good life while you're carrying, and don't stay pregnant long enough to feel that you've lost something once they've taken it. Honestly, Terry, what more can you ask for?"

The question was just short of being exasperated, about as far from the rote response of conditioning as you can get, and she knew well enough she'd made at least one valid point. Just as she and I had been raised in crèches, our children, the children of any other empaths, and the talented children of any normals would be raised the same way. That had not only been a government requirement it was an out-and-out necessity, especially where normals were concerned. When a newborn baby is empathetic, it doesn't simply cry the way other babies do. It doesn't yet know how to read emotions, but general broadcasting is something you don't have to be taught. If you suddenly find yourself feeling very uncomfortable, starving-to-death hungry, or cranky because you're so tired, you can be fairly certain there's a baby empath around. If the baby happens to be colicky or delightfully engaged in nursing, there's no "fairly" about it. You *know* there's a baby empath around, and either you take yourself out of its limited range, or see to it that *it's* the one taken away while you still have your sanity. Adults experience a wider range of emotions than babies do, but they usually don't experience them so *intensely.* A little of that goes a long way, and it takes trained workers to put up with it for any length of time. But I was letting myself be distracted off the track, and it was time to get back on it.

"All you're doing is rationalizing," I told the girl Mera, able to see it where she couldn't. "They talked you into believing you had no chance fighting them, so you rationalized your decision to back down. I'm not interested in their opinions one way or the other, so I don't have to rationalize anything."

"Garbage," she came back with a snort, leaning forward to put her brush back into the box under her cot. "I'm not rationalizing anything, but you haven't been here long enough to know that. Once you are, you'll see I'm right. Now listen, when we go into the dining room, I want you to stay right next to me. That way you won't have to worry about being noticed, which should speed things up a little. Some of the guys don't want anything but those icky, cooing, clingy types who still believe they're being honored, but most of them prefer a woman who knows a little something about flirting. They don't believe what I say any more than I do, but they get a kick out of hearing it and always come back for more. Let me tell you, I haven't spent a night in this menagerie since they brought me back straight, and with just a little effort you won't have to either. And in case you're wondering, you don't *want* to spend a night here."

She gave me a look of solemn assurance, the voice of experience instructing innocence, and all I could do was blink a little. She had enough self-possession for someone twice her size, and I couldn't ever remember being—taken over—like that before. After the surprise passed I found I didn't like it much and was about to say so, but she wasn't through imparting the store of information she'd gathered.

"And don't let these stupid cover-ups bother you," she went on, flicking a finger at the smock she wore. "These are just for daytime use, and to be worn to places like Medical and the General Offices. If you get asked to stay in someone's apartment for the night, they'll give you one of the dress-up outfits as a reward for your efforts. You may end up having it ripped off you and then you'll need to come back bare, but that isn't anything to worry about. The male Secs in the men's sector won't ever put a finger on you, and the Secs in our own areas are all female. I happen to think the male Securities are drugged or conditioned against touching any of us, and not just for our protection. We're special, and meant only for the guys. I hate to think what they would do to a Sec who tried to touch what was theirs."

Her shudder wasn't completely muffled as she shifted to sitting on the cot, and somehow I knew she was right to be upset at the thought. We who were Primes could do terrible things to people, worse than just about anyone knew, so bad I didn't *want* anyone to know. That was something else I couldn't get the details on, something else gone with the rest, but enough was left for me to know better than to comment. Mera began talking again, back to giving me information and advice, but this time I had no interest in listening. I lay down again on my cot, and stared up at the ceiling stretching high above me.

Only a few more minutes went by before a sound suddenly began echoing through the room, a very low, pleasant gonging that awoke eager movement everywhere it touched. Women began putting their brushes and combs away and getting to their feet, and Mera broke off her monologue to lean forward and tap my arm.

"Lunchtime," she announced, standing up to stretch high. "And since I took care of my exercises this morning, I can spend the time after lunch having fun. Come on, Terry, we don't want to be last."

"Since I'm not very hungry, I think I'll stay right here," I answered as I looked up at her, making no effort to get off the cot. "You go ahead and have a great time for both of us."

"Terry, why do you have to be so thick?" she asked in exasperation, putting her fists to her hips. "They're not going to let you skip lunch, so why bother pretending? If you don't walk to the dining room alone they'll drag you, and that's not the kind of first impression you want to make. Let's go in now and get something to eat and meet the guys, and just save the defiance for some other time."

The suggestion was so reasonable I smiled, but not with anything like real amusement. If I cooperated now to avoid an unnecessary confrontation I could always resist later, but if I went along with that line of thinking I'd find that later was always ahead, never at a place of arrival. I'd cooperated to the point of letting them put me in that zoo of a dormitory room, but that was as far as I was willing to go.

"I've always been really bad at saving things," I said, letting my smile fade. "And what's that saying about putting things off? It would be a shame to start developing bad habits after living so long without them."

"People who won't listen to good advice are *dumb,*" she pronounced, leaning forward a little to emphasize the opinion. "You're lucky I like you, or I'd leave you to get into all the trouble you're looking for. If you're all that good at fighting you'd better get started now, otherwise we're about to go in to lunch."

Just for a moment I didn't understand what she was talking about, and then the two big women in security white reached my cot and leaned down to take my arms. I struggled and tried to keep from being pulled to my feet, but as far as fighting ability went I didn't have any.

The two women were about as distant as it's possible to get from the bumbling incompetence of the man Gearing, and each one of them alone weighed more than I did. I was pulled along between them behind a calmly strolling Mera, cursing under my breath, wishing I *had* learned how to use a sword—

You can't really stiffen when you've been straining with all your strength to get loose and you certainly can't stop short, but I know I made a respectable effort to do both. Where in the name of everything that's real had that thought about a sword come from? *Me*, learn how to use a sword? When? How? And even above that, why? What in hell was going on with my mind, and if I knew all those things were there, why couldn't I *remember?*

The frustration flared so sharply through me that I barely saw the ramp I was dragged up and the double swinging doors I was hauled through. There was a short, wide corridor beyond the doors and another set of doors at the end of the corridor, and then I was in a room even larger than the dormitory room. The walls had pastel designs with dark-colored accents, the floor was softly carpeted, low, pleasant music was playing, and large, round tables were scattered from one end to the other. As involuntary as my entrance was it took me a moment to notice, but the tables closest to the doors I'd come in by weren't quite the same as the ones farther away. The nearer ones were just as large but plain, with ordinary-looking chairs circling them in an uninteresting way. The closer I looked at the ones toward the far end of the room, however, the more attractively designed they and their chairs appeared. The tables had brightly colored cloths and rich-looking settings, the chairs were more like overstuffed and contoured armchairs, the carpeting seemed thicker, the . . .

"Well, what do you think of them?" Mera murmured to me over her shoulder, just as though I'd accompanied her willingly and now stood without being held there. "Aren't they yummy and delicious?"

The "they" she referred to were the men, of course, and I'd been trying very hard *not* to look at them. They had been filling the room even as we came in, talking and laughing together and strolling casually in our direction, and the women I stood among were so anxious and eager they were practically holding their breath. I could almost feel a hum in the air from their hovering, and I hadn't missed the fact that none of them were moving toward any of the tables. It was as though they first needed permission before they could sit and eat, and I hated the thought. I kept my eyes on the inanimate parts of the room or looked down at my feet, making no answer to Mera's question, but I should have known better than to think that would stop her.

"Oh, I know you'll be one of the ones they take down to the other end, Terry, I just know it!" she enthused, practically jumping up and down where she stood. "Some of them saw me and started over, but now they're looking at you, too! They're our kind, Terry, more so than any other men anywhere, and it's right that we belong to them. Come on, girl, smile at them!"

Smiling was the last thing I wanted to do right then, most especially after what she'd said. I'd never even so much as met a male of my kind, a male Prime, and as a young girl I'd had daydreams about what wonderful things would happen if I ever did. I *wanted* to know them but I couldn't even bear the thought of looking at them, of finding them attractive, of enjoying their company, or ultimately shuddering to their touch. I would *not* do what all the rest of them were doing, would not sell my self-respect and my body in response to the psychological manipulations of lowlives. What the Amalgamation was doing was *wrong,* and if I let myself be coaxed into going along with it, I'd be just as dirty as they were.

"And how are you today, Mera?" a male voice said suddenly, almost bringing my eyes up from the floor to the group that had stopped near us. "I'm happy to note you're looking as tasty as ever. I don't remember having seen your friend before, but she's being treated like a hatchling. We were wondering why that is."

"In a way she *is* a hatchling," the girl answered, light laughter and eager attention in her voice. "She only just got here but she's already broken out, so of course she doesn't know how silly she's being. Other hatchlings are frightened and confused, but all she is is stubborn."

"Then, by all means, let's bring her along and show her what she's missing," another male voice said, heavy amusement in it. "If she still tries being stubborn after that, we'll have to do something about it."

The comment caused chuckling in everyone in the group including Mera, and then they were moving away with me being forced along behind them. I was aware of the way others of the women had been claimed and drawn toward the far side of the room, but there were still some left who made their dejected way to the nearer, plainer tables. It was clear there weren't as many men as there were women, which meant the women were being made to compete with each other for attention. I didn't know what happened to them if they didn't get that attention, but it wasn't likely they escaped the fate of those more popular. Most probably they were left alone to suffer and agonize, which would make them swear to themselves to do better next time.

With jolly thoughts like that for company, I was taken to a table and forced down into a very comfortable chair. The table was more than halfway across the room and was nicely set, but it wasn't the best of what the room held. The security woman on my left took my hand and pressed my fingers onto a narrow print-plate to the left of my setting, the one on the right bent to slide a padded metal cuff around my ankle which quietly clicked into place against the chair leg, and then the two of them let go of me.

"For future reference, you're to identify your position in the room at every meal before you do anything else," the woman on my left said softly, obviously not wanting to interrupt the conversations going on around the table. "The chef has been programmed with a different diet for every woman here, but it has to be told where you are before it can deliver it. We'll be back for you later, and in the meanwhile you'd be wise to behave yourself."

They both turned and walked away, leaving me alone in the midst of quite a lot of amusement. Others of the women had been brought to the table by the men, and the whole bunch of them, men and women alike, considered my being locked to the chair the funniest thing they'd seen in a very long time. I could feel my discomfort over that, burning in my cheeks like a flame, but all I did was sit there, staring down at my hands in my lap.

"Stubborn or not, she's certainly pretty enough," observed a voice to my left, a drawling male voice. "And she even knows how to blush. I expect to enjoy myself quite a lot with her, even before she starts to moan and squirm. I think, after this morning, no one can deny I'm entitled to firsts."

"You don't have to look for challenges that aren't there, Jer-Mar," another male voice said from a different place around the table, a faint hint of petulance to the words. "You've placed higher than anyone else on our level, and we know it as well as you do. If you can hold that place for another four days, you'll be leaving us to move up to the next level."

"When, not if," the man to my left corrected smugly, shifting in his chair. "Once you take that one major step it starts getting easier rather than harder, so much easier you'd have trouble believing it. It was hell dividing that first projection in half, but now I can hold the result for more than thirty seconds before starting to tire. Once they move me up to the next level, who knows what I'll find I can do."

"You might even cause Kel-Ten to start worrying," a third voice said, and this one was chuckling. "If you keep going the way you've begun, you won't only be able to challenge him, you'll have first dip ahead of him. Which might be more of a favor, or so I hear. The word going around is that he's bored and making some trouble."

"Only a man with something wrong with him could get bored with first dip," the man to my left, Jer-Mar, said with a very cultured sneer. "When I get firsts on that level, you won't find *me* getting bored. And speaking of firsts, sweet thing, your food is on the table in front of you. Eat up fast like a good little thing, and then Jer-Mar will take you to his apartment for a while. No need to let it go until after dinner."

The man reached over to me and put his finger to my ear, caressing the outer edge before poking abruptly inside. I jerked my head away with a feeling of disgust, but he just laughed, took my face in his hand, and forced me to look over at him. It was something I hadn't wanted to do for a very specific reason, and as soon as my eyes were on him I knew I'd been right. That woman Quatry, the one who was the leader or whatever, had told me I'd been "helped" for my first meeting with the men, and she hadn't been joking. The desire that shivered through my body wasn't my own idea, and certainly wasn't being caused by the brown-haired, blue-eyed man who held my face. The arrogance in his stare was that of a grown-up spoiled brat, but I was partially wrong about his not being the cause of the way I felt. His very presence was the cause, that and whatever they'd injected into me, and the flaring anger behind my eyes did only a little against the rising heat lower down.

"Well, well, what pretty green eyes the sweet thing has," the man drawled with a grin, obviously knowing what he had made happen to me. "I do believe she's now ready to eat up fast, so Jer-Mar can get to his fun. She really needs him to have his fun, don't you, sweet thing?"

"Stop talking to me as though I were a worthless pet," I choked out as I pulled my face from his hand, ignoring the laughter coming from those around the table. "I'm a Prime just the same as you are, and you have no right talking to me as though I weren't."

"Oh, stubborn indeed," the man said with brows raised high, but he was still grinning and enjoying himself. "Yes, sweet thing, you *are* a Prime, but certainly not the same as I. I am a male and you are a female, and that means you squirm while I make you squirm. We simply aren't on the same level, you and I, so why waste time discussing it? Being a Prime for you means you get to serve those of us who are the best there are, and that's as close as you can come to any sort of importance. But just look at how much they've given you to eat. Surely that's an indication of some sort of importance—or maybe it isn't. Maybe it's just that they think you're too skinny or undernourished. Let's take a look and see if they're right."

With no more warning than that his hands came to the front of my smock, and then he pulled it open while his friends roared with laughter. The women were laughing too, even Mera, and I was so furious I couldn't control myself. Without an instant's hesitation I slapped that weak-featured, arrogant face with every ounce of strength I had, wishing I could slap it in an entirely other way. He wouldn't have tried doing that to me if—something—was different, but I still refused to allow it to happen. I was alone—I was alone—but I still wouldn't let it happen.

It took a moment before I became aware of the dead silence that had fallen at our table, and of the odd pressure that I could feel in what seemed to be the very air around my mind. The man Jer-Mar had jerked back to stare at me with mad-eyed, voiceless fury, his entire body trembling with the rage, and for an instant it seemed as though he were attacking without moving, attacking, attacking . . .

It was ridiculous, of course, because he really *hadn't* moved except to pull back, and that's not the way someone or something attacks. It would have been understandable if I were trembling the way he was, but I found to my surprise that I wasn't. My hands were steady when I went to reclose my smock, no more than a tingling in the right palm from the slap I'd delivered, and then it came to me that it wasn't so surprising after all. I hadn't been threatened by a dangerous man, I'd been pawed by a little boy, and how frightening is *that* supposed to be? It was closer to being annoying, especially since I was beginning to wish more and more that there *were* real men around there. . . .

"You have to be out of your mind," Jer-Mar said at last, bringing my eyes up to see the way he was still breathing hard and glaring hate-daggers into my flesh. "No other female has ever *dared* touch one of us like that! How I wish you weren't protected against me, shut down and safe inside your little shell! I'd show you then what you were stupid enough to challenge, I'd show you. . . !"

"Please accept the profuse apologies we offer, Prime Jer-Mar," a voice said from behind me, and then two security females were to either side of me again, a third woman in a yellow uniform accompanying them. She stopped to my left, near the angry little boy's chair, and her skin actually seemed pale even in the soft, intimate lighting of the room. "The girl is new and has no idea of your true importance, so we beg you to forgive her. We, ourselves, will punish rather than forgive, and will deliver her back to you later for your pleasure. When you find her sufficiently chastened, we hope you will accept her."

I was free of the ankle cuff and chair by then, my arms again in the possession of the two Secs, but I still stood where Jer-Mar could see me. He looked up at my face and then he deliberately smiled, leaning back comfortably in his chair.

"Yes, do return her to me afterward," he drawled, his narrow chest swelling from all the bowing and scraping he'd been given by the woman in yellow. "I expect to enjoy that quite a lot, possibly even more than the ride I'll take. Later, sweet thing, definitely later."

He turned then to talk to one of the other men at the table, and I was taken after the woman in yellow when she gestured to the Secs holding my arms and then hurried off. A last glimpse of the people at the table had shown the men outraged and the women disbelieving, all but Mera. She alone had looked frightened and very upset, but obviously not on her own behalf.

I was taken back to the dormitory room and through it, and from there to the office of the woman Quatry. By then my arms were hurting from the grip the two Secs had on me, but the older woman in the yellow uniform was not in the least concerned with my comfort. She froze me with her stare until I was brought to a stop in front of her desk, and then she folded her hands on top of a neatly placed folder.

"Tell me what she did to the Prime Jer-Mar," Quatry said to the woman in yellow who had entered with us, talking to her but looking only at me. "I want to hear it all, with her listening."

"She—she—slapped him," the woman said after swallowing hard, as though she were reporting a murder and mutilation. "He went so far as to take an interest in her, telling her to eat her food quickly so that she could follow him back to his apartment, and she had the nerve to announce that he couldn't talk to her like that, that she was a Prime, too! I thought he would be insulted and almost intervened then, but he was gracious enough to laugh off such childish boasting, and tried to show her he still found her attractive. That was when she hit him."

"I have never in my life heard anything so inexcusable," Quatry pronounced, her dark eyes glowing with cold fury. "If I hadn't had you watched closely and carefully, there's no telling what you might have done next. Is it possible you have anything at all to say for yourself about this insanity, that you can in any way attempt to excuse it?"

"You seem to have chosen the right word when you picked 'insanity,' " I said, rubbing arms that had been released while trying to adapt to the idea that I was asleep and having a nightmare. "Nothing about this entire situation is sane, not you and not those—those—overgrown children. I am a free woman and a Prime; I will not be spoken to as though I were a bauble of little value, and I certainly won't be groped and pawed. I was not being done a favor, I was being insulted; and if it ever happens again I'll do the very same thing. If all of you are crazy here, that doesn't mean I have to go along with you."

The woman in yellow had gasped in shock over what I'd said, but Quatry was stronger than that. She simply stared at me for a full frozen minute, then slowly nodded her head.

"I should have seen this sooner, from your earlier behavior," she said, sounding as though she had found a solution to a puzzling question. "You're not bright enough to understand the quality of those around you, to see how truly superior to you they are, so you simply reject everything and anything you come across. Those men are *trained* Primes, trained in a way you could never be and *will* never be. Through them and the offspring they produce, Central will be made supreme over every other planet in the Amalgamation, not merely the elected leader among equals. Whatever it is they want, that is exactly what you will give them, and that while quietly bearing their children. You, someone who hasn't even established her percentage level yet, will not even *speak* to her betters unless spoken to first, and then she will respond properly and politely. Do you understand me, girl?''

''What I understand is that you would certainly do better in my place than I would,'' I said, understanding even more fully the futility of arguing with mindless fanatics. ''Why don't you and I trade places, and then you can kiss the feet of those—marvels—in person?''

''I've already had the privilege of being in your place,'' she answered, and the ice in her eyes cleared briefly to show pride and pleasure and fierce satisfaction. ''I served their sires all the years I was permitted to do so, and some of the present generation have to be my sons. If you weren't a Prime you would never be allowed near them, and even as a Prime you barely qualify. It's my job to see to it that you do as you're told, and believe me, you *will* do as you're told. For inexcusable behavior I sentence you to First Punishment, the hardest sentence I'm able to give a first offender. If you should prove to be too thickheaded to learn from that, it will be my pleasure to go on from there. Get her out of my sight.''

The two Secs took my arms again, and I was pulled out after the other woman in yellow who led the way with a grimly satisfied expression on her face. She was younger than the woman Quatry but not what might be considered *young*, which probably meant she was the same sort of retired servant. I'd had my own ideas as to what was done with female Primcs who could no longer give them the babies they wanted, but apparently some were made further use of instead of merely being put quietly to sleep. It took a really sick mind to guard a program with the conditioned aggressiveness of former victims of that program, and I couldn't decide whether to feel angry or nauseated. Even mass murderers didn't destroy their victims more than once.

I was distracted with my thoughts for a moment or two

after leaving the office, but was brought back to what was going on around me when I noticed I was being taken away from the dormitory doors and up the corridor to the branching. When I'd first been led in it had been up the lefthand fork, but now I was taken past the guard post and to the right. Passing the curve brought to sight three unmarked doors, one to the left, two to the right, and it was into the first of the righthand doors that I was taken. The room was small and pale yellow, with nothing in it but a padded table and a narrow cabinet against one wall, not enough to be called ominous or to cause unease. The woman in yellow closed the door behind the Secs and me, and the smile she wore finally forced me to consider the question of what they were going to do to me.

"Put her on the table," the woman in yellow said as she walked to the cabinet, the anticipation in her voice so laced with a sense of—justice, you might say, that I began to be aware of a flutter inside me. I hadn't spent much time thinking about what they would do to me for refusing to cooperate, the refusal itself had seemed much too natural to generate thoughts like that. They were wrong and I was right, and what else was there to consider? I had thought it possible they might kill me, but now I could see they weren't going to kill me.

The first thing the Secs did was take away my smock, and then I was forced face down onto the padded table. The material of the table was warm and comfortable rather than cold and hard, and my wrists and ankles were closed into soft, gentle bindings rather than unyielding metal. For some reason my heart was beating rather hard by that time, just as though I were being threatened with some barbaric torture, but that was ridiculous. Misguided or not, those were still people of a civilized culture, as far from naked, screaming savages as—

"Hold her thigh," the woman in yellow directed, and as soon as two strong hands had complied I felt the stinging stab of a needle. Something was injected into me and then the woman went back to the cabinet, returning to the table a moment later with a bottle of clear liquid in one hand and a wad of cotton in the other. The smile she looked down at me with was just short of gleeful, and I discovered I was trying to pull my wrists free from where they were bound below the edges of the table.

"So you have the unmitigated gall to think you were right in what you did," she said, a definite edge of fanaticism to her voice as she continued to smile that same smile. "You offended a man so far above you that you should have fainted in delight at his even noticing you, and you aren't even sorry you did it. I think, dear, we now have to search for that sorrow, and when we find it you're to tell me at once. If it's deep enough and sincere enough it might get you something of a reprieve, but don't expect the reprieve to come too quickly. Living with sorrow for a time brings a bad girl regret for having been bad, and you were a very bad girl indeed. You'll tell me that, too, that you were a bad girl, and then you'll tell me how sorry you are. Are you ready?"

I had the impression that her question was for me, but one of the Secs took it as a cue. She gathered my hair together and pulled it away from my back, and then the woman in yellow came too close to the table for me to see her where she stood. I heard the sound of a bottle being uncapped and then the slosh of liquid, and a moment later a wet line was being drawn across my back. The line went from left to right before it ended, I heard the slosh of liquid again, and then another wet line was being drawn. My heart had really begun hammering when the first of the liquid had touched me, but the second line was completed and a third started, and I still felt nothing but wet. No pain, nothing but the mildest of discomfort—I didn't understand what they were doing.

I didn't understand, that is, until I was completely covered with lines, and then those lines began to dry.

# 4

I was able to keep from screaming for a while, but the more the liquid dried, the more the pain intensified. It began by stinging just a little, like a faint and not very serious rope burn, but then the sting changed to a sharpened throb, and then to a flaming that felt as though it were eating into my flesh, and finally it began searing so deep that I thought I would be burned to nothing by it. When the pain first started I tried to free my hands to rub at it, to try to brush or rub the liquid off before it dried any more, but I *couldn't* free myself no matter what I did. The bindings on my wrists kept me pressed flat against the table, my breasts crushed under me, my head able to raise up no more than a matter of inches. My ankles, too, were held gently but inflexibly, allowing my toes no latitude for digging in, no purchase of any sort. I wanted to get off that table and *claw* at myself, but it just wouldn't let me go!

"Am I mistaken, or did I just hear a whimper?" the woman in yellow asked in a faintly interested voice, moving a bit to her left so that I might see her. I had my right cheek pressed hard into the padding of the table as my mind fought to deny what was happening, and she looked down at me and smiled.

"You might be interested to know that no real damage is being done to you," she said, her easy, conversational tone making me shiver. "Your nerve endings may not believe that, but it's entirely true. You may *feel* as though the skin is being whipped off you in strips, but it isn't really happening. Doesn't that put your mind at ease?"

Just then my mind was too busy clanging with shock, as more and more of the lines dried in turn. I couldn't believe how high the pain was growing, how the entire back of me felt as though it were being set on fire. I tried to pull at the bindings again, then couldn't keep from crying out, my own movement having made it all flame even higher. After that I fought to lie still, to breathe as shallowly as possible, to do nothing that would add to the rising agony, but then an unexpected cross-line flared and my body twitched and then I screamed and the scream made it worse and I wanted to convulse but the bindings wouldn't let me and I screamed again and again and again and—

After an endless time surrounded by burning red I must have fainted, but I think I was screaming again even before I completely woke up. It went on and on like that, agonizing consciousness occasionally slipping into black times of no real relief, determination forgotten, noble intentions forgotten, only a very small me left right in the center of it all. Finally, after ages of knowing nothing but intense agony, I awoke to find that the level of pain had fallen just a little, enough so that my raw throat could settle for mewling instead of screams. I think I was terrified, but there wasn't enough sense of judgment left in me to be sure.

"You poor dear, you look exhausted," a female voice said from somewhere to my left, and a hand touched my sweat-soaked hair. "I tried to give you enough time to search for that sorrow we were talking about, and you've apparently used every bit of it. Were you successful, or do you need just a little longer?"

"No, please, no," I whispered, unable to open my eyes, helpless to stop trembling, the small bit of me left inside shuddering in terror. "I'm sorry I did that, please, I'm so sorry, I swear I'll never do it again, I swear! Don't bring the rest of the pain back, please don't . . ."

"Oh, what a good girl you're starting to be," the woman's voice said with heavy approval, the hand patting my hair again. "But we still remember what a bad girl you were. Are we going to see any more of that bad girl?"

"No, no, I'll be good, I swear I will," I babbled, my chest heaving against the padded table. I suddenly thought I was back in the crèche, facing the Head after having been found doing something wrong. "Please don't hurt me like that again, I swear I'll be good."

"Of course you will," the woman's voice said, satisfaction now mixed in with the approval. "To help you keep that in mind some of the pain will be left with you, but not too much of it. Tell me: what will you do if the Prime Jer-Mar is generous enough to find interest in you again?"

If my eyes had been open I would have closed them, in a useless attempt to keep the tears from flowing out and running down my cheeks. That time, with my eyes already closed, it didn't help at all. The tears slid down my face to the padded table under my right cheek, starting a pool that would unfortunately not be deep enough to drown in. The only thing available for me to drown in was pain, that and deep, curling shame.

"I'll do anything he wants me to," I whispered, the sobs already beginning. "Anything, anything . . ."

Anything I had to in order to keep that agony from touching me again, to put an end to the need to scream. I'd thought I was strong and noble and brave, but all I was was a coward, shivering at the thought of being hurt like that again. To be brave I needed something I didn't have, something I couldn't even remember, but something I knew I'd never have again. I'd been lying to myself, thinking I could do it alone, and now I'd been taught that I couldn't. When you're all alone all you can really do is cry, and they were cruel enough to let me learn that.

I was so exhausted I fell asleep, and when I woke up there were two more women in the room. They were slender, young, and seriously quiet, both dressed in one-piece things like uniforms that weren't uniforms, made of heavy material in a dull green color. They watched without comment while I was released from the table, possibly wondering why I moved so slowly and carefully, possibly already knowing. The all-consuming agony was gone, but I still felt as though I'd been whipped over the entire back of me, as far down as my ankles. Worse than that was the sense of defeat I was sunk into, but defeat doesn't make you draw your breath in sharply if you accidentally lean back against something without thinking. All it does is make you not really care that you've caused yourself unnecessary hurt; you've already accepted so much hurt, what difference can a little more make?

The two women in dull green had brought a freshening kit with them, the sort that people take with them when they go off on vacation to leave civilization behind, but would rather not part with certain essentials. The kit used sonics or something to clean you when water wasn't available, and most people agreed it did a better job than water. The only thing it didn't do was satisfy the way water did, but you can't have everything. If you wanted to be clean you used the kit, and waited until you got home to your bath to be satisfied.

The freshening kit took away the smell and sweat of too much pain, and I couldn't even find enough curiosity in me to ask why I hadn't been taken instead to the shower stalls I'd been told about. The two Secs and the woman in yellow watched while I was made clean again and my hair was brushed, and then they watched while I was dressed. My thin cloth smock had been put somewhere, and in place of it the women produced something I couldn't at first believe they were serious about. The underneath layer consisted of having my nipples brushed with something wet before golden glitter was sprinkled on them, and a very thin, fine, glittering, golden metal chain girdle was closed around my hips. The girdle also had a thin section that went down between my legs and up again to be fastened behind, but when I tried to tell the women they'd made it too tight, I discovered it hadn't been an accident. My unimportant observation was ignored the way all petty distractions are, and the women went on with their work.

The top layer of my new outfit was something like a robe, high to my throat in front, down to my toes, and almost to my fingertips. In back it was open from my neck down to below my waist and closed from there, with a single thin chain of gold across the middle of my back to hold it properly closed and make it hang right. Wearing it hurt a little despite the fact that the material was so thin it might well have been cobwebs, but the pain wasn't what bothered me most. The robe was a lovely green and very graceful and delicate, but it was also completely transparent. Under it I was more than naked, much, much more, and everyone who looked at me would be able to see that. I was given nothing for my feet, but that felt more appropriate than surprising. The people around me wore shoes or boots, but not being a people meant I didn't get to do the same. The woman in yellow came closer to look me over, and then she smiled.

"We've taken care of seeing to you this one time, dear, but from now on you're responsible for dressing yourself," she said, putting a hand under my chin to raise my head a little. "If and when you're claimed for a night, you'll tell someone so that you can be given an outfit that will please the Prime who claimed you. And what will you do for that Prime or any other?"

"Anything he wants me to," I answered tonelessly, making no attempt to meet her eyes. It didn't matter what I said or didn't say, nothing mattered, not any more. There was nothing in the way of fight left in me, and I just didn't care.

"What a good girl you're going to be," the woman said, patting my cheek in approval before taking her hand away. "Leader Quatry and I have discussed the matter, and we've decided that although you'll be going in to join the men at dinner, you needn't bother letting the chef know where you're seated. Since you've refused nourishment twice today, we've decided that it won't really hurt you if it's not offered again until tomorrow. By then you'll know better than to refuse what's given you, won't you, dear?"

I could almost feel the smile that was being sent toward me, that and the enjoyment which seemed to fill her. They were going to make me go hungry until they were ready to graciously forgive me, but that wasn't the added punishment they thought it was. Despite the fact that I couldn't remember the last time I'd eaten, I didn't expect to ever be hungry again. When I'd looked down at my body I'd thought I was thinner than usual, thinner than I was somehow supposed to be, but that was nothing but more help. The end would come sooner that way, with less time that had to pass while I did "everything and anything." I still couldn't remember my previous reason for wanting to die, but having a brand-new reason made remembering totally unnecessary.

Since there was nothing left that needed to be done to me, the two women in dull green were allowed to leave, and then the woman in yellow led me and the two Secs back to the dormitory room. When we reached it I could see through the wide windows that it had grown dark out during my time in the other room, and small, distant lights had been lit around the walls to replace the lost sunlight. It still wasn't anything like bright and cheerful in that big, circular place, but none of the women in it appeared to notice or care. They were all putting the finishing touches on themselves, either happily adjusting gaily-colored, provocative outfits or miserably brushing hair that fell onto nothing but plain, cloth smocks. Possibly one or two looked up as I was led back to my cot and left there, but I really didn't care. The stares of my fellow victims weren't what would soon add terribly to the shame I hadn't been strong enough to keep from touching me.

"Terry, are you all right?" Mera demanded in a whisper as she came away from her cot, glancing nervously at the retreating figures of the ones who had brought me there. "I knew they would punish you for doing something that dumb, I knew it! Sometimes hatchlings are so confused they try refusing to do what they're supposed to, and when they bring them back they're always crying but ready to be reasonable. I don't see any tears, but there's something—different about you. What did they do to you?"

They defeated me, I thought as I turned away from her, wishing I could lie down. But I'd been told I wasn't permitted to lie down, that it would ruin my outfit if I did, so all I could do was stand. Mera herself wore a pair of trousers with billowy legs and a very short tunic top in a lovely and transparent pink, and being barefoot didn't seem to bother her any more than it bothered me. We both were obviously used to going barefoot, but I couldn't quite recall how *I* had gotten used to it.

"No, Terry, don't start doing that," Mera said with something like fear as she came around to stand where I could see her. "Don't withdraw into depression and simply go through the motions, or they'll hurt you again. They want you to be eager and attractive for our men, they won't accept anything else. You have to smile, and laugh at the jokes you hear, and show them that you're really *trying*. I've seen the results of what they do to bring girls out of depression, and I don't want that happening to *you*."

I think I shuddered at the thought of their doing something else to me, my hand going to my mouth to keep the violent illness inside, and Mera put her own hand to my arm in the only gesture of comfort she could give. She and I both had outfits on that weren't supposed to be ruined, and if she'd hugged me the way she seemed to want to do, someone would have been displeased.

"Okay, we've just decided we're not going to let something like that happen to you," Mera said quickly, then put on a smile that almost seemed real. "I know it's Jer-Mar you have to go with tonight and that you don't like him, so we're going to work very hard at understanding and remembering that it's only for the night. He never pays attention to any one girl for longer than that, so it's just tonight you have to get through. After that the others will try you, and some of them are really nice. You'll stay with me as much as you can and do what I do, and then everything will be fine. You just wait and see, they won't have a reason to hurt you again."

By that time she sounded completely convinced, but I was convinced of something else entirely. They weren't going to let me die, they were going to force me to keep on living, and if they couldn't talk me into it they would hurt me into it. I didn't know what to do, didn't know what I *could* do, but the panic that had begun rising in me wasn't allowed the time to fill me completely. Musical notes sounded, telling us we had to go in to dinner, and Mera quickly urged me along with her, whispering words of encouragement and reassurance.

The dining room had been subtly changed to project an aura of evening rather than noon, and most of the women were already inside it before the men appeared. It was fairly clear they were making an entrance, their casual clothing of earlier in the day having been changed to the most elegant evening wear it was possible to have. Every imaginable color in the shape of formal suits erupted into the room with their arrival, brilliant ascots adding to the breathless display, and although the women around me had undoubtedly seen the same thing many times before, they gasped as one with awe and delight. I found myself gasping right along with them, but for an entirely different reason. The arousal I'd been made to feel at lunch had been overcome by the presence of pain, but suddenly it was back again, three or four times worse than before. I gasped at the burning itch that flared between my thighs, not understanding why it was happening until I remembered the injection given me by the woman in yellow. I'd thought the injection had had something to do with the liquid fire she'd put on me, but maybe it hadn't. . . .

"Well, well, what *do* we have here?" a voice drawled from very near, a voice that made me look up. The man Jer-Mar and his friends had reached us, and he stood just a few feet away letting his eyes move deliberately over me. He wore a green formal suit and boots and a gold ascot, and the green of his suit was exactly the same shade as my transparent robe. If I'd had any doubt as to who I'd been given to for that evening, the color scheme was meant to lay them to rest. I hated the look of that arrogant, foolish face, but when he stepped forward to get even closer, my body responded with a gush of moisture that nearly made me gasp again.

"Were you well punished, sweet thing?" he asked with that same insulting amusement, raising one hand to brush a finger across my cheek. "I'd venture to say you were, so I'll have my apology now. Tell Jer-Mar how sorry you are for being bad, and he'll tell you if he forgives you."

"I'm—sorry I was bad," I managed to get out, completely unable to look at him. "I didn't know what I was doing, and I won't do it again. I don't know what else to say, except that I hope you'll accept my—"

My words broke off with a grunt as his hand moved to my breast, and I had to close my eyes against what he was making me feel. I couldn't remember ever needing a man so much in my entire life, and the too-tight chain of the girdle was suddenly turning it a good deal worse.

"I just noticed how stiff your nipples are, my pretty little thing," he said, laughing at me as he all but ignored the apology he'd asked for. "You're going to give me a real good ride when I'm ready to take it, aren't you? I love the taste of eagerness, so I think I'll have a sip of it now."

His fingers left my breast to raise my face, and then he was holding me to him as his lips covered mine. I didn't want his kiss and yet I needed it very badly, a kiss that usually led to something I needed even more. The way he was holding me made my back hurt, but the pain wasn't enough to distract me from the more demanding feelings flashing through me. He took the kiss hard with no attempt to share, something that upset me but also did nothing to help, and then he suddenly ended the kiss, let me go, and stepped back.

"And now on to the meal, I think," he announced to his grinning friends, clearly satisfied over having gotten what he wanted and caring nothing about what it had done to *me*. The others made sounds of agreement and the ones who hadn't yet chosen a woman began doing so, the ones with previously chosen founts of adoration spending the waiting time teasing or examining their victims. I discovered that victim really was the perfect word when Jer-Mar blessed me with partial attention of the same kind. His hand slid into the open back of my robe and began to stroke my bottom, but when I moaned and tried to press myself up against him in wordless begging, he pushed me away in disinterested refusal.

It took only a few moments before everyone was ready, and then we all went to a table. The men walked ahead talking to one another, none of them looking back, but there was really no reason for them to look back. Their simpering satellites hurried in their wake as though they were on leashes, their gazes clinging to the backs of the men who had honored them. Mera acted as though she wanted to do almost the same, but she hadn't lost her determination to watch over me. She coaxed and urged me along with the group, constantly reminding me that it would all soon be over with.

By the time the happy group was seated and meal orders had been given to and received from the table's autochef, I found I was as completely forgotten about and ignored as the rest of the women. The men were having a friendly disagreement over the best way to attack while still defending, but made no mention of how they were attacking or who, or what they were defending with. Nothing in the way of food was delivered to me, and no one was so unreasonable as to offer me any of theirs.

Sitting in the very comfortable chair was painful in various ways, but it didn't take long to discover that my mind wasn't paying attention to the pain. I still felt horribly defeated and crushingly shamed, but there was a very small core of anger beginning to glow under those feelings, the heat of it starting to burn upward and outward. I'd been hurt so badly that the thought of having to face the same agony again made me immediately and automatically ill, but the core of anger was refusing to be affected by any part of that. It was growling with the insistence that no one had the right to treat me the way those people were treating me, and seemed to be demanding that I do something to make them stop. If I hadn't been so confused and upset I might have laughed at the idea, the completely outrageous idea that *I* could make them all stop what they were doing to me, but I had the impression the anger inside would have ignored the laughter. It seemed to believe I *could* do something other than just sit helplessly by, and therefore refused to stop heating up and spreading.

The dinner turned out to be a rather long one, and I would have had to have been dead not to notice that Jer-Mar was purposely dragging it out. The other men seemed to be used to following his lead, and when he ordered another bottle of wine and then sat back to discuss how he intended decorating his new-level apartment, some of his cronies looked faintly surprised but none of them objected. A few of the women around the table had been allowed a taste of the first bottle of wine, but not all of them and none got a second taste. I remembered then what I'd been told about diet restrictions, and the anger inside me took that, too, as fuel.

By the time the mighty Prime finally decided he'd made me wait long enough, the small core of anger in me had grown to triple its original size. The entire back of me felt as though I'd suffered a low-intensity burn, and the tightened chain between my legs had become more than painful. That chain was probably supposed to have added to the raging need I'd been made to feel, but it had done a more effective job on my anger. I remembered thinking I'd never before needed a man so much, but during the time everyone else was eating my mind had apparently been working, and now I seemed to recall an episode when I'd been forced to feel the same way. I couldn't bring any of the details back, but I was convinced there *had* been such a time; I'd feared the people who had done that to me, but somewhere deep inside I'd also been furious.

"And now, my friends, I believe I'm in the mood for some entertainment," that fatuous voice came, accompanied by his rising from the chair next to me. "Come along, sweet thing, and we'll learn exactly how eager you are to please Jer-Mar."

This time he waited for me to get to my feet rather than simply moving off, and once I was standing he took my hand and led the way to the center of the dining room. Since I'd been expecting him to show me to his apartment I didn't understand what was happening, not until he picked me up and then went to one knee to put me flat on the carpeting.

"No, no, my pretty little thing, I don't want you up again," he said as I tried to struggle back to my feet, his left fist closing painfully in my hair. "Those in charge of you may have punished you for being a bad little girl, but I haven't given you all of *my* punishment yet. I remember what caused your misbehavior; you'll remember what you earned with it."

He gestured to one of his now-laughing friends and the man came to take over holding my hair, which freed both of Jer-Mar's hands. The crony's fist was almost as tight as his leader's had been, and although I knew I shouldn't be struggling, I couldn't seem to help myself. More and more faces were starting to join those already circled around where I'd been put on the carpeting, and *all* of them were laughing. They knew what that—*man*—was going to do to me, and I couldn't stand the thought of being humiliated like that.

"You do indeed have a sweet, eager body, little thing," Jer-Mar said as he used both hands to slide the robe up on me, his crouching to one side letting him avoid the kicking of my legs. "We're all going to see every bit of it and more, and then you're going to please me. And you do need very much to be pleasing, don't you?"

He took both of my nipples between his fingers then, squeezing them harder and harder, but not so hard that the pain was a distraction. The people watching laughed at my moan, a reaction I wouldn't have had without that "help" I'd been given, and I couldn't keep from closing my eyes in shame. My hands went from trying to push the fist from my hair to beating blindly at the man touching me like that, but apparently that was exactly what he'd been waiting for. His fingers were gone before my wildly swinging hands could reach any part of him, and suddenly there was a body forcing itself between my frantically kicking legs.

"Are you blushing, my precious?" Jer-Mar asked with real amusement in his voice, his elbows keeping my knees to either side of his body. "How sweet to see modesty in a little thing like you, and also how touching. Well, will you look at this. What *do* we have here?"

Just as though he didn't know what it was, his hands went to the chain that was now so easily in his reach. I choked when he touched me and tried to get away, but his free hand got a grip on my thigh and then he went on investigating his "find." It didn't take long before he had me screaming, but the laughter of the crowd almost drowned me out. Half of the laughter seemed to be vicious delight, maybe even more than half, but part of it felt like desperation to fit in, and knee-weakening relief that it was someone other than them who was being treated like that. It came to me in a vague flash that I was not only frantic but wild enough to imagine strange reactions around me, and then Jer-Mar grew bored with toying with his little "thing." His fingers detached the chain from the front of the girdle, left me for a moment to presumably see to his own preparation, and then he was thrusting inside me.

I knew how terribly bad off I was, how desperately I needed the attentions of *any* man, and for that reason was surprised when Jer-Mar's heavy stroking didn't drive me deeper into helpless response. After a couple of minutes my mind began to clear, and that was when I noticed I wasn't doing anything more than accepting what was being done to me. I wasn't moaning with delight, or begging him not to stop, or frantic to give him anything and everything. What I felt most strongly was pain in my back, a good part of that due to the fact that Jer-Mar didn't seem to know better than to rest so much of his weight on me. Like an inexperienced boy he was too wrapped up in working off his excitement, hips pounding and eyes closed in self-centered pleasure. He paid no attention to the woman he used, and might just as well have been using a woman-shaped doll.

By the time he spasmed with release, I was back to being filled with almost nothing but fury. I was so humiliated by what he had done to me that I wanted to scream with the rage of it, and the fact that he hadn't satisfied me only added to the rest of it. Those fools who were standing all around were still laughing, just as though they had the right to look down on me, but I knew better than that. They *didn't* have the right, none of them did, and some *how,* some way, I would prove it.

"And so the sweet little hatchling has been given her first ride," Jer-Mar said as he lifted himself off me, using one hand to see to his clothing before rising the rest of the way. "I never realized how stimulating public punishment could be, and regret now that I didn't try it sooner. I'll certainly have to try it again, though, and possibly even with the same mount. You may now apologize again, little thing, and thank me for having honored you in a way you didn't really deserve."

He stood there looking down at me with a superior sneer, accepting the chuckling and backslaps from his friends as nothing more than his due, watching as I turned to my right side on the carpeting and then sat up. He was probably hoping he'd hurt me, definitely expecting me to be devastated, but he hadn't hurt me in the least, and all I felt was mad.

"I apologize for having tried to fight you off, Jer-Mar," I said, looking up to meet his eyes directly. "If I'd known you were going to go at it for so short an amount of time, I wouldn't have bothered protesting. I really appreciate the way you honored me, but I do have a question: when does it get to be my turn to be satisfied?"

There were so many gasps and choking noises from the people all around, that it sounded like a windstorm rising in a forest. The blood drained out of Jer-Mar's face and then it came back to make him look like he'd been slapped, a bright flush of crimson humiliation that went a good distance toward getting even for what he'd done to *me*. In my imagination I could feel the way the men in the room were now laughing at *him*, not aloud but still plain enough to sense, and again there came a feeling of pressure around my mind, as though something were trying to squeeze me to nothing.

The man who had tried to add to my shame stood with fists clenched, eyes bulging, and no expression for a very short time, and then he seemed to grow even angrier with frustration. His face twisted with savage fury, and he made a gesture of dismissal.

"Turned off is untouchable, but only in that way," he said with a snarl, then shook off the hands of his friends who tried holding him where he stood. "I don't care *what* the policy against really hurting them is, nobody talks to me like that. Nobody."

With that he started toward me, his right hand still clenched into a fist, and it wasn't hard figuring out what he intended doing with that fist. I got to my feet as quickly as I could, but made no attempt to back away from the oncoming attack. I'd known Jer-Mar was the sort who could be goaded into something that wasn't supposed to be done, someone who could be pushed until he pushed back just a little too hard. No one in that place was willing to let me die, but if it happened before any of them could stop it . . .

It took only seconds for the man to reach me, wonderfully brief bits of time that I happily greeted the end of, his fist beginning to rise to the ready point while his eyes filled with vicious satisfaction. It was just about to happen and too late for any of the Secs to interfere; he was going to do it— But then his rush faltered as he looked past me, and stiffness replaced the readiness in him.

"That's a good boy, Jer-Mar," a deep voice said from behind me, a calm and easy voice filled with the faintest hint of amusement. "Trying to hurt one of the girls will get the boy's ears pinned back hard, but not by the fools who run this place. And you have to admit she was telling the truth. That's not the first time I've heard it suggested you'd still be the next thing to a virgin if the girls had anything to say about it. If you were smart, you'd look into the possibility of taking a few lessons."

"From *you?*" Jer-Mar came back with all the scorn he was capable of, but there was still an almost-trembling inside him, a fear of sorts that limited him to the use of no more than words. "The story around *here* is that you're having trouble cutting it, Kel-Ten. Everyone's waiting for the time you're defeated, so a real man can take over firsts. That time may not be too far ahead of us."

"That's right, you *are* due to move up soon, aren't you?" the deep voice said, and the amusement in it had increased. "I've been meaning to come by and tell you how much I'm looking forward to that. And the story you should have been hearing is that I'm bored with cutting it, but I doubt if you're capable of understanding something that deep. You're not smart enough to know there's more to life than working up to a challenge, and in between dipping your brains out. Come to think of it, maybe that's *why* you're not smart enough."

"So to cure your boredom, you come slumming," Jer-Mar said, his eyes glittering with the wish that he could go beyond that. "You stroll in and act the great protector, but what you've really accomplished is doing *me* a favor. They would have drawn and quartered me if I'd managed to hurt the pretty little thing, but now I've calmed down enough to step back and let *them* do it. She took their first efforts hard enough to start out this evening with a real attempt to apologize. I can't wait to see what the next set does to her."

The look on his face was pure vindictive glee, and closing my eyes in defeat didn't stop me from knowing about it. I'd been so torn apart when my plans hadn't worked out, that I hadn't even turned to see who had ruined them. Now I was more than torn apart, more like close to stark terror, and the next words I heard began to freeze my blood.

"We humbly beg your pardon, Prime Jer-Mar," the voice of the woman in yellow came, the tremble in it undoubtedly caused by anguish and anger both. "We returned her to you thinking she was now worthy of your attentions, but obviously we were wrong. The next time she's brought back, there won't be any possibility of our being wrong."

That was the signal for the hard, uncaring hands to close on my arms again, hands that would drag me back to agony I couldn't even bear to think about. Opening my eyes again was something I couldn't bring myself to do, as though the nightmare would dissolve and drift away if I didn't look at it, leaving me safe and unhurt. The hands closed tighter and began pushing and pulling me, refusing to dissolve the way they were supposed to, forcing me to take the first steps toward crushing horror. Part of me wanted to whimper and beg for forgiveness, to swear that I'd never do anything like that again, but the rest of me refused to let the words come out. Women were lucky in that they didn't have to be strong at all times, I remembered from somewhere, but most of me dismissed the thought as unacceptable. Some women couldn't let themselves be anything but strong, especially if they were alone—without someone really strong beside them whose strength they could share—

"Where do you think you're taking her?" that deep,

calm voice came again with no warning, a big hand suddenly on my shoulder in company with the words. "Were you given permission to take her?"

"But—but—Prime Kel-Ten, you don't seem to understand," the woman in yellow began to stutter, choking up in horror over having to disagree with one of her gods. "The girl was obscenely, unbelievably insulting to a *Prime,* a man who's one of your own! She has to be punished for that, she simply has to be, it would be unthinkable to allow anything else! I do hope you're not upset over my having spoken to you like that, but . . ."

"But you're missing the point," the deep voice interrupted, surprisingly sounding gentle rather than annoyed. "Prime Jer-Mar hasn't yet reached the point where he's one of mine, and even if he does eventually get there that doesn't change the fact that *I* want the girl. I was about to take her with me when you and your Secs interrupted, but I'm prepared to forgive you for not knowing that. If you like, I'll punish her for you, but I'm still taking her with me."

"You have no right taking that girl!" Jer-Mar snarled with frustrated fury, while confusion forced my eyes open to see how close he was to throwing a fit. "She belongs here with the rest of the no and low percentage fluff, not . . ."

"Wrong again, big man," the deep voice said, all gentleness having disappeared from it. "I can take any girl I care to, from highest to lowest, and no one will do anything but smile and nod. It's one of the privileges you get when you reach the level I'm at—something I really do hope you manage. Until and unless that happens, I can't do any challenging of my own. Tell your Secs to let the girl go, woman. They're not Class Zeroes, and I don't want to have to hurt them."

"Of course you don't, Prime Kel-Ten, of course you don't," the woman in yellow said hurriedly with worry, while Jer-Mar paled and stepped back to fall silent. "See, they've already let her go, so she's yours to take. You *will* punish her while you have her, you did say you would, didn't you? No permanent physical damage, of course, but that leaves quite a lot . . ."

The woman's voice faded away into the distance as the hand on my shoulder directed me out of the dining room through the doors the men had used to enter, the man belonging to the hand still nothing but a disembodied presence behind me. The Secs had turned me loose so fast the woman in yellow hadn't had a chance to give them the order, and the fact that they had actually looked frightened added to my confusion. I was so relieved I wouldn't be going with them that I wanted to tremble, but unbelievably I was also beginning to feel angry again. I'd been claimed by one of those—*men,* one of those so-called Primes, and my emotions were running in so many different directions I didn't know *how* to feel.

"Don't harm yourself rushing to thank me for getting you out of that," the deep voice said once we were through the doors and out into a wide, lobbylike area, one that seemed at that moment deserted. "You have very little to be grateful for, after all, so why be fanatic about it? Or are you still so frightened that you're not capable of anything more than putting one foot in front of the other?"

The last part of his commenting was an afterthought that took the dryness out of his tone, but all it did for me was add burnables to that inner fire that was giving me so much trouble. Everyone in that place was made of solid arrogance, and I'd long since had more of it than anyone might be expected to want.

"So you're waiting for me to thank you for appropriating me," I said, trying to pull loose from that hand still on my shoulder. "As soon as I'm able to recall asking you for the honor, I'll be sure to show my gratitude as fully as I can. If by some chance you're also waiting for me to beg you not to send me back, I think I ought to mention that you're wasting your time. I fully expect to end up back with those sadists eventually, so I've decided not to waste good begging. And now that I've insulted you as well, we can just turn around and . . ."

"If you don't mind, I'm the one who's supposed to be giving the orders around here," he said, his big hand refusing to turn me loose. "If I decide I'm getting tired of it, then you can take over, but until then it stays my privilege alone. That, of course, includes deciding when and if I've been insulted. And you really should understand I can't take you back yet. We have to work on getting you to remember when you asked me to help you, so you'll have the opportunity to be fully grateful."

He sounded so very amused that my core of anger grew furious, just as though it were a separate, living person inside me. The rest of me was also more than mildly annoyed, and both together gave me a good enough reason to begin struggling to free myself from his grip. I swung wildly with my arms and managed to hit the arm of the hand holding me, and very briefly I was rewarded with being entirely free. I used the opportunity to start to run, to what destination I had no idea, but being free and alone was a good enough intention to begin with. I must have taken three or four steps before a hand closed on my arm, and then I was pulled back to a broader chest than I'd been picturing.

"You're trying to leave already?" he asked, looking down at me with laughter in his eyes as his arms held me to him. "Without first showing me how grateful you can be? People have always told me how beautiful and desirable I am. Are you trying to say they were lying?"

At that exact moment I wasn't trying to say anything, most especially because I couldn't seem to find the words. Seeing his face had been something of a shock, but I couldn't understand why. Rather than being boyish-featured he had a broad, manly face, one that was really quite handsome. It made me feel very odd to look at him, almost fluttery inside and the next thing to shy, but I didn't understand why that should be. After all, it wasn't as though I'd never seen a handsome, blond, blue-eyed man before.

# 5

"This is it," Kel-Ten said after opening the door and pulling me inside by the hand he held, then closing the door behind us. "What do you think of your new cage?"

The room we had entered was just short of enormous, and was more opulent than anything I'd seen in a very long time. Deep, luxurious carpeting and expensive drapes in gold, shimmering crystal decorations and accompaniments, couches, chairs, tables, sideboards—everything perfectly matched in varying tones of gold, a visitors' room unlikely to find its equal anywhere but Central's State House. Getting to the apartment had been like moving through the most expensive and exclusive visitors' Residence ever built, and remembering the dormitory room and narrow corridors of the women's section of that facility, I couldn't help but find my new surroundings annoying.

"I believe it would be more accurate to say that this is *your* cage," I answered, pretending to dismiss the room after the single glance around. "After what I've seen, I can't deny that you and those like you *need* cages; it would just be more appropriate if there were heavy bars and keepers with whips to go along with the rest."

"What makes you think there aren't?" he asked, looking down at me with that amusement lurking behind the light of his eyes. "This isn't *my* apartment, it's the apartment of the highest ranking male Prime, whoever that happens to be. Right now I'm it, but that could change the very next time I'm challenged. Take my word for the fact that the next lower apartment is about a third the size of this one."

"Oh, you poor thing," I commiserated, shaking my

head with the tragedy of it all. "If you lose you have to move into an apartment a full third smaller than this. Why, that would make its visitors' room only ten or fifteen feet square, with a mere eight-foot ceiling. However would you stand it?"

"I get the feeling you're not experiencing much in the way of sympathy for me," he said, folding his arms as he tried to look stern, the effort doing nothing to extinguish his continuing amusement. "And after I went to all the trouble of finding and rescuing you from the bad guys. I think I'm going to have to remember the promise I made to punish you, but first there are other things to be taken care of. Right this way."

He unfolded his arms to take my hand again, and then I was pulled after him toward an arch in the somewhat distant righthand wall. The arch gave onto a short hall containing three closed doors, one directly ahead at the end of the hall, one to the left a bit before that one, and one to the right which was also the closest. The one to the right turned out to be our destination, and once we were through the doorway it also turned out to be a bathroom. Not your simple, ordinary bathroom, though, but one that went well with the acre of visitors' room.

"The first thing you need is a bath," my appropriator said, dropping my hand to go toward the giant's tub sunk halfway into the thickly carpeted floor. "Water won't do anything to counteract the reagent already absorbed through your skin, but it *will* get rid of what's crystallized and clinging to the outside. The crystallized portion isn't being diluted and washed away by your bloodstream, so that's what's continuing to cause you most of the pain. When we get rid of that, you'll find yourself feeling a good deal better."

So that was why they'd used sonics to clean me instead of taking me to the shower area. I remembered wondering about that, and now I'd been given the answer. But I'd also been given another question or two, and there was no reason not to ask them.

"How do *you* know what they did to me?" I asked his back as he studied the bathtub dials set in the wall behind and to the right of the tub. "I wasn't aware of the fact that their procedures were general knowledge. And why should you care whether or not I'm in pain? Your—own kind—by the name of Jer-Mar was delighted to have me that way, and would have been more delighted still to have the pain increased. I don't see that much of a difference between you two."

"Now, *that* is an insult you won't be getting away with," he answered, turning his head to give me a hard look over his shoulder. "When the day comes that I'm defeated, it won't be by a low-class incompetent like him. And even if everyone in this facility gets to the point of being able to walk all over me, he still won't be anything like my kind. My kind is human, and Jer-Mar doesn't qualify. As soon as the tub is full, get out of that window pane and start soaking."

His finger poked at a stud on the wall, and water began pouring into the tub from four separate spouts, each one shaped like a golden pitcher set on its side. The faint scent of perfume began rising into the room on the warm air shimmering up from the rapidly filling tub, a scent very much like that of flower petals.

"I don't like having perfume added to my bath water," I said, noticing that he was walking over to a dry-chair rather than leaving. "And I also don't like having an audience while I bathe. If you're afraid I'll try sneaking out with the washing only half done, you can set up a guard post and inspection station at the front door. This isn't . . ."

"That's enough," he said as he settled into the chair, loosening the golden ascot at his throat just a little. He hadn't raised his voice to anything like a shout, but the way he was looking at me turned the two words into a flat-voiced order he didn't seem prepared to have ignored. "I know I've been letting you say just about anything you cared to, but that doesn't mean you're in charge. *I'm* the one who's in charge, so stop telling me what you do and don't like. You haven't been here long enough to have an opinion, and even if you had been, mine comes first. I'll be very upset if these facts of life do anything to ruin the beautiful friendship that's started between us, but I'm also certain I'll survive. Now, get out of that thing and into the water."

Once he'd said his piece he turned his attention to flipping open the arm of the dry-chair to reach the drink-order pad, and a moment later a glass of wine rose up on the small stand put out from the right side of the chair. I turned my back as he reached for the glass, having no interest in waiting until his eyes were on me again, and then began getting out of the transparent green robe. If bathing hadn't meant I'd be rid of that still-burning pain I would have turned and walked out of there, but I knew well enough I'd need all the help I could get once he sent me back to the women's section. Which would probably be in a short enough time, if his annoyance meant what annoyance usually did. I felt nothing in the way of desire to *be* sent back, but that permanently angry, stubbornly refusing part of me would not let me do anything to make sure that I wasn't.

The robe part of my outfit came off easily enough, but when I tried unhooking the golden metal girdle, I found myself with something of a problem. I'd apparently been too out of sorts to notice that Jer-Mar had reattached the short chain to the front of the thing, and I couldn't quite see the way of opening it again. Because of that I had to reach around to the back of the girdle rather than slide it to where I could see what I was doing, and had to try getting it open by touch alone. Since it hadn't taken long to put on it must have had a relatively simple catch, but all my fingers found were rounded links with nothing that seemed made to be opened. I worked at it long enough to begin wondering if I could slide it off over my hips once I was wet and soapy, but before I could decide definitely to try it, an alternate suggestion was put forward to me.

"Come over here, and I'll get that open for you," my audience said, sounding as though he'd been watching my struggles for a while. I didn't have to think about it very long to know I didn't like the idea, but when I tried pretending I hadn't heard it I was firmly disagreed with.

"I said, get your tail over here," he repeated in a harder voice, but not one that seemed totally out of patience. "If I have to come over to *you*, you won't like what happens."

"I'm not likely to enjoy it either way," I pointed out, still not turning back to look at him. "The question I'm wondering about now, though, is which one will turn out to be the worst of the two. Since I have my suspicions, I think I'll stay right where I am."

I'd been fighting with that stupid girdle even as I'd spoken, hoping I could get it off and solve the problem that way, but nothing had worked out right for me since I'd opened my eyes that morning. Instead of finding the catch I was looking for, I suddenly found myself being pulled into two strong arms. A hand came to my face to turn it upward, and then I was being kissed with an odd kind of full attention, as though something in particular was being looked for. I was given two or three kisses of the same sort, and then Kel-Ten raised his brows.

"That's strange, you *do* taste like a girl," he said, sounding as though he thought I wouldn't. "If you taste like one you probably are one, but I didn't think there were any girls like you left in the entire universe. Back-talk instead of breathless agreement, thinking for yourself instead of expecting me to do it for you. I'd love to be able to get used to that again, but I'm afraid my enjoyment would be your eventual pain. You can't act like that around here, soft and lovely, or they'll take everything from behind your eyes and leave nothing but the shell. We both know they've tried delivering that message to you, but until now you've been refusing receipt. We're going to have to work on teaching you how to be a good girl before sending you back, or you'll end up just like all the others. And *that* is something I won't allow."

He finished his speech on a more sober note than he'd started it with, and the look in his light eyes had developed a stubbornness to match. I still didn't understand what he was after—or trust him in any way at all—but he wasn't waiting for a show of cooperation. As a matter of fact, he didn't wait for anything at all. Before I knew what was happening I was turned around, the girdle was opened, and then a smack to the bottom sent me forward toward the tub.

"Now you can get into the water," my volunteer assistant said, the amusement back in his voice. "I added the perfume to discourage myself from joining you, but if you take much longer perfume won't be enough of a discouragement. Of course, if you *want* company in there . . ."

Glancing over my shoulder showed he was grinning as he let the words trail off, but that didn't mean he was joking. His one-piece, gold formal suit would not take long to get out of, and his fingering of my bottom while opening the girdle had definitely been deliberate rather than accidental. My answer to his uncompleted question was to quickly climb the tub steps and then move down into the water, and by the time I'd lowered myself into the wet, delicious warmth, he was already on his way back to the dry-chair.

I hadn't been completely sure he'd been telling the truth about the water easing my pain, and for the first couple of minutes it didn't. The smack to the bottom he'd given me hadn't been gentle, and that combined with the remnants of the liquid treatment I'd had made sitting on the tile of the tub uncomfortable. I was trying to figure out what I would do if the water *didn't* help, when I noticed that what had been left of the glitter on the ends of my breasts was just about all washed away. Right after that the pain began thinning in a way I could feel, and once started the withdrawal didn't stop until there was only a shadow left of what it had been. I took a deep breath and moved myself over to a headrest, able to relax for what felt like the first time in a thousand years.

"Now that you're rid of most of what they did to you, you might consider taking a break on the biting and scratching you've been doing in my direction," Kel-Ten said, drawing my eyes to where he sat in the dry-chair with his glass of wine. "I know that the treatment you got was partially my fault, but I think I made up for it by not letting it happen a second time. Do *you* think you might try seeing it that way?"

What I thought was that I didn't understand a word he was saying, and the way I frowned at him must have told him so. He sipped at his wine while showing a very faint smile, and then he shook his head.

"No, Kel-Ten, dear, I don't think I can see it that way without having everything explained to me," he said in a high, squeaky voice accompanied by a very bright smile. Then he changed the brightness to a wise-looking, very solemn smile and said in his own voice, "I suppose I was expecting that, girl dear. You're not yet ready to take my word for things, foolish though that proves you to be. And by the way, what name is there for me to use in place of 'girl'? Just in case you happen to end up in a crowd of females, and I need to call you."

By then he was looking at me again, this time waiting patiently for an answer. I knew that everyone I'd met in that place was a good deal stranger than average, but Kel-Ten topped them all by quite a bit.

"The name I've so far gone through life with is Terrilian," I grudged in reply, half wondering why I was bothering. "Are you always this crazy, or are you making a special effort on my account?"

"Sometimes I'm even crazier," he said with more of a grin than a smile, nodding at me as though in thanks. "Not long after I got here I learned that I *had* to act crazy, or I'd end up going crazy. The only time I refrain is during a challenge, but that's not what *this* is. Or at least not exactly. I take it, Terrilian, you'd like those questions you asked earlier to be answered now."

"I would have preferred having the questions I asked earlier to be answered earlier," I answered, splashing some of the delightful water over my shoulders. "Now I have even more questions, and since there's going to be a wait between asking and answering, I'm going to have to keep track of them all. The only problem is, I'm getting too sleepy to keep track."

"If that's the only problem, you can forget about it," he said, his grin widening. "Once you're out of that tub, I'll see to it that you're feeling something other than sleepy. But to get back to our original topic of conversation. What makes what happened to you partially my fault is the fact that I heard about you not long after they let you wake up, but I couldn't come looking until after you'd already gotten into trouble. I was in the middle of a training session when the word reached me, and even the First Prime doesn't get to walk out of a training session."

His expression had gone from amusement to tight-jawed anger, what seemed like the same sort of raging, burning fury feeding my own core of anger. I still didn't know why he would feel that way, but he seemed to mentally brush the emotion aside and then went on.

"It isn't often one of the incoming girls breaks out as soon as you did," he said, pausing to take a measured sip of his wine. "That in itself would have started the word on its rounds, but the better part of the story made it move even faster. We heard the new girl had marked up that fat fool Gearing, and the Secs vine was confirming it even before we stopped laughing. That was when I knew I had to try getting my hands on you, but I couldn't rush out of the training session. I couldn't even sneak out, not when everyone else's efforts were being measured against mine, so I had to wait until it was over. Once it was, I showered and changed clothes, then rushed over to the low dining room—only to find you'd already had a run-in with Jer-Mar. If cursing had the ability to dissolve metal, this whole facility would right then have come down on everyone's head."

He allowed himself a swallow of wine that time, his expression a sour grimace, and the wine didn't do much to sweeten it.

"I'd been hoping you would be on the unattractive side to keep the boy Primes in the low world from noticing you, but it didn't work out that way," he said after the wine was swallowed. "I didn't waste my time hoping you'd be smart enough to go along with the usual routine; what you did to Gearing proved you wouldn't be, and when I found I was too late I thought it was all over. There have been others over the past couple of years who started making something of a fuss when they first broke out, but none of their fussing lasted beyond the first punishment. I suppose I went back to the low after dinner to see the latest ex-human I'd missed out on, and imagine my surprise when I discovered there was no ex about you. You were giving me a second chance to play rescuing hero, so I lost no time in doing it and here you are.''

''And here I am,'' I agreed, pleased to find there was soap in the water as well as perfume. ''Kidnapped—excuse me—rescued by a total stranger who heard about the sparkling conversation I was capable of, and who therefore rushed right over to make sure it was him I spoke to. That has to be the most touching story I've ever heard.''

''You're thinking I'm interested in something other than conversation from you,'' he said, crossing his legs as he grinned at me. ''I can't imagine what would give you an idea like that, because it so happens it *is* conversation I'm after. From someone like me, someone who remembers a real life among real worlds. You have no idea how few of us there are.''

I had no doubt that this time I could see pain in his light eyes, a kind of pain I was sure he didn't usually show to people. He emptied his glass and ordered another glass of wine from the chair, and when it came he took it and smiled at me.

''I've been here more than five years,'' he said, gesturing with the glass. ''Exactly how much more than five years, I don't really know. Time has a habit of moving strangely in this place, and sometimes you lose track. I grew up on Nopalt and spent my adult life working as a Prime for the Amalgamation—and then I was sent here. I thought it was just another Mediation assignment, but they gave me a room, took away my personal possessions, and told me my real name was Kel-Ten. It was the name I'd been assigned when I was born here on New Dawn, and had the sort of meaning the name I'd been using all my life didn't. They told me I'd been brought back to see how my training results compared with the results of Primes not only born here but raised here as well. And then they told me I had my pick of the women—after the Primes of higher level first made their choices—but that I was responsible first for covering the women assigned to me. I'd most likely be able to handle pleasure as well as duty, but duty always had to come first.''

Another swallow of wine went down his throat, one that gave me the impression he wanted to drain the glass, but he didn't drain it. He took only that one swallow, then rested the glass on the arm of his chair.

''At first I couldn't believe how lucky I was,'' he went on, an odd smile curving his lips as his eyes examined a scene in the elsewhere. ''I was going to have my ability trained beyond anything I'd ever thought was possible, and while that was going on I could have just about any female I wanted. The other men I met who had grown up among the worlds felt just the way I did, like we'd died without noticing it and had found there *was* such a thing as a final reward. We were worked hard in our training classes, but any time we weren't working it was party time! Party time.''

He repeated the words with something of a small laugh that might have been part sigh, and then his eyes were on me again.

''Have you any idea how boring partying can get to be?'' he asked, but not in a way that showed he expected to be answered. ''I'll admit it took a while before *I* found out, and the revelation came not long after I began being seriously involved with challenging. It felt as though I were going from one level to the next with hardly a pause in between, and people stopped betting on who would win when I issued a challenge. It always turned out that *I* won, and the defending Prime never got off easy. I finally noticed how much time my ex-opponents were spending in Medical recovering, and then I noticed that being idolized by each and every woman I took to bed was beginning to turn my stomach. I thought about it for a little while, and then I went to my section leader and told him I wanted to go back to Nopalt and the life of nothing more than a Mediator.''

He was watching me fairly closely at that point, and the expression I surely developed brought back his amusement.

''No, don't bother telling me you said the same thing as soon as you found out where you were,'' he interposed, raising one hand. "I can almost hear you doing it, but I was a bit more courteous than that. And don't forget that I'd been here a while, and had done everything asked of me. I walked in expecting them to try talking me out of it but eventually agreeing, and very quickly found out how naive I was being. My section leader laughed and told me to go back to doing what I was supposed to be doing, and then ignored the few protests I managed to get out before the Secs showed up. I was escorted back to my apartment and left alone, after being reminded that I had a training class in a little while. I also had two women I was supposed to thrill after the class was over, but I decided then and there that I didn't give a damn. I'd go to no more classes and issue no more challenges, and to hell with the women. When they found they couldn't make me do things their way, they'd have no choice but to turn me loose.

"I can't believe I really was that naive," he said, and this time there was no doubt about the sigh. "When I didn't show up for the class they sent someone to find out if I was sick, and when they saw I wasn't I was scheduled for the full treatment. I didn't find out my wine had been drugged until I woke up most of the way, and then began learning what life would be like in place of what it had been. I was in this tiny cell of a room on the floor, mainly because there was no bed or any other kind of furniture, and I'd been stripped almost naked. Refusal to participate meant removal of privileges, all of them, with nothing but duty slipped in to fill the vacancies. I was mad enough to start out not caring *what* they took, but that didn't last long.

"The first thing taught me was that although I refused to go to class and learn, I wasn't finished with challenges. The only difference was that I wasn't the one issuing them, and the upper level Primes had been released from needing to refrain from working over someone not yet up to their abilities. Several times a day I was forced out of the cell by Secs to walk around the complex, and every time I came across an upper level Prime he slammed me. Half the time I was too groggy to know what was happening, and another quarter of the time I was in too much pain to care. The last quarter was when I made my trips to Medical, and they always made very sure I experienced every minute of the visit.''

He paused again at that point, and his eyes had gone to the wine instead of staying with me. He seemed to be having trouble putting what he wanted to say into words, and somehow I was certain that embarrassment made up a good part of his hesitation. He struggled very briefly in silence, and then, still without looking at me, forced himself to go on.

''Remember that I said duty was all they left me,'' he groped, trying to make the words come out round instead of square. ''One of my very first duties was seeing to the women they assigned me to, and the quality of the stock had improved as I moved higher up the ladder. When I lost everything I also lost access to those women, but I was still responsible for covering them. They dragged me to Medical every day, and—made the process less direct and a hell of a lot less pleasant. I knew damned well that it didn't have to be every day, that just once should have taken care of the matter for a good long time, but they weren't interested in my opinions. They waited until I was stupid enough to yell out something to that effect, and then they punished me. They gave me an injection to make sure I would be more cooperative the next time I was brought there, and locked me into a special—belt—to keep me from lessening the urge to cooperate on my own. After that I was walked around the complex again to give my former peers a chance to laugh at me, and then I was thrown back in my cell to suffer without distraction.''

The anger in him had grown so high that it was a good thing the glass he held wasn't really glass. If it had been, the hand wrapped around it would have been badly cut when the delicate thing shattered. The symglass actually squeaked in protest at the pressure he was putting on it, something I'd never seen happen before, but he didn't seem to notice.

''After that the injections became a regular thing, and they added a special stop to my schedule,'' he continued, still not looking at me. ''Once a day I was left in a small room that was all viewing window, and given the chance to look at the higher level girls I would have been covering if I'd still been cooperating. The viewing room looked out into the falls and streams area built for the girls to play and bathe in, and although I could see and hear them, they didn't know I was there. When the Secs discovered I was trying to beat down the walls to get to the girls, the word was passed along and from then on I was tied before being put in there. They kept me at it until I began screaming mindlessly twenty minutes or more before I was due to be put in, and then they sprang something on me I wasn't prepared for. Instead of being sent to the viewing room, I was tied and put in a room that held six real, true, breathing girls. Six willing girls, eager to be honored.

"At first I was stunned, and then I was too crazy to be stunned," he said with a growl. "It had been weeks since the last time I'd touched a female, and I would have been hurting even without those injections. With them I was a madman, and I was so happy it didn't even bother me that I was tied. Those girls didn't have to be chased, they were ready to beg me to honor them, so what did a few straps matter? I ordered the nearest one to her back, went to my knees next to her—and only then remembered the belt I was locked into. I'd tried getting it off before and hadn't even been able to dent the damned thing, not even when my hands were free. The girl I'd chosen began whimpering and begging, and the last thing I remember is her hand touching my thigh. That started the screaming again, but everything after that is a blank."

He stopped to take another measured swallow of wine, and I couldn't help but admire his self-control. If those had been my memories pouring out like that, I would have needed to compensate with a comparable flow of something bracing pouring in. My mind searched for appropriate comments, didn't find any, and then it was too late.

"I don't know how long I was out of it, but when I woke up I was in a small apartment, dressed again in civilized clothing, and no longer hurting," he went on, slumped back in the chair with his eyes on his knees. "It was almost possible to believe I'd dreamt the whole thing, especially when the assistant section leader came in, greeted me as though I'd been away a short while on vacation, then walked with me to the challenge room. Inside the room was the Prime I'd been next scheduled to challenge, still laughing at me the way he'd been doing for weeks. I suddenly found myself with this terrible need to flatten him, and although he was harder than the ones I'd faced before him, it didn't take long before I did it. Once he was down a whole crowd of people came in to pound my back and congratulate me, just the way they used to do, and the assistant leader waited only a few minutes before laughingly rescuing me from the crowd. After that I was led to a room where two upper level females were waiting, and was told they were all mine. It wasn't until I was lying flat in exhaustion and the females were gone, that I really understood what had been done to me. They'd led me right back to the point I'd strayed from, and were giving me the chance to start over again with no hard feelings."

"Which you apparently took," I said, having finally found a comment to make. It might not have been the most diplomatic comment ever uttered, but I'd been waiting to hear that they'd found they couldn't break him and had offered something to make him change his mind instead. That they'd defeated him was something I didn't want to hear, not then and not ever. For some reason I felt it was wrong that he'd been defeated, wrong and totally unacceptable.

"Damned right I took it," he said, finally looking up at me again. "I'd been taught the hard way that I couldn't hope to beat them by bashing my brains out against the walls they'd built around me. All that would have accomplished would have been to make me a smear on the floor to be washed off and forgotten about. Just in case you have no personal knowledge on the subject, let me assure you that that isn't the best of all possible things to be."

"You consider it better to be someone who's sold out?" I asked, noticing almost peripherally that the water I sat in had begun to cool. I moved away from the headrest and wet my hair, then used both hands to squeeze it out.

Since I knew I wouldn't be there for much longer, I decided it would be best if I washed as much of me as fast as I could.

"The position and outfit I found you in said you did some selling of your own," he came back, but not as sharply as I was expecting. "And Jer-Mar did mention something about you starting out the evening apologizing to him. Pain has a way of turning even someone with the most inflexible code of bravery practical, and only its easing and disappearance lets the nonsense come back. Don't get out of the tub without first showering off in clean water. You don't want to leave a film of that reagent still on you in places, just waiting to dry out."

I had already begun standing when he said that, and I didn't need to think about it to know he was right. At least about the showering part. I moved over to the white and gold shower block and stepped up onto it, waited while the clean water came at me from both above and below, then left the block to walk the tub rim to its edge. Just beyond the tub on the floor a section of the carpeting had been turned into a drip-mat, and a fluffy white towel sat folded on a raised pedestal beside the mat. I stepped off and got the towel, and only when it was wrapped around me did I turn to Kel-Ten again.

"Sometimes pain can force you into making the wrong decisions," I said, watching him sip his wine as he listened and watched me back. "It lies to you and tells you everything will be all right if only you give in, but everything *doesn't* turn out all right. You find that giving in hurts more than the pain did, but doesn't even allow you the luxury of unconsciousness when it reaches the unbearable level. I've heard it said that enough pain can kill you, even if those giving you the pain are trying to keep you alive. People *do* make mistakes, a possibility not too farfetched to spend your time hoping for. Or, maybe I should say it's something I'll be spending *my* time hoping for. And I'm ready to go back now."

"To the hope of that possibility," he said, his light eyes filled with something very much like anger. "You still don't understand why I brought you here, do you? Did you somehow get the idea I have a thing about wanting to bathe female newcomers? Or that I enjoy being insulted by idealistic infants who have managed to move through life without learning anything about it? Come over here."

"I can see and hear anything I have to from where I am," I returned, holding the towel more tightly around me. "To prove it, I can show you what I've already seen. For you, giving in means being forced to enjoy the satisfaction of success over your competition, of having to—cover—all those women, of needing to live in luxury. For me it means becoming little more than a slave, accepting constant humiliation and even more constant rape. Someone once told me you can't enslave a free man or free a slave, no matter how hard you try. A free man will still be free even with chains weighing him down, and a slave, unchained, will soon crawl back to his fetters. I can't quite remember who said it, but I have the feeling he meant it to refer to women as well as men. I've been spending enough breath saying I'm not a slave; I think the time has come to try proving it."

I somehow had the feeling he could be swayed to my way of looking at things if I spoke with enough belief and conviction, which I thought my speech had had. When he put his wine glass aside with a sound of annoyance and got to his feet, I began wondering if I weren't mistaken. He didn't *look* very convinced, and the closer he got the less swayed he seemed to be. It occurred to me it might be wise to take a step or two back from him, but the thought came the least bit too late. Even before I could decide whether or not that would constitute backing down as well as up, he bent and lifted me off the floor in his arms.

"You're going to learn that when I tell you to do something, you'd better do it," he said, ignoring my yelp of startlement as he turned back toward his dry-chair. "The practice will come in handy for use around section leaders and Secs as well as the Primes you're assigned to, and won't turn out to be a waste with me, either. Unquestioning adoration may make me queasy, but I've discovered I enjoy having women obey me. Life turns out less complicated that way, and at the moment I have all the complications I need.''

By that time he was sitting back down in the chair, settling me into his lap as though carefully tending to an infant. My being all wrapped up in that towel may have given him the impression he was dealing with a child, but just because he thought it didn't make it so. The volume of air inside the dry-chair's radius was as moisture free as the rest of the bathroom was steamy, the object, of course, being to keep any nonbather from wilting. Being brought out of the heat like that may have felt good, but it didn't do anything to cool me down.

''I think you'd better have your hearing checked,'' I stated, trying to bring my arms out of the towel without completely uncovering myself. ''I have no need to learn anything where section leaders and Secs—and most especially Primes—are concerned, because I have no intentions of being anywhere near any of them. I will *not* cooperate with what everybody considers unavoidable, and that decision will stand no matter how much they hurt me. Now, let me go so I can get out of here.''

''Don't you think it's time to leave that fantasy world behind?'' he asked, his left arm firmly around my waist to hold me where he'd put me. ''The leaders would enjoy having your cooperation, but the full, dirty truth is, they don't need it. If you don't come around permanently the second time they give you pain, the next thing they'll give you is a vacant smile, which will mean they never have to worry about the problem again. Don't you understand that they'd prefer having your mind left alive, but all they really need is your body? Do you want to be turned into a willing and agreeable vegetable incapable of any sort of thoughts at all?''

He was looking straight at me as he asked his question, and because of that didn't miss seeing my shudder. Most people believed that to kill the *I* in someone was the same as killing their body, but what would happen if it wasn't? What would happen if some very tiny portion of that *I* was left, deep down and too small to change anything, but not too small to know what was happening? How could I go on living like that—and how would I find it possible do anything else?

"Okay, now, you're finally beginning to understand," he said gently as he held me to him, his arms tight to keep my shuddering from getting out of control. "You thought you were ahead of the game by being able to tell them to go ahead and hurt you and be damned, but now you know that isn't true. You weren't lucky you weren't cowed into submission by the first punishment they gave, you had the bad luck to be shifted into line for a lot worse. If you can bring yourself to believe that, and believe as well that you have no choice about cooperating, we'll have exactly the starting point we need."

"How can you call that a starting point?" I demanded, sick to my stomach as I tried to push away from him. "Is it totally impossible for you to understand what they want me to do? I don't *want* to be *covered* at somebody else's direction, bred like an animal over and over and over! I can't let them do that to me, and I won't!"

"You can't stop it," he told me bluntly, the patience gone from his eyes as he refused to let me go. "You can do as they ask and be a part of the program, or you can try fighting them and be *made* a part of the program. The second way you haven't any chance at all of ever stopping it; the first way you can cooperate with me as well, without them knowing it, and together we might just find some way out of this. If you don't understand yet that I want out as badly as you do, you may not be the one I've been waiting for after all."

The look in his light eyes had hardened so far I wished fleetingly that I could move back from him, and then I really heard what he'd said. He thought I might be the one he'd been "waiting" for, that he and I might do—something—together. Irrationally bright hope flashed briefly inside me, then dimmed fast when it found nothing in the way of fuel to feed on.

"Of course you've been waiting for someone like me," I said, finding disbelief easier to deal with than a hope that would almost certainly be betrayed. "I'm so very special that even those who run this place were waiting breathlessly for my arrival. What sort of reward do they give you, I wonder, if you manage to talk one of the animals into being good? I believe that they're not very anxious to burn my mind away, probably for the same reason they got such bad results from their *in vitro* experiment, but what do you get out of helping them? What do they give someone already so burdened with privilege and luxury?''

''What in hell was done to you to make you so full of distrust?'' he asked in turn, narrowing his eyes as he ignored everything I'd said. ''You can't be reacting just to this place alone, not with only a single day behind you. After what you went through you should be confused, frightened, unsure, maybe even bitter—but not so completely unwilling to trust anyone. What were you involved in before they brought you here?''

''I—don't remember,'' I said, finding his stare uncomfortable. ''For some reason they don't want me remembering, so they took the memory away. But that doesn't change anything at all. Since there's absolutely nothing I can do to help you, your wanting me to 'cooperate' can mean only one thing: you let them buy you, just the way you let them convince you to be good. I won't . . .''

''You won't keep your mouth closed long enough to let anybody disagree with your flawless logic,'' he interrupted, now looking annoyed. ''And if I hear you tell me one more time that I sold out my humanity for comfort and reward— Well, you won't like what happens. For now let's talk about all that nothing you can do to help me. What makes you think there's nothing you can do?''

''Only the admittedly obscure fact that I'm still right where they want me,'' I answered, unable to understand what point he could possibly be trying to make. ''And if you wonderful male Primes, with all your secret training and experience meeting challenges, can't do anything to get out, what do you expect me to be able to do?''

''Nobody said we *couldn't* get out,'' he returned with a headshake and a faint grin. ''We wonderful male Primes slip out of the complex all the time as a joke, but that's all the others see it as: a joke. None of them would ever seriously try to leave, most of them enjoy it here too much. The ones who don't enjoy it also don't have the guts to try making a break, so that leaves me as one of a kind. I know what's necessary to get out of here, but I can't do it alone. I need another Prime to do it with me."

I opened my mouth to say something else, but suddenly the words refused to come. His expression had turned serious and the least bit strained, as though waiting for my reaction to what I'd been told. For a moment or two I *had* no reaction, and then I slowly shook my head.

"But I'm not whole," I said, knowing it for a fact even though I wouldn't have been able to explain the statement. "They've—done something to me, and I'm not whole. I can't be of help to you like this, and you should know it. And if you've already learned what's necessary to get out of here, you shouldn't need anyone else. A trained Prime *shouldn't* need anyone else."

"I wish that were true," he said with a smile, raising one hand to smooth back my still-damp hair. He didn't seem to believe what I'd said, but I somehow *knew* it was the absolute truth. A trained Prime who was complete should be able to do anything she wanted to do. *Had* been able to do anything she wanted to do. My arms tightened the towel against my body as my mind searched for the basis of that conviction, but I simply couldn't reach it. It was with the rest of my memories, locked away out of prodding range, closed behind a door I still battered uselessly against.

"It might be true under other circumstances that a Prime doesn't need any help, but not when it comes to getting out of here," Kel-Ten went on, still with an indulgent smile on his face. "This complex has the highest number of Class Zeroes ever assembled, and just about all of them are in male Prime territory. It takes a minimum of two active minds to slide around enough to avoid them, but you won't understand that until you can see and feel the situation for yourself. Which you will when I key you awake."

"But how can you possibly do that?" I demanded, only his hold on me keeping me from straightening indignantly. "I may not remember *much* about it, but one thing I can bring back is that empaths don't have that sort of information, not even First Prime empaths."

"You can thank the boyish high spirits this place breeds for the fact that *this* First Prime *does* have it," he said, deep satisfaction brightening in his eyes. "A couple of years ago some of us cornered one of the medical staff, and forced a bottle of wine down his throat. We didn't like the man, and had decided to turn him loose drunk among some high girls after telling them he was a newly-arrived Prime. That would have gotten him fried for sure, only we made the mistake of doing our own drinking while we poured his into him. Instead of setting him up, we all ended up laughing and joking like old friends, and when we mentioned our secret about what we'd intended doing with the girls, he was so touched he began to cry. No one had ever told him a secret before, and after he'd heard ours he thought it was only fair if he told us one. The only secret he knew was the keying word to awaken female empaths, so he told it to us. By the next day no one could remember anything that had happened—except for one Prime who stopped drinking after getting this idea about escape. . . ."

"Awake," I said, feeling an oddness deep inside. "You can key me awake, and then I'll be whole. But I don't understand what you mean by Class Zeroes. What are they?"

"If you're an empath, you know them," he answered, making something of a face. "They call them Class Zeroes around here, but out in the worlds they're known as nulls. It was explained to us that they don't like that name, so it's never used. But you'd better take it slower, because you're getting ahead of yourself. I can key you awake, but that won't make you entirely whole. Before we can get ourselves out of here I'm going to have to give you some training, the sort of training *we've* been given. How fast you pick up on it will depend on your inborn abilities, but it has to be done. That's why I told you you'd better get used to accepting what they have you scheduled for. Even the most basic sort of training will take time, and we can't get along on basics. We'll need more than that if we're going to get out, and into a ship, and away. If you still think I'm working for the enemy you'd better say so now, and I'll send you back to try out the plan you were talking about earlier. If you decide to go along with me you have to trust me completely and do everything I say, otherwise we're both wasting our time. I need a decision from you *now*, but you can have a minute to think it over."

He leaned back a little in the chair, his arm still around my waist, his eyes unmoving from my face. The choice of accepting or rejecting his offer was mine, but it wasn't simply a matter of saying yes or no. If he was telling the truth I very much wanted to be a part of his plans, but if he was lying in order to get me to cooperate I would find nothing in agreement but betrayal. I could feel something inside me telling me not to trust him, that I would be sorry if I trusted him, but that something was patently ignoring the one point that kept me from outright and immediate refusal. If he *was* as important as he'd told me, and I had the reactions of the woman in yellow and the Prime Jer-Mar to show that he did seem to be exactly that, what would he get out of betraying me? There could be something to give him that I didn't know about, but if there wasn't, then he had to be telling the truth. Maybe. I bit my lip in vexation, wishing I had more than that minute to make a decision, then tried a temporization.

"You said you can key me awake," I stated, trying to keep the eagerness out of my voice. "Do it now, and then there won't be any doubt about our being partners. If you really do want me to help you."

"Yes, I do want your help, but no, I won't key you now," he came back, firm decision in both eyes and voice. "In actual fact we *will* be partners, but there won't ever be a time that I treat you like one. You have to remember that they're not stupid, and if you forget even for a moment that I'm in complete charge they're bound to get suspicious. Your—sisters in service—would never dare think themselves as good as a male Prime, so you won't be given the chance to do it either. And we won't ever discuss this unless we're where we are right now, in a place whose usual field distorts any listening devices they may have planted. I won't key you awake until *I* want you awake, and that's it. Take it or leave it."

He really was pushing the thing, almost as though he were trying to make me decide *against* saying yes—or was trying to be absolutely honest and straightforward about what I had to expect. It was much easier—and safer—believing he was hiding something, but until and unless I could find out if that was true, I couldn't justify refusal. I had to take the only way out offered to me, no matter what I had to do to achieve it.

"All right, you win," I grudged, not terribly happy about having to do things on his terms. "I help you after you train me, and then we leave together. It just better not take *too* long, or I won't be able to keep up the pretense."

"Terrilian, you'd better understand right now that you won't be pretending," he said with a sigh, not as pleased as I'd thought he'd be. "If you try pretending it simply won't work, so I'm going to give you my first decision as absolute leader of this effort: no matter how ready you turn out to be, we won't make our try until after your first pregnancy. It may take even longer than that, but it won't be sooner. Again, take it or leave it."

The flatness in his tone brought the illness back to my middle with a stab of—I don't know, fear, horror, flaring disappointment, maybe all three if not more. I wanted to scream out my denial of what he'd said, wanted to push away from him and just run without stopping, but his arms had closed around me again and he wouldn't let me go.

"No, if you're going to refuse you'll do it in here, still in this chair,"he said, keeping me from struggling out of his hold. "I had to make you know that I don't want your agreement unless you're ready to commit yourself *completely* to my plans, just as completely as I'm committed. I've waited years for this chance, but I'll wait years again rather than throw away all hope of success by having you ruin things. They know the difference between cooperation, no matter how reluctant, and a pretense at cooperation, so you can't pretend. You have to accept the reality of one or more pregnancies before you can leave here, and you have to decide if you're willing to pay that sort of price. One or two pregnancies against years and years of the same, and the decision has to be yours. Every other decision will be mine, but that one has to be yours."

I still sat stiffly in his arms, trying to push away from him, but then my eyes closed, almost by themselves. I was tasting the awful sourness of defeat again, nailed tight into a box with no way out, forced to accept what he'd said or completely reject the only real hope I was ever likely to find. It felt so wrong agreeing to allow what they would do to me, wrong in a way even I couldn't completely explain, but it was either that or fall back on the flimsy hope that was really no hope at all.

"I would rather be dead," I said in a whisper, my arms braced flat against his chest. "The only problem is they won't let me be dead, will they? Why won't they let me be dead?"

"Because they need you," he answered, the words completely unsoftened by pity. "Just the way I need you, and for exactly the same reason. You're a Prime, girl, and no one in their right mind wastes a Prime. You don't yet really know what that means, but you'll sure as hell be finding out. And if we're going to be working together, you'd better learn to stop the dramatics. They're not going to be cutting you into a whole lot of bloody pieces, they're going to have men put babies in your belly. As someone who has been doing that to women for years, I think you can believe me when I say you might even get to the point of enjoying it. Other women do, so why should you be any different?"

My eyes opened fast to look at him, wondering if his expression would match his tone, and it certainly did. He was studying me with something very much like impatient ridicule, and that made me mad.

"I can be as different as I like without needing to justify it to you or anyone, simply because I *am* a Prime," I grated, wondering how well *he'd* take to having the same done to him. "I may have to go along with all this, but I 'sure as hell' don't have to like it. If you're expecting me to force myself to the point where I do, you're wasting your time and mine. If that's what you need to make your plan work, we might as well forget about it now."

"If that speech was meant to prove to yourself that success is impossible so you can simply give up, you're the one who's wasting time," he came back with a snort of faint amusement. "As long as you understand and accept what will be done to you, I'll take care of everything else. Are you understanding and accepting?"

"How about understanding and not accepting?" I asked, trying to dent his rising good humor. "Or at least not accepting on an emotional level as opposed to a physical one? What will they do to me if I take it without the requisite smiles and sighs of delight?"

"They'll increase the dosage of your injections," he said, a grin forming despite my attempt to deflate him. "If you think you'd rather hop around whimpering than bat your eyelashes and smile at a man, go right ahead and try it. Once you get it through your head that no one is going to let you do things any way but theirs, you'll relax and look for the easy road instead of the hard. If you're capable of recognizing easy, and distinguishing it from hard."

Which, his tone suggested, he didn't think I could. I felt the flush in my cheeks caused by his amusement over what would be done to me, added to by his obviously low opinion of my way of doing things. I was about to be insulted all over again, but he didn't give me the chance.

"If you're finished with your little-girl pouting exercises for today, I'm still waiting for a final answer from you," he said, a directness in his gaze despite the amusement he still clearly felt. "Do we do it my way without argument, or do we not do it at all?"

"I'd still rather be dead," I answered, this time glaring at him. "If I can find any way of arranging that instead, you can consider our deal canceled. Until then, though—we do it your way."

"Do you really believe that if you mumble the words binding you to an agreement, you won't be bound as tightly as you would if you pronounced them clearly out loud?" he asked, his wide grin showing how funny he considered that idea to be. "I think I'll have to try that some time, to see if it actually works. Right now, though, let's celebrate our agreement by trying something else. Raise your face to me."

He put a hand under my chin and bent his head to kiss me, and I couldn't help but notice how much—ownership—there was in the doing. I had committed myself to agreeing to whatever he wanted of me, and I had a terrible, sinking feeling that even that quickly it was already too late to back out. I might have told myself I was imagining things, but I wasn't given the time to indulge in false assurances. The kiss was a brief one, and as soon as it was over his hands went to the towel I was wrapped in. I could feel myself reddening and silently choking over the swallowed protests I wanted to voice but wasn't allowed, and that made him chuckle.

"What a good girl you're being," he approved even while he laughed softly, taking the towel out of my grip to open it slowly and deliberately. "Not that trying to refuse would get you anywhere. Did I mention that they switched from giving me shots to adding to my food? It was all I could do to hold back while we were talking, no matter how important I knew the conversation to be. Being First Prime means I have a lot of women to see to, and they want to be sure I'll be up for it. They also want to keep me too well occupied with thoughts of other things, to make sure I don't start thinking about making trouble again. Isn't it nice of them to help me out like that?"

His voice sounded as though it wanted to be a growl, but with his palm sliding over my breast it came out as a murmur. He had uncovered me completely and was slowly moving his hands everywhere, but when he reached my thighs I had an unpleasant surprise. Despite the fact that I didn't want to be touched like that, I was very suddenly finding it extremely hard to sit still. The heat I'd earlier thought was gone had abruptly returned, and when his fingers left my thighs to stroke elsewhere, I found myself giving in to the urge to gasp.

"Trying to push my hand away isn't being a good girl," he said, his grin as strong as his hand was impossible to move. "Hold onto my wrist with both of your hands, as though encouraging me to do anything I like. After all the argument I've had out of you, you *owe* me some encouragement."

I didn't in any way agree with that, and found that I couldn't even try to go along with it. I struggled against the way he was touching me, fought to dislodge his hand, but couldn't get free or make him stop. He was so much stronger than me that even *trying* to fight was a useless gesture, but instead of him becoming angry with me he started to laugh.

"I knew I could count on you for what I needed," he said through the laughter, his tone and expression full of arousal. "None of them make the least attempt to struggle, all they want to do is give me everything. But I'm tired of being given, I'm bored with it, what I need is something else. You'll give me that something else, and no one will get suspicious because they know I really do want it. You'll learn not to behave like this with the others, to be sure they don't do to you what I'm going to do, but for me you'll continue on with it, and that will be my reason for keeping you as long as I can and taking you back when your assignments are over. One day soon we'll beat them and be gone from here, but until then we're going to have *fun*."

He pushed me off his lap, then took my wrist and pulled me out of the bathroom with him, dragging me along behind as he headed for his bedroom. The towel had fallen to the bathroom floor to lie in an abandoned heap, and even with the burning in my body I couldn't help but think how lucky it was.

# 6

He held me tight in his arms as he stroked with all his strength, grunting and moaning out the delight he felt. He'd worked me into such a frenzy, that I couldn't have kept myself from moaning along with him even if I'd wanted to. I needed what he was giving me, needed it badly, and only distantly wished that he'd also let me hold him instead of him alone holding me. I wanted to feel that I was sharing with him rather than just being given what he wanted to give, but he didn't care to allow that. He was making it my place to take whatever I was given, and I was in no state to argue even a little. I burned for what he was giving me, and would have done almost anything to get it.

It wasn't over quickly, not until he had given me what I needed and had taken what he wanted, and then we both lay unmoving for a while in the wrinkled, sweaty linen. I'd felt fairly well rested from the previous night's sleep before the bout had begun, but the end of it hadn't left me with anything like the same impression.

"You'll find the injections will do that to you," Kel-Ten said when he'd gotten his breath back, turning to his right side to put a hand on my thigh. "Make you uncontrollably hot, I mean. Twice last night and once this morning, and if I started you up again you'd find you couldn't refuse. But you're going to try refusing anyway, aren't you, 'sweet thing'? Just to make Kel-Ten happy?"

I looked up at his grinning face, feeling no least urge to share in his amusement. Three times now he'd goaded me into trying to deny him, and then he'd laughingly gone ahead and done as he pleased. Once he was in me, my interest in resisting him was thoroughly stroked away, but by then it was cooperation he wanted and not denial. I no longer doubted that he really did mean to try escaping that place, and that was a shame. I was beginning to want very much to walk away from him, but I couldn't afford to do that.

"I think I'll have a shower, and then we can sit down to breakfast," he said, giving my thigh a last squeeze before starting to get up. "I have training classes this morning, and you'll be going to them with me. You won't be able to appreciate them, but I'm not doing it for you. I want to show off my new acquisition to those who come closest to sharing my point of view, and maybe lure them into asking to borrow you. Whether or not I'll agree is something you won't know until it happens—or doesn't happen. That should keep you on your toes."

His grin was chock-full of amusement, but during his speech he'd glanced at me in a way that said I was to pay close attention to what I saw in those training classes. His reasons for taking me there were more involved than the one he'd mentioned aloud, but that didn't mean he'd overlook the spoken reason. Do nothing to arouse suspicion was his motto, and he'd stick to that no matter what I had to go through to see it done.

"Personally, I'd like a bath," I said, pushing myself to sitting before running my hands through my hair. "You've made the one I took last night absolutely worthless."

"Not absolutely," he contradicted, still enjoying himself. "We got rid of that reagent, which might have made you think twice about trying to argue with me. But don't bother getting up. You don't have my permission to take another bath."

"But why not?" I demanded, more than startled by his refusal. "How can it possibly matter to you if I bathe?"

"It doesn't matter to me," he answered, grinning down at me where I sat on the bed. "What does matter is that you have to learn how to listen to me, and I think this is a good place to start teaching you the lesson. Eventually you won't be doing anything without my permission, but that's a point you'll have to work up to."

"And if I decide to take a bath anyway?" I asked, pushed into putting the question by his insufferable attitude. "What will you do if I simply ignore you and act as I please? Hurt me? Send me back to be worked over by those low-grade sadists? What if I don't care what you do?"

"Oh, but you do care," he contradicted, still grinning as he brought his big, naked body back to the bed. I'd been trying to tell him there was only so much I was willing to take even with escape as an objective, but the message didn't seem to be getting through to him. "You won't care if I hurt you or let others do it, but you do and will care if I decide on something else. Would you like to spend the morning—and maybe the afternoon as well—as hot as you were just a few minutes ago? With no one to kiss you and make it all better? Under those circumstances, which do you think would be worse: being tied up and left here to squirm at an empty apartment, or be taken with me so my friends can see you? Friends who might even help the squirming along a little. Would you like to make your decision now, so I can get started with it?"

He put one knee on the bed and leaned forward onto his palms, as though about to come back to where I sat. I tried telling myself he would never really do that to me, humiliating me in front of everyone, but that was a lie that didn't even need thinking about. In order to avoid suspicion he was prepared to put me through hell, and for some reason I wasn't surprised. Just looking at him seemed to tell me he would always do exactly what he had to, whether or not I agreed, even if I were hurt. He was really a very handsome man, blond, blue-eyed, broad-shouldered and strongly made, but the one most important thing in his life wasn't me.

"It looks like you win again," I said, moving my eyes to the very big gold and white bed I sat on. "Another challenge successfully met for you to take pride in."

"And don't you forget it," he said, but the satisfaction I'd been expecting in his voice didn't surface, and the previous amusement he'd shown had faded. "No one will ever have any doubt as to which of us is boss. Now get belly down facing the door, and keep watching for me to get back. I also want you to learn to be eager to see me."

I didn't hesitate long before stretching out the way he'd told me to do, but I was expecting some sort of comment about how he'd have to teach me to move faster. When it didn't come I glanced up to where he was standing, but didn't understand the expression on his face. There was more disturbance in his frown than impatience, more upset in his eyes than amusement. Then what I'd thought I'd seen was gone, and he moved forward to pat me on the head.

"That's a good girl," he said, as though talking to a pet. "You wait right there, and when I get back we'll feed you."

After praising his little animal he strolled out of the room, leaving me an empty doorway to watch breathlessly until he returned. I wondered in passing if I could disobey him by watching breathfully instead, shook my head at the ridiculousness of it all, then spent some time glancing around the room. I hadn't seen much of it when I'd been dragged into it the night before, but my impression that any number of athletic games could have been played in it without the players feeling crowded wasn't far from from the mark. It was only a little smaller than the visitors' room, and someone must have decided to bring a bit of relief to the overall color scheme of the apartment. Instead of being all gold it was gold and white, but use of the second color had been minimal. The giant octagonal bed I lay on had some of the white, specifically in its wooden headboard and thick but nearly weightless cover. The sheets and pillowcases were a gleaming gold, though, and I'd been surprised to find they weren't silk. Couches and chairs and lounges and tables were scattered neatly all through the rest of the room, and one wall, the one currently to my left, was all mirrors. If it hadn't been part of an apartment that had to be earned, it would definitely have been too much.

Kel-Ten took his time at showering, and when he strolled back in he grinned in my direction as he made his way toward the mirrored wall. His grin said he liked the idea that I was right where he'd left me, to be taken advantage of or ignored as he saw fit. Personally I hated the idea, but with nothing else to do I'd been forced into thinking about what he'd said and was finally seeing the point. He was trying to show those watching how much fun he was getting out of keeping me, establishing a reason for continuing our association. I had the feeling I was supposed to keep on grumbling and complaining before obeying, but wasn't to try *not* obeying. He was going to do everything he could to get me mad, and then would force me to listen to him. An unending time of fun and pleasure, but not for the little animal chosen to amuse him. He was boss so he was the one who had to be pleased, and the little animal didn't matter at all.

My happy owner slid one section of the mirror wall aside and took out clothing for himself, the sort of very short pants and sleeveless shirt the men had been wearing the day before at lunch time in the dining room. He also chose a pair of tie-on athletic shoes, and it wasn't long before he was dressed. I couldn't understand how he wasn't sick to death of the color gold, now the color of everything he wore, but his glance into the mirror was pleased rather than nauseated. After confirming the perfection of his reflection he reached into the closet again, pulled something out before reclosing it, then turned and came toward me carrying what he'd taken out.

"You need something to wear, and this is what I've decided on," he said as he neared the bed, then tossed me what he was holding. "I don't *have* to dress you in anything, but I don't care to leave anyone in doubt as to whose you are. Put it on and let me see how it looks."

There wasn't much to the thing he'd thrown to me but I sat up and pulled it on, getting to my knees to urge it as far down as it would go. It was no stunning shock to find that my new clothing was gold in color, and it didn't take long to recognize the thing for what it was: a sleeveless shirt like the one he wore, only one that had been torn at the front of its rounded neck. It was made of that new material that has an unbelievable amount of stretch in it, so that a single size will fit a very wide range of forms. Its twin fit Kel-Ten tightly but apparently not uncomfortably, which meant I couldn't quite believe how tight it was on *me*. It also stretched down to the middle of my thighs, but that was not what I considered a positive point. Positive would have been if it came down, at the very least, to my knees.

"Don't tell me," I said, looking up at him after inspecting myself in that—shirt. "You've decided you don't like the smock I was given to wear yesterday morning, but not because it matters. Only because this is the way *you* want to do things. If I complain, I get to wear nothing at all."

"Certainly not," he disagreed with a grin, getting a good deal of enjoyment out of looking me over. "If you complain you get to wear a gold neck ribbon and bow, which certainly can't be called nothing. Come over here so I can make that look a little better."

If I'd had any choice at all I would have stayed right where I was, but choice was something I'd given up in the name of escape. I crawled to the end of the bed and then got to my feet, and Kel-Ten came closer still wearing his grin. His hands reached out to raise my chin a little, and then he was pulling hard at the material, adding to the tear already in the top of the shirt. He kept ripping until the cleavage was almost to my navel, and then he let go and stepped back again.

"And to think I almost threw that shirt away when it was torn during a friendly little tussle in physical exercise class," he said, so pleased with what he'd done that his grin had widened. "That just goes to show you never know when something will turn out handy rather than damaged. I think I have more of an appetite now than I did before, so let's go get something to eat."

"You can't seriously expect me to walk around in this," I said, caught unawares when he simply turned and headed out of the room. I had to hurry after him in an effort to catch up, which made me feel even more ridiculous. "This may well be worse than what they forced me to wear last night! Kel-Ten, listen to me!"

"But I am listening to you," he answered, stopping in the doorway to turn and look at me. "What I'm not sure about is what I'm hearing. Did I hear you say you'd rather go naked?"

I slowed abruptly, more because of his stare than to keep from running into him. He was still having a lot of fun, but that doesn't mean he was joking. I could feel my cheeks heating up badly at the thought of being dragged around that complex naked, and that was the answer he was looking for.

"I thought so," he said with a pleasant nod, reaching to take my hand. "Let's go and have breakfast."

The bedroom had turned out to be the door to the left off the hall past the bathroom, which made the door in the end wall the only one we hadn't used. Kel-Ten remedied that by opening it and pulling me through, into a kitchen that matched the rest of the apartment. This time there was a bright rose to relieve the monotony of the gold, an effort to make the room look cheerful and happy rather than cold and formal. I was taken to the golden table and pushed into a comfortable gold and rose chair, and then my hand was released.

"You go ahead while I decide what I want," Kel-Ten said, indicating the oblong in the table where my fingers were meant to touch. "I'm in the mood for something different this morning, but I don't yet know what."

He had taken the chair right next to mine, and with a touch of his hand under the table had made a menu appear in the table top. It seemed to be a menu with quite a lot of listings, and I didn't understand that.

"I thought all diets were carefully regulated," I said, startled by the two or three entries I could read without craning my neck. Most chefs didn't stock dishes requiring such complex preparation, and there was even one I'd heard about but had never managed to taste. "Or does that go only for dining room meals?"

"Location has nothing to do with it," he answered, glancing at me with an amusement that should have warned me. "It's you girls who have carefully regulated diets; we men can eat anything we please as long as we stay in decent physical shape. We're not the ones who get pregnant, after all. A girl who stays the night in a Prime's apartment is sometimes given a special tidbit if she's been especially good, but even we aren't allowed to ruin what the the dieticians decide on for you. Touch the plate, and my chef will deliver whatever it is you're supposed to have.''

He went back to his perusal of the menu then, leaving me to sit silent but furious. I *hated* being watched and controlled so completely, hated having everything decided for me without my own wishes being consulted. My stomach had been letting me know about the meals I'd missed the day before, but the hunger pangs were a lot less than I would have expected them to be. It was just as though I hadn't been eating so regularly lately that missing a few meals was something to take special notice of, but that was silly. I always ate regular meals, and I'd grown more slender than I was usually was because—because— Well, probably because I'd been on a diet or had been working especially hard. I ran a hand through my hair, frustrated over not being able to remember, but there was something I *did* remember. If you miss enough meals you'll die of malnutrition no matter who doesn't want it happening, no matter how hard they try to stop it. The realization made me feel a good deal better, and Kel-Ten couldn't say I hadn't warned him. I'd said that if I could find a way to die I would take it, and it looked like I just might have done exactly that.

''Touching the plate won't do me any good,'' I said, trying to sound surly and resentful instead of filled with satisfaction. ''I was told yesterday that I was being punished, and wouldn't be allowed to eat until someone decided I could and I was specifically given permission. I haven't been given that permission yet.''

''That's ridiculous,'' Kel-Ten said, looking up from the menu with a frown. ''You're already clearly underweight, and you're starting to lose color. In all the years I've been here, I've never heard of them doing anything so—''

His words broke off as he looked at me, and I suddenly had the awful feeling he was remembering what I'd told him as clearly as I did. If I'd had any intelligence at all I would have kept quiet and not *given* any warning, but some part of me had insisted that wasn't fair. I'd found it very necessary to be fair, but the next minute that fairness did me in.

''So you're being punished,'' Kel-Ten said, no longer

in any way amused with me. "If that's true, then touching the plate will prove it. If they don't want you eating, they'll have directed the chef not to give you anything. Let's just see."

I tried to keep him from taking my hand, but he had very little trouble ignoring my efforts. After forcing my fingers open he pressed them to the plate, then sat back to stare at me while I rubbed at my hand. He'd hurt me in his attempt to test his theory, but not so much that the pain became my greatest concern. I knew his chef would cause considerably more damage, and it wasn't long before I was proven right. Much too quickly the delivery slot in the center of the table raised up, and an unreasonably large number of dishes were pushed out.

"What was that you said a minute ago?" Kel-Ten asked, moving angry eyes from the delivery to me. "You're not being allowed food, or you're not being allowed everything edible in the complex? From the looks of that meal, the dieticians are even more unhappy with your weight than I am. I don't know what you thought you'd gain by lying to me, but I guarantee it'll turn out to be nothing like what you were expecting. As soon as I have the time, you're getting punished. Now take that food and start eating it."

"And if I don't?" I countered, his anger making mine flare in response—even if I did feel as though I were repeating myself like a faulty recording. "I'm not used to eating when I have no appetite, and every time I turn around in this place something happens to ruin what appetite I do have. If you and they want me to eat, you can all leave me alone. Maybe not being bothered for a while will make me hungry again."

"If you don't eat on your own, they'll force-feed you," he came back, his angry gaze sharp as he answered only my question and ignored the rest of what I'd said. "I saw it done a couple of times, and you won't believe how unpleasant it is until you're the one it happens to. They make everything as close to a liquid as they can, and then they use a tube to put it directly into your stomach. One of the girls I watched tried throwing up, and to teach her not to do it again they took what she'd brought up and made her swallow it without the tube. If you'd prefer doing it that way go right ahead, I don't mind watching it again."

Meaning there was no way he would lie for me and say I'd eaten when I hadn't. I moved around in the chair he'd put me in, completely nauseated by the story he'd told, feeling his eyes on me even though I wasn't looking at him. Considering the fact that a dead partner would be of very little use to him, his attitude wasn't terribly surprising. He was going to keep me alive until we could escape, another unpleasant truth I was wasting my time trying to ignore. I hesitated no more than an additional moment, staring at the edge of the gold table in an effort to regain control of myself, then reached for the first of the dishes.

"How nice to see reason prevailing," he said, his tone dry and not quite back to being amused. "Don't even think about leaving any of that over, or I'll make sure your section leader finds out. I happen to know what she'll have done to you, and you really won't care for it. *I* will, but you certainly won't."

Good humor had returned to him with the last of his words, and the mood seemed to help him make his breakfast decision. He dialed his choice from the chef and took it eagerly when it came, then proceeded to make the rest of the meal more silent than the beginning had been. His food smelled a whole lot better than mine, something I was sure he was aware of, and he even went so far as to offer me a taste of it. I ignored the offer and just kept working my way through the plain and very healthy food I'd been given, having no desire for anything better. I didn't even have a desire for what I was eating, but others had decided on desire for me.

By the time the meal was over, I was thinking seriously about being depressed. I'd expected to have trouble finishing so many different items of food, but each portion had proven to be exactly the right amount, and before I knew it everything was down my throat. Even the large glass of swed was just right for the meal provided, and it really bothered me that they knew my capacity and needs so well that they'd known just what to give me.

Being still hungry or terribly stuffed would have been much more pleasant, but they weren't trying to make things pleasant for me. They were trying to keep me alive and healthy, to make sure I served their high and noble purposes.

"It's time for us to get going," Kel-Ten announced into the brooding silence I was wrapped in, taking the empty swed glass out of my hands before getting to his feet and pulling me up after him. "My first class is a relaxer, to let me digest my meal in peace, and after that the heavy stuff starts. I also haven't checked my schedule for today, so we'll begin with that. Come this way first."

His "this way" turned out to be a stop in the bathroom, where I was allowed to see to my bodily functions—but not privately—and then had my hair brushed by him. Hair brushing without first bathing and/or washing was ludicrous, which meant the action fit in very well with the rest of what had been done to me in that place. When I was groomed to my owner's satisfaction, we left the apartment.

Since we'd taken a lift up to the apartment the night before, it wasn't entirely unexpected that we needed a drop to go down again. We emerged onto a floor different from the one the dining room was on, but not different where posh was concerned. The red carpeting was top quality, the walls paneled and hung with artwork, the lighting source excellently invisible, the ceilings high enough to accommodate a gathering area that large. Men dressed like Kel-Ten filled the area, some sitting on the cream-colored furniture, some standing around, some strolling from group to group or place to place, all looking perfectly relaxed and at home. I was led into the midst of them by a briskly strolling Kel-Ten as though I were nothing special or of particular importance, but most of the conversations slowed and died as we passed. We went through a good part of the area before stopping in front of a large glass board with electronic notices neatly posted all over it, and that was where some of the men suddenly decided to go as well.

"Good morning, Kel-Ten," a man in red greeted my companion pleasantly but respectfully, looking at me rather than at the man he addressed. "I hadn't noticed what a really pretty morning it was until *you* got here, but now I can see it clearly. Yes, sir, more than clearly."

"It's supposed to rain today, Ank-Soh," Kel-Ten said without turning away from the board, his observation casual and accompanied by his tapping a finger against one of the items in the glass. "The window I looked out of earlier seemed to confirm that, but maybe my windows don't face the way yours do. I hate running outside when it rains."

"Oh, it shouldn't be all that bad," the man Ank-Soh came back, a grin on his face as he continued to stare at me. "Who cares if you come back wet and cold, as long as you have something to dry you off and warm you up? You wouldn't find *me* minding if I had all that, especially if it was scowling and blushing with embarrassment instead of bouncing with eagerness. You never know how much you'll miss having a woman trying to say no, until you don't have it any more. And what did you do to get them to let you keep her like that?"

"Her?" Kel-Ten echoed, as though he had no idea what the other man was talking about, and then he turned away from the board to show heavy, overdone revelation. "Oh, you're talking about sweet thing here. I'd almost forgotten I had her with me. I didn't do anything, Ank-Soh, except for what I always do, which is continuing to be First Prime. I'm teaching her to behave herself while I keep her, so maybe they think I'm doing them a favor and that's why they're not trying to take her back. She's been fun so far, but who knows how long the fun will last? By the time she's ready for her first covering, I might be bored again."

"If you are, then I'm next in line to try for the privilege," Ank-Soh murmured, his dark eyes bright as he reached two fingers out and used them to stroke the side of my breast. The extended tear in the shirt made a touch like that easy to accomplish, but in my opinion he didn't have the right to do something like that. Without even thinking about it I stepped back away from his fingers, and his grin widened as he and Kel-Ten both began to chuckle.

"Don't forget I said 'might,' " Kel-Ten stressed to the other man, his amusement clear as his hands came to my arms from behind. "Even when she obeys me she does it reluctantly, and that's one of the things I like best. Go ahead and touch her, and you'll understand what I mean."

The hands on my arms tightened to hold me in place, which meant I couldn't avoid Ank-Soh's casually reaching fingers a second time. The man in red stroked the side of my breast lightly, then deliberately reached his entire hand inside the shirt to squeeze my breast gently but possessively. I tried to twist out of Kel-Ten's grip and away from the insult of being touched like that, but the man behind me held me in place while the one in front of me kept on with his amusement. It continued for a time that was short but infuriating, and then Ank-Soh's grin widened again.

"Those green eyes would broil me to a cinder if they could," he said with a laugh of pure delight, still moving his fingers on my flesh. "Not only is she damned good-looking, but she'd hate it if I started dipping her. What's your schedule like, Kel-Ten? Any chance you'll be so tied up you won't notice if someone borrows her for an hour or two?"

"Sorry, Ank-Soh, but I only have three scheduled for today," my owner answered with a laugh of his own, nothing of regret to be heard in his voice. "I'll need sweet thing to keep me entertained the rest of the time, so you're out of luck—at least for now. Tomorrow could turn out to be different."

"Then I'll check with you again tomorrow," Ank-Soh said, withdrawing his hand with what seemed like real reluctance. "Right now I think I'll skip relaxation class and find one of the rings *I'm* assigned to cover. If I don't, I'll never survive heavy ex. And if they try taking her away to make her like the others, let me know and I'll help you organize a general riot. See you later, my friend—and you, too, sweet thing."

He tapped me lightly under the chin before turning and walking away, and Kel-Ten chuckled as he finally let me go.

"I knew you'd be popular, sweet thing," he murmured, patting me on the backside. "Ank-Soh is one of the two Primes one step directly below me, and thinks that when he gets around to challenging me he'll win. One more minute of touching your knob, and he would have projected his rock to every man in a thirty-five foot radius. The board says he has a challenge of his own to meet today, and how much would you like to bet he wins it without half trying?"

"Why don't I bet everything I own?" I muttered in answer, trying to control a temper that was rising much too fast. "And what will you do if I suddenly decide to play cow to every bull you stand me in front of? No novelty means no interest, the best way I can think of to keep their hands off me."

"You, stand there and play cow?" he asked, coming around to stare down at me with brows raised high. "Are you forgetting *I'm* the one who's supposed to make the jokes? If you ever stood there and took it without complaining, I'd rush you to Medical to find out what was wrong with you. Let's get going, and I'll give you a tour of this place."

He took my hand and moved off again, through the crowds of men who were now for the most part staring. A number of them were staring with interest, but at least the same number were staring with disapproving frowns on their faces. I thought I was the only one to notice that, but once we were past them and walking up a very wide corridor with lift doors on either side, Kel-Ten made a soft sound of disgust.

"Those jerks," he muttered, making no effort to look back. "They'rc afraid to face any woman who isn't crazy about them from first to last, but they still expect to win challenges and make it to the top of the list. They still haven't figured out that the name of the game is confidence, something you have in everything or don't have in anything. To your left over there is the rec area for high girls, to the right the exercise areas for Primes. Physical exercise is taken by all Primes together no matter what their grade, and they separate only later on, when it's time for serious work. Low Primes get to look at high girls, but touching is out until they make high status. Most of the high girls are no better than the low girls, but it's the principle of the thing."

We'd stopped at the end of the corridor to look around at the very large open area that stretched both left and right, but open only in the sense that it was made of windows that let anyone standing there look out. Couches and chairs of leather covered the uncarpeted area, making it a nice place to sit and take in the sun on days when there was visible sun in the sky. That particular day was dark and overcast with the promise of rain, which was enough to make the wide expanse feel cold despite the warmth of the interior heating system.

"What's this high and low you all keep talking about?" I asked, suppressing a shiver as I looked away from the heavy clouds not far above the transparent roof. "And why does the term 'Prime' refer only to men in this place? I've been a Prime long enough to find the differentiation petty as well as stupid."

"That's only because you weren't a Prime *here,*" he answered, faintly amused again. "Once you're here a while you'll understand that that's the only way it can possibly work, the only way they can get what they want. The men here are trained hard to use their abilities in a way empaths have never before been trained, and once they get to a certain stage they're out-and-out dangerous. Considering what they need from the women, how smart would it be to train them to be just as dangerous? A trained Prime can say no and make it stick, which would put an end to the breeding of even more Primes. They need their supply more than they need trained women, so the females around here are just girls."

He looked around, spotted a couch he seemed to approve of, walked over to it, then pulled me down next to him as he sprawled comfortably.

"High and low status," he said, getting ready to lecture on the subject as he locked his hands behind his head. "For Primes, high and low comes about by how quickly you learn and how well you do in challenges. As soon as your mind starts opening out you can get involved in challenging for higher level positions, but some men never get to that point. Their minds seem frozen and totally inflexible, unable to get much beyond where they already are. They start out low and never get past that, but since research shows they can sire sons who *can* get past the block or whatever it is, they aren't kicked out to panhandle on street corners. They stay low, and service the girls who are low.

"All girls are low when they first come into this facility, even the ones who were raised in the crèches a few miles away. Low for girls means unrated, and rating comes only after their first Prime fetus is brought to term by one of the host mothers. Average output in this place has come to be one Prime offspring for every ten pregnancies, and any girl who does better than that is raised to high status and assigned to high Primes. They also have better living quarters, areas to relax and have fun in, and contests to see which of them can produce the most male Prime offspring. They're given parties and fussed over for every fifth male Prime baby, and there are charts in their quarters showing where each of them stands in the contest. Every time the reports are due to be updated, they get so excited you can hear them jumping and squealing from three floors away."

"If you were trying to make me nauseous, you've managed it," I told him from where I sat on the very edge of the couch, not joking in the least. "I now understand why they use conditioning, and how compassionate they are to do it. Are they gentle with the ones who go crazy from living a life like that?"

"None of them go crazy, and you won't either," he said, unlocking his hands to lean up and pull me to him. "I doubt if anyone will be expecting you to jump around clapping your hands and squealing, so no one will be disappointed when you don't. Your spare time will be filled by me and those like me, so you won't have much opportunity to brood. All in all it should be a lot of fun."

"Fun!" The one word exploded out of me with such outrage that he began to laugh, something I could feel through the chest I was being held against. I could also feel his hand where it rose beneath the hem of my shirt to rub my bottom, but before I could even start to struggle out of his grip a gentle chiming sounded. The chiming was obviously a signal of sorts, as he immediately let me go, got to his feet, then pulled me up beside him.

"That's the official signal for the start of the day, and for the first time in a long time I'm eager to start with it," he said, sending me a grin before moving off to the right of the couch we'd been on. "I knew you'd be good for me, but I hadn't realized just how good. Yes, sweet thing, we *are* going to have fun."

Which was the last we had in the way of conversation for a while. He pulled me with him to a large room where I was put into a corner, then was left to watch while he and the other men who entered spent their time on their knees with their eyes closed, alternating between breathing strangely and remaining absolutely unmoving. The goings on held my fascinated attention for a good ten seconds, and after that there was nothing to occupy me but boredom. Over the last couple of days I'd been given enough to think about, but the picture drawn for me of the life of a high female Prime in that place had made me too depressed to *want* to think.

After breathing and playing tree, the men went to a big gym area and I got to go with them. They were put through quite a lot of exercise that got heavier and more complex as it went along, and after an exquisitely monotonous amount of time they were led toward a set of doors and through them. The doors obviously led outside, an observation reinforced by the presence of white-uniformed male Secs, but although that was one destination I wouldn't have minded being dragged to, I didn't get to go along. I'd been left in the keeping of one of the Secs, and he made sure I stayed seated on the floor where Kel-Ten had left me, amused over my annoyance but firm in his decision. Kel-Ten didn't want me wandering around, so seated was the way I would stay until he came back.

That, I suppose, was the point I gave up trying to keep from thinking. There's only so much boredom you can take even when you're depressed, and I had the distinct impression the men would not be coming back in anything like a little while. If there had only been the major points of disturbance coming at me I could have held them off a good deal longer, but I was being prodded by minor points that were more confusing than upsetting. None of them seemed to fit, and my thoughts went to poking at them even before I sighed and joined in.

The men were being trained to be "dangerous," and the higher the level they reached, the more dangerous they were considered to be. No one seemed willing to discuss what they were being trained *for,* but that wasn't the part bothering me so much. I *knew* a fully developed Prime was dangerous; even with the reasons for the knowledge locked behind that door in my mind, I was far from uncertain. What didn't quite match that unsupported knowledge were the things I'd heard Kel-Ten and even Jer-Mar saying, things that made no sense. Jer-Mar had boasted that he'd been able to split a projection in two and hold it for a full thirty seconds. Kel-Ten had said that Ank-Soh, one of the two men right below his own exalted position, would have projected to "every man in a thirty-five foot radius" if he'd lost control of himself.

Those were supposed to be high accomplishments? *That* was what brought them promotion and rewards and even fear from Secs who didn't happen to be nulls? Baby tricks like that?

I made a sound of frustration as I leaned back against the wall I was sitting in front of, drawing another amused glance from the Sec standing near me. He hadn't been shy about inspecting me with his eyes when I'd first been left with him, and he'd obviously considered it very funny when I'd kept my knees together by bending both my legs to the left beside me after sitting down. I had the distinct impression he would have enjoyed making use of me, but Mera had been right when she'd said we had nothing to fear from the male Secs in the men's areas. It wasn't that they weren't interested in us, only that they weren't permitted to touch us, and I wondered if it really was fear of the Primes, as Mera had suggested, that made sure they obeyed the rules.

Fear of Primes who strutted around because they could do baby tricks.

I couldn't hold back another sound, this time one of

annoyance, but my attention was no longer on the Sec or how he was taking my involuntary reactions. I knew beyond doubt that *I* could do more than the trained wonders the facility was so proud of, but that was all I seemed to know. Trying to reach my own ability was almost enough to make me forget I *had* an ability, the harder I tried, the more the memory faded. Obviously I had their conditioning to thank for that, and trying to press the point wouldn't have made much sense. I was "turned off," a state Kel-Ten said he would change, a state I wished I could stop thinking about. Some part of me seemed to consider the phrase very important, a key to something vital, but the rest of me hadn't the faintest idea what that could be. It was adding to my frustration so badly, I almost wished it was one of the things I'd been conditioned to ignore. They didn't want me reaching what I could do, but knowing why I couldn't do it was perfectly legal.

I fell so deeply into the mud pit of confusion and frustration, that the first I knew Kel-Ten was back was when he leaned down to tickle me in a rather sensitive place. I gasped and jumped, embarrassed and ready to be outraged, especially when the Sec joined him in laughing at me. The great Prime was covered in sweat, his blond hair hanging in strings, his pretty gold outfit soaked through and looking as though it should be thrown in the trash, but his blue eyes said he was still enjoying himself.

"I asked how you would like to take a shower with me," he said, his grin more than mocking. "The number of other men showering with us shouldn't bother you, not the way you like water, and if I should happen to think of something to do in addition to showering, you'll be right there and handy. What do you say?"

"I say I'd rather stay dirty for the rest of my life," I answered, getting to my feet to glare at him. I almost went on to tell him how little a shot he really was, but the anger inside me refused to let me be stupid. I could get as mad as I liked, as long as I kept quiet about things that could turn out to be an advantage at a later time.

"I wonder how I knew you were going to say that?" he mused, the grin still there and strong. "I think I'm learning to read your mind even if I *can't* reach it. And what a handy talent it's proving, too, since I've already made arrangements for you to do something else while I'm showering. Come along, sweet thing."

He took my hand and then I was being pulled along behind him again, toward the door leading out of the gym into the corridor. I would have hated being treated like that even if his hand hadn't been as sweaty as the rest of him, but there wasn't much I could do to stop it. I was his brand new toy, and people played with their toys just as they liked.

Rather than going back toward the central area of couches and windows, Kel-Ten led me more deeply into the men's areas. A couple of minutes worth of walking brought us to an unmarked, light brown door, and before I could ask any questions my owner had it open and I was being taken through it. Inside were two men, one in Security white and one in Medical brown, and they both looked around when we appeared.

"Right on time, Prime Kel-Ten," the man in brown said with a smile as he walked toward us. "We appreciate this more than words can say. Your generous cooperation won't be forgotten, I can assure you of that."

"I'll make certain it isn't, Gerdoh," Kel-Ten answered with a grin, pulling me closer to the other man by the hand he still held. "If you need to check her to be sure I haven't damaged her, go right ahead and check away. The only other thing you also have to make sure of is that when I come back to get her, I find the same girl I'm leaving. If you—improve—her the way you and your group like doing to everything female coming past you, you'll be gifted with something besides generous cooperation that won't be forgotten. You have my word on it."

"Now, now, Prime Kel-Ten, we have no intentions of taking her away from you or doing anything that would displease you," the Medical man said in a soothing way, raising one hand but not using it to touch the hard-eyed Prime he spoke to. "You've earned the right to have the girl any way you wish, as long as she's well cared for.

We'll simply assure ourselves of her continuing good health, and then you may have her back."

"As long as we both know where we stand, she's all yours," Kel-Ten said lightly, finally letting my hand go. "You can tell your Class Zero Sec over there to relax, I need a shower more than I need a fight. Right now, that is."

He gave the man Gerdoh a very amused grin, then turned and left the room without bothering to see to the door he'd left open. The Sec followed behind and closed the door quietly, and the Medical man took a deep breath and let it out slowly.

"I don't care what anyone tells me, I can feel their minds pushing at mine whenever one of them talks to me," he muttered, possibly to the Sec or maybe to the empty air. "If that's what they're like when they're reasonably calm, I don't ever want to get one of them angry at me. Most especially not *that* one."

He shuddered just a little at the thought, clearly impressed with the man called First Prime, then put his disturbing ideas behind him. He was a fairly tall but rather thin man with very straight black hair and brown eyes, and I knew he was ready to get down to business when he squared his narrow shoulders and smiled patronizingly in my direction.

"And how are we feeling this morning, Terry?" he asked, his tone suggesting we were friends of long standing. "The Prime indulged himself rather extensively between last evening and this morning. Are we possibly a bit sore now?"

"Maybe you are," I answered, trying to ignore the warmth in my cheeks as I folded my arms and looked at the man. "I hadn't realized he'd indulged himself with you as well as me, but I feel fine. If *you've* developed a problem, though, I'd suggest abstaining for a while."

The man Gerdoh blinked at me in confusion for a moment while the Sec chuckled, and then he sent me a frown.

"My dear girl, there's really no need to be insulting," he said, less in anger than in wounded protest. "We've had you brought here to be certain you haven't been harmed, and will continue to see to your well-being as best we may. It's a pity the Prime wants to keep you as you are, he has no real idea how difficult he's making things for you, but he mustn't be denied. My superiors are delighted with the change in him, and don't care to see him returned to the—destructive—frame of mind he was previously in. Since you now know my question was far from idle, I would appreciate your answering me."

"I've already answered you," I said, feeling that strange anger beginning to rise in me again. "As though it really mattered. If it turns out that he did hurt me, will you take me away from him or punish him for doing it? Of course you will, why am I wasting time asking? As concerned as everyone is about me, how can there be any question?"

"Now, now, you have your value just as he has his," the man tried to soothe me, his properly correct smile meant to be reassuring. "If he's hurt you he'll be spoken to, to see that it doesn't happen again. Come over here and lie down on the table, please. I'm afraid I'll need to examine you."

He turned away from me and began moving toward the table he'd mentioned, the same sort of table there'd been in the room the woman in yellow had taken me to. Even if I hadn't been angry I wouldn't have gone near a thing like that again, but I'd forgotten about the Sec. As soon as he knew for certain I wasn't about to move from where I stood on my own, his big hand circled my arm and pulled me forward with no difficulty at all. He was one of the biggest men I'd ever seen, larger even than Kel-Ten, the difference between them enough to be noticed.

"When you're given an order, pretty girl, you'd better learn to obey it," he said, his dark eyes looking down at me with something not too different from amusement. "The doctor wants you on the table, so that's where you're going to be put."

"Gently, man, gently," Gerdoh cautioned him nervously, turning back to watch as the Sec ignored my struggling and lifted me onto the table. "If the Prime returns to find her bruised, there's no telling what he may do."

"There isn't much he can do to *me*," the Sec answered

with almost total unconcern, paying more attention to holding me down on the table than to the man he was talking to. "If he closes his eyes he can't see me, which means all he can try using is his hands. If he's stupid enough to do that, he won't be in any condition to even *look* in your direction."

The arrogance in the Sec's eyes added to his faint smile as he held me down, and the shudder that had touched Gerdoh earlier came back to see that I had my own turn with it. A Class Zero was a null, and the thought of nulls had always frightened me in a way I couldn't completely understand. I remembered that nulls couldn't be touched by empaths, that their emotions were hidden away on a level none of us could reach, which meant even the strongest of us had reason to be wary of them. Wary, yes, but wariness doesn't account for the presence of fear—and didn't explain why something he'd said had struck me as strange. *If he closes his eyes he can't see me,* he'd said, but does not seeing something mean it isn't there? If it doesn't, what *does* it mean?

"Now, now, you know well enough our superiors don't want him hurt," Gerdoh fussed in agitation, sounding as though he were the one who needed the soothing and reassurance. "If we do nothing to antagonize him, it won't be necessary to concern ourselves with the possibility of official censure. Young woman, if you don't stop kicking like that, I'm going to have to bind your ankles."

From the sound of his voice Gerdoh was now annoyed with me, but I couldn't have cared less. The Sec hadn't let me go once he'd put me on the table, and he was leaning so close I couldn't even see the Medical man where he stood a few steps behind him. Dark-haired and dark-eyed, the man wasn't all that unattractive, but the point bothering me was what he was, not what he looked like. I tried telling myself my heart was hammering because of the way I struggled to get free from his arms and hands, an explanation that might also have covered why my mouth was dry, but if I'd said any of that aloud the Sec would have laughed. He knew I was afraid of him, and the knowledge made him grin as he stared down at me. I twisted harder against him, trying to push him away, then had to cry out in protest even though it was already too late.

"Now, now, you *were* warned, you know," Gerdoh said distractedly in answer to my wordless shout, undoubtedly watching as the soft cloth he'd looped around my ankles retracted toward the table. "We haven't all the time in the world, and if you refuse to cooperate like a good girl you'll just have to pay the price. If you like, Adjin, you can use the wrist bindings instead of having to hold her."

"It's no trouble holding her," the Sec answered, sounding casual but showing a wider grin. Then he leaned even closer to me and said in a very low voice, "I'll bet you're a good girl even when you don't cooperate. Oh, yes, a very good girl."

I refused to shiver where the null could see it, but that doesn't mean the shiver never happened. He had his left arm around my body and his right hand holding my right wrist, the arm of that hand doing far too much in keeping my left arm down and pinned between us. With my ankles tight to the table I could scarcely move, but I still gasped and tried to jump when Gerdoh began his examination. Those in charge of the facility were anxious to know if their top stud had damaged the little mare with his boyish enthusiasm, but not because they gave a damn about the mare. They were worried about her because they still had to breed her, and if she were damaged they would lose the use of her.

It's difficult to be angry and frightened and embarrassed all at the same time, but somehow I managed it. Gerdoh's examination was as far from arousing as you can get, and being held like that by the Sec while it was going on made it worse than any internal I'd ever had. I squirmed as hard as I could in an effort to stop it, and got just as far as one would expect; Gerdoh was ignoring me, and the Sec Adjin was simply enjoying himself. I really believed it was as bad as it could reasonably become, forgetting briefly how *un*reasonable that place actually was until the Sec's fingers left my wrist after pushing my arm more nearly under his body. He wanted his hand free so that he could slide it into the tear in my shirt, that tear everyone seemed to find so irresistible. I gasped again as his fingers closed painfully on my breast, trying for the fiftieth time to struggle free, but nothing had changed. The null held me down while he groped me, and Gerdoh never knew anything was happening.

It wasn't all that long before the examination was over, it only felt like forever. When Gerdoh got off the stool he'd been perched on, Adjin's hand left its comfortable nest, no abrupt movement, no guilty start, just a calm shifting from one place to another that the medical man never noticed. Very briefly I'd considered telling the man supposedly in charge just what was being done to me while he was so engrossed in his work, but I couldn't seem to do it. The look in the Sec's dark eyes really frightened me, a heart-fluttering coldness that said nothing so terrible would happen to him if I told, nothing that would keep him from coming after me later to show how unhappy he was. I didn't want him coming after me later, didn't want him near me ever again, and just keeping quiet seemed like the best way to make that happen.

"I'm pleased to report that you've taken the Prime's vigorous efforts with no difficulty whatsoever," Gerdoh said, actually sounding as pleased as he claimed to be. "It's almost as though you've been accustomed to use of that sort, but such an idea would be ridiculously outlandish. Most probably you're merely adapting well, and we need to do no more than remain alert against any possible future difficulties. The Prime is extremely fortunate in having chosen a woman so well suited to his situation, and we, of course, are even more delighted than he."

He'd been moving around as he spoke, doing something I couldn't see with the Sec in the way, but that didn't last. He reappeared at the foot of the table and moved around to the other side of it, then gestured at the null with the injector he held.

"Turn her a bit more toward you and hold her still, Adjin," he directed, back to being partially distracted. "She won't enjoy this, and I don't want her jumping at the wrong time and hurting herself."

"What are you doing?" I demanded, vaguely wondering if words as shaky as mine could be called a demand.

The Sec had shifted his hold to turn me part way to him, the ankle bindings and his hand clamped tight to my thigh keeping me just the way Gerdoh wanted. I hated the idea of being given any more injections in that madhouse, but laboratory animals are never offered their choice. The needle went into me just above the Sec's hand, and this time it hurt enough to make me cry out.

"There, there, it's just about all done," Gerdoh soothed mechanically as he paid attention to what he was doing, finally withdrawing the needle no more than an instant before I would have screamed. "We do have to be sure you'll continue being able to accept what Prime Kel-Ten wants to give you, and my superiors were somewhat displeased with the way you attempted to refuse allowing Prime Ank-Soh's touching of you. The Prime may have been amused by the novelty of the thing, but there's really no reason for him or any other Prime to have to be subjected to something like that. If the next occurrence of a similar happening shows you being more amenable, your dosage will be reduced again."

I detested self-satisfied voices like Gerdoh's, almost as much as I detested the way the null ran his hand slowly over my bottom before letting me go completely. The Medical man had already turned away to rid himself of the injector, of course, and I just lay there on the table, tears trickling down my cheeks. I suppose I would have been happier if the tears were from frustration or anger, but even I was incapable of giving me happiness in that place. I was too miserable to be frustrated, too sunk in hopelessness to be angry, and pulling that ridiculous shirt back down to the middle of my thighs did nothing to make me feel better. Even a full uniform wouldn't have kept me from being a walking invitation to violation, and the tears I cried were the terrible tears of helplessness.

By the time Kel-Ten came back for me my ankles had been freed and I was simply sitting on the table, but the flow of tears from my eyes hadn't stopped. He was no longer covered in sweat and his gold outfit had also obviously been cleaned, but the grin he walked in with faded when he saw me. A heavy coldness darkened his light gaze as he strode to where I sat, and Gerdoh was already speaking even before the Prime's arms went around me.

"Now, now, Prime Kel-Ten, she's quite unharmed," he said more hurriedly than soothingly, his nervousness obvious even to me. "She's merely begun feeling the effects of her injection, effects which are making her extremely unhappy. She'll need seeing to in the near future, but I would recommend not sooner than after lunch. A touch of discipline will do her no end of good, and we *were* asked by her section head to administer punishment to her if we found an opportunity."

"Oh, yes, I'd forgotten about that," Kel-Ten said, raising my face with one hand to examine me critically. "I can see from the way she's blushing and squirming that *is* the only thing wrong with her, so you can stop thinking about which direction to run in, Gerdoh. And since I owe her some punishing of my own, I'll take your suggestion about after lunch and may even add to it. I was going to cover one of my three rings after lunch, and if she doesn't show me something to change my mind, I'll make her sit there and watch."

"An excellent thought, Prime Kel-Ten, an excellent thought," Gerdoh laughed in relieved agreement, finally coming away from the side of the Sec he'd almost put himself behind. "Just to show my appreciation of your noble generosity, understanding and cooperation, I believe I'll tell you now of the decision made by my superiors. They've concluded that an experiment of sorts is definitely in order, so they've altered the rules in regard to this female. When her first fertile period arrives, it's *you* they mean to assign to cover her. In that way you won't need to give her up for the time, and afterward there will be other high Primes doing the same. If her percentage turns out to be significantly higher than the norm, other unconditioned females will be experimented with."

"Say, now, I really appreciate that," Kel-Ten said with a wide grin, his arm tightening possessively around me, his tone clearly delighted. "I can see you people are going out of your way to please me, and I won't forget it. Come on, sweet thing, let's go to lunch."

He took my hand and pulled me off the table, then strode out of the room with me hurrying behind. He whistled as we moved along, obviously in the highest spirits, and didn't think to glance in my direction until we were almost back to the bank of lifts. Once he did the whistling cut off abruptly, and he stopped to put a hasty arm around me. I wasn't crying any longer, but if I looked the way I felt my face must have been absolutely ghastly.

"Now, now, none of that," he said in the softest of voices, for an instant giving me the crazy impression it was Gerdoh who was speaking. "I know what's bothering you, but you can't let it. You have to accept it the way we agreed you would, or at least wait until we can discuss it in private. Do you hear me and understand what I'm saying?"

There wasn't much for me to do besides nod, which didn't in any way change anything. Despite all the open spaces in that part of the complex, I could feel the walls closing in from all sides. My body was burning, the arm Kel-Ten had around my shoulders making it considerably worse, and I finally understood to the very core of me that when it came time for him to see to his newest assignment, I'd have no choice about accepting it. I'd find it necessary to pull him to me rather than push him away, and then it would be irrevocably done.

"I'll bet one of your problems is that you're hungry," Kel-Ten said with a smile after seeing my nod, his free hand smoothing my hair as he began leading me forward again. "It's been hours since breakfast, and as soon as we get some food in you, you'll be right back to snapping at me again. Come on, it's not much farther."

At least he was right about that. The doors to the dining room were only a short way beyond the lift area, and they opened into a much fancier dining room than the first one I'd been taken to. Crystal and silver sparkled among gracefully beautiful flowers, but here, too, the opulence went from high to higher. We made our way past tables filled with males and females together, lovely music keeping step with us, until we reached the very center of the room. There was a single, smaller table there, the decorations golden rather than silver, and the only ones to sit at it were we two.

"You'd laugh if I told you how many of my distinguished peers tried angling for an invitation to join us for lunch," Kel-Ten said as he deposited me in a chair then took the one next to it himself. "They all wish they'd gotten to you first, the ones who are real men, I mean. For a little while I was thinking about using one of the high tables in the low dining room instead of coming here, but I changed my mind. I certainly don't belong there, and now you don't either."

He leaned over me with a good deal of satisfaction and pressed my fingers to the print-plate in the table, then called up a menu for himself. The dial for the table's chef was disguised amid all the glitter and sparkle, but he had no trouble finding it and using it once he'd made his selection. By then my own meal was being delivered, and I couldn't stop the surge of fury that rose in me over the continuing fact that he ate what he pleased while I ate what was given me. I hated it, all of it, especially when I felt a sharp twist of hunger I should have been too out of sorts to feel. I knew at once I was being manipulated again, either by something that had been added to my breakfast or by something in that injection, and it was all I could do to keep from jumping up and running out of there. If there hadn't been a promise of escape . . .

But, as slim as it was, there *was* a promise of escape. Kel-Ten chattered away while I ate mechanically and silently, finding nothing of any interest in the meal. This time I'd been allowed a small cup of kimla to be drunk after I'd finished my glass of swed, and I took a small amount of grim satisfaction in ignoring it completely. I neither needed nor wanted their version of treats for the little child, the thrill of being allowed something normally reserved only for grown-ups. I was willing to bet they'd also approved a taste or two of wine for dinner, and was looking forward to refusing that as well.

As was to be expected, Kel-Ten's meal lasted longer than mine. This time he didn't offer me any of it, and when he'd discovered I wasn't answering any of his conversation he'd stopped talking and spent his time simply watching me. By the time he was through I could see he was really amused, and the glare I sent him only added to his fun. I'd been uncomfortable while I'd been eating, but once the food was gone there was nothing to distract me from the results of the injection I'd been given. I'd thought the shot from the day before had been bad, but right then I was learning the true meaning of bad.

Everything touching me was sending flashes of heat through my body, even the brocade of the chair against the bare part of my thighs, the brush of the tablecloth against my leg, the very movement of the air around me. My breathing was ragged and I couldn't sit still no matter how hard I tried, and the music playing was more sensually suggestive than anything I'd ever heard. By rights I should have been in pain, but pain would have been too distracting so I felt nothing like that. Only desire and need, desire and need, over and over and only just short of whispering in my ear. I swallowed hard as I fought to hold it down, then grunted when Kel-Ten reached over to tug at my ear.

"You look like you could use a little dessert," he remarked, the laughter heavy behind his voice. "Why don't you come over and sit in Kel-Ten's lap, and tell him what you'd like in the way of dessert?"

"I'd like to see you drop dead for dessert," I whispered, keeping my eyes away from him. "Could you arrange that, please?"

"See, I knew a little food would put you back in better spirits," he said, this time laughing out loud. "You're going to have to say please, you know, so why don't you say it now and get it over with? If you don't, you'll find yourself sitting and watching me do it to somebody else. Do you think you'll be able to stand that, watching me take another woman in my arms, kissing her as I put her to her back, entering her . . ."

"Stop," I moaned, closing my eyes in a useless effort to block out the picture he was deliberately painting for me, my hands clamped tight to the arms of the chair. "Stop that, Kel-Ten, it isn't fair! You don't know what you're doing to me!"

"Of course I know," he said with a chuckle, and then

his fingers were stroking the back of my hand closest to him. "I'm teaching you that if you want what you need, you have to be a good little girl and ask me the way I prefer being asked. Even if I did pick you out of the rest of the herd, my services aren't automatically yours for the wanting. And you'd better understand that if you pass on it now, your next earliest opportunity will be very late this afternoon. Do you have any idea what you'll be feeling like by then?"

The shivering darting through me from the mere touch of his fingers to my hand, told me exactly what I'd be feeling like by late afternoon. I'd be ready to crawl to him and kiss his feet and beg for his favors, mindless from the terrible, burning need consuming me. Waiting would only make everything that much worse, as though it weren't already bad enough. Bad. Again. Just like everything I touched that also touched me.

"Please, Kel-Ten," I whispered, my eyes still closed and my hands wrapped tight around what they held to. "You want me to say please, so I *am* saying it. Please take me somewhere and make this stop."

"Why, that was very nicely said, sweet thing," he answered, and I could see his grin even without seeing it. "I think you're learning to appreciate Kel-Ten. Well, you did what I asked you to do, so you'll get what you asked for. As soon as I finish one more cup of kimla."

I just sat there in the chair after that, hearing the music and the sound of voices all around, seeing nothing in the darkness behind my eyelids. I felt no surprise that he was making me wait even longer after I'd done as he'd demanded, it was something some part of me had apparently been expecting. I couldn't sit still in the chair or let go of the chair arms, couldn't breathe normally or stop feeling what was rapidly overcoming the ban against pain, but the one thing I didn't feel was surprise. And all I could do about it was sit there and wait.

It takes forever for a cup of kimla to cool enough for you to drink it, two forevers for you to be led by the hand through a room full of people, some of whom start conversations with the one leading you. The trip from a dining room, up a lift, and over to an apartment is five forevers in duration, but walking through that apartment to the bedroom is only three forevers long. I made the last part of the journey carried in Kel-Ten's arms, and when he put me down on the bed he was breathing almost as hard as I was, but not from exertion.

"I don't know what it is about you," he panted, already thrusting the shirt up to my armpits as I lay on my back in the middle of the bed. "I can have any woman in this complex and *have* had most of them, but ever since I first saw you you've become the one I most want to do it to. Say please again, and tell me you want it."

"Please, Kel-Ten, please, please, please," I moaned, wrapping my arms around his neck and trying to pull him to me. I barely knew what I was saying or doing, and when I pressed my lips hungrily to his, he forgot about everything but what we'd come there for.

It was quite some time before it was over, quite some time before our minds could think again rather than simply feel. I lay curled up on the wrinkled bed that had been neatly made up when we'd gotten there, trying to memorize the sensation of bodily satisfaction. Without knowing how long it was going to last, I didn't want to chance taking it for granted and then finding it gone before it could be appreciated. Kel-Ten stirred where he lay beside me, and then he lifted a strand of my hair.

"I think you just had a harder workout than I had in exercise class, sweet thing," he drawled, heavy satisfaction in the words. "I'll have to send you off to your own exercise class in a few days or they'll start to scream, but for now you'll make do with being ridden. You can't deny you enjoyed the ride, but I'm not enjoying all that sweat it left you covered with. Looks like it's time you got a bath."

The thought of a bath should have made me feel considerably better, but as I was forced to sit up and follow Kel-Ten by the strand of hair he still held, all I felt was that useless anger rising again. The man wanted his pet bathed so his pet would be bathed, and no one in that entire complex would stop to wonder what the pet wanted. I kept getting the idea I'd been through something like that before, that what *I* wanted hadn't even been considered by the people around me. The hatred and bitterness and frustration were all so familiar, as though I'd lived with them for quite a long time, and Kel-Ten seemed to suit it all especially well. Big and blond and blue-eyed felt terribly right, a figure that brought pain, a sight to stir that hatred and bitterness and frustration. I'd felt odd the first time I'd looked at him, but now I was beginning to know what the oddness had meant.

I was taken to the overdone gold bathroom, made to stand quietly while my bath was dialed, then was ordered into the water. Kel-Ten sat himself in the dry-chair with an "Ahh" of appreciation for the cooler air, but his grinning stare never left me. He knew I hated what was being done to me, and that seemed to make it all the better for him. The water was perfumed again, and when I leaned back into the headrest to let my hair be washed, so was the shampoo. I wasted no time soaking and trying to enjoy something absolutely devoid of enjoyment, and when I stepped out to wrap the towel around me, Kel-Ten gestured me to him.

"Now you can come over here and let Kel-Ten enjoy how clean you are," he said, patting his still-naked lap. "You'll be needing him again later, and if you aren't a good little sweet thing you won't be getting him as fast as you did this time."

As fast as I did that time. It was all I could do to keep my lip from curling as I walked over to him, and his grin said he knew what I was prudently refraining from showing or commenting on. He pulled me onto his lap and settled me the way he had the first time, and then his arms were around me as he sniffed appreciatively.

"Wildflowers," he said with a good deal of enjoyment. "I love the smell of wildflowers." He moved his face to the side of my neck, as though getting closer to enjoy the perfume more, but instead said very softly, "Why did they give you that heavy a shot? Did they tell you anything more than they told me? Try to conceal the movement of your lips when you answer me."

"They said it was because of the way I acted with Ank-Soh," I answered after pretending I was burying my face in his chest, partially startled by having forgotten that

that chair was where we supposedly could speak freely. "They knew *he* hadn't minded, but they didn't feel the same way about it. If I make sure I don't refuse to be touched again, they'll be gracious and not do that to me again. But why are we hiding the movement of our lips? I thought it was safe to talk here."

"Soundwise, I'm sure it *is* safe," he replied, moving his face around in my headrest-dried hair. "If they knew what we were discussing last night you'd be back in low having your personality Xed out, and I'd be—having problems of my own. Since I don't know whether we're being watched as well as listened to, I decided not to give them any more distorted conversations to wonder about. Everything is going much too well for me to chance ruining it now."

I let my face rest against his chest just in case he was right about our being watched, but this time said nothing because there was nothing I cared to say. He picked up on my silence faster than I'd expected him to do, and his right hand reached across to move the towel off my left shoulder.

"It may not seem like it to *you*, but things *are* going unbelievably well," he murmured, rubbing the top of my arm gently with his palm. "Not only did they give you to me without any of the argument I was expecting, they made it even better by coming up with a reason for me to keep you longer than I thought I could. I've decided not to waste any part of the opportunity, so tomorrow morning I'm going to awaken you."

"Tomorrow morning," I breathed, feeling a jolt of excitement coursing through me, almost forgetting to bury the words against him. "But why not today, right now, this very minute?"

"Not before you've visited my afternoon training classes, he demurred, his hand sliding down my back under the towel. "I have to get everyone used to seeing you, and knowing they can't reach through to you. You'll have to make sure you stand well back out of everyone's range, as though you're afraid they'll hurt you, and that way no one will be able to tell you're awake when you *are* awake. While you're pretending to be frightened you'll be paying very close attention to the exercises and instructions, getting yourself taught without my having to take the chance of doing it. Afterward I'll help you practice, and I'd like to see them detect *that.*''

I only just kept myself from making a sound of amusement, knowing as well as he that no one had equipment capable of detecting the use of emotions. Our escape was about to start, *would* be starting the very next day, and after that it would only be a matter of— A matter of allowing myself to be—to be— The elation drained out of me as I became very aware of the hand moving on my body, a hand that touched me as though I belonged to its owner. And I *would* belong to its owner, more completely than I'd ever belonged to anyone, and he knew that, and had begun heating me up again to prove it. . . .

''Don't worry, sweet thing, by the time it happens you won't even notice,'' he murmured, obviously knowing where my thoughts had gone. ''In a little while you'll understand that it'll be *my* baby in your pretty belly, and you'll be as hot at the idea as I am. I want to do you, girl, more than I ever wanted to do any other female, and I mean to see you wanting it just as much. Use that squirming to shift around to face me, and then give your Kel-Ten a big kiss. If they're watching, we're about to give them something interesting to look at.''

He held my towel while I did as he'd told me to, miserable but having no choice about listening to him. I could almost hear the bubbling in my blood starting up again, and had no illusions about what it would be like for me if I tried refusing. He let the towel fall on his knees behind me as I raised my face to him, and once our lips met his hand made sure we met in another way as well. I moaned deep in my throat and hated myself for it, feeling that it was somehow my fault I couldn't stop what that drug was making me do and feel. It had me so tight that when Kel-Ten didn't shift closer to me, I whimpered and went to him. He chuckled and used his thumb to encourage me in my efforts even more, but just before I lost myself to wildness I was able to whisper deep inside, ''Tomorrow morning . . . tomorrow morning . . . tomorrow morning . . .''

# 7

But tomorrow morning was still a long way off. When Kel-Ten was through with me he laughingly ordered me to the thick, soft carpeting on the floor, belly down while he showered off the sweat of his most recent exertions. He left me there while he went to throw our clothing into the wall cleaner in the bedroom, already having refused me another bath even before I'd asked. He seemed to be trying to get me used to the idea of having his spending inside me with no opportunity to rid myself of it, the way it would be when my protection finally wore off. I spent my time on the floor trying to pull handfuls of silky carpeting loose, my thoughts too black even for me to dwell on.

Once we were back into our newly-cleaned clothing, we left the apartment again. For some reason the sight of all that gold was beginning to bother me even more than it had when I'd first seen it, as though I'd once seen something similar and hadn't enjoyed the occasion. Rather than wasting time trying to pin down memories made purposely and permanently elusive, I simply accepted the annoyance and dislike I felt and followed Kel-Ten back down to the area where his classes were to be held. Paying attention to something important would rid me of useless, extraneous feelings like the ones clashing around inside me, and the classes were definitely categorized as important.

The first one we went to was a large room with about thirty men, and once I'd been fussed over by some of them Kel-Ten was able to put me into a far corner with no one bothering any more about me. The room, I saw, had no windows, and from the flat sounds of voices and such in my ears I decided it was probably shielded in some way. The floor I sat down on had thick white lines painted on it, with numbers on the walls apparently corresponding to the lines. When a man wearing a black uniform came into the room and closed the door behind him, the Primes who had been milling around joking with one another began moving to different places on various parts of the lines.

Once everyone was arranged in the way they were apparently supposed to be, the man in black stood himself on a short line in front of the room. Rather than being all the way in front himself, Kel-Ten stood on a line farther away from the front than anyone else, and the man in black looked at him and smiled.

"Good afternoon yourself, Prime Kel-Ten," he said, nodding with what seemed to be satisfaction. "Were any of you in the first line able to feel that greeting? No, of course you weren't, because despite the strength of the projection, Prime Kel-Ten was using a tight beam to me alone. Your own strength will develop as you go along, but precise control is something you have to practice. This is the place you'll be practicing it, and at increasingly greater distances. Once you're able to reach me from the same line Prime Kel-Ten is standing on, you'll know you're ready to challenge him. I would not advise trying it before that."

A ripple of laughter went through the room, and those in the first line stirred in what seemed to be discomfort. I had the impression they were new to the class on control, and the man in black's joke had somehow been at their expense. For a while the class went silent as the man in black looked at each Prime in turn, nodded as though he were getting something from him, then went on to the next. After the last of them was done and nodded to, the man in black looked around again.

"Now everyone will take the same place one line back and try the greeting again," he said, giving most of his attention to the front line. "As you can see from the wall the distance between each line is two feet, and those are the increments of extra distance you'll be trying for. We start newcomers off at a distance short of the twenty to twenty-five feet you're already capable of covering, and then you work your way up to more and more distance. Please don't forget that control is the important part here, so when you can reach me from thirty feet away, you won't really be reaching me until you can reach *only* me. If the man standing next to you or in front of you feels it too, your control isn't what it should be."

He nodded to the members of his class then, a gesture which sent them back the one line he'd asked for, and then everyone went silent again. I noticed that Kel-Ten also stepped back one line even though no one was close enough to crowd him, and out of curiosity looked at the number on the wall of his new line. The numbers were large and bright, a glowing yellow easily read against the dark brown paneling of the wall, and I had to be very careful to keep all expression off my face. The First Prime of that complex, the man everyone was so in awe of or proud of, stood on the line with a 47 beside it, meaning the new range he was trying for was forty-seven feet. Forty-seven whole feet.

I stirred where I sat on the floor in the back corner of the room, momentarily enjoying feelings of ridicule and superiority, but then common sense came along to bat me between the eyes. Kel-Ten had decided to turn me back on the very next morning, but what would happen when he did? I already knew I couldn't try pressing for memory of what I could do, but wasn't there something that would show him the difference between our minds? Everything I'd seen and heard about so far had struck me as no more than baby tricks, which logically meant I was capable of doing a good deal better. What would happen when Kel-Ten found out about it? Would he be delighted and decide to move up the date for our escape attempt, or would he feel so threatened and jealous that he would quickly try turning me off again? If he decided against using me to help, could I stop him from making me helpless again? What in hell was I going to do?

I spent the rest of that class time fretting and trying to consider the problem unemotionally, but didn't have as much of an opportunity as I'd thought I would. It wasn't very long before the man in black told them that was it for the day, and I looked up to see a group of very wilted men heading for the door out of the room. Kel-Ten was coming to me instead of leaving, and although there was still a lot of spring in his step I could see the sweat on his forehead when he bent to take my hand and pull me to my feet.

"Did you see that?" he asked, satisfaction in the light eyes looking down at me. "Before very long I'll have that new mark established, and then I'll only be eight feet away from the all-time record. You have no idea how badly I want to break that record, sweet thing, and every day that passes brings me closer to it. Once I have it it'll be *my* name on the golden plaque, *me* everyone else has to measure up to. There'll be a celebration the likes of which hasn't been seen in this place in years, and you'll be there to share it with me. I have to admit I've been letting it slide lately, but now that I'm back to it I'll be trying harder than ever."

He put his arm around me and began leading me out of the room, and I almost gave in to the urge to bite my lip. Was he serious about how much he wanted to break that record, or was he simply announcing to our unseen listeners another reason why they'd be stupid to take me away from him? I didn't know which the truth was and would have immediately started worrying about it, but a question had occurred to me that he should be able to answer.

"Kel-Ten, who set the record you're trying to break?" I asked, turning my head to look up at him as we walked. "And for that matter, what became of the Prime you won first place from? Was he knocked down to one of the two second places? How many times has he tried getting first place back?"

"Yes, sir, that celebration will really be something," he said, his grin widening as he shook his head just a little. "All classes will be canceled for the entire day, everybody will dress up in the best they have, and no one will do anything but party. I'd better stop thinking about it, or I'll be useless in my next class."

He laughed lightly and squeezed me gently with the arm he had around me, and then fell silent for the rest of our walk up the corridor. For my own part I wanted to shiver violently, because I'd been watching his face when I'd asked my questions. He'd started out listening, I knew he had, but once my first question was out his face had gone slack until I'd finished. Once I was done he'd come alive again and had talked about the celebration, just as though I hadn't said a word! He wasn't ignoring me, he'd been—programmed—against hearing or thinking about anything like that! What happened to the First Prime once he was bested was a taboo subject, most probably right along with what happened to *every* Prime once they'd reached their limit. And I'd been jealous of the men in that place for being free of the conditioning the women were subjected to!

Wondering about what they did with Primes who had reached their full development occupied me until we got into the next room, and then I gave up on the question as a complete waste of time. There was no way of knowing *what* they did with them, but it was highly unlikely the men were accorded anything as simple as the death given to women who could no longer bear children. I was certain that that was the fate of most women who were beyond being bred, but the same thing wouldn't be done to men who had been put through that very thorough training. You don't go to such lengths to train people who are slated for nothing more than death, but what could they possibly . . .

"This next class may frighten you, but I don't want you interrupting it by making any noise," Kel-Ten said, bringing me back to where I was supposed to be. "Just sit in your corner like a good girl, and it'll be over before you know it."

He patted me on the head as I sat down in a room exactly like the last one, then he went to join the other men who were there. They weren't the same men who had been in the previous class, and when a new instructor in black came in they all spread out along a single line. That let me see there were fewer of them, at least until three Secs herded in a matching number of men dressed in bright orange coveralls. The newcomers were somehow different from the men already there, thinner and looking less well cared for, shambling rather than walking normally. They were prodded into line opposite Kel-Ten and the others with twenty feet between the two groups, and then the Secs moved back to the now-closed door and the instructor inspected his students from where he stood at the lefthand wall.

"All right, everyone at once," he said, sounding and looking downright bored. "Let's start with fear."

Some of the men in orange had come in looking deathly frightened, but the next instant it wasn't a matter of just some. I gasped back into my corner when every one of them began screaming, some with eyes stretched wide, some with eyes and fists squeezed closed, all of them sounding as though they'd been pushed off a tall building or were about to be jumped on by a starving carnivore. The instructor let it go on for about ten seconds, and then he shouted, "Defeat!" and the screaming cut off as if someone had thrown a switch. Half of the men in orange collapsed to the floor and one or two covered their heads, the rest just standing where they were with rounded shoulders and heads down low. Their attitudes said it was all over for them, everything was all over, but that was just the emotion they were made to feel. Everything wasn't all over, it was only just beginning.

After that the instructor had the Primes manipulate their victims one at a time, hopelessness, doubt, bitterness, hate, and even cruelty. Every dark emotion there was was practiced on the men in orange, but Kel-Ten had been right when he said it wouldn't last long. Even with taking turns the Primes were quickly too tired to go on, and in significantly less than half an hour it was over. The men in orange were sprawled on the floor, most of them twitching from the series of terrible emotions they'd had forced on them in such quick succession, the Secs in charge of them coming away from the door to stand over them. Once again the Primes heading out of the room looked wilted, and as Kel-Ten approached me I could see he wasn't doing much better.

"Now we get to take a short break," he said, looking faintly pleased that I was rising to my feet alone. "That one really takes it out of you, even more than all that exercising I did this morning. We'll use the lounge just a couple of doors away from here."

He took my hand and led the way back to the door, paying no attention to the way the Secs were prodding at the men in orange to get them to their feet. One of the men was crying openly, sobbing out the pain of what he had just been put through, the sound of hopelessness so heavy in it that everyone listening should have felt the emotion as claws along nerve endings. We came closest to them as we passed through the doorway, and it was then that I became aware of the conviction that the men weren't normals, but empaths like us. Since it wasn't likely they were Primes, I shuddered at the sure knowledge that that had to be what became of some of the babies who weren't—*lucky*—enough to be born especially gifted.

"Just take it easy, you did fine in there," Kel-Ten said, dropping my hand in order to put an arm around me. "We do have to have someone to practice on, after all, and there are certain things you can't aim at an instructor and still expect him to be able to go on instructing. That's their purpose, to be targets for us, and it really isn't as bad for them as it looked to you. Come on, the lounge is in here."

The new doorway off the corridor he urged me through brought us into a room decorated in browns and tans and grays and greens, all deep calm and deep relaxation colors being used and appreciated by the five men already in the lounge. The couches and chairs were very soft leather and the accompanying tables matched, and when Kel-Ten dropped onto a dark brown couch he immediately used the arm server to order himself a drink. It came fairly quickly and wasn't all that large, so four swallows later he put aside the empty glass and smiled at me where I sat beside him on the couch.

"Now I've got to rest for a while, so you might as well take it easy yourself," he said, drawing his legs up onto the couch and folding them in front of him. "If any of those jokers tries bothering you while I'm out of it, just remind them how fast I'll be back—and how well-rested

I'll be. I'll even be ready to take on *your* usual temper again."

He grinned as he tried chucking me under the chin, grinned wider when I moved my head to avoid it, but he didn't pursue the matter. He looked close to being totally drained with even the grin appearing forced, and he'd already gone as far as he could. He turned his face from me and took three very deep, very slow breaths, and by the end of the third he was completely under. Deep trance through self-hypnosis, something I'd learned myself a few years earlier, but had never thought to use to return my own strength when I needed it. I actually spent a minute wondering why I hadn't before the disgust set in, causing me to slump back in amazement at the unbelievable stupidity I seemed capable of. If you know you've been conditioned, how can you wonder about the things it never occurred to you to try?

After a couple of minutes of soaking in self-derision, I straightened on the couch and drew my legs up to the left of me. One of the other men in the room had been eyeing me and the way I'd been sitting, his lazy grin aimed at how high that shirt was on my thighs. Not being particularly anxious to encourage trouble I decided I'd better watch what I did a bit more closely, but sometimes trouble doesn't need encouragement to find you. No more than five minutes after Kel-Ten went under, a shadow fell across me, and there was a white uniform standing directly in front of me. I looked up slowly, somehow knowing who I would see even before my eyes touched him, and the Sec Adjin looked back down at me with a faint grin on his face.

"The people in charge of you think you need a little more body fat, so they sent me with this midafternoon snack for you," he said, gesturing with the cup and packet he carried before crouching down closer to me. "I happen to think you look fine just the way you are, but we'll still do it their way. Here, take it and eat it."

He handed me the cup of meat soup and the packet of crackers, and I couldn't seem to do anything but take them. My heart was hammering again and my hands felt cold, my insides were turning and my mind had gone numb, all of me overwhelmed by the fear reactions coursing through me. I didn't know what it was about that null, but just looking at him made me want to run and hide and never come out. His dark eyes stared directly at me, the enjoyment in them showing he knew exactly how frightened I was, and then his right hand rose and slid under the bottom of my shirt to touch the inner part of my right thigh. I closed my eyes for a moment as I fought to keep a lurching whimper inside, and then I hurried to eat the food that had been sent me.

Square food goes down in lumps no matter what its original texture and consistency is, and the soup and crackers more than qualified. I swallowed it all without tasting any of it, desperate to get that null away from me, praying that finishing the snack would accomplish that end. Once again no one knew what he was doing to me, his broad body blocking the view of whatever men were in the room and probably doing the same for any observation or recording devices there might be. His hand held to me as two of his fingers moved in a teasing way, but I was too terrified to find the gesture at all arousing. I took the empty packet and stuffed it into the emptied cup, set it down on the couch to my left, then found that my desperate hope hadn't been in vain. The null squeezed my thigh one last time before withdrawing his hand, and then took the empty cup and straightened.

"And they said I might have trouble with you," the Sec commented with a good deal of amusement, not minding in the least that he was talking to the top of my head. "You won't ever give me trouble, will you, pretty girl? See you again some time."

With that he walked away, leaving the lounge without even a single glance back. I found I was trembling so hard I might have had the chills, and if I hadn't been controlling myself rigidly I would have thrown up what I'd just eaten. I put one hand to my head and leaned back against the soft leather trying to calm down, trying to understand why I felt like that when that one Sec was near me. He was far from being the only null in the place, so why did I go into a panic only when *he* was anywhere near me? What could my reaction possibly mean?

Thinking about it got me absolutely nowhere, and all that came out of the time was a reconfirmation of my decision not to tell what he was doing. No one in that facility cared enough about me to stop him from doing just as he pleased, at least not on a permanent basis, so what was the point in saying anything? There wasn't anyone anywhere who really cared about me, something I'd understood and accepted a long time ago, so getting used to that new situation wouldn't be all that hard. It really added very little to the hurt, but the cold was something else again.

It wasn't more than another few minutes before Kel-Ten's breathing rate changed again, showing he was coming out of it. When he did he stretched hard and called up another drink, downed it as fast as he had the first, then pulled me off the couch and out of the lounge. He was all recovered and ready to go back to it again, and I had just enough time to wonder what was in those drinks he'd had. I'd thought at first that they might be alcoholic, but they seemed, instead, to be bracers of another sort. I could just remember that alcohol ruined control and concentration more than almost anything, which meant they were giving him something else. If there was one thing they *didn't* want, it was having their star Prime lose his control and ability to concentrate.

His next class was already assembled and waiting for him, and this time it was a matter of delicate handling rather than gross manipulation. The Primes had a different group of men in orange coveralls to work on, and what they did was have a victim walk from one side of the room to the other, each Prime deciding when he would cause his target to trip, or fall, or forget where he was going, or suddenly become unsure of himself, or any one of another half dozen things. Some of the targets were set to putting something simple together, like a child's building toy, and the object then was to keep them from doing it right. The Primes were scored on the unnoticeability of what they did, the largest number of points being given to Kel-Ten when he caused his target to put a piece in wrong but fail to notice the error. The target was confused when his building collapsed, not knowing why it had happened, but the other Primes cheered and the black-uniformed instructor grinned and offered his congratulations.

Again the class didn't last very long, but this time we didn't go anywhere when it was over. Kel-Ten sat cross-legged next to me in my corner and closed his eyes, this time in a light trance rather than a deep one, waiting only until the room was cleared of its previous occupants and the new ones had arrived. The newcomers turned out to be an instructor and five strange Primes, and when the men were standing along one of the lines and the man in black was to the far side of them, Kel-Ten opened his eyes and got to his feet. He strolled more than walked to the short line previously used by an instructor and stood himself on it facing the five men, and then he smiled at them. Although their backs were to me I had the impression they weren't returning his smile, and when the instructor told them all to get ready they seemed to stiffen. Kel-Ten, twenty feet away from their line, was the only one who didn't.

"Number one, please begin," the instructor said, and the man at the extreme right stirred when Kel-Ten's eyes went to him. They stared at each other in silence for a while, the seconds ticking heavily by, and then the man with his back to me grunted and staggered backward from the line he'd been standing on. It was almost as though he'd been pushed away, and I looked over to see that Kel-Ten's smile had returned.

"Not bad, sir, not bad," the instructor said to the man who wasn't returning to the line, true satisfaction in his voice. "Your strength is improving quite a bit from what it was, and this time you were able to hold your ground for eight seconds. You other gentlemen will take your marks from that, and please note that the Prime is remaining back from the line now that he's been forced away from it. Number two, if you please."

Kel-Ten looked at the man who had been second from the right, and again his stare was returned. This time, however, there was less of a wait before the man stumbled back, and then it was the third man's turn. Seconds for him and seconds for the last two, and then none of them remained on the line they'd started from. Kel-Ten was sweating hard and looking drained again, but his smile was one of triumph as he stood proudly on the same spot he'd started from.

"For four of you gentlemen, that was your initial experience against the strength of the First Prime, Kel-Ten," the instructor said to the men who were standing where they'd been forced to, most of them also looking drained. "This exercise lets you compare your own strength to his, and tells you how far you've yet to go before you can consider challenging him. I'm sure each of you noticed that the distance was minimum rather than maximum, which is another point for you to consider. When you think you've made significant progress you'll ask to come back here, and then, like the fifth of your number, you'll find out whether or not you have. This is a practice rather than a challenge situation, something you'll find out more about as your growth continues. That's it for now, gentlemen, and I hope to see you all again quite soon."

His dismissal of them was polite but cuttingly casual, especially when he turned his back on them to go to Kel-Ten, and began pouring out congratulations and praise. The five men were silent as they filed slowly out of the room, but their sullen anger and jealousy and airs of vindictiveness were so strong I could almost feel them where I sat. Kel-Ten was being used as an object of hatred to goad the others on to try for his level of ability and position, but I doubted that he realized that. He must have thought they were simply after the golden prize, the thing his masters wanted him to believe.

The First Prime was stroked hard and long for his excellent performance, and then the man in black left the room. I was already on my feet and waiting by then, not exactly patiently, which Kel-Ten noticed with a grin when he finally called me over to him.

"I know you couldn't appreciate that, but you can take my word for the fact that I was great," he said, putting an arm around me. "Doesn't it give you a thrill to have been chosen by the best man here?"

"I'm absolutely overcome with awe and gratitude," I said with a yawn, ignoring the rough arm around my shoulders. "What heart-stopping excitement do we go to from here?"

"From here we go back to my apartment so I can shower and rest up for dinner," he answered with a laugh, squeezing me a little before heading us out of the room. "You have to be on the receiving end of that before you learn what tired really is, so don't be surprised when you don't immediately find me all over you. I'll need a short nap before I can do a proper job of assault."

"I'm glad you told me," I answered, still pretending to be extremely bored. "If you hadn't, I might have begun worrying that I was losing my attraction for you. If that ever happened, I don't know how I'd console myself."

"Oh, right," he agreed with even more of a laugh, heading us directly down the center of the corridor and making everyone else walk around us. "I can just see you crying yourself to sleep—which I just may decide to see that you do anyway."

He was still chuckling when we reached the bank of lifts, but then he was distracted by a knot of men standing in the area laughing and talking together. He seemed to know what was going on, and when we moved closer to them I got my own idea. Ank-Soh was standing in the middle of the knot being congratulated, and when he saw us approaching he left his admirers to come over to us.

"He didn't have a chance, Kel-Ten," he announced with a grin, confirming my guess. "Another challenger met and bested, one who seemed to have overlooked the fact that I'm also growing and improving. What's your range these days?"

"I'm reaching for forty-seven, Ank-Soh," my companion answered, the blandness in his voice worse than smugness would have been. "And you?"

"My win was at forty-two," the other man answered, a faint smile accompanying his own blandness. "A couple of days ago, I began reaching a little higher than that.

Everyone says my growth has really improved over the last few weeks, more than they would have expected. And how are *you,* sweet thing? Have you been enjoying yourself spending the day with the First Prime?''

''It's been an unforgettable occasion,'' I muttered, stiffening as his hand went into my shirt the way it had that morning—but making no attempt to back away. He grinned down at me as his fingers and palm enjoyed my flesh, and then his eyes moved to the man standing to my left.

''Congratulations, Kel-Ten, you've made quite a bit of progress with her since this morning,'' he said, stroking the pet while he spoke to her master. ''I look forward to the time you're too busy to give her the attention she needs. I'll check with you again tomorrow.''

He took his hand back without looking at me again, bowed sardonically to Kel-Ten, then ambled away to return to his friends. Kel-Ten dialed open a lift door, pulled me inside with him, and fumed silently only until the doors closed us in.

''That son of Ejects!'' he snarled then, his good humor entirely vanished. ''He still thinks he has a chance of besting me! And wouldn't they love seeing that, one of their hot-house Primes besting the wild and captured First! Those of us raised outside of this complex and only brought in later have always been best, but Ank-Soh is more interested in advancing than in being pampered. Damn him and his ambition!''

He lapsed into silence after that, a dark roiling silence that took us all the way back to his apartment. I didn't have to be told he was in no mood for swapping clever conversation, but keeping quiet didn't keep me from getting singed on the edges of the flames. The fingers around my arm had grown painful by the time we reached the golden bathroom, and being thrown to the carpeting in the middle of the floor was almost a relief.

''Stay right there until I tell you to get up again,'' my owner growled as he kept moving past me, pulling his shirt off over his head as he went. ''Belly down and cheek to the carpeting, and don't let me hear a word out of you.''

The only thing I would have said to him wouldn't have done any good for me with anyone listening, so it was just as well that I'd been told to continue with my prudent silence. I turned my head from him and put my cheek to the carpeting in accordance with the rest of my orders, then closed my eyes and fought to gain control of my body. Ank-Soh's touching me had started the burning again, not as badly as it had been earlier but bad enough, and I didn't want to feel that way. If I couldn't get it under control I'd have to beg Kel-Ten for relief a second time, and I especially didn't want to do that. His mood would make it more than simply unpleasant for me, that I knew beyond doubt, and my backing down in front of Ank-Soh had been humiliating enough.

As it turned out, I didn't have to worry about begging Kel-Ten. He moved around very briefly before the sound of water came, took his shower fast, then strode out of the room. I waited for him to come back and tell me I could get up, fighting all the while with the need that insisted on rising, and finally it came through to me that he wasn't coming back. He had walked out without paying the least attention to me, possibly even without seeing me, and had gone to take his nap. He must have known I'd have a problem after Ank-Soh's little gesture, but since he wasn't up to doing anything about it he'd just gone ahead and ignored it. It was easy to see how really concerned he was about me, just like everyone else.

I suppose it would have helped if I could have fallen asleep, but my body saw to it that I wasn't able to sleep. Kel-Ten napped for hours and I experienced every minute of the time wide awake, my mind uninterested in thinking, nothing but sensations and emotions occupying it. It was a painful, endless time, but one that somehow seemed very familiar, almost as though I'd gone through the same thing before. Being too alone in an unendurable situation, afraid to let yourself think about what was being done to you, knowing that if you started to think the tears would come, marking the end of all your attempts to be brave. I wanted to give up but I couldn't afford to, not when giving up would mean much more than simply losing. There *are* things worse than death, living being one of them, or more properly being forced to live on under certain conditions. I rubbed my cheek against the carpeting, wondering why I kept thinking of it as fur, wondering why my mind took hope from that—then rejected the hope completely. Why did I have to be haunted by supposedly buried memories. . . ?

"Well, now, will you look at what a good girl she is?" a blurry voice said suddenly from behind me, lazy amusement in it. "Put her to her belly and tell her to stay that way, and that's exactly what she does. I wonder if she did it because she's hoping for a reward. Did you want Kel-Ten to reward you, sweet thing?"

If my eyes hadn't already been closed I would have closed them, not far from wishing the man had stayed asleep no matter how I felt. I didn't even want to look at him, not to mention talk to him, but he had recovered too much of his good mood to let my obvious reluctance bother him. He came over and crouched beside me, used two fingers to get a more direct answer to his question than words, then closed a fist in my hair and pulled me to my feet.

"I really enjoyed that ride you took this morning, so much so that I think I'll let you do it again," he said, grinning down at me as he guided me toward the dry-chair by the hair. "After this, though, we're going to find another chair. It's handy doing it in the bathroom if you want to shower afterward, but otherwise the surroundings don't do much to encourage my mood."

He chuckled at his cleverness as he seated himself and pulled me into his lap facing him, and then he proved how restorative sleep can be for some people. It was exactly what I needed and I groaned as I inched closer to him, but his casual comment had disturbed me enough to keep the pleasure from being overwhelming. He had said we would probably not be using the dry-seat again, meaning we would not be speaking privately again, but I didn't know why until he put his arms around me and began kissing my shoulder and face.

"I've decided our talking like this is too much of a risk," he whispered, letting me do most of the work while he simply enjoyed himself. "We'll end it now, before I awaken you, giving them less to be suspicious about. But we had to have this last time because I've been thinking about tomorrow. Being awakened will jar you a little, but you have to get used to the feeling because it will be happening on and off during the entire day."

"What are you talking about?" I whispered back, my lips very close to his bent head. "Why will it be necessary to do it more than once?"

"I can't keep you permanently awake the way I thought I could," he answered in a murmur, beginning to move just a little under me. "We're liable to run into Ank-Soh at any time, with at least one meeting already guaranteed, and he'll know at once if you're awake. I'll have to turn you on before every class and then turn you off again, then on again here in the apartment so you can practice. If for some reason it doesn't work, I'll have to think of something else."

"But why can't I shield?" I asked with difficulty, almost completely lost to what he was doing to me—and what I was doing to him. I knew the conversation we were having was important, but my body considered other things even more important. If I'd had the attention to spare I would have cursed that injection, but I was much too far beyond the ability to curse.

"What's that supposed to mean?" he came back, nearly forgetting to keep on enjoying himself. "What sort of shield are you talking about?"

"I don't know, but I think I'll know when I'm awake," I said mostly in a moan, kissing at him in between the words. "No one will know my mind is active . . . I don't think they'll know . . . Let's wait and see, Kel-Ten, and do something else now rather than talk. Please move a little more, and harder, Kel-Ten, please harder."

I took his face in my hands and pressed my lips to his, but it seemed like a very long time before he began to respond the way he usually did. If I hadn't been so far gone I would have known he was thinking about something, but I didn't understand that until we had finished up and he had left me to rinse himself off under the shower. By then it was too late to discuss whatever had been bothering him, but not too late to worry about it. I didn't know myself what I had meant by a shield, the thought had just come without my looking for it, but if it made him change his mind about awakening me I'd bite my tongue out. I ran a weary hand through my hair as I sat on the floor waiting for Kel-Ten, trying to tell myself it wasn't yet time to be depressed. If the next day came without my being awakened, that would be the time to start thinking actively about suicide.

Dressing for dinner was more of a distraction than I'd expected it to be, since Kel-Ten wasn't the only one who had something to dress up in. He must have told someone what he wanted at some time during the day when I wasn't around; when he slid a mirrored door aside at the end of the wall, it was all there and waiting for him. More than half a dozen different creations hung on a rack behind the door, for the most part flimsy things that fluttered in the breeze generated by the door being opened, all of them one shade or another of gold. Kel-Ten inspected them for a moment before choosing one, carried it over to me, then helped me put it on. I'd been expecting to be pleased when I no longer had to wear that shirt, but the new outfit was not what might be called an improvement. The wide jeweled collar had a broad strip of gold material attached front and back, and although the material was solid rather than see-through and came down to my ankles, that's all there was to it. No belt, no ties, and nothing at all under it aside from me. When Kel-Ten took my hand and began to stride out of the apartment the back panel billowed out like a cape, something he found a good deal more amusing than I did.

Dinner was a glittering affair with everyone in one sort of finery or another, but I couldn't help noticing that the men were dressed to please themselves while the women were dressed to please the men. I decided to ignore it all and concentrate on eating, but the table chef didn't deliver the sort of plain meal I was expecting—and hoping for. Plain food is much better when you're in the mood to brood rather than enjoy yourself, but what I got was sautéed valmin and creamed sinrows mixed with unsalted nuts, tessin soup and dreff salad, baked gimels and glazed finfaws. Again there was just enough of each, something I could tell simply by looking at the portions, and behind the rest of it was a very involved, very high-calorie dessert. That in itself would have been enough to depress me, but the whole thing together was simply too much. I didn't know if I was being rewarded for proper behavior or simply fattened up for the eventual kill, but it made no difference. I ate no more than half of the food and none of the dessert, also refusing the glass of wine Kel-Ten said I could have. He threatened me half-heartedly when he saw the food left over, saying something about how unhappy everyone would be with me, but he was too distracted to pursue the matter. His mind was very clearly on other things, which meant mine was, too.

After the leisurely dinner was over we joined a number of other people in the "open" section of the floor, standing or sitting around with rain pouring down outside while the men discussed the best ways of achieving this or that desired effect when practicing on a target. Kel-Ten's advice was asked more often than anyone else's, which meant he had no trouble letting the discussion distract him. I, on the other hand, was not quite as fortunate, and watching the rain batter mindlessly against the windows all around did nothing to raise my spirits. Again I felt as though the situation was familiar, that I'd watched the pouring rain once before as I waited for something important to happen, something that wasn't guaranteed to go well. Kel-Ten let his hands move over me beneath the cloth as he spoke to the others, but that, too, was becoming easier and easier to ignore. All I could think about was the next day, and because of that regretted the little I'd eaten.

The discussion was interrupted after a while by the same sort of gentle chiming I'd heard that morning, and the wonderfully free and fearsomely powerful Primes immediately broke off what they were saying and began heading for the lifts. They still talked to one another as they moved, just as they'd been talking all along, but they obeyed the chime without the least argument or sense of rebellion. It seemed obvious they were being sent to beddy-bye like the good little children they were, but not a single one of them realized that. The men were too conditioned to notice, and the women were too intent on the men for it to penetrate the fog. I wondered briefly what they would do if someone was able to make *all* of them understand what was happening, but then the lift doors opened and I let the pleasant get-even wish simply slip away.

We shared the lift part of the way up with others, but when we reached Kel-Ten's floor we were all alone. The First Prime didn't only stand above everyone else he also lived above them, a fact my companion got a lot of pleasure from. There was no trace of his introspection left as he pulled me out of the lift and along the corridor to his apartment, my dinner costume flying out behind me again, and he even chuckled as he watched.

"There are a lot of men in this building who are going to have an easier job of it tonight because of you," he said, taking my left hand as well to keep it from capturing the flying cloth. "The front section of that thing teases you about what's under it, the back of it lets you see only enough to tease even more, and all that soft, bare skin to either side makes you lick your lips. The ones with rings to cover will be seeing you instead of the rings, just the way I'll be doing, but the difference is once tomorrow comes it *will* be you under me. It's too bad it can't be tonight."

"You've got another date?" I asked, finding the news more than heartening as I followed him into the apartment. "What a terrible, awful, horrible, crying shame. Will you be gone all night, I hope?"

"I won't be gone *any* of the night," he answered with a laugh, seemingly glad I was back to starting up with him. "The girls I'll be covering will be brought to me here, and we'll be using the bedroom. You'll come in to sleep there after they've gone so I can get to you in the morning, but until then we've got to find some place to put you. I'd enjoy having you around to watch me perform, but after a day like today I won't be up to any more than those three—which means you won't be able to get in line. If I want you to sleep—which I do—I have to put you somewhere until I'm through."

"If you're asking whether I'd prefer this visitors' room

or the kitchen, I have to tell you that's not much of a choice,'' I said, looking around the giant room we'd stopped in without much enthusiasm. ''There isn't anything to do in either place, but I suppose in here I can curl up on a couch until your admirers leave. I *am* a little tired, so . . .''

''So we don't want you bothered by all that traffic going in and out,'' he finished for me, suddenly back to showing a very wide grin. ''We need a place where you won't be disturbed while you spend your time missing me, waiting breathlessly until you can return to my side. I have a feeling you *will* end up hoping it isn't all night.''

''Kel-Ten, what are you going to do?'' I demanded as he took my hand again, already beyond suspicion. I *knew* he was going to do something I'd hate, and I wasn't wrong. Rather than answer me he simply led the way to the golden bathroom, stopped in the middle of the room, then pointed to the floor.

''Belly down with the front panel smooth underneath you,'' he ordered, his blue eyes gleaming from all the fun he was having. He knew I had no choice but to do as I was told, and he was absolutely correct—no matter how I detested that position. I refrained from muttering under my breath as I got into it, but then he crouched down beside me to make it even worse. His hands took the back panel and folded it neatly upward until it reached my waist, then he left the roll of material there as he straightened again.

''Now anyone coming in here to make use of the facilities will have a pretty, round bottom to look at while they do,'' he said, the laughter in his voice showing he knew I couldn't keep myself from blushing with embarrassment. ''The girls could come in or I could—or I might even invite a few friends over simply to see how I've decorated this room. Are you still hoping my—date—will take all night?''

''What I'm hoping is that you suddenly find yourself impotent!'' I snapped, furious with him for doing that to me. He didn't have to tell me I'd be staying like that until his rings were gone; that went without saying, something I wished he would do.

"Have fun while you're waiting for your first visitor," he said with a chuckle, bending to pat my bottom before beginning to leave. "And try not to blush so hard, I'd hate to see my carpeting singed."

The door closed behind his high good humor, cutting it off rather abruptly, something I would have preferred seeing happen to him. Telling me to stop blushing had only made the problem worse, just as he'd known damned well it would. I leaned on my elbows as I looked down at the carpeting between my arms, trying to convince myself that there wouldn't *be* anyone coming in to see me like that. He'd only been trying to torture me for not appreciating him properly, or at least for saying I didn't. I was sure he thought I really found him absolutely irresistible, just like every other female in that place. If that had been the only point he was dead wrong about, things might not have been all that impossible around there.

It took a while for the extreme embarrassment I felt to fade, but I had the while and then some. I'd been listening hard for the arrival of the women, just to know when my actual wait would start, so I heard the faint sound of giggling in more than one voice pass my door. The next few minutes after that were hard, agonizing over the possibility that he would bring them in to look at me and laugh, but enough time passed that the chance of it became more and more remote. I really hated being put on display like that, humiliated so that someone could enjoy my discomfort and embarrassment, but it looked like I'd gotten away with—

"Oh, now that's what I call considerate," a voice said from behind me, a very soft voice that I still had no trouble recognizing even as it froze me where I lay. "Someone knew how bored I'd be, so they left me a toy of my own to play with. I really will have to find out who it was and thank them."

People who talk about feeling terror spreading through them are ones who have never experienced the real thing. Terror doesn't spread; it appears full-grown in every muscle of your body, turning you to quivering liquid, turning your mind numb and dead, turning your flesh cold and trembling. I didn't have to look around to know it was the null Adjin who had come in, and my fingers closed convulsively in the carpeting under my hands.

"Just between you and me, I was expecting to find a toy of my own to play with," the null said, his voice still very soft but now much closer. "When I saw who I'd be escorting those girls to, I knew there would be someone around with nothing to occupy her. Since I hate seeing idleness and waste, I made certain arrangements to be sure nothing would be wasted, especially not the opportunity. We have this time to ourselves now, but let's just make sure the Prime isn't disturbed while he's seeing to his duty."

By then he was so close I could hear the sound of his uniform as he moved, and then the roll of material lying on my back was lifted away. If my throat had been able to break through the ice closing it off I would have screamed, and it quickly became clear that he knew it. A moment later the now-unrolled material was in front of my face, his big hand wadding it up, and then the wad was thrust into my mouth. He didn't want me screaming, at least not then, and had taken steps to be sure I couldn't.

What happened after that is a memory I would love losing forever, even to forced oblivion. There was no doubt he'd made special preparations for that visit, ones that suited the sort of personality he was. I'd been expecting him to take physical advantage of me and he did just that, but not in the way I'd been anticipating. He'd brought along a pack of sharp, tiny pins, small metal clamps, and a number of feet of thin, rough rope that felt as though it were cutting my skin open even though it really wasn't. He began by tying my wrists together behind me, and then I was turned to my back for the real start of his fun. Before he began I had no true idea of just how sensitive the "sensitive" portions of the human body are, but before he was very far into it I had learned the lesson all too thoroughly. Clamps produce pain without leaving marks, pin holes can't be detected easily even when you can feel the burning agony, and thin, sharp rope discourages you from pulling against it in an effort to escape it all. I couldn't even scream full out, let alone escape, and that made it infinitely better for the null.

By the time he was through with me and the rope was gone I was no longer even whimpering, the red flame of pain encircling me so completely that all I could do was lie unmoving on the carpeting with my eyes closed. Some men enjoy giving nothing but pain, a quiet voice in my numbed mind told me, they can't find pleasure of their own unless they're hurting someone. This one knew that any damage he did would be the next thing to invisible, and that I would most likely not try proving it had happened without supporting physical evidence. The carpeting was silky soft under my left cheek, a grotesque counterpoint to the way the rest of me shrieked, and then I felt a finger gently stroking my right cheek.

"I'll knock on the door on my way out with the girls," the null whispered, his voice heavy with extreme satisfaction. "You'll stay exactly where you are until then, and won't make a fuss either now or later. The only thing a fuss will bring you is trouble, and I think you know that. Next time we'll probably do something different, to make sure neither of us gets bored. We'll just have to see."

He chuckled as he stroked my cheek again, and then he was gone as silently as he'd come. After a moment or two I reached up and pulled the wad of cloth out of my mouth, but aside from that didn't move. I also didn't think, which was something of a blessing; the only thing to think about was pain, and it was enough that I had to feel it.

I waited a short while after I heard the knock before trying to get up and walk, finding even then that neither action was easy. I might have stayed in the bathroom despite Kel-Ten's orders, but it had occurred to me that he would be waiting for me and would at least be able to hold me in his arms. Right then I needed holding very badly, more than I could ever remember having needed it, even when I'd been very small. I made my slow, painful way into the bedroom, knowing the effort would be worth it, forcing myself to keep going until I reached the bed. Kel-Ten was there and would be waiting for me, waiting to hold me and tell me everything would be all right, waiting to stroke my hair and comfort me the way I needed to be comforted. It was very dim in the room, almost dark, but he was there—

Sound asleep on his stomach, his arms buried under the pillow his head rested on, his breathing deep and even and slow.

I took off the costume and crawled into the very large bed, then lay at the very edge of it on my side in one small spot. All I really needed was that one small spot, somewhere to stay until the pain left me. It was lucky I didn't need anything more, because there was nothing more to be had. It was useless for the quiet tears to trickle down my cheeks, because there was nothing more to be had.

# 8

I awoke to find that I'd been pulled against a large male body, two warm lips kissing my face and neck. I felt confused but knew I didn't want to be kissed and held like that, knew I just wanted to be left alone the way I'd been alone all my life. I moved against the arms that held me as I began to struggle, but the kissing suddenly turned into very soft words.

"Stop trying to push me away," Kel-Ten whispered, so low there was almost no sound to his speaking. "I'm going to key you awake now, and I need a reason for being this close."

It came to me with a heart-thumping shock that that was it, the time I'd been waiting for, the time I'd been afraid would never come. What had happened the night before had also come back to me, but that was less important than what was about to happen, a good deal less important. I quickly stopped struggling and put my arms around Kel-Ten, as though I had just realized who he was and didn't want to get away from him, and he made a sound of satisfaction and then spoke a word. The word registered in my mind without my ears being able to hear it, a word I didn't know and would never have been able to repeat, but because of it I was suddenly—

Alive.

Truly alive and whole again.

I could feel everything there was to feel in that place, the faint, distant murmur of very many minds, some active, some not, some below and some outside, beyond the walls of the buildings we were in. I took a very deep breath after ages of suffocation, then finally paid attention to the man in whose arms I lay. His mind was bright and strong, clearly active rather than latent, but I had the distinct impression I'd seen stronger minds somewhere, in some place I couldn't quite remember. I could also feel the growling desire in his mind, a desire that didn't seem totally natural, and he was balancing between the desire and a curiosity tinged with apprehension. His mind poked at mine in the same way his tongue tickled my ear, and I could feel that he was somewhat disappointed.

"You're not as strong as I'd hoped you'd be," he breathed, beginning to move his hands around on my body. "All we can do is get you started on the exercises, and try to make them do you some good. What about that shield you mentioned yesterday?"

His saying I wasn't very strong startled me, but then I realized he was experiencing my mind through the curtain over it, not even knowing the curtain was there. I was able to remember about the curtain then, knowing it had formed because of my need for it, because of my worry that Kel-Ten might be jealous of a mind stronger than his. I was about to replace it with my shield, when I suddenly realized I had two shields to choose from, one the small, strong shield only I could get around, and the other the light shield I'd developed first that had so many holes in it. It came to me that an impervious shield might attract unwanted attention of its own, and also that a shield with holes would be handy for me to look out through. I'd had enough of being locked away in the dark, and wanted no more of it.

"How's that?" I murmured as I kissed his face, allowing the light bubble-shield to surround my mind. Once it was there I found that I *could* look through it with just a little effort, but the startlement in Kel-Ten's mind said he couldn't do the same.

"Absolutely perfect," he murmured back, almost distracted. "I can't reach you at all. How do you do it?"

"I don't know," I lied in a whisper, immediately deciding that was the smartest tack to take. "One day it just happened. No one will know?"

"Um um," he grunted, a satisfaction to the sound, and then he dropped the dangerous discussion and began to let the desire in his mind take over. He was going to complete what he'd begun and not only to make it look right, not only to be sure no one grew suspicious. His body constantly tore at his mind with need, sometimes easing up on him but never for long, never leaving him entirely free unless he pushed himself to the absolute end and deep into exhaustion. It was the drug that made him feel like that, the drug they'd been feeding him so long, but although he had my pity I couldn't simply let him do what he had to. I had been hurt too badly the night before, and there was no longer a reason to accept what I didn't want.

I couldn't have fought him off if I'd tried, but even if I could have that would have brought its own consequences. All actions and consequences had to be his, whatever happened his fault rather than mine. There's a certain point of desire we all work up to in sex, a point that must be reached before anything more than touching and kissing can be accomplished, most especially on the part of the male half of the effort. Kel-Ten had already reached that point just as he always did, but that was the results of the drug working on him, not of his own desire. I touched the man holding me with a shadow of the urge to procrastinate, giving him a reason for continuing on as he was doing rather than going on to other, more undesirable undertakings, and was relieved when he followed the urge without realizing it wasn't his own. Kel-Ten hadn't felt me in his mind, and that meant I could look at what the drug was doing to him a little more closely.

It usually takes a while to see—or guess at—what it is that's supporting a particular emotion, but when drugs are involved the effort is minimal. I *knew* what was feeding Kel-Ten's need to use me, and only had to see just how it was doing that. Probing into the growling roar of his thoughts was difficult and not terribly comfortable, but the effort quickly turned out to be worth it. There seemed to be a single point of compulsion feeding everything else, and if that could be blocked off—

"I'm thinking about how you looked last night, sweet thing," Kel-Ten murmured to me, his hands everywhere, his desire spreading like a flame through his mind. "Remember what I said about everyone else wanting you, but me being the only one who would have you? It's just about that time."

I could feel his thoughts and desires beginning to break through the urge to put things off that I'd touched him with, but I couldn't afford to let that happen. I felt my own urge when he stirred on the bed beside me, the urge to panic, but if I did panic I would lose all control over my abilities and would be helpless to stop him. Realizing that made the rising fear inside me worse instead of better, turning my muscles weak with anticipation of what the pain would be like—and then something odd happened. All sense of fear disappeared under the shower of cool calm that spread quickly through my mind, and I was able to strengthen the need to wait in Kel-Ten's mind, and then begin to construct a block for the compulsion ruling him. It was almost as though I simply watched while someone else did the work, and then I remembered about having found a tool to help me control my emotions when it was really necessary. I'd needed the tool for—something, somewhere—and now had it available for the here and now. I couldn't remember why I'd needed it, but that didn't mean I couldn't use it.

Setting up the block seemed strange, as though I'd never done something like that before, but it wasn't terribly complex and didn't take very long. Kel-Ten continued to kiss me and touch me, unaware of what was being done to him, his mind straining unconsciously against the hold I had on it. He wanted to get on with doing what he had to, wanted it—wanted it—then suddenly wanted it less. The urgings of the drug were being shunted past the center of his desire by the block, freeing him from the constant, driving need he'd been in the grip of so long. What the mind believes it feels is what the body feels, and Kel-Ten's mind was beginning to feel that he didn't want me after all. Too much of *anything* can sour a normal human being on it, and the man who held me had had too much for far too long. His feelings slowly retreated away from the point where he could do anything but touch and kiss, which eventually made him raise his head to look at me.

"I'm sorry," he said, some of the confusion and embarassment he felt showing in his expression. "It looks like I may have extended myself a little too far yesterday, and now I can't—quite get into the mood. I'm afraid we're going to have to get back to this later."

Instead of waiting to find out how *I* felt about that, he simply rolled away, then got out of the bed. If I'd needed relief he could have given it to me without being more than marginally involved, but that wasn't the way things were done around there. If he'd gotten me hot, so much the better; by the time he was back to being interested, it would simply be a bonus for him.

"Let's not forget what we're supposed to be doing now, sweet thing," he said as he stretched hard, the words lazy and his attention elsewhere. "While Kel-Ten is under the shower, where does pretty sweet thing wait for him?"

He turned back to look at me with the question, a faint grin on his face, a satisfaction in his mind that he could give me embarrassment to partially offset his own. I gave him the glare he was expecting before acknowledging my helplessness by crawling to the foot of the bed and lying there the way he wanted me to, and he laughed softly as he came over and patted me on the head.

"Now that's a good sweet thing," he said in icky-smooth tones, really enjoying himself. "Belly down and watching the door is the way I want her. I'll be back in just a little while."

I kept my eyes on him until he'd strolled out of the room, still pretending to be annoyed, in reality feeling ten times the satisfaction he did. The emotionless calm had left me as soon as I'd finished doing what needed to be done, and the best part of it all was that Kel-Ten had no idea he was acting to the urging of someone else. There had to be quite a lot I'd be able to do with that, but before I even thought about it there was something else of higher priority that needed seeing to. Moving around on the bed had shown me how much pain was left from what had been done to me the night before, which meant it was time to work with pain control. There were decisions I would have to make that day, and they would be hard enough without distractions.

By the time I heard Kel-Ten coming back, there was only a faint soreness from the way I'd been savaged. I hadn't remembered until I'd started that I'd gotten better at pain control too, and after all the ugly shocks I'd had, a pleasant surprise was a nice change. I watched the man walk to his closet and begin taking out things to wear, wishing I hadn't decided against "asking" him to let me have a bath. I didn't just want a bath I needed one, but I couldn't afford to suddenly have everything going to my advantage and comfort, even if outwardly it seemed to be no one's decision but Kel-Ten's. The people in that place had to be used to seeing the results of mental manipulation, and if they were given the least reason to believe the First Prime was being twisted around, the game would be up and my neck would be in a noose. I had no doubt that they would be very interested in finding out about what I'd learned to do, which meant bath time would have to be put off until it really was Kel-Ten's idea.

After dressing in a slightly different short outfit of gold, my partner in deception came over to the bed with something for me to wear, in point of fact the same something I'd worn the day before. It had been cleaned by the bedroom wall unit and was therefore fresh and ready, and Kel-Ten got a lot of amusement out of seeing me put it on again even though I so clearly didn't want to. Once again it was a matter of wearing the torn shirt or wearing nothing, a choice I didn't have to be reminded of, a choice I was still limited to even though I was awake. All I could do was follow a chuckling Kel-Ten into his kitchen with my jaw clamped tightly shut, knowing my expression was the reason he was chuckling.

I would have enjoyed being able to think during breakfast, trying to decide on a time and a way to tell my partner we would not have to wait to make our escape after all—among other things—but Kel-Ten had shifted into too good a mood. For the first time in a very long while he wasn't being tormented by the demands of his body, even though he didn't really understand why he felt so good, he apparently decided to enjoy the time by tormenting someone else. The breakfast delivered to me was different from the one of the day before in that it was richer, showing that the eyes-in-charge still weren't pleased with my caloric intake, and that meant to Kel-Ten that he could force some of his own breakfast on me without worrying about being reprimanded. I made short but nasty comments to him while he stuffed me almost to the exploding point, and finally managed to get him to stop by saying I wasn't feeling well at all. If he got me sick he knew they would bother him about it, but he'd had such a good time he was still chuckling when we left the apartment.

We left the drop at the same level we had the day before, but although the crowds of men were the same the experience was more of a first encounter, at least for me. Even before the drop door opened I could feel their minds, every one of them actively alive, some calm and calmly controlled, some roiling at one level or another of agitation. As Kel-Ten and I left the drop and lift area and entered their midst, the vast majority of them seemed to draw back mentally even though physically they didn't move. They still stood in their small groups, engaged in conversations, but they knew Kel-Ten was there and they gave him what amounted to a clear mental aisle. The expression never changed on the face of the man I walked beside, but his mind smiled with satisfaction over the deference paid him, a deference that was his due. I wondered how he could feel that way with all the resentment and hatred muted behind those withdrawals, and then I spent some time wondering if he could sense it. None of the minds were shielded, but they seemed to have learned to do their feeling on two separate levels. The upper levels were filled with random thoughts and properly deferential feelings, but the lower levels—

We stopped in front of the large glass board again and Kel-Ten began studying it, giving me the opportunity to look casually around. Most if not all of the men there seemed to know who I was—or, more to the point, what I was—and to a small extent the First Prime had been right about their feelings. A large number of them resented my being there, but of that number only a few were actually "afraid" of a woman who wasn't conditioned into adoring them. The rest were more outraged over the presence of a lesser being, feeling that their sacred precincts were being invaded by someone who didn't and would never belong. They were superior, and knew it without doubt because they'd been told they were.

Of the ones who were jealous of Kel-Ten's possession of me, again only a few were jealous because they considered me more attractive than the women *they* had access to. The rest saw me as a symbol, one of the benefits of Kel-Ten's position, a benefit they were burning to enjoy as a foretaste of that very position. They were all determined to work very hard until *they* became First Prime, and no more than a handful doubted they would one day make it.

I stirred where I stood beside Kel-Ten, certain I'd interpreted all those emotions around me correctly, and because of that felt rather upset. Dedication to a particular goal is all fine and well, but those men weren't dedicated, they were obsessed. Or conditioned, which isn't exactly the same thing. There was a burning need inside each of them to prove themselves, matching a similar need in Kel-Ten to improve on what he'd already accomplished. My partner in conspiracy thought he wanted to escape; was that absolutely true, or simply an outlet the conditioning was allowing him to keep him from exploding into uselessness? Had he put off the time of our leaving because he really thought a wait was necessary—or because he'd never actually do what he was being allowed to dream about? If I told him I was ready to go and no further delay would be necessary, would he laugh with delight and get us started, simply be unable to hear me, turn me off and send me back to the low dormitory, what? I didn't go so far as to turn to stare at him, but couldn't help noticing that the hall we stood in had suddenly become a good deal chillier.

"Looks like I have a heavier schedule today than I did yesterday," Kel-Ten said, drawing me away from increasingly depressing thoughts. "Two intro classes for new arrivals from low, five rings to cover with another two as standby possibilities, and a formal challenge.

Which doesn't even count my regular classes. I've had days like this before, and I hate to tell you how wiped out I'll be by tonight. I'm surprised Ank-Soh isn't here waiting, all ready to give me a hand with looking after you."

He chuckled as he made the observation, putting an arm around me to hug me, but there wasn't much in the way of amusement inside him. I could feel a heavy sense of worry, tinged faintly with fear, and only then realized what he was worrying about. The women he was supposed to take care of, when he'd mentioned them the fear had appeared—because he was still being protected by my block! His body didn't even want one woman, not to mention five for certain and maybe even seven, and the First Prime was wondering if he would be able to handle it.

I reached over to him gently with my mind, touched the block to make it dissolve, then watched the rate at which the drugs began affecting him again. He was able to feel it a good deal sooner than he'd stopped feeling it, leading me to believe they'd increased his dosage because of the sort of schedule they'd given him. I stood with his arm around me as he continued to look at the board, waiting for his reaction to being released, really afraid he'd start wondering what was going on, but it didn't happen. His mind suddenly surged with elation as he knew himself able again, but there wasn't the least sign of suspicion, most certainly not of me. He didn't seem used to questioning what happened to him, and rather than making me feel better, the realization drove me deeper into worry of my own.

I had another couple minutes of quiet to use for a stern inner talk with myself about the stupidity of having forgotten about the block, but I didn't have to belabor the point. I could have had real trouble by letting it slip my mind, and I had already sworn to be careful not to do the same again. I'd also had the time to add my curiosity to Kel-Ten's about where Ank-Soh was, but not because I missed the other Prime. I couldn't very well make Ank-Soh *not* want me after everything he'd said the day before, but I thought it might be possible to convince him his own schedule was too heavy to fit me in. It was a risk I'd been wondering if it would be smart to take—no matter how I felt about it emotionally—and his not showing up was a bigger break than I'd been expecting. Wherever the other Prime was, I couldn't help hoping fervently that he stayed there.

My thinking time was ended by the sound of the chime that officially started the day, and once again my hand was taken in Kel-Ten's as he set off to his first class. When we got to the room I was put in the back corner the way I'd been the day before, but once the class started I got a surprise I hadn't been expecting. Rather than having it be the relaxing class of the day before, it turned out to be a mental exercise class filled mostly with beginners. The black-clad instructor welcomed six of the fifteen men to their new level, made sure they knew the First Prime was there and watching them, then began them on their exercises. He called out an emotion and they all projected it together, then he had them do the same only one at a time.

Right from the start I'd had to be very careful of my expression, making sure I gave the impression of being as bored as I'd been the day before. I sat in the corner leaning up against the righthand wall, my legs again bent to the left, my hand now and then patting a yawn, my mind busily taking in everything I was being shown. Kel-Ten was again at the back of the group, and when he'd joined in the general broadcasting he'd been careful to use only a part of his strength. With the others it didn't matter; only a small portion of their weakly sloppy projections were reaching the trainer, and I thought I knew why. They had the control we were all taught for close-up work, but none of them was really used to projecting at a distance. They could just reach the trainer where he stood, his mind braced against what was coming at him, and some of them were even letting their efforts spread in my direction.

The trainer himself was a surprise, and although I looked at him closely with my mind, I made sure not to touch him. The man wasn't a Prime but he *was* an empath, and someone had taught him how to recognize what was coming at him without letting it affect him. His braced mind in effect *slid* the emotions past him once he knew what they were, just as though he held up something mental to cause that sliding. It was an interesting technique, requiring nothing of the effort fighting off the projections would have demanded, something I would have had to do in his place.

Again, even with individual efforts the class didn't last very long, and by the time it was over I understood that the class I'd seen with the targets would be what the men in that class would graduate to once they had control and strength. The man in black ended the class with another sort of competitive comment about Kel-Ten, and while everyone was leaving spent some time talking to the First Prime. I could feel Kel-Ten purring from what was being said to him, most likely the usual stroking he was given, and then the purring stopped in order to let him pay closer attention to what he was being told. His mind registered faint surprise and an odd mixture of satisfaction and regret, and then he left the trainer to come over to my corner. For some reason I felt I ought to be very curious about what he'd been told, and came *that* close to asking straight out as I got to my feet. Luckily I was able to bite my tongue before the giant size of it let Kel-Ten know I'd been able to follow what was going on at that range, but didn't have to waste time trying to think of a way to trick the information out of him. As soon as he put his arm around me, he came right out with exactly what I'd wanted to know.

"I just found out why Ank-Soh wasn't waiting at the schedule board to try taking you over for the day," he said, beginning to lead me out of the room. "He'd originally been scheduled to be in this class too, to work with me giving the former lows a demonstration, but at the last minute they canceled him so the trainer canceled the demo. What he was told is that Ank-Soh suddenly got very sick after eating breakfast this morning, and they think it was food poisoning of some kind. Right now they're busy sample-checking all the dishes in the main facility chef, especially what Ank-Soh ate. He's not going to be answering challenges for a few days, or covering rings, or attending classes.''

''Or asking about standing in for somebody with a heavy schedule,'' I added, wondering why the information was giving me such a funny feeling. It was relieving to know I would not have to take the risk of manipulating him, but there was *something*—''He must have been the only one to be affected, or they'd know if it was one specific dish or an entire line of meals. That's really strange, I don't think I've ever heard of something like that happening in a carefully run establishment. Does it happen *here* very often?''

''Only once before that I heard of, nearly five years ago,'' Kel-Ten answered with a shrug, leading me up the corridor in a new direction. ''It turned out to be an isolated case, only that one dish being affected, and the man, a rather high Prime, nearly died. He was never quite right after that, and lost his position on the very first challenge.''

His face briefly went blank then, showing me again that he wasn't permitted to think about what happened to high Primes who lost, and when the blankness faded the subject was over with and closed. We were simply walking along the corridor going somewhere, saying nothing at the moment, no unanswered questions hanging in the air. Rather than shivering I just felt sick, and took my own opportunity to find something else to talk about.

''Your having a practice class instead of the relaxing class surprised me,'' I said, making sure my voice was steady and unconcerned. ''Are they just trying to confuse you, or don't you ever follow the same program every day?''

''If I had to do the same thing every day, I'd be crazy in no time,'' he answered with a snort of faint ridicule, glancing down at me. ''I might have two days that are almost the same, but never more than two and never exactly alike. Today I get to do heavy ex in the afternoon with breathing ex after it, and they've thrown in some light ex for now. I won't be working up too heavy a sweat, not with two of my rings waiting to be taken to my apartment, and after that are more practice classes. If you're a good girl I may let you into the bedroom for your own turn before we go on to the classes, but only if you come up with a really pretty please. I've got you around to break up the boredom, after all, and if you like you can even look at it as practicing before we get to the real thing."

He grinned as his arm tightened around me, and then we were turning into a room that was a smaller version of that physical exercise room. I was glad getting to the room kept me from commenting, but that was just about the only thing I *was* glad about. The room held two fully uniformed Secs and one who wore a short outfit of white, and after I'd been left in charge of one of the uniformed ones, Kel-Ten and half a dozen other Primes jogged out of the building behind the one with short clothes. I ignored the grinning inspection I was getting from the one in whose charge I'd been left and sat down on the floor, then tried to understand what was going on inside my head.

For some reason I didn't understand at all, it felt as though a heavy alarm was going off in my mind, insisting on so much of my attention that I couldn't pick up the emotions around me without putting effort into it. I couldn't remember ever having experienced something like that before and it bothered me, so much so that I leaned back against the wall with a hand in my hair, trying to *force* myself to understand. I had the definite impression that something was terribly wrong, and that if I didn't figure out what the something was fast, I might as well not bother. Maybe starting from the beginning, when I'd first felt the feeling, would help to clear away the murk.

The beginning wasn't very far away, only a matter of a minute or two, just before Kel-Ten and I had reached the room. It had been about the time he'd told me we'd be practicing for the real thing, a comment that had upset me, but certainly not nearly as much as the first time the subject had come up. I'd have to be there for Kel-Ten to be able to "cover" me, and if things went my way even a little, that would never happen. No, it wasn't the practicing or even the covering that had started it, it had to be something else, something said at just about the same time—

The breath caught in my throat as I straightened away from the wall, and I found it impossible to keep myself from shuddering. Kel-Ten had said his rings would be "brought to his apartment," and that was the phrase that had done it. I suddenly knew beyond all doubt that it would be the Sec Adjin who brought them, and once again Kel-Ten would be occupied while I wasn't. He had a really heavy schedule that day, so heavy he'd never be able to pay more than token attention to me, and the man who would have "looked after me" during that time had suddenly come down sick that very morning. Accidentally sick!

I put a hand to my middle as I felt worse than Ank-Soh possibly could, wasting not a single moment trying to tell myself I was imagining things. In a place like that, where everything was so carefully controlled, someone who wanted to do his own controlling would have very little trouble slipping his machinations in between those of everyone else's, especially if he was one whose job it was to guard it all. The null Adjin wanted me again, and even if I didn't know why his interest was so high, that didn't make it untrue—or avoidable. My being awake meant nothing when it came to a null; I couldn't touch him any more than any of the others could, and if I panicked and asked Kel-Ten to intercede for me he could very well end up like that high Prime he'd mentioned, the one who had nearly died and afterward was never the same. If I learned that the Sec was responsible for that as well, it would hardly come as a surprise.

To hell with surprises, what was I going to do? I sat bent over with my hand to my mouth, trying to keep the terror inside, trying to think of something to escape what was coming. I hadn't been able to face the null even before he'd hurt me; right then the thought of trying to cope with him made me want to run and run and run and—

"Are you all right, girl?" a voice suddenly asked, a properly dutiful concern behind the words. It took me a minute to understand it was the Sec in whose charge I'd been left who was talking, the man leaning down a little trying to get a better look at me. Since I undoubtedly looked as pale as I felt, his frown deepened, and then he said, "Maybe you ought to be checked over by someone in Medical. We already have a Prime down sick, and there's no sense in taking any chances."

I instantly panicked at the thought of being taken to the man in Medical whose guard was Adjin, but just before I could babble out a refusal a different thought came to me. If I could get myself to the women's area and the female doctor I'd seen when I first got there, maybe something could be done to protect me. Male Secs weren't allowed in the women's areas, Mera had told me, and although it felt like ages since I'd heard it I immediately got to work on the only out I had.

"Yes, please, I do need to go to Medical," I said weakly as I rocked back and forth a little, but there was nothing weak about the total agreement I fed him. The man was a Sec but not a null, a bit of luck I didn't mind taking full advantage of. "Cataran Olden is the doctor I want to see, back in the women's section."

"Cataran Olden it is," he answered with a calm nod, reaching down to help me to my feet. "I'll take you as far as I can go, then turn you over to someone else. Can you make it?"

Obviously I didn't look all that steady to him, but I was so desperate to get out of the men's section I would have crawled if I'd had to. I nodded to show I was well enough to walk wherever necessary, fidgeted only on the inside when he stopped to tell the other Sec where he was taking me, and then we were leaving the room.

The fear didn't start loosening its hold until we reached the low dining room, finding it empty of all obstructions to our crossing it. On the other side of the dining room was a short corridor, and beyond the corridor was the area the null would not be able to reach me in. The Sec holding my arm was moving faster than he had to begin with, the faint urgency I'd brushed him with taking care of the need I'd felt so desperately. It had only just been within the realm of possibility that the null Adjin would appear suddenly to end my escape attempt, but it hadn't been unlikely at all that Kel-Ten would get back from his jogging to do the exact same thing. He would certainly have made difficulty over my being taken back to the women's area, and although I could have changed his mind easily enough, doing it would just have added to my problems.

Problems. Mountains ten miles high that needed to be climbed was more like it, hard, cold mountains I was tackling barefoot and practically naked. We had crossed almost half the dining room when my mind refused to let me avoid the major question any longer, the question of what I would do once I got to Cataran Olden. I could tell her I was terrified to go back to the men's area, could even tell her why, but what good would it do me? She wasn't in charge of anything but examining people, and had as much as said no one listened to her any more than they did to me. Even if she screamed and demanded that I be left alone and in the women's area, would that stop one of the low Primes from claiming me for any night he cared to? It sure as hell would be useless if Kel-Ten demanded me back, most especially in view of the new experiment I was supposed to be a part of. No, going to Cataran Olden would only prove to be a temporary escape, and even wasting my breath on that Serdin man wouldn't—

I almost gasped as the answer suddenly came to me, and I knew I had to be looking pale again. I'd said it over and over, the only thing I could do, but my attention had kept shying away from it, as though totally incapable of facing that sort of truth. And I'd been wondering and worrying about how *Kel-Ten* would respond—

I had to escape, and I had to do it right then.

"Just take it easy, we're almost there," the Sec holding my arm told me, apparently becoming aware of the way I'd begun trembling. "They'll find out what's wrong with you and they'll fix it fast, and then you'll be feeling fine again. Just hold on a little longer."

He increased his pace a bit, anxious to get me turned over to someone else before I passed out or died, I think, but he hadn't the least idea of the meaning of the word anxious. Bad enough was the fact that I would have to try getting out of that place alone, without any idea of where I was going or what I'd be doing if I did get out. Far worse was the fact that I would at the same time be deserting the man who had made my escape possible, the one whose desperate urge to be free had started the whole thing in the first place. If I could have stopped and gone back for him I would have, but even if I did go back there was no guarantee he would be able to make the try with me. He was at least partially conditioned, and without knowing how far that partial extended meant I couldn't take the chance he would ruin everything without even knowing he was doing it. No, all I could do was continue on alone, promising both of us that if there was any chance of coming back to help *him* get out, I'd do it.

If I didn't die of heart failure first. No more than minutes earlier I'd been deathly afraid I would never make it to the swinging doors leading to the women's dormitory room, but when the Sec pushed through one of them, helping me along with him, I almost hung back. When the thought of going on is just as terrifying as the thought of retreating, you most often find yourself in the position of wanting to stand absolutely still, moving not an inch in any direction. At that point in time I didn't have the option of standing still, a truth I hated but couldn't do anything to change. The male Sec called a female Sec over, explained to her that I was sick and was to be taken to Cataran Olden in Medical, and all I could do was let her take my arm and begin leading me across the crowded floor.

I was too busy trying to find frantic plans to make to notice the trip over to Medical, but suddenly there were quite a few women in smocks around me, all of them apparently waiting on line for attention. Most of them seemed to have no idea they were doing something as boring as waiting on line, and even worse than that none of them laughed at the short, torn shirt I was still wearing. It made me ill to know I would have preferred it if they *had* laughed, and very happily I wasn't left to stand around with them. I was taken directly down the hall to one particular door, the Sec holding my arm waved a hand in front of it, and then the door was being opened and I was taken inside.

Cataran Olden looked up when we entered, her mind tired, her expression neutral, but when she saw me she started, her thoughts registering concerned surprise. It was clear she hadn't expected to see me there, and she put aside the papers she'd been reading and moved away from the wall she'd been standing near.

"What's wrong?" she asked the Sec who still had a hand around my arm. "It's too soon for her next checkup, so why is she here?"

"She was brought in from the men's area, and you're the one I was told to take her to," the Sec answered, her shrug mostly referring to her lack of knowledge. "They're having a food poisoning problem over there today, I hear, and the guard who brought her thought she ought to be looked over. Do you want me to wait in here?"

"No, outside if you please," the brown-haired woman answered with a faint frown, her eyes already examining me. She put a hand to my shoulder and began leading me farther into the room as the Sec turned me loose and left; I waited only until I heard the door close, and then I gently but firmly brushed her hand away.

"I don't have food poisoning," I said, quickly calming her automatic protest. "What I do have is a problem, and I need your help with it. Are you still willing to help?"

"If there's anything I can do," she answered, more hesitant and unsure on the inside than she let the words come out. "You know what I have absolutely no control over; if it's something other than that, I'll do my best."

I nodded as I returned her stare, then began telling her what had happened to me since the last time we'd met. I wasn't talking for any purpose other than to kill time, time I desperately needed to decide what to do. They say stampedes are hard to stop, but when it's one single female Prime who's doing the stampeding, the saying doesn't necessarily hold true. If I could think of something else to do other than panic and run, I'd certainly find myself better off when I finally did get around to escaping. And if I had enough time, I also ought to be able to find out if Kel-Ten was really able to go with me. Two against the odds felt like a much better idea to me, so I pondered my options as I spoke and then tried to find out if there were any I hadn't yet considered.

"So you can see why I don't want to take the chance of his coming after me again," I finished up to a silently listening Cataran Olden, having edited the story just a little to eliminate what could easily be considered nothing but paranoia. "He's a Sec, one of those in charge, and he told me he would come to hurt me again. When Kel-Ten told me two of his rings were going to be brought to his apartment right after he came back from jogging, all I could think about was what I would do if he was the one who brought them. Not being able to think of anything made me so sick they thought there was something wrong with me, and somehow I managed to talk them into bringing me here. That man Serdin told me to come and see him if I had any problems, but I wasn't sure if he would consider this a real problem. He isn't female, so he couldn't know how I— Will talking to him do any good, or just make things worse?"

The woman stood leaning against one wall of the examining room with her back, her head down, her arms folded, and for a moment she didn't move or speak. I could feel that her mind wasn't anywhere near as quiet and unmoving, and when she raised her head to look at me there was no smile inside to match the one on her face.

"I really must learn not to offer help before finding out what the difficulty is," she said, clearly forcing herself to meet my eyes. "The problem you have is twofold, and is most easily described as follows: the man who hurt you is not just a Sec, he's a null, and considering how important nulls are around here, he pulls more weight than most would believe. Serdin told you everyone wanted you to be happy here, but there are alternate methods of making you happy if your natural happiness interferes with the happiness of someone who has pull. Frankly, what I think will happen is that Serdin will simply make a note to be sure the null stops visiting you soon enough before your fertile period to avoid any complications, and in the interim will use an alternate method to make you happy, say through injections or in your food. If you don't talk to him and let him know what needs to be done, all you'll have to look forward to is suffering, so I think it's clear you have very little choice.''

She fell silent then and just stared at me, her self-hatred so strong I could almost feel it without reaching through my shield. She'd told me the truth for *my* sake, to keep any false hopes from rising, but would have been much happier if she could have pretended she was able to do something to give me real help. It's extremely painful to admit you're helpless in a situation where you don't want to be, a contention I happened to know personally as the truth. She'd been right when she said I had no choice, and had been wrong only in believing she knew what that no choice was.

''So I get to visit Serdin again after all,'' I muttered, using one hand to rub at my forehead as I tried to put my thoughts in order. ''That might be the best move in any case, considering how important a man he is. And he *is* important, isn't he, even though he isn't a null?''

''Yes he's important, and no he isn't a null,'' she answered with a frown, replying to both of my questions without noticing the faint urge to speak freely I'd brushed her with. ''Terry, you're not thinking about trying to—influence—Serdin, are you? They have women brought in for men in special positions like his, women who are just as special for the purpose they serve. You can't . . .''

''I can't not see him, and I can't not try,'' I interrupted, gesturing with one hand while soothing her agitation again. ''If I can make him understand how badly I need his help, he may make more of an effort than he would normally. Will you at least wish me luck?''

I held my arms out to her, asking to be hugged, and the flare of compassion inside her needed only a little help from me before sending her toward me to give that hug. When my lips were right next to her ear I whispered to her, my mind working along with the words, my heart pounding just a little as I realized I was committing myself with no turning back. I intended trying to influence Serdin, all right, but not the way Cataran Olden thought, and I didn't want anyone hearing the instructions I gave to the woman doctor and begin wondering. I needed something to help Serdin's efforts, and Cataran Olden was just the one to give it to me.

"Say, since you're going to Serdin, I wonder if you would do me a favor?" the woman said when I let her let the embrace end, her words completely natural as she stepped back from me. "I have something he should have, and if you take it I won't have to send someone to make a special trip."

"I don't mind helping," I answered, watching nervously as she walked to a small, recessed locker in the righthand wall. "Being helpful might even do me some good."

To anyone watching, the woman was acting completely on her own and doing something *she* wanted to do. In point of fact she was completely under my control and doing what *I* wanted her to, something I needed badly to have done. If I was going to use Serdin to get me out of there as I intended, I couldn't very well walk out in the short, torn shirt I was wearing and expect to get very far. I needed clothing and shoes, and with Cataran Olden so close to my size, there wasn't likely to be anyone better to supply my need. I had made the woman believe she really was sending a package Serdin was supposed to have, and as I watched her put the spare uniform and short boots into a package-pouch I didn't allow her mind any freedom at all. When she was all through and handed the thing to me with a smile, I took it and then fed her a large jolt of forgetfulness. She had just given me as much help as she would have liked to, but if I'd let her remember it the fearful side of her nature would not have let her enjoy it. I couldn't recall ever having used forgetfulness before, but now that I had I didn't know why I hadn't. It was a lot easier to do than I would have thought possible, and was more the result of my having acted without thinking than a carefully planned-out action.

"Now, what were we just talking about?" she said as she looked at me, the curiosity she would have felt over what I was carrying pushed aside by my mind. "Oh, yes, wishing you luck with Serdin. I certainly do wish you luck, and you'll have to let me know how you make out."

"I guarantee you'll know," I answered as she walked me to the door and opened it, finding no amusement in my own comment. "And I have a feeling it won't be long before you do. Thanks for supplying the shoulder I needed."

"Any time," she answered with a real, warm smile, then looked at the Sec who was still waiting for me. "Take her to Serdin's office now. It's important that she see him."

The Sec nodded with uninterested agreement, took my arm as I stepped out into the corridor, then led off away from the remaining lines of waiting women. The end of the corridor had a closed and guarded door that we had to be passed through, which reminded me that that wasn't the way I'd gotten to that area to begin with. I wondered if it made a difference which way you went, tried to tell myself it did and that I should think about it, but the try was useless. The only thing I could think about was what would happen when I got to Serdin's office—and what would happen if I failed to make my escape attempt good.

I know I should have paid more attention to what was happening around me, but my thoughts were so full of desperate plans and counterplans and contingency plans that before I knew it a door was being opened in front of me. Serdin sat behind his desk as he had the first time I'd seen him, gray-uniformed, white-haired, light-eyed and absorbed in what he was doing, but not so absorbed that he didn't take a moment to glance up. Faint surprise flickered through his mind, and then he gestured toward the chair I'd sat in the last time I was there.

"Sit down over there, Terrilian, and I'll be right with you," he said with familiar distraction, going immediately back to what he'd been doing. The Sec released my arm and left without asking anything or waiting to be told, an indication of just how sure of himself Serdin was, but there was no reason why the man *shouldn't* be sure of himself. Primes could be dangerous but I wasn't really a Prime, and I could have felt his automatic dismissal of me at twice the distance. Anger began to stir in me at that, the sort of anger that had been so useless until then, but it wasn't yet time to let it have its way. I moved forward to the chair I'd been told to take and sat, putting my package on the floor by my feet, letting the anger build slowly inside against the time I would need it.

"All right, that should do it for now," Serdin said after nearly five minutes, closing the folder he'd been working on and putting it on a small stack of others just like it before bringing those eyes up to me. "I'm glad to see you took my advice about coming to talk to me. If there's something bothering you, I'll do everything I can to take care of it."

"The something bothering me is a Sec named Adjin," I said, not really using the complaint to waste time. I wanted to see for myself how Serdin would take it, which would, in turn, determine how I finally handled him. "The man delivered Kel-Ten's rings to the First Prime's apartment, then decided to kill some of the waiting time with me. He hurt me badly, Mr. Serdin, and I want to know what you intend doing to *guarantee* it never happens again."

Serdin frowned at what I'd told him, spending no time on trying to pretend he didn't know I'd been appropriated by Kel-Ten. His mind went annoyed rather than concerned as he reached to his right on the desk, and then his attention centered, showing he was beginning to read something. I decided he'd called up a dot list to his desk screen and was checking it to see exactly who we were talking about, and knew at once when he found the entry he'd been looking for. The annoyance faded quickly and entirely, was replaced just as quickly with the set of emotions that translates to, "Oh, well, now I understand," and then his attention was shifted back to me.

"You know, you have every right to be proud of yourself," he said, his faint smile probably meant to show just how proud *he* was of me. "Not only have you attracted the attention of the First Prime, you've also been noticed by one of the highest-rated Class Zeroes this facility has. There hasn't been another woman able to do that since I've been here, a statistic that makes you more than a little special."

"That's not my idea of an answer to the question I asked," I said, feeling how he expected me to puff up and preen from what I'd been told. "I don't care if that null is the favorite son of the creator of the universe. He *hurt* me, and I want to hear that it won't ever happen again."

"A beautiful woman sometimes has to pay the price of her beauty," he returned, more annoyed than surprised at my response, his body relaxing back in its chair. "If her looks cause men to lose control of themselves, it's the fault of those looks, not of the men who respond to her. And let's not forget that that's the reason for those looks in the first place, to attract the attention of men. Judged on that basis, your effort is very, very successful."

"An effort you're suddenly interested in responding to yourself," I said very low, my crackling anger in no way keeping me from feeling the type of curiosity he'd developed. "You aren't the sort of man who lets beauty influence him, but you've begun wondering what it is about me that the others find so compelling. You have no intentions of helping me, only a brand-new desire to help yourself."

"Now, now, Terrilian, you mustn't let the ability for observation you've developed over the years turn you bitter," he said, folding his hands over his middle as that faint smile came back to his face. "Men are *always* in competition with each other, even when actual challenges never occur, which means what one or two have, others want. I won't keep you for very long, certainly not long enough to upset your other admirers, and afterward we'll give you something to make sure none of this upsets *you*, either. Everyone will be happy, because happy is the way we want all of you."

"You know, I really am delighted that happy is the way you want me," I responded, giving him something of my own smile as I realized he still didn't understand I was awake, despite the heavy hint I'd supplied a moment ago. "Happy is also the way *I* want me, and I think we ought to get started seeing to it right now. You very much feel that you'd like to take me somewhere, and I agree that you should. I'll be ready in just a minute or two."

The faint smile froze on his face, but not specifically because of what I'd said. My mind had flowed into his, taking complete control of it, and although he began struggling almost automatically the struggle didn't last long. I was making him believe he *did* want me happy and *did* want to take me somewhere, and was more than willing to let me do whatever I had to in order to hurry the time until *he* could do what he had to. The urge for sex was a large part of it, the very urge he'd developed himself now amplified by me, and everything he felt revolved around the desire to make me happy. He watched me slip out of the foolish shirt I wore and begin to get into the uniform and boots I'd brought along, and his anticipation of the delights to come made the passing time sweeter for him.

It didn't take more than the couple of minutes I'd specified before I was ready, and once I was Serdin stood up from behind his desk and came around to join me where I stood. His light eyes were very bright and the faint smile on his face reflected only a small portion of what he was feeling inside, but we weren't as ready to go as he thought.

"That female Sec outside needs to be sent back to where she came from," I told him, mixing the desire to wait with his anticipation, the result causing him to change his mind about touching me. "I'll stand behind the door while you take care of it."

He nodded pleasantly because of the strong need for agreement holding him so tight, turned to the door, then took care of getting rid of the one person who would question what was going on. After that he came back to me and simply stared until I felt we'd given her enough time to leave the area, and then I took his arm and told him we were ready to go and get a ground vehicle.

I'd almost forgotten how quickly underlings obey someone with a great deal of power. No one asked *why* Serdin wanted a ground vehicle, and when he also dismissed the one who would have driven it for him there was some faint surprise in the minds around us, but nothing of suspicion. The man was free to do anything he pleased, and if it pleased him to drive away with a female member of Medical, there was nothing anyone could say about it. I would have been a nervous wreck while Serdin handed me into the vehicle and then walked around to the driver's seat, but the part of me in charge of calm and cool made sure I wasn't. It let me smile at the man I rode with while the gates to that part of the complex were slowly opened for us, rather than letting me faint dead away. Fainting would have felt a lot better, but wouldn't have been quite as useful.

I had Serdin pretend we were heading for the big building I'd first awakened in at the very beginning of that madness, but once the gates were solidly closed behind us had him head for the distant forest instead. The trees and brush had been cleared away from the complex for quite a distance from its walls, and seemed to be given periodic treatments to keep it like that. The major complex we had just left was about a quarter of a mile from the building we were supposedly going to, and clearly took up more space than the tall but single building. As we bounced over the uneven ground I felt giddy from the realization that I'd actually made good on my escape, but then the more practical side of me insisted on stamping all over the delight of the feeling. I'd escaped, all right, but only from the complex. I still had to face the fact that I had, as yet, no way off the *planet*.

"How do people come and go from this world?" I asked Serdin, still holding his mind tight with mine. "Where do the transports or their transfer slips land?"

"There's a good-sized port behind the main administrative building," he answered, gesturing with his head toward the building we were no longer heading for. "It's carefully walled and guarded, of course, even more carefully than the rest of the complex. It would hardly do to have one of our—guests—come out of it far enough to decide on an unauthorized trip to somewhere else. There aren't many in the Amalgation who know about this world, and we'd like to keep it like that. Can we stop for a while now?"

"We'll be stopping soon," I assured him, giving him the urge to believe along with the words, carefully keeping my own frustration and fear to myself. When they found out I was on the loose they would close and seal that port, making sure it was impossible for me to gain access to it. One single null in the right place would do it, one single mind I couldn't control and I'd never *reach* a transport let alone get clear away. I felt trapped and walled in, almost as much as I had before getting out of the complex, and to say I didn't like it wasn't telling half the story.

"What the hell are you people *doing* here?" I demanded, trying to keep down the roiling inside me. "Why are you breeding Primes, and why is it so important that no one find out?"

"We're getting ready to take over the Amalgamation," he answered in such a matter-of-fact tone that it didn't seem real, his eyes busy with watching where he was driving. "Right now Central heads the Amalgamation, but only with the agreement and approval of the other member worlds. Once we have enough trained Primes we'll take over the other worlds, and there won't be anything they can do to stop us. How effective will a hastily scraped together volunteer army be against men who can feed them terror at a distance? How dangerous will the Kabras, the only professional fighters in the Amalgamation, turn out to be, when our people can intensify their feelings that to fight an equal force of their own is useless, and that any force of ours they face is just like one of their own? The Kabras won't lift a single weapon, citizen police forces or armies will spend more time running away than standing and fighting, and no leader of any of the worlds will be able to lie about being loyal to us. After we've taken over, our Primes will be everywhere, making sure people do as they're told, making sure that those who harbor the strongest resentments are arrested and dealt with before they can be troublesome. Our regime, once begun, will go on and on in perpetuity, and no one and nothing can stop it."

The vehicle slid around a little on the rutted ground as the shock I felt transmitted itself to the man who was driving, and although I cut it off quickly that doesn't mean I stopped feeling it when he did. They were not only going to take over the Almagamation, they were also going to use empaths to do it, to see that everyone was enslaved as completely as only their pet tools now were! The desire to rule was theirs, but me and mine would be the ones who got them that desire! I felt so sickened I put a hand to my mouth, trying to keep the uneven ride from adding so much to the sickness that it erupted out of me, almost finding I couldn't do it. Those people were crazy, but their craziness would work unless someone discovered a way to stop them. I *had* to get free and stay that way, and hope that eventually they relaxed enough to let me sneak or force my way into the port.

"When we reach the edge of the forest you can stop the vehicle," I said after a moment or two of trying to pull myself together, frantically searching for something I could do right then that would help rather than be useless or harmful. "Is there anything out there it would be especially wise to avoid, anything someone even with my mind strength would have trouble handling?"

"Only the Ejects," he replied, a faint shadow of annoyed disgust crossing his mind when he spoke the word. "They hate everyone and everything connected with the complex, and don't even care that we rid this entire area of dangerous predators in order to give them more of a chance to survive. They take the babies we leave out and raise them as their own, but start a riot any time we come by to claim the rare Prime baby *they* manage to produce, or take some of their number to be targets for our Primes. Way back in the beginning we even gave them people to show them how to live in the wild, but even that means nothing to them. They're simply and basically incapable of feeling gratitude."

"You expect them to be grateful for being thrown out instead of killed, don't you?" I asked, not really requesting an answer. That was exactly what he expected, he and the others like him. They wasted nothing, apparently, not even the empaths who weren't born Primes, turning them out into the wilderness to live or die as they could. Killing them would have been kinder, but if they'd killed them the occasional Prime they produced would not *be* produced, so they graciously let them live. The Primes in the complex had no idea what was done with their offspring, and in that way everyone was kept happy.

"You're—hurting me," a faint, choked protest came, bringing me back to awareness of how erratic our progress had suddenly grown. Serdin's hands were clamped to the drive wheel, the knuckles white against the pain he felt, his body trembling with the need to keep on as we were going even though his mind was on the verge of being crushed. I was suddenly feeling more enraged than sickened, more furious than frightened, and the strength of my mind was squeezing at the mind I held, wanting very badly to hurt it the way it had caused others to be hurt. I was very much aware of the pain Serdin was in, could see the sweat beading on his face, but felt nothing in the way of guilt even as I stared at him. Yes, I *was* hurting him, but no, I wasn't regretting it.

"It's really too bad I still need you," I said, a part of me wondering why I wasn't trembling and confused and unsure of myself. My mind-tool of calm was giving me very little help just then, doing no more than waiting against the possibility of need, so both feelings and actions were *mine*. I was the one giving pain to someone who most often gave it to others, and I realized it might be wise of me to stop—before I began enjoying it *too* much.

"Since we're almost to the forest, you might as well stop here," I said, releasing the mind I held captive to the extent of eliminating the pain the man was feeling. "As soon as I leave the vehicle you'll turn around and go back, taking it as slow as you can, thinking about nothing but the fun you've had and how right you were to spend a little time on experimentation. Do you understand?"

"Yes," he answered in a breathy whisper, and it was a good thing I'd had him stop the vehicle. I was right then feeding him complete physical satisfaction as I'd taken it from the minds of other men at some other time, and he was shuddering in delight with his eyes half closed, the rapture completely in possession of him. I would have preferred giving him something other than pleasure, but the mind clings to memories of pleasure and tries to hold onto them, while an equal measure of agony and pain is forgotten as soon as it can possibly be managed. The longer he remembered what had been done to please him the longer it would take for him to understand what had really been done, and that extra amount of time was what I needed. The last thing I did was force confusion deep into his mind, a confusion that would not be noticed or felt until after he was well out of my area of influence. It would surface again and again in the hours to come, playing havoc with his ability to remember and reason clearly, and that, too, would help me.

I got out of the vehicle and slammed the door, then watched only long enough to be sure my orders were being obeyed before turning and hurrying into the waiting brush. It felt odd being completely clothed again and shod, odd in a way I couldn't immediately pin down, but I had very little time to waste thinking about it. I broke into a slow run as I went deeper into the forest, changed direction once I thought I was completely concealed from observation, then tried increasing my pace. I didn't know how to disguise the trail I was leaving, so I had to do something to destroy it as quickly as possible, before they discovered I was gone. That could happen at any time, and then they would be after me.

Panic comes in two varieties, and I would have much preferred being a victim of the first, which is four-fifths terror. It descends on you fast, taking your breath and your muscle control, trying to freeze you where you stand or cripple you in the midst of movement. It's an emotion that does, very often, generate its own opposition in you once the initial shock is over, helping you to overcome it as soon as possible. The second variety is only half terror or less, which means it comes slowly but firmly over you, creeping up and getting a good, solid hold before you understand completely that it's there. You find yourself racing along like a mindless animal, wasting strength and breath, almost running into trees in your need to get away from whatever it is that's coming behind you—or will be coming behind you. It tells you that even if nothing's behind you now there soon will be, and gives you no time to think, no opportunity to stop and use reason on your problem. Most of the time you don't even know it's happening, not until a countershock jars you free of it.

My countershock came when I slammed hard into the ground, facedown among twigs and thin grass and leaves. My knees and palms got the worst of it, but my left ankle also ached a little from the way my left boot had gotten caught on something I hadn't seen. My breathing was still ragged and I still felt the urge to run without stopping, but having to brush my palms clean and then rub at my ankle meant I also had the opportunity to look around. I hadn't seen much of what I'd been running through, only a blur of trees and bushes marking my progress in my memory, but it didn't take long to see it was a damned good thing I'd fallen hard enough to be snapped out of it. Without realizing it I'd been running *beside* a brook, the sort of shallow little waterway I needed to disguise my trail, and I hadn't even seen it.

I gave myself a minute to catch my breath, begrudging every second of it but knowing it was necessary, then got to my feet and walked over to the brook. It was fast-moving and shallow, coming up to no more than ankle-height on my boots, and once I stepped down into it found that keeping my balance against the movement of the water was one of the things I had to be careful about. Another was the slick stones the water ran over, not to mention occasional hidden holes, but it had the overwhelming advantage of not showing a single one of my footprints. I moved around a bit to get used to walking in it and convince myself about the lack of visible passage, then turned in the direction opposite to the one I'd been running in and continued on my way.

I suppose I started out congratulating myself on my cleverness over having turned in a new direction, and truthfully it hadn't been a bad idea. I'd run headlong into the forest as far as I could until the brook had stopped my straight-line progress, and then had chosen a different direction and had simply kept going. Right or left really didn't matter just then with one way as good as another, but turning back again after entering the water should have confused everyone and anyone trying to follow me. I felt so pleased it took a while before I discovered how cold my feet were growing, courtesy of the brook water I was walking in. My borrowed boots were watertight but uninsulated, and I hadn't known before how cold it's possible to get while still remaining dry.

I found out how cold it's possible to get, just before I also found what seemed like the best place to leave the brook. I'd walked on for quite a way against the flow of the water, slowly feeling my feet freeze solid, slowly discovering just how much of my strength I'd thrown away in blind panic, and just before I gave in to the urge to sit down right there in the middle of the brook I saw exactly what I needed. Most of the ground beside the water had no more than thin grass, the dirt under it obviously created for the sole purpose of taking footprints and holding them forever with a smirk of laughter. What I finally came to was a wide table of stone that jutted out just a little over the water, stone that looked almost swept clean of dirt by a broom, and that was my way out. I waded over to it, used strict self-control to keep myself from getting down on hands and knees to kiss it, and simply left the friendly brook behind.

I forced myself to walk on a short distance before sitting down near a tree, leaned against it with my back, then concentrated on resting while at the same time getting pain control ready for when my feet would start coming back to life. It had felt as though I'd been walking on wooden feet for quite a while, and the surprising part was that I hadn't at any time fallen. I closed my eyes as I leaned back against the hard wood of the tree bark, feeling the way my body ached, trying not to think about whoever would be coming after me. I couldn't afford to believe they would give up the search easily, which meant I had to keep going as long as humanly possible and then add a little more distant to *that.* How I would find food and shelter I didn't know, but—

My eyes flew open as I straightened away from the tree, my mind belatedly feeling the presence of other minds, minds that were very close. I'd been too deep inside myself to notice them immediately, too concerned with what I had done and would do next, but the hatred that had suddenly begun welling at me had forced me to notice. My sight confirmed what my mind already knew, that there were ten or twelve men and women standing and staring at me, their approach having been so silent I hadn't heard anything of it, but vision added shock because of their appearance. They were *thin,* those people, as though they'd never had a decent meal in their lives, and their hair and beards were long and totally unkempt. What they wore in the way of clothing wasn't clothing at all, but what seemed to be hides and pelts of various animals, badly made, badly kept, and smelling so foul that I experienced a very strong urge to throw up. The barefoot people themselves were as dirty as what they'd wrapped themselves in, but one fact stood out even more clearly than the stench coming at me in waves: every one of them had an active mind, which meant every one of them was an empath.

"Watcha doin' here?" one of them suddenly demanded, a man larger than the rest who stepped out in front of those he stood with. "Watcha up to, huh, thinkin' y'c'n sneak up 'n us? Ain't got enuffa watcha want whur y'cum frum?"

It actually took me a minute to understand what he was saying, the words were so garbled and the accent so thick, and all the time I had to fight off oceans of hostility and hatred trying to roll over me. As empaths they had no control of their minds at all, no discipline to keep them from projecting what they were feeling, and I had never been exposed to such completely raw emotions. I retreated most of the way behind the thin shield I'd been looking through, trembling in spite of myself, then forced myself to stand and face them. The men of the group were carrying heavy sticks of some kind, almost like long cudgels, and the women were gripping thinner but still nasty-looking versions of their own weapons.

"I've run away from those people and I need help," I said to the man who had spoken, wishing my heart wasn't making so much noise. "I can't let them catch me again,

I have to stay free, but I can't do it alone. I hate them as much as you do, so won't you help me?"

I'd been trying to keep my words as simple as possible so they would understand, but understanding wasn't a problem. Most of the group immediately began to mutter, and the man I'd addressed snorted out his disgust and disdain.

"Y'din like it there, so y'run t'us," he said, looking me up and down with no approval at all. "Whole buncha ya don' give a damn 'bout us till y'need us, then y'cum lookin'. We ain't had none a ourn took fer killin' in a whole long while 'cuz they don' know we's here, an' we ain't gonna do nothin' t' change thet. We's gonna drive ya a good long ways away, an' then whin they git ya they still ain't gonna know whur we's at. Them others bin mens steada girls, but it don' make no nevermind. They's gonna git ya but ain't gonna git none a ourn."

"Please, wait a minute, I don't understand," I protested as some of them started toward me, finding myself taking an involuntary step back. "The people there don't ignore you because they want to, but because the ones in charge *make* them do it! And what do you mean, they're going to get me like they got the others? If I hide well enough they won't be able to find me; didn't the others try to hide?"

"Hidin' don' do none a ya no good," he said with another snort, now close enough to wrap a filthy hand around my arm. "They's got boxes t' tell 'em whur y'all's hidin', an' them boxes don' miss nothin'. Whin they find ya they ain't gonna find us, that's fer damn spittin' sure. We's gonna run ya far's we gotta."

The hand on my arm pulled me away from the tree and shoved me toward the center of the group that had closed in, but my mind was so numb I barely noticed it happening. The people from the complex used *tracking* devices, which meant there had to be a fix thread or a spot dot somewhere on or in me. I'd never find it soon enough to get rid of it, especially if it was under some part of my skin as they usually were, and I didn't know what to—

"Git outen here!" a woman's voice shrilled from behind me, and the next instant I screamed at the pain from the sharp blow of a stick across my back. I half-jumped, half-fell forward, trying to keep from being hit again, trying to merge with my mind-tool so that I could drop my shield and protect myself, but there were too many of them. Blows struck at me from all sides, some even landing on my head to make me dizzy, and then they were all screaming and shouting and beating at me with mindless fury. As though from a great distance I noticed that only the women were using their sticks, the men using no more than hands and fists, and then I was running with my arms wrapped around my head, running in an attempt to get away from the pain of those blows. I whimpered as I ran, fear adding to the flame of agony as they kept hitting me over and over, and I couldn't seem to get away from them. They were running with me, still beating me as they kept up, which made me run even faster. I had to get away from them, had to escape that terrible pain, but I couldn't, I couldn't, I couldn't . . .

Just how long a time passed I have no idea, but it was still full daylight out when I again became aware of the forest around me. I was on my knees beside a tree, holding to it and trying to hide myself in it, and it came to me that I hadn't been unconscious, only separated from all awareness of self. It felt as though I'd been trying to bury myself in the tree for quite some time, and hadn't managed it because of the utter exhaustion and raging pain I burned in. That didn't sound exactly right for some reason I couldn't quite put my finger on, but it didn't matter in the least. I knew where I was, knew the people called Ejects were gone without a trace, and knew it was only a matter of time before those from the complex came and captured me again. They would find me no matter how far or how fast I ran, find me easily, and there was nothing I could do to stop it or them. Matter, matter, matter, no matter what it didn't matter.

I scraped my cheek against the rough bark of the tree, but something inside me refused to allow me to let go. I needed endless strength to lean on, endless gentle caring to help me past the pain, endless love to warm me against the chill starting in the air. Where I was supposed to get those things I didn't know, but it was almost as though the tree was— connected in some way, reminding me of—something—or someone—no longer there and maybe never there—I didn't know and I was so confused—

Distantly I was surprised at the tears running down my cheeks, tears from a source other than the flaring pain I felt. If I hadn't been using pain control I would have been unconscious from the terrible beating I'd been given, the beating that had driven me away from people who were too bitter to give up what little they had for a stranger. I didn't blame them for that, it wasn't their fault, but giving things up—and giving people up—there was something about that that brought me tears—tears I didn't understand—

I froze where I knelt beside the tree, everything forgotten but the sound I'd thought I'd heard, all my senses trying to flare out in an attempt to search and pinpoint what it was. Most of my strength was going toward supporting the pain control, the possibility of broken ribs making it more a necessity than a luxury, but when I touched human minds I knew it. Male alone, distant but coming closer, a strong sense of searching and an even stronger sense of confirmed anticipation. Whoever it was knew I was there, knew they would find me very shortly, knew I couldn't hide from them. They were already there, already on the verge of recapturing me, and although I knew more running would be as useless as what I'd already done, I still used the tree to help me drag myself to my feet. If I just sat there waiting for them I would be helping them, and as long as there was life and awareness left in my body helping them was the last thing I would do.

Standing up made me dizzier than I had been, but I held to the tree until the dizziness went away and then I went stumbling off into the forest. I couldn't move very fast, couldn't even walk straight, but I wasn't going to help them catch me. I waited for the panic to come to add to my lost strength a little, but the panic refused to cooperate. It didn't come, not even a shadow of it, and I discovered I was muttering curses at it under my breath. Never there when you need it, that's what a waste panic was, never there, not even nulls there, stupid not sending nulls, why are the trees blurring, the ground getting mushy without any water around, everything going in slow circles, that strange sound in my ears, getting dark fast, too fast, not late enough, not—

# 9

I was awake instantly, faster than I could ever remember waking up before, faster than I knew it was *possible* to wake up. I raised up on my left side on the bed, using a slightly sore elbow to brace me, confused not so much about what had happened before I'd lost consciousness, but about what was then going on. The plain metal room I lay in wasn't anything like what they had in the complex, and in fact looked most like a cabin aboard a transport, which didn't make any sense. I hadn't been anywhere near the complex port when the last of my strength went, and couldn't quite believe I'd found it and gotten into a transport while still unconscious. And those men I'd felt in the forest, the ones coming after me; if they hadn't been there to take me back to the complex, then what—

I was just about to put a hand to my head when I heard a sound at the cabin door, a sound that meant the door was being unlocked. I forced myself to sit up all the way, paying scant attention to the sheet that covered my otherwise bare body, banishing the light shield that covered my mind and leaving only my curtain. I didn't know whose hands I was in that time, but whoever they were they would learn what it meant to be in a fight if they thought I was going to let myself be taken advantage of again. I'd had enough of being pushed around to last *ten* people a lifetime, and I'd be damned if I took any more at all.

The door in the wall opposite the foot of my bed opened with no special hurry, and by then I knew there were four people outside, three male and one female. There were other minds farther away, quite a few minds, but two of the nearest four clearly intended entering. The other two minds were concerned with nothing but waiting—which made them guards for my door—but the third man and the woman were coming in. I couldn't reach the woman's mind without moving through her shield, but the man's mind was unshielded, and there was something familiar about the rigidly controlled worry in it. As the door opened I was sure I knew that mind, and then the woman walked in and quickly turned to help the man—

"Murdock McKenzie!" I blurted, watching him move his twisted body toward the only chair in the room, leaning heavily on his cane. His gray hair was as neat as always, his clothing as plain, and the ever-present pain in his mind was so well-controlled that it was flatly refused access to his awareness. The woman helped the head of Central's XenoDiplomacy Bureau to the chair then waited while he sat, the bending he had to do almost the hardest part for him, but nothing of his struggle showed on his face any more than it ever did. He got himself settled with a minimum of fuss, then raised those cool gray eyes to me.

"Yes, Murdock McKenzie," he agreed, the words dry as he studied my face. "A bit late, perhaps, in his arrival, but nevertheless here. Are you all right, Terrilian? Did they harm you in any—permanent—way?"

"You're not asking about what happened in the forest, are you?" I said, suddenly knowing it for a fact. "You're discussing those people at the complex, which means you know all about them. Are you one of them, Murdock? If you are, don't think you have me safely captured because you don't. I'll fight before I'll let anyone take me back there."

"I see you've changed quite a lot since the last time we spoke," he said, a faint, cold smile just creasing his lips as he continued to study me. "I believe I know the reasons for the changes, and I couldn't be more pleased. And no, my dear Terrilian, I am *not* 'one of them.' I'm one of those opposed to them, a group they happily know very little about, but who now, even more happily, know the location of their most secret nest. It's thanks to you that we have this very vital knowledge, and now we may move with all speed to begin stopping their madness for all time."

His mind, unlike his narrow, sunken face, showed warm delight and the gratitude and appreciation he'd spoken of. I didn't want to relax away from the unyielding sense of resistance I'd put up in front of me, not while I still suspected the motives of everyone I met, but I knew Murdock McKenzie wasn't lying. I could feel the truth of what he'd said, and the ache I was also feeling was beginning to convince me that leaning back and resting a short while would not turn out to be self-betrayal.

"If you're all that grateful to me, then you won't mind if I insist on joining your major effort to stop them," I said, easing down to my right elbow so that I could still look at Murdock. "I want to be there when you hit them, and I want to do my share of the hitting. You don't mind humoring me to that small an extent, do you, Murdock?"

"Absolutely out of the question," the woman interjected in a flat, final way before Murdock could answer me. I'd forgotten all about her during my brief conversation with Murdock, but the way she spoke put her quickly center-stage. She was my height but carried more body weight, was a good deal older, had light brown hair and blue eyes, and wore a drab-green, one-piece ship's uniform with what seemed like full familiarity. She had also opened her shield to look at me with her mind, and those back at the complex probably would have been upset to know her strength was very close to that of Kel-Ten.

"Absolutely out of the question," she said, folding her arms where she stood beside Murdock's chair. "Her mind is so feeble she'd be flattened in an instant, and it wouldn't take the best they have, either. I still don't understand how she could have been declared a Prime to begin with. And if *you* have no modesty, girl, you might consider the feelings of those around you. That sheet should be covering you, not resting forgotten across your hips."

She was right about my having forgotten the sheet, but suggesting I had no sense of modesty was as ridiculous as the rest of what she'd said. I was as modest as the next woman, but there are, at times, things more important than worrying about whether or not you're covered. I took a handful of the sheet and pulled it over me, then met the annoyance in the light eyes staring at me.

"Please accept my apologies for having offended your sensibilities," I drawled, knowing the tone would add to the woman's annoyance. "If I'd realized you've never before seen what I was showing, I would certainly have been more careful. And since my question was addressed to Murdock rather than to you, why don't we let *him* answer it, hm?"

The woman stiffened where she stood, unfolding her arms as her mind also went stiff with insult, the expression on her face turning coldly angry. She was all ready to come back at me with a blast of words, but this time Murdock was the one to interrupt.

"Now, now, ladies, let's not have hostility between allies," he said, the command so smooth and soothing that it almost seemed like a casual interjection. "It's come to me that you two don't know each other, so you must forgive me for being remiss in regard to introductions. Prime Ashton Farley, I would like you to know Prime Terrilian Reya, and you may both accept my word that you are *not* enemies. Ashton has been in charge of training our own force of empaths, Terrilian, and from what I hear Terrilian has been struggling with very special training on Rimilia, Ashton. If you like you may address her as *'Chama,'* for that's the position she won to in Vediaster."

"*She's* the new *Chama* of Vediaster?" the woman Ashton Farley demanded, her disbelief so clear even Murdock must have felt it. "That's not possible, Murdock, not with the small amount of mind-strength she has. I have ordinary empaths with more mind-muscle than that, so someone must be pulling your leg. And if she was on Rimilia, why didn't I know about it?"

"My dear Ashton, she wasn't there to train with your forces," Murdock answered with faint amusement for the woman's continuing annoyance, his fingers turning his cane just a little. "She was there for another purpose entirely, one facet of which was to be five-banded by

Tammad, the *denday* Rathmore Hellman believes is uniting Rimilia for him. What the esteemed head of the Centran Amalgamation on Central doesn't know, of course, is that Tammad is in reality working in the interests of his own people, and therefore in our interests as well. He and Terrilian have been together for months, and—''

Murdock's words broke off a bare moment after his eyes returned to me, leading me to wonder what my expression must be like. It had taken me a little time to realize that Murdock knew what was missing from my memory, knew where I'd been and what I'd done during the time that was only a blank to me. He clearly didn't mind talking about it, but for some reason I felt very reluctant to ask him to go into details.

''Of course,'' he said almost at once, his gray eyes narrowed as he studied my face, his mind close to outrage. ''They've conditioned you into forgetting all that, haven't they? They wanted nothing to interfere with total dedication to the new commitment, and with no memory of what was, their wishes were fulfilled. Have no fear, child, their wishes will very shortly no longer obtain. As quickly as your system rids itself of the drugs you were being fed, that quickly will you begin to remember—and more quickly still with the assistance of my own memories. Would you like me to begin now?''

''I—think I'd like to rest for a while first,'' I said, knowing I was being a coward but helpless to do anything else. ''And I think I'd also like to hear first how it was that you were right there to rescue me from what I thought was a hopeless situation. Is it modern science we have to thank for our now being able to grow coincidences to such an unusual size?''

''Our being there was hardly a coincidence,'' he answered, his tone warmly reassuring despite the snort of ridicule voiced by the woman beside him. ''It's all part of the story, but not a part you're likely to remember on your own. You never knew the entire story, you see, but it's more than time that you did. Perhaps you'd care to join us for a meal once you've rested, and we can talk then.''

''I think—I'm suddenly more hungry than tired,'' I

found myself being forced to say, the decision having been made almost on its own. Something told me I would not be too pleased to hear what I'd been doing during the time that was blank to me, but I discovered I *had* to know. I didn't want to know but I did want to know, and since I would remember eventually anyway there was no sense in putting it off. "You don't happen to have something I can wear, do you?"

"That uniform you had on when we found you is hanging in the closet over there," the woman Ashton said, nodding her head toward the wall to my left. "The bloodstains have been cleaned out of it, and the rips and tears aren't so bad that it can't be worn. Would you like us to wait while you dress, or would you prefer bringing the uniform out to the common area and getting into it there?"

"Ashton and I will go on ahead and get the food ordered," Murdock said as he began to struggle out of his chair, the words so quick and smooth I barely had time to glare at the woman. "There's no need of your hurrying, Terrilian, take what time you require and join us at your leisure. Come, Ashton, I find I've an appetite of my own to see to."

I was ready to swear Murdock had never accepted as much help from anyone as he did from the woman right then, forcing her to pay more attention to him than to me. It seemed fairly clear she was spoiling for a fight as much as I was, and although I didn't know the details of what was motivating her, I was more than ready to oblige. The only thing that had held me back until then was the difference in the strength of our minds, a difference the woman had no real idea about as yet. If she pushed me one more time she would learn about the difference, though, no matter how unfair it was. Enough is enough, but with her it was too much.

Once the door closed behind my two visitors, I was faced with the need to get out of bed. Doing it wasn't as easy as deciding on it, and although I didn't have to use pain control, I did have to move a lot more slowly than I wanted to. Getting into the uniform first meant sitting back down, and if the boots hadn't been flexible enough to more or less step into I would have had a problem. By the time I was dressed I knew the beating I'd taken hadn't broken anything on me, not even the ribs I'd first thought it had, but that didn't mean it didn't still hurt.

It wasn't unreasonably long before I left the cabin for the common area, but even before I reached the single, round table set up in it I could see that plates of food had already been brought. Murdock was settled into a special chair that both supported and comforted his body, a cup of kimla in his hands, for the most part ignoring what he'd said he was developing an appetite for. The woman Prime was still his companion, sitting in a standard chair and sipping from her own cup of kimla, her gaze more inward than on her surroundings. Murdock's mind was still under its usual calm control, but hers, as unshielded as it was in the cabin, was a whirlwind blend of annoyance and confusion and frustration and anger. As I neared the table, heading for the last unoccupied chair, she looked up and purposely smoothed the turning in her mind, but didn't say anything.

"Ah, Terrilian, happily sooner than I had expected," Murdock said, touching a stud that raised the back of his chair just a little. "The ship's doctor informs me that you're doing very well, considering the fact that you might have been seriously hurt by so vicious an attack. Whatever possessed those people to hurt you like that?"

"Those people," I echoed, looking at him as I carefully lowered myself into a chair that was usually very comfortable. "Am I mistaken, Murdock, or are you under the impression this was done to me by those of the complex?"

"Why—of course I'm under that impression," he said, exchanging faint frowns with the woman Ashton. "Who else might there be on that world, a world noted on the charts as having no higher life forms of its own?"

"Murdock, they're breeding for Primes," I said, leaning back slowly enough so that what pain I felt increased only a small amount. "When empaths mate you may always get more empaths, but you don't necessarily get Primes even from Prime parents. I was attacked by one group of those who didn't happen to be born Primes."

"You can't mean they simply—kick out—the ones who aren't Primes?" the woman Ashton demanded, her body straightened by the same outrage filling her mind. "Empaths are empaths, some stronger, some weaker, but all the same! How can they do such a barbaric thing, such a—a—!"

"They do it as easily as they do all the rest," Murdock interrupted, his thoughts as cold as his face was devoid of expression. "Clearly, I should be unsurprised by anything I hear of them, and yet just as clearly—"

His voice stopped for a moment while he fought with the urge to do something useless but violent, and then his normal self-control reasserted itself. "I refuse to waste my strength on rage," he stated, possibly more to himself than to us. "As we may now begin to finalize our plans against them, I shall content myself with the knowledge that they will soon be made to pay for *everything* they've done. At the same time their wrongdoing will be righted, as quickly and as thoroughly as we find it possible to see to. And I believe we would do well to speak of other things now."

He paused while a steward stopped beside me to supply a cup of kimla like those my companions held, and I found I was more than happy to have it. The kimla was warm and smooth and properly sweetened, the first sip of it showing me how badly I needed something like that in my stomach. I felt as though my insides were just about empty, which meant it was time for one of the questions I hadn't yet asked.

"How long ago did you people find me?" I put to Murdock, leaning forward carefully to check the contents of a tureen already on the table. It held a creamed soup that positively beckoned to me, and when the steward saw I wanted some of it he took over the job of filling a bowl.

"We've had you aboard almost a full day now," Murdock replied, nodding with absent approval over the bowl being filled for me. "Our doctor treated your cuts and bruises while muttering things best not repeated under his breath, then put you to bed with orders that you weren't to be disturbed by anyone. He felt that it would likely be quite some time before you regained consciousness, but it wasn't that long at all before the empath assigned by Ashton to watch you told us you were beginning to come awake. The doctor also thought you would be bedridden for quite a while, but he seems to have been in error on that score as well. Once you've eaten and we've talked, we'll let him know you're up and about again."

With a bowl of soup in front of me and a small scoop in my hand I didn't feel the need to comment on that, most especially since I wasn't terribly anxious to see his doctor. It was true that I still hurt, but if the doctor could have changed that he would have, which meant seeing him would be a waste of time for both of us. Right then I preferred wasting my time in other ways, and Murdock shifted in his chair before beginning on one of them.

"Perhaps it would be best if I tell Ashton what's been happening to you, with you simply listening in," he said, apparently aware of the upset still felt by the woman and wanting to distract her. "If you happen to hear something that strikes you as wrong or partially inaccurate, don't hesitate to speak up. It will mean your memory is beginning to return, an occurrence I would like to see completed as soon as possible. We will all need to be in our clearest minds before this thing is over and done with.

"As you know, Ashton, Rimilia was chosen for the construction of the all-planets conference complex because of its location in space. With all member planets just about equally distant from it it was considered perfect, but it also had another attraction not as well publicized. With a population not far above the level of barbarism, Rathmore Hellman and the others felt that when the proper time came to deprive the other planets of its seasoned leadership, that very population could be pointed to as the perpetrators of the bloody-handed deed. In order to manipulate permission for the complex out of the Rimilians as well as gain control over them, we gave our backing and wholehearted support to a Rimilian leader named Tammad.

"From the very beginning Tammad appeared to be nothing more than our ally, and Terrilian here was sent to Rimilia to assist him in convincing the others of the

Rimilian leaders to allow the complex. She was told by everyone involved that she would be returned to Central when her mission was accomplished, no one finding it necessary to mention that Tammad had indicated such a strong desire for her that he insisted on purchasing her in the accepted Rimilian way. Rathmore Hellman was amused by such naiveté, that Tammad would believe Central would simply sell one of its best Primes to a primitive, but still allowed the insistence. Tammad's price for her was his promise to unite as many of the diverse people of Rimilia under his own personal banner, so to speak, as possible, which was exactly what Rathmore wanted him to do. His own broaching of the subject made the arrangement much sweeter to Rathmore's way of thinking, and through me Tammad's offer was accepted at once. When Terrilian was returned to us at the embassy on Rimilia after the complex was approved at the Great Meeting she had been sent to attend, we all believed Tammad had changed his mind about keeping her. For that reason, I immediately returned her to Central on my own transport.

"No more than a small number of days passed before I learned of the misunderstanding we were all in the midst of," Murdock said, pausing to sip at the kimla he still held. "Tammad appeared at the embassy with a large number of his warriors, offered me polite greetings, then asked to have his woman returned to him. It developed that he'd sent her back only because he'd given his word to her to do so, fully intending to reclaim her once he'd made good on that word. When he discovered she was gone he grew furious, and demanded that he be provided with the means to follow after and recover her. By the time my transport returned I discovered she was due to Mediate on Alderan, so I sent Tammad and some of his men off in the transport, telling the captain to give Tammad all the help and advice he was able to provide.

"The mission proved successful and Tammad returned to Rimilia with Terrilian, but in the interim there had been occurences neither of them knew about. Word had come to me with Rathmore's authorization behind it, stating that Terrilian was to be returned to Central for a 'highly classified and extremely important' assignment. I had no doubt as to what that would be and immediately decided it was time Terrilian joined *your* group, Ashton, but the step was never taken. Although Terrilian clearly had no desire to return with Tammad to the midst of his world, Tammad refused to release her. He spoke of our 'returning the price he'd paid for her,' a promise of the withdrawal of his cooperation and alliance which Rathmore most certainly did *not* want at that point. When I admitted my inability to return his price he simply turned and strode away, taking Terrilian with him."

"I remember how frustrated and furious you were after that confrontation," Ashton said, a faint smile on her face as she looked at Murdock. "No one in the entire community dared ask you what had happened, but we gathered we could forget about our supposed new arrival. Why didn't you tell Tammad how dangerous it was for the girl to be away from our protection? 'Highly classified' assignments for female Primes have always meant the end of their lives as rational individuals, and if he really cared about her he wouldn't have refused to let her go with you."

"Speaking to him privately at that time was out of the question," Murdock replied, a faint look of distaste flitting across his face. "Not only had he been angered by Terrilian's refusal to accompany him—and another incident involving her which I won't mention—but one of those who accompanied *me* was Rathmore's man from first to last. I couldn't speak out without betraying my own stance, and therefore had to stand there and watch Tammad walk away with Terrilian as well as the two people sent from Central who were meant to replace her. After that I used ill health as an excuse to leave all but one of my aides behind in the embassy, supposedly to rest in orbit while they awaited further orders from Central, and instead used a landing slip to visit the community and plan our next move."

"Just a minute," I interrupted, frowning down into what was left of the bowl of soup. I wasn't precisely upset, not when everything I'd heard sounded as though it had happened to someone else, but something didn't fit in with what I *did* remember. "You keep talking about a community on Rimilia, as though you mean a Centran community of some kind, but I can't recall ever having heard of a Centran community on that world. All I ever heard about was the Rimilian barbarians."

"That's all anyone was *supposed* to hear about," Murdock said, a faint smile on his face to match the satisfaction in his mind. "Our community on Rimilia isn't a Centran-sponsored one, nor is it large enough or accessible enough for even the natives to know about. It's made up almost entirely of empaths, mostly of Centran stock but well leavened with the addition of Rimilian blood, and was established generations before Rathmore and his cronies decided on the world as a site for their complex. When we first learned of their plans we nearly began an immediate campaign to sabotage their efforts, then decided we'd be best off allowing them to continue. We were, after all, already there. What better position might we have to keep very close track of what they were doing?

"At any rate, quite some time passed before our agent in Tammad's entourage contacted us frantically by radio. He had reported from time to time of the events transpiring around and about him, among which were Terrilian's abduction by savages, her having been kept as a slave by the Hamarda, her escape from the Hamarda across the desert to Grelana, her forced assistance to the *Chama* of Grelana, her part in the breaking of the *Chama*'s power, her flight to Gerleth, her capture there, and finally her journey to Vediaster. When Tammad and Terrilian and Cinnan, another Rimilian, were taken prisoner by the then-*Chama* of Vediaster, Dallan, the fourth of their party who was also a Prince of Gerleth, sent back word to his father the *Chamd* that he and his companions were in dire need of assistance.

Cinnan's *l'lendaa* from Grelana and Tammad's *l'lendaa* joined the warriors of Gerleth and all rode as fast as possible toward Vediaster, but by the time they reached the city of Vediaster everything was over but the shouting. Those who had opposed the former *Chama* had attacked her palace in force and, with Terrilian's assistance, had defeated the hated ruler. Everyone was safe and sound, and by the law of the land Terrilian was the new *Chama*, circumstances which should have pleased all concerned. It certainly pleased the Rimilians, but for some reason not quite clear to any of them, Terrilian wasn't equally as pleased. She had agreed to help out a short while until they chose someone else to be *Chama*, had seemed to be honoring the agreement she'd made, and then, on the very day the small army of *l'lendaa* from Gerleth arrived, had suddenly disappeared. No one had any idea where she might have gone, and then they discovered she'd taken a *seetar* and had ridden alone out of the city."

Murdock sighed and used the pause to swallow down more of the kimla, but that wasn't all he used the pause for. He also spent a short time studying my face, probably searching for some sign of returning memory, but there weren't any returns for him to see a sign of. Everything still sounded as though it had happened to someone else, and when he saw that he shrugged inside himself and simply went on.

"Groups of *l'lendaa* and *w'wendaa* began a search for her both inside and out of the city, and one group, the one containing our agent, found something more than the faint, cold trail they would have been willing to settle for. Once they had left the city behind them, they were contacted by a completely unexpected ally—the giant black *seetar* that was Tammad's usual mount. How the beast had gotten out of the city no one seemed to know, but his recognition of some of the riders had brought him from the forest surrounding the road the riders were on, his thoughts positively frantic. Our agent was already familiar with the *seetar*'s emotion-symbol for Terrilian, and since most of the agitation in the beast's mind centered around that symbol, he knew at once that the *seetar* had seen her. He worked for a short while calming the beast, then began the very difficult task of extracting what information he could. By the time he was through he was exhausted, but was also certain he understood what the *seetar* had been trying to tell them.

"Apparently he had seen Terrilian riding past him on

another *seetar*, felt confused as well as annoyed as to why she would do that, then decided to follow her. She didn't go very far before she stopped, dismounted, and sat down in the woods beside a tree, but before he was able to approach her she suddenly fell over unconscious. He was trying to decide whether to go for help—and how to get the only man he could count on to give that help—when two strangers appeared, picked up the unconscious woman, and disappeared back into the forest. He followed them to something that smelled a little like a sword but was very large, watched them enter the thing, then had to stand helplessly by while the thing rose silently into the sky and out of his reach. He waited a short while to see if it would return, and when it didn't he started back for the city to find help. The emotions signifying 'high' and 'gone' were so clear to our agent, he lost no time calling us to say Amalgamation people had taken Terrilian."

"And how right he was," Ashton said with a snort and a flash of remembered anger. "We located their private transport in orbit, and were able to lock onto them before they left that orbit. If it hadn't taken them so long to get around to leaving once they had the girl, we most probably would have missed them completely. I wonder what they were so busy with, that it took them that long to get started."

The question was put very casually and only to Murdock, but there was something in the woman's mind that sneered faintly in my direction, and that on top of the way she was pretending I wasn't there at all. I didn't have to know what she was hinting at in order to resent it, but once again the option of replying was taken from me by Murdock.

"They were certainly overconfident through being in orbit around an undeveloped world," he said, his tone suggesting his guess was the only reasonable one. "It never occurred to them there were others around who would be able to detect them, so they took their time and no precautions at all. We hadn't planned on using you as bait to help us find their hidden base of operations, Terrilian, but once presented with the opportunity we could hardly refuse to take it. We were in the midst of trying to decide whether it would be possible to free you before we returned to our people with the news, when our instruments told us you had effected your own escape. We sent people down into the woods to intercept you, found you senseless from the vicious beating you'd been given, and quickly took you to this transport. Now, happily, you are once again among your own."

The faint, icy smile he sent me was very familiar, so familiar it was probably meant to distract me from what he'd said to the great amount of very real satisfaction he was feeling. Unfortunately for his intentions, though, I was too annoyed by the snide attitudes of his woman companion to be anything but critical of what I'd been told. Murdock's narration was as neat and outwardly complete as anything I'd ever heard from someone in the XenoDiplomacy Bureau, but a small figure named logic was jumping up and down inside my head, pointing eagerly and insistently at the gaping holes in the fabric so recently constructed for my benefit.

"You know, I have the strangest feeling I've been told that before," I remarked, doing my damnedest not to slump in the chair the way my body wanted to. "I'm referring to your comment about me being among my own, Murdock, and I also have the feeling I've doubted the sincerity of those who previously told it to me. Maybe that's why I'm being so ungrateful as to feel no hesitation about lumping you in along with the rest of them."

"A reaction like that is no more than to be expected after what you've so recently gone through, child," the head of Central's XD Bureau said smoothly, his mind as unconcerned and convincing as his expressionless expression. "When one is forced to spend time among those who cannot under any circumstances be trusted, one most naturally transfers the attitude to all who are thereafter encountered. Only a lack of betrayal can serve to alter the attitude, so you must expect to spend some time among us before. . ."

"Before easy explanations and overblown sentiments can blind me to the truth again?" I interrupted to ask, my brows raised with the question. "I've always admired your ability to weave blindfolds, Murdock, but this time you were a little sloppy. I wonder if that's because you thought I was hurting too much to notice. I certainly hope it wasn't because you decided I would never notice even under the best of circumstances. I've learned to resent having people dismiss me like that."

"You're in no position to resent anything, girl!" the woman Ashton snapped out, her mind filled with heavy annoyance rather than any sort of guilt or regret, her light eyes hard. "Right now you owe your life to us, and you'd be smart to understand you're not important enough for Murdock or anyone else to bother lying to. All you Central bigwigs are alike, so full of yourselves you think the universe stops and goes only when you press the switch. Once you've been in my group for a while you'll learn better, and until then you'll keep your mouth closed and your opinions to yourself!"

The woman's words started out heated and rose in temperature from there, her mind reaching out toward mine and quickly surrounding it before beginning to squeeze. Murdock was saying something in protest that both of us ignored, and although I now knew the main reason the woman didn't care for me, that didn't stop me from being as furious as she was. I'd taken all from her I intended taking, and it was time to fight back.

The Prime Ashton Farley was sitting up and forward in her chair, her hands clamped tight to the armrests, bracing herself physically for the mental assault she was in the midst of. For me, just sitting there normally was almost too hard, but then I didn't need to brace myself in order to drop my curtain. Ashton's mind was strong and trying hard to impress me with that strength, the pressure she exerted aimed toward making me ask her to stop—or begging her to, which was probably more like it. The instant I dropped my curtain I began exerting my own pressure outward, hard against her efforts but not as hard as I could have. First I let her see what she was trying to contain and then I flung her mind away from mine, more contemptuously than I had ever done with anyone.

The woman had been very surprised when my mind

didn't immediately quiver and collapse under her efforts, but the surprise paled into shock when my curtain disappeared to show her what she was working to hold down. She gasped and tried to continue squeezing even as the blood drained from her face, choked as she tried to throw herself back in the chair, but nothing happened the way she wanted it to. When I thrust her away from me she was even beyond the ability to scream, her mind clanging with shocked disbelief and fear, her body shuddering and gasping. Her feet had been pushing at the floor to get her farther away from the table, and when she had the chair facing far enough away, she staggered to her feet and ran. There was silence for a moment after that, and then Murdock brought his eyes and attention back to me, looking more shaken than I had ever before seen him.

"You—appear a good deal less than wearied from that exchange, Terrilian," he said, his thoughts whirling so fast I found it impossible to separate one emotion from the next. "Ashton is one of the strongest we have, and yet you bested her with almost no effort. We were told your abilities have grown over the last months but details were not included, save that the process causing the growth was far from pleasant. I dislike the implications of that, but—our needs are too great to ignore any avenue presented us. Did the—disagreement—harm you in any way?"

His cold gray eyes were now trying to look inside me, his mind so quickly calmed and back under control that it was possible to believe he'd never lost that control. I found myself just as impressed as ever, but not swayed in the least.

"You know, Murdock, I really do wish you would stop trying to show how concerned you are about me," I said, reaching for my unfinished cup of kimla. "Every time you do it you remind me again about how you used me, so why don't you just give it up? If you had an agent in with whatever group of people I was with, you *could* have warned me about what was most likely going to happen. That you didn't warn me means you *were* using me as bait, and were waiting for me to be taken so that you and your friends could follow. The fact that you were able to detect me in the forest means you were keeping close track of me with some sort of tracer device, so don't even bother denying it. And that you people who are my 'own' were also prepared to abandon me in that place once you had what you wanted is also pretty clear, since you made no effort to get me out and only picked me up once I'd gotten myself out. Why don't you tell me again how grateful I ought to be?"

Staring at him over my cup rim didn't show me anything but the same lack of expression anyone ever saw, which wasn't the same as touching his mind. The guilt he felt over what had been done was fully accepted, but neither that nor the real, true pain he experienced ever reached his narrow, sunken face.

"You're completely correct, of course," he conceded, nodding fractionally. "To warn you might have also given warning to our enemies, but that's neither here nor there. We used you as necessary to gain the ends we simply *had* to gain, but would not have forever abandoned you to your fate. You *are* one of us, child, and would have been freed as quickly as we organized our people and attacked. What you were made to suffer is certainly. . ."

"Regrettable?" I finished for him, replacing my cup on the table. "It was that, all right, but it was also something a lot worse than you'll ever be able to understand. 'Abandoned' is a good word, but you'll have to remind me some day to give you the emotions that go along with the word. The experience should be—an experience. I'd like to know now what world you intend dropping me off on, so I can begin making plans. In consideration of everything that's happened, I don't think we would be wise to spend any more time in each other's company than absolutely necessary."

"Terrilian, I thought you understood you'd be returning with us to Rimilia," he said with a frown, disturbance now touching his mind. "Not only have we an attack to plan and carry out, but Tammad must be told that you're safe. He'll most certainly be beside himself with worry, and once your memories have returned you'll know. . ."

"Please, Murdock, I'd really rather not hear any more

about that,'' I interrupted impatiently, beginning to start the process of getting to my feet. ''If your narration was meant to show me anything other than that I want nothing to do with this Tammad of yours, you failed to accomplish your aim. The man 'buys' me without any regard to what feelings *I* might have on the subject, kidnaps me and forces me to go with him when even you knew I didn't want to, and then concerns himself so little with me that all sorts of horrendous things are able to happen to me. This is the person I'm supposed to be concerned about? Somehow I think not. As far as your attack goes, I'll probably join in just to make sure there won't be anyone left to come after me again, but once it's done there will be an absolute parting of the ways between us. Do you understand me?''

Having managed to stand—with the help of the table edge—I looked up at him, and for once his cold gray eyes were mirroring the throbbing pain his mind sent out. He wanted to argue with me, reason with me, talk and talk until I saw things his way, but the pain refused to allow that.

''I understand,'' he said in the softest of voices, a two word admission of total defeat, and when I let go of the table and headed back for my cabin, no other words followed me.

# 10

I wouldn't have asked for the help I could have used in getting back to my cabin, which means I barely made it to the bed before I was asleep. How it's possible to sleep when you're hurting that much I still don't understand, unless it's more a matter of passing out than sleeping. Whatever it was I indulged in it for quite a while, then awoke to find myself out of the light-brown uniform and under the covers again. I hadn't been able to get out of the uniform on my own, and had just collapsed onto the bed still in it. Its being gone told me I'd had visitors while I was out, which supported the unconscious as opposed to asleep theory. I didn't care for the idea much—the unrealized visitors, that is—and decided I'd have to see if there was anything to be done about avoiding such deep lack of consciousness in the future.

I stirred in the bed and then began to sit up, trying to find out if being out of things so completely had at least helped me a little, finding myself surprised when I discovered it had helped a good deal more than a little. Sitting up didn't hurt at all, no more than faint stiffness and a shadow of aches whispering from somewhere in an effort to get my attention. They *weren't* getting my attention, at least not much of it, and that made the dim transport cabin around me almost as pleasant as a sunny day in springtime. I took a deep breath and stretched a little, enjoying being able to do it again, then reached out with my mind to learn where the others were—

And ran into nothing but blankness. I stiffened where I sat, as tense as the woman Ashton had been during our fight, trying to understand what had gone wrong. I was awake, I knew I was awake, but I couldn't reach anyone or anything—not the slightest murmur or overtone—just the way it had been in the complex—

Just the way it had been in the complex. I leaned back again onto one elbow, not knowing whether to be hysterical or furious, my thoughts so violently entwined with my emotions that I couldn't separate them. It was fairly obvious my clothing wasn't the only thing that had been taken from me while I was unconscious, and I didn't have to wonder why. People are always afraid of what they can't control, especially if that item has previously indicated it isn't feeling very friendly toward them, and fear doesn't invariably paralyze. Sometimes it pushed its victims into action, possibly badly thought out and hasty, but action nevertheless. My—'own' had been pushed into action, and now I was turned off.

Turned off. Through the anger I felt that phrase began signaling in some way, almost like a frantically waving hand trying to get my attention. I remembered having the fleeting impression back at the complex that that phrase meant something important to me, represented something I ought to know and think about. If I'd been talking to someone else I would have snapped out impatiently that it didn't mean anything, it was only two words that described the condition I was now suffering from, a condition inflicted on me by my "friends."

But a condition it shouldn't be *possible* to suffer from. I stiffened again as the realization came, a flood of protest from the part of me that normally engaged in arguing against things that were accepted as truth but were patently not so. How do you turn off one of your senses? that part of me demanded, a thought I knew I'd had before even if I couldn't remember when. To turn off your hearing you had to plug your ears, to turn off sight you needed a blindfold, to avoid smell you had to hold your nose, and to keep from touching things you needed gloves. Keeping things out of your mouth took care of taste—in the absence of strong odors, that is—but without using special means, senses could *not* be turned off. To keep them from working you had to block them off, shield them from what was around them, interrupt the flow of data—

Shield. The single word-thought set me sitting up straight again, feeling more like an imbecile than anything else. That, of course, *had* to be it, but it had taken me so long to see even with all the clues I'd had! That Prime Jer-Mar, the one I'd insulted in the low dining room. How many times had he mentioned in passing that he couldn't "reach" me with his strength, not even when he was furious? None of the Primes at the complex knew about shields, none of them used one, and even Kel-Ten's amazement over the one I'd shown him hadn't rung any real bells. I was stupid, that's what I was, which is a hell of a lot worse than just being ignorant. Conditioning or no conditioning, I should have realized a lot sooner that the only way to "turn off" an empath is to key a shield into being around his or her mind.

"With intelligence like yours, you would have made a good brain surgeon," I muttered to myself, moving my legs under the cover so that I could sit cross-legged and lean my arms on my knees. "Are you going to test the theory, or just sit here and admire it for the rest of your life?"

I didn't quite sigh at the question I'd asked myself, but only because I would rather have put off answering it for a while. The theory was sound, no argument there, but I had a fairly good idea of how many sound theories never worked out in practice. I really *needed* it to work out, but that didn't mean it would; all it meant was that I had to try as soon as possible, even if there was nothing but disappointment waiting for me as a result. After all, disappointment wasn't all that bad or unbearable, not with all the practice I'd had living with it. . . .

The second time I did sigh, but that was only a necessary prelude to making the effort that had to be made. If there was a shield imposed around my mind I was the only one who could be generating it, which meant it was subject to me and my decision to banish it. Theory, theory, that was the theory, but how do you make something go away that you never asked for in the first place? Banishing a shield—banishing it wasn't the hard part, letting it form to begin with was harder. You had to encourage it to come nearer to form it, but to banish it you just—

Let it drop. It was almost like taking sound-deadeners off my ears at first, but in an inexplicable way was more than that. Even that drab cabin brightened in color, I could breathe deeply and freely again, and best of all could feel the presence of other minds on the transport. I was free of the shackles they'd tried to put on me, and couldn't help grinning at the thought that those particular shackles should never work again. I was awake, but hadn't been "turned on" with the usual keying word or phrase. Two "offs" in a row shouldn't work with conditioning any more than it did with a mechanical switch, but that was a theory I was in no hurry to test. What I did instead was allow the shield to form again, that light shield I could see through when I tried—and *had* seen through, the strange impressions I'd had in the complex proving that—then got up to look for the clothes that had been taken from me. Ever since my eyes had opened I'd been feeling as though I were starving, and I was suddenly eager to see how my dear friends would treat their poor, helpless little capt—ah—guest.

When I left my cabin the single table in the common room was neatly set but unoccupied, which I took to mean that it was waiting for me. As soon as I sat down the steward appeared, looking faintly startled but making no attempt to refuse the food order I gave him. It didn't take him long to return with my meal, which meant I was able to get more than halfway through it before two people came out of the passageway that led to or from the command deck. Murdock McKenzie was being helped by his friend Ashton Farley again, but I paid very little attention to them until they were both settled at the table. By then I was ready to acknowledge the fact that I couldn't eat any more, so I simply pushed my plate away, picked up my cup of kimla, then leaned back to stare at Murdock while I sipped in silence.

"Whether or not you're prepared to believe me, I'm glad to see that you appear better than you were yesterday," Murdock offered, the words a shade calmer and more quiet than usual. "The doctor was furious with us for allowing you to leave your bed, but happily it did you no real harm. Would you like an explanation of why it was necessary to do—what else—was done to you?''

''Not really,'' I answered, holding my cup in the fingertips of both hands. ''I'm more interested in what you intend doing next—and also in hearing more of how terribly concerned you are about me. And you *are* concerned, aren't you, Murdock?''

''It so happens that's exactly what he is,'' the woman Ashton put in when the man I stared at didn't respond, at least not in words. That pain I'd seen the last time we'd spoken was there again, and maybe that was why I shifted my gaze to the high and mighty female Prime. She was looking at me with a good deal less than sisterly love, a reaction I more than shared.

''Not that it will do any good telling you this,'' she went on, ''but the only reason we were near New Dawn long enough to pick you up is that Murdock refused to just leave. He kept arguing with the rest of us, trying to convince us we had to do something to get you out of there, even though he knew as well as we did that there wasn't anything we *could* do. I kept telling him he was just wasting time, and then when you turned up in the woods I understood that was exactly what he'd been doing: wasting time to give you a chance to do what we couldn't. How long do you think you would have lasted out there if he *hadn't* given you that chance?''

Her question was surprisingly calm considering what had previously gone on between us, but there was a faint bitterness behind it that I could just feel filtering through my shield. Her light eyes were making no effort to avoid mine, which meant I could see the brief flash of surprise in them when I made a sound of scorn.

''That touching story is very—touching, but what do you expect it to accomplish?'' I asked in turn, making it clear that now *I* was holding *her* gaze. ''Am I supposed to be so overwhelmed by his thoughtfulness and loyalty that I stop thinking and just emote? You told me he made everyone wait around when they didn't want to, so would you like to tell me what he was making them wait for? *I* didn't know there was anyone out here waiting to pick me up if I got out of the complex, so what good did his delaying tactics really do me? It was pure luck I was not only forced to run, but also able to do it when I had to. If he makes a habit of expecting the intervention of luck like that, you're all a bunch of fools for listening to him."

"You don't know anything about us at all, do you?" the woman asked, her sudden frown and faint pity making it my turn to be surprised. "You're one of us, no possible doubt about that, but you haven't the faintest idea of what you're one of. There are a number of us who had to leave the community at a very young age and grow up elsewhere, but we always knew who we were and who we came from. I don't know why they did it differently with you, hadn't realized they did do it differently, and don't much like it. Of course my brother was counting on luck like that, but we aren't fools for listening to him. When he gets the feeling something wildly improbable will happen, it usually does. His only mistake was in thinking *we* had to make it happen, when we had no real part in it. Sometimes his talent works like that."

Just a minute or so earlier I'd been all ready with a large number of words, each one designed to tell those people exactly what I thought of them. The words were still inside my head somewhere, still bouncing with indignation and huffiness, but they were no longer first in line and maybe not even second. I don't like revelations, especially startling ones, and too much of what I'd just heard fell into the wide-eyed, what-the-hell-are-you-talking-about category.

"What the hell are you talking about?" I demanded almost at once, only glancing in the direction of Murdock, who wasn't looking at me. "He can't be your brother, you don't even have the same last names. And what do you mean, his 'talent'? Murdock's from Central, and he doesn't *have* a talent."

"Murdock grew up and lives on Central, but like the rest of us he was born in the community," the woman Ashton corrected, and if she wasn't the sort to be gentle, she had no trouble managing patience. "Of course he and I have different last names, we were raised in different places by people who have no connection with each other except for wanting to be sure we don't all end up living in chains. Our natural parents don't use last names, so those of us raised away from the community simply keep the last names we grew up with when we go back. As for Murdock's talent—our people were very upset when he wasn't born an empath, and with both Rimilian and Centran blood in him couldn't understand why he wasn't. They didn't know about his talent until he learned to talk, I'm told, but it was so strong and definite in him that they began checking others for the same thing. They discovered then that quite a few of us have it, but none are able to be quite as accurate as my brother. When he gets a flash of prescience, it usually can't be argued with."

This time I turned my head to look directly at Murdock, vaguely wondering why he still wasn't looking at *me*. There wasn't the least expression on his narrow face, but it was almost as though he were ashamed of what I'd just been told. The pride I'd heard in Ashton's voice made his attitude something I couldn't understand, which only added to the crowding in the compartment of my mind meant to hold confusion.

"I think you can see now why his making us wait really was for your benefit," Ashton went on, unbothered by the fact that I was no longer looking at her. "None of us could imagine how you could possibly get out of there, most especially with all that conditioning they use, but Murdock's talent kept us from giving up and leaving. And he was the only one of us who didn't want you turned off again, too. We insisted because we can't afford to have someone with your strength walking around thinking we're practically blood enemies, but it will only be until we get you home to the community. Once you share that with us and *know* you're one of us, you'll also know that what we did was in no way uncaring use or abandonment."

I didn't need my abilities to know the woman believed everything she was saying, believed it deeply even though she didn't expect me to believe. My innermost thoughts were carefully searching everything I'd been told, looking for loopholes and inconsistencies and flaws running counter to simple logic, but I suddenly realized I didn't expect them to find any. What I'd been told was what the people telling it considered the absolute truth, and then something else came to me with the same feeling of total conviction.

"Murdock, there's something bothering you that has nothing to do with what Ashton just told me," I said, the statement considerably softer than the words I'd previously addressed to him. "I'm too confused right now to know *what* to think, but this is a point I'm not uncertain about. I think you have something else to talk about—that I won't be terribly happy to hear."

"Intuition that accurate is almost certainly much more than mere intuition," he answered, a faint smile curving his lips before he turned his head to look directly at me again. Once he did I could see that the smile wasn't reflected in his eyes, a lack that made me even more uneasy than his words. "Terrilian, child, there's one important point you haven't yet commented on or questioned," he said, something of a sigh behind the words. "Both Ashton and I have told you you're one of us, but you haven't yet asked how that could be. It's possible you don't believe us, or perhaps so much else has been told you that you haven't yet gotten around to considering the contention. Will you do me the favor of thinking about it now?"

Reaching through my shield showed that Ashton was puzzled and concerned, undoubtedly because of the way Murdock's mind was behaving. He was absolutely determined to go through with discussing what he had begun on, but the rest of him was so filled with the desire to avoid the subject that he was just about trembling inside. From Ashton's reaction I could see I wasn't the only one who wasn't used to seeing Murdock like that, but at least I had his request as a partial distraction.

"I don't really know *what* to think about it," I admitted, finally remembering I held a cup of kimla I could drink from. "Murdock, have you forgotten that I know my parents even though they didn't raise me? They were the ones who turned me over to the Centran government so that I could be raised in a crèche with other empaths like myself. The authorities considered them my parents, and with all the checking routinely done, *I* don't consider it likely that they weren't."

"Terrilian, we were expecting and prepared for all that checking, that's why it showed the authorities nothing we didn't want it to show," he answered, gray eyes still sober, mind still burdened. "Not many of our people have ever been placed on Central itself, but not because doing the placing was all that difficult. Keeping in contact with them was the hard part, making sure they didn't forget us—or talk about us when they were too young to realize what danger the talking would put us all in. We usually provided one older friend and confidante to support them with understanding companionship until they were old enough to be discreet, and then they were told the truth about where they came from. Once they knew, they were able to make occasional visits back to the community, to grow closer to those they came from, but, child—none of them were ever Primes."

"Central tends to spoil Primes for any position lower than Ruler Of All Creation," Ashton put in, her tone dry, her thoughts totally disapproving. "We've had Primes raised on other worlds relocate to Central, and after a couple of years there, there was no living or getting along with them. When the time came to pull them out of public life and bring them home for good to keep them from disappearing forever into what we then thought of as a Prime-maw, the very first thing they tried on the very first day was taking over direction of the community. They didn't need or want to join any of our training classes, they just wanted to run everything in sight because they were so special. They had to be flattened hard before they listened to anything told them, and with most the lesson had to be repeated more than once."

"Which should explain the rather—cool reception you had from Ashton at the very beginning," Murdock said, the faintest of smiles on his face. "She herself took over heading our training program only after she was convinced she really was the strongest and most advanced in the community, and most of the difficulty she mentioned—and more she didn't mention—became hers to contend with. But we seem to have strayed from the point

I was attempting to make. What few empaths were placed on Central itself we kept in touch with, and none of those were Primes. Should you accept our contention that you were, indeed, born in our community, then your first question must be obvious."

"Overly obvious," I agreed, but only to the comment he'd made. I still wasn't anywhere near convinced that what they thought was true really was the truth, but to continue the discussion the point had to be conceded. "If everyone placed on Central was kept in touch with and wasn't a Prime, then what was I doing there without a friend on the world?"

"Exactly," Murdock said, a totally unnecessary counteragreement—which had been forced on him by all that reluctance. "In order for you to have been placed there in virtual—abandonment—someone must have caused standard practice to be discarded in your case, someone whose opinion carried enough weight to override any objections made. There were objections aplenty, I can tell you, and the debate raged on for quite a while, but in the end the needs of everyone in the Amalgamation had to come first. You were taken away from your real parents, placed with people who could pass you off as theirs, then were left to grow up without ever being told what had been done."

"A heinous crime if there ever was one," I muttered, really beginning to be worried about the state of his mind. "Murdock, I'm more than willing to admit how lonely I've been most of my life, and I'm also willing to bitterly accuse anyone who was responsible for making that happen to me. What I'm not quite up to is making it the absolute tragedy of the ages, especially since I have no idea what growing up among my 'own' would have been like. I was dissatisfied on Central and very alone, but Central isn't the only world I've ever seen and I've never found one I thought I'd like better. If you want the complete truth, I'd rather believe I've been lonely all this time because my true companionship was callously and heartlessly stolen from me—not because there's no one *anywhere* I'd get along with and like, a concept I've toyed with a few times over the years. I'm at this moment willing to bet even the deck plates of this transport have figured out that you're the one who caused me to be put where I was, so can't we stop the bush-beating and get on to whatever's rattling your mind like a shack in a windstorm?''

"You're not believing any of this,'' Murdock said, really *looking* at me for the first time in many minutes, his light eyes narrowed. "No one could be so cold-bloodedly reasonable after being told their entire life was the result of someone else's manipulation, most especially not when they're also an empath. Damn it, Terrilian, I will not have you humoring me!''

"You prefer the thought of being accused?'' I asked, blinking just a little at the way he'd nearly raised his voice. I'd also rarely heard him swear like that before, and found it disconcerting. "Yes, I can see you *would* prefer being accused, to help bleed off all that guilt you're feeling. It's fairly clear you think you're telling me the truth, Murdock, and for all I know it might be true. My only problem right now is that I'm not accepting any of this, not the least, smallest part. I feel as though I'm walking through a very clear dream, parts of my past just as uncertain as most of my future. When and if I get my memories back that might change, but *your* best bet would be to get every painful confession off your chest right now, while I'm still unlikely to get hysterical. And if a time comes when I am prepared to believe, having heard it earlier just might make it easier to accept.''

"I hadn't thought of that, and you may very well be correct,'' Murdock said with faint surprise, now more thoughtful than upset. "There's a saying about even the darkest of days being brighter than the lightest of nights, and this may be a prime example of the brightness in the dark.''

"Did you say a *Prime* example, Murdock?'' I asked, sipping my kimla in relief at seeing the awful agonizing loosening its hold on him just a little. "Most people would be ashamed, but I don't think diplomats are really considered people.''

"That was most inappropriate, young woman,'' he came back with lowered brows while Ashton half groaned and half chuckled. "You will do me the courtesy of waiting until I'm free of distractions before offering a bout of verbal fencing. As you stated, I am indeed the one who caused you to be done as none before you, but that's no more than a part of my—concern over the matter. You were a lovely infant full of a great deal of promise, but the moment I first looked at you I knew you must be sent away from us—without being told, like the others, that you did indeed belong somewhere. Considering who you were that in itself would have been bad enough, but the fact of the matter is—I wasn't able to give any concrete reasons for doing such a thing. The need for it was so overwhelming I was able to argue down anyone who disagreed, but Terrilian—to this day I have no real idea whether or not I was correct. The possibility remains that you were severed from your rightful heritage for no good reason at all, and *that's* what I felt you should know. What was done to you was my fault, but worse than that—I can't justify it."

The cold gray eyes were looking at me with no attempt on his part to move them, no attempt on his part to avoid seeing whatever condemnation I felt it necessary to show. It's possible for some people to do terribly heartless and low things without feeling guilty, but only if they have a really good reason to justify, at least to themselves, having done those things. What was causing Murdock's agonizing was the fact that he had no such reason, and in an odd, strangely detached way, I was almost beginning to believe his story.

"But Murdock, didn't we find New Dawn because of her?" Ashton asked, reaching over to put a hand on his arm in an attempt to ease the pain. "If she'd known about us like the others, we would have brought her home before she could be taken, leaving us knowing nothing more than we knew then. Couldn't *that* be the reason you did what you did?"

"I wish it were," the man answered with a sigh, patting the hand on his arm without looking at the woman the hand belonged to. "We were almost to the point of using a volunteer, one properly conditioned to forget all about us, of course, but when Terrilian was taken while we were in a position to follow immediately—as we'd hoped we would be—we did that instead. Ever since the possibility first came up I've been sniffing around it, hoping to find that *it* was the reason I hadn't been able to discover earlier, but I'm afraid it isn't. When you come across the real reason behind something you did while acting blindly, you *know* it without any doubt. This, my dear, unfortunately isn't it."

"What did you mean when you said, 'considering who I was'?" I asked, finding the phrase standing out in my memory. I'd been very detached from the whole thing at the beginning of our discussion, but I felt myself being drawn more and more deeply inward with every new thing I heard. I was starting to believe I'd be much better off all alone in my cabin, but the part of me I'd been having so much trouble with lately had asked a question I couldn't escape having answered.

"Terrilian, child, this all started only moments after you were born," Murdock said, the gentle words an odd contrast to his usual expressionlessness. "The reason I was there to see you at all, let alone that quickly, was because you were the firstborn of my youngest sister. I knew your mother better than any of my other brothers and sisters because, unlike the rest of us, she wasn't gone very long from the settlement. From the moment she first began walking and talking, she also began fighting against life in a crèche, finally making it necessary for her 'parents' to take her back. No planet ever releases an empathetic child unless he or she is considered not only incorrigible, but also unable to learn what's being taught. Your mother flatly refused to learn, flatly refused to let them force her to learn, and therefore ended up back in the community before she was ten years old. She spent a day or so looking around and getting acquainted with our real parents, then settled in without argument or fuss. It seems she approved of the settlement a good deal more than she did the creche, but that doesn't mean she never argued or fussed again."

"Is that why she was married to one of the recruited Rimilians, instead of one of the men of the community?" Ashton asked, a grin of amusement now on her face. "I'd always thought it was simply good luck for the rest of us, since no one ever told me that story before. Irin could have had my place, if she'd worked at developing a little more self-control."

"Irindel has always had her own priorities in life, and has also always pursued them in preference to anyone else's," Murdock returned, his faint smile back. "And marriage with Rissim was completely her choice, just as most of everything else occurring around her has been. If she had been stronger when I first spoke of what had to be done with her infant, I truly believe she would have ended me somehow, to keep me from convincing the others of the necessity. She has never quite forgiven me, but *has* left active acrimony for the time when we discover whether or not I was right. If events fail to justify what I caused to be done, I'll have no need to worry about guilt plaguing me."

"Yes, that certainly sounds like our sister," Ashton said with wry agreement, then moved her gaze to me. "And must also account for why Terrilian there seemed so familiar to me right from the first. She looks only a little like Irin, but that irritating mental attitude is very nearly a carbon copy. Well, girl, don't you have anything to say? Not even a polite hello for your newly-found but loving aunt?"

Ashton seemed to be rather amused, and I could have sworn that what was causing her amusement was a memory of the fight we'd had the day before. I really did wish I could find things just as funny, but suddenly I was feeling worse than I had when I'd awakened in the complex. I'd believed for so long that I knew all about myself, but the skepticism I'd begun with had faded to a ghost of its former strength, what was left being too weak and transparent to support the weight of my growing doubt.

"Are you distressed to learn we all share the same blood, child?" Murdock asked, no sign of Ashton's amusement in him. "You've no need to acknowledge those blood ties, you know, most especially not where I'm concerned. You may continue to think of me with whatever enmity you wish, for as long as you wish, just as your mother has done. I've never needed to be protected from the strength of her mind, of course, but only because she does have rather tight control of herself when she feels the occasion warrants it. She's pledged herself to wait before taking vengeance on me, and can usually be counted on to keep her word."

"Something we'll have to find out about *you* before we can turn you loose again," Ashton said, taking Murdock's sobriety when she found he wouldn't share her amusement. "My brother may be guilty of everything he told you about and lots more besides, but none of us wants to lose him—or any of the others who were talked into agreeing with him. I don't know where you got the strength you have, girl, but it isn't something we can play around with. You'll have to convince us you can and will hold yourself in check, and then we'll be able to welcome you the way you should be welcomed."

"Welcomed," I repeated, discovering that the word had been said and echoed so much in my mind that it no longer had any meaning for me. I was staring down at the table we all sat around, groping for a solid reality I could throw my arms around to anchor me in the windstorm I'd been tossed to, but there was nothing in reach. I was like my mother, they'd said, my *mother*—not that strange woman I'd never felt any link to, but my own, real, actual, warm person.

"You don't have to worry about my self-control," I said, aiming the words in Ashton's direction without actually looking at her. "If there's one thing I've managed to learn, it's control over what I can do. As long as I stay shielded or curtained, I won't be a danger to anyone."

"Just a minute!" she came back, the words sharp as I began pushing myself away from the table and to my feet. "How do you know about shields, and what do you mean by 'curtained'? If you think what you said is enough to get us to release you, you really must be . . ."

"I'm already awake," I interrupted, telling it with a lot less scorn and satisfaction than I'd expected to, raising my eyes to look at her frowning astonishment. "I don't need anyone to turn me loose, because I've already figured out how to do it for myself. And now, if you don't mind, I'd like to be alone for a while. There's so much—!"

I couldn't go on in words with explaining how I felt, but I dropped my shield for an instant just to show I could—and to briefly share what I couldn't speak about. Ashton made a sound of strangled pain and put her hand out to me as she rose from her chair, her face suddenly full of tragedy, but that wasn't what I wanted or needed. Those who are used to being alone have to work things out that way—alone—before they can possibly discuss it with others. Even if the topic for discussion is no longer needing to be alone. I turned away from the two people who had told me so much, and went slowly back to my cabin.

# 11

"Stop bothering me," I said for what seemed like the ten-thousandth time, finding it impossible to keep the annoyance out of my voice. "If you're trying to find the limits of my self-control, be smart and take my word for the fact that you're almost there."

"It's very bad manners to be so high-handed with people who are only trying to help you," Ashton came back, her own annoyance reaching for the heights mine had already achieved. "The doctor said you're doing a lot better than he'd expected you to, but you should still be taking it easy, preferably in bed. Instead of that you've been wandering all over the transport, and now you insist on going down in the slip with Murdock. Why can't you wait the hour or two until we're home?"

"From what you people yourselves have told me, Murdock can't be trusted to be alone with Rimilians," I returned, looking down at the bland expressionlessness of the subject of my comments with very little friendliness. "If he *is* left alone with them, he seems to get this overwhelming urge to sell things—like me, for instance. I'm just going along to make sure it doesn't happen again."

"But my brother *can't* sell you again," Ashton pointed out with a purr while Murdock used one finger to rub gently at his lips, trying to keep the amusement off his face. "You belong to someone else now, so if there's any selling to be done Murdock won't have a part in it. What if we promise to let you know the instant any deals are concluded?"

"That's very funny," I said with no expression at all, staring unblinkingly at her grin. "And also please accept my congratulations. You've just put yourself one step away from being on my "flatten first" list, right along with the ones who run the complex on New Dawn. I didn't think I'd find anyone outside the Amalgamation government with enough talent to achieve that."

I turned away from them both with that, and went to sit in a chair by myself until the transfer slip was ready for boarding. Murdock had a couple of men hovering a short distance away who would take over Ashton's job of helping him for a while, but that didn't mean Ashton had no intentions of going along with him. The slip would be landing in the courtyard of the palace in the city of Vediaster, and Murdock had said something about considering it prudent if he had a woman with him.

The steward materialized in front of me with a tray holding cups of kimla, but a shake of my head continued him on his way to the others in the common area. I was no more in the mood for eating and drinking than I'd been for the last few days, and as was becoming usual, as soon as I stopped thinking of other things and talking to other people, my mind began working on its own. I not only had what I'd been told about my supposed beginnings to clamor at me, I was also starting to remember some of what the New Dawn people had conditioned me into forgetting.

I stirred in my chair as flashes of Vediaster began coming through again, a time that seemed to be composed of no more than various levels of unpleasantness and unhappiness. Faces flashed in front of me, women's faces with names like Farian and Leelan and Deegor and Relgon and Roodar and Siitil. Some of the faces carried the sense of being friends, other the feel of enemies, but even the moment of triumph I could almost reach had an overimage of some sort of pain and loss. I'd been in that city for no more than a short while, but not one of the memories coming back to me was a happy one.

And yet, I was supposed to be *Chama* of the place, the Rimilian word meaning something like "absolute ruler of all." That triumph I couldn't quite recall had won me the position, but it hadn't been something I'd been trying for because I wanted it. It seemed to have just happened, and I'd seen clearly enough that I had to go down there with Murdock to tell the people involved that I wasn't going to keep the position. I knew I owed them that much, and simply sending a note or word of my intentions wouldn't have been right, even if that's what I would have preferred doing.

I sighed as I moved in the chair again, but the sound had more than a little impatience and annoyance to it, two emotions I would have enjoyed being able to avoid for a while. The previous days had practically been made of impatience and annoyance, not to mention indecision and uncertainty and doubt and fear, all wrapped up into one big ball of upset. I didn't know if what Murdock had told me was true, and didn't even know if I wanted it to be true; all I could do was go to where they were taking me and try to find out about all of it. My emotions had taken quite a beating at first, as I worked at imagining what it would be like to meet people who were supposed to be my parents; would I want to know them, would I like the looks of them, would they like and want to know *me?* Those and a thousand other questions had kept me going around and around for hours, not one of them the sort I could answer but all still refusing to leave me alone. I'd finally fallen asleep in exhaustion, and when I'd awakened I'd found the strength to push away questions and flying emotions alike. When I got there I'd know the truth and could then make decisions, so all I had to do was wait until I got there.

All. I put my hand to my hair as I fought to keep the impatience and annoyance behind my curtain where it belonged, convinced that to use the word "all" with the concept of waiting was like using the phrase "a little" with the concept of dying a horrible death. I'd started out doing the waiting in my cabin, found that my thoughts were taking advantage of the solitude, and so had left the cabin to find something to occupy my attention. What I had found, unfortunately, had been Ashton and Murdock and the others, all hovering around and anxious to help make me feel better. When I refused to discuss their community they accepted my decision, but that was the only thing they were willing to be reasonable about. All of them including Ashton began fussing over me and refused to stop, and Murdock decided to explain why he really had no choice about dropping in on Vediaster for a very brief time.

"If you like, you may consider it a matter of honor," he'd said, looking up at me from his special chair with a faint smile on his face. "As I was the one who arranged your banding by Tammad, and inasmuch as I know precisely how worried he is about you, I have no other choice than to inform him of your safe recovery. He'll certainly want to see you, so I will most likely bring him back here to . . ."

"No," I'd interrupted at once, for some reason feeling that the last place I wanted to see the object of Murdock's concern was on a transport. "I tell you I don't know the man, and don't want to know him. From what you've said he could decide to take me away from you again, just as he did once before, and in order to stop him I'd probably have to hurt him. Is that what you want? To see him hurt because of *your* concept of honor?"

"Terrilian, child, you mustn't hurt him," Murdock had said, an odd look in his cold gray eyes, an even stranger feel to the tenor of his thoughts. "I truly believed Tammad would be the first thing you remembered, knowing as I do what your own feelings for him are. If you cause him harm, you'll likely never forgive yourself. Hasn't there been enough pain in this episode for everyone involved? His love for you is quickly becoming legend on Rimilia, and you need only allow him enough time to remind you of your own love for *him.* Surely such a small thing . . ."

I'd turned around and walked away from Murdock at that point, unwilling to listen to any more of his diplomatic attempts at matchmaking. Did he think I was an idiot who didn't realize that if I *was* in love with someone, he would certainly be the first thing I remembered? All I could feel was the way my mind held the offered folder marked "Tammad" at arm's length, as though it had no interest in letting it come nearer, and that was good enough for me. All I wanted to know about right then was the community Murdock said was mine as well as his and Ashton's, and I didn't need some love-struck barbarian trying to distract me.

"If you're going with us, now's the time," Ashton's voice came abruptly, bringing me back from the recent past. "The transfer slip is ready to go, and so are the rest of us. And if you don't take it really easy down there, the doctor'll have a fit. A couple of those bloody welts on your back haven't closed all the way, and if you rip them open he'll do the same to Murdock's throat and mine for letting you go down with us. I don't want you taking a stroll anywhere unless I'm with you, and that's an order."

"Ashton, try to remember you're supposed to be my aunt, not my mother," I came back, barely glancing at her as I got to my feet. "If you're suffering from role confusion, you'll be best off staying away from me for a while. Hanging around will only make it worse."

"Once we get home, you'll learn the difference between hanging around and being in charge, honey," she answered with a grin, having no trouble keeping herself from feeling insulted. "And remind me to have a word with you about eating when we're back aboard. The doctor isn't happy about your trim little figure, and I got him to let me talk to you before he loses his patience, ties you down and starts stuffing your face with edibles. I've known that mild little man for years, and never realized before that he had such a violent side to his nature."

"That mild little man is almost as much of a pain in the neck as you are," I said, following behind Murdock and his assistants at the slow pace necessary to keep from running them down. "I'm beginning to remember how I used my ability to get rid of someone else who was a pain in the neck once, and if he doesn't leave me alone he's going to find out all about it—first hand."

"It isn't his job to leave you alone," Ashton returned, but with a distracted tone to her voice. "It's his job to pester the life out of you until you're so desperate you get better just to get rid of him. Terrilian, once we're home we're going to have to sit down with a couple of other people, and talk about your ability and how you've been learning to use it. That curtain trick, for instance, and how you developed the strength you have. We need to know whatever you can tell us, especially with the attack against New Dawn so near. That won't ruin things for you as far as getting to know the community goes, will it?''

I turned my head to see the way she was looking at me, her mind involved with three or four different lines of thought, but her surface concern supporting only the question she'd asked. She had meant the question seriously no matter how much amusement she got out of bothering me about other things, and the headshake I gave for an answer brought her more satisfaction than it did me. Whether anything in particular would have to ruin my experience with the community—aside from just being there—was a topic I didn't care to consider right then, which meant I paid a lot of attention to getting aboard the transfer slip.

The trip down to Rimilia's surface in general and Vediaster in particular didn't seem to take very long, but only because I'd lost the battle against not thinking about the community. I didn't slip so far that I let my mind tangle with specific worries, but that still meant I looked up to find that everyone was getting ready to leave our transportation. Ashton was talking to Murdock as he struggled to his feet, telling him something that her mind said wasn't very important, and it was all I could do to keep from insisting that they hurry. I refused to guess about what was waiting for me in the place they called the community, but I was almost painfully anxious to get there and find out what it would be.

I could feel a large number of minds waiting outside even before the slip ramp opened and extended; disembarking brought sight of them all, as well as of the newcomers who were streaming up in smaller and larger bunches to see what was going on. It was a warm, pleasant, sunny day on that planet, the air smelling fresh and clean, but the level of astonishment and surprise and curiosity coming out of the largely female welcoming committee made me glad my curtain was firmly in place. Quite a few of them had active minds, and I could tell from their reactions that they were more or less expecting us. Apparently they'd known we were coming, but hadn't known *how* we'd be coming.

"Terril, how pleased we are that you have been returned to us unharmed," one of the women called up, her grin matching the true happiness I could feel in her mind. She was a big woman, blond and blue-eyed the way most of them were, wearing sandals, trousers and a shirt as well as a sword. My still-incomplete memories stirred at sight of her, and then I was smiling and raising a hand to a friend named Leelan.

"You all must forgive Terril if she seems somewhat different," Ashton called out in Rimilian, the language Leelan had used, her eyes moving from one side of the crowd to the other. "Those who took her also took her memories of her time on this world, memories which are only now beginning to return for her use. She will come to recall each and every one of you, only now such a thing must not be expected of her."

A dissatisfied mutter moved through the group of women, a sound to match the growl of anger in their minds, but it wasn't Ashton they were angry with. My—aunt—stood a little ahead of me to my right on the ramp, which put her head level a bit below mine, and when her face turned to the left I could see she was squinting against the late-morning sun the way I was. Her narrowed eyes were checking what her scanning mind brought to her, and when she also found that the anger wasn't for her, she smiled faintly.

"You need not concern yourselves that those who committed so vile an act will go unpunished," she called out again, raising her voice to make it carry over the mutter. "We who are blood-kin to Terril will see to her rightful vengeance upon those who are our enemies as well as hers, and may well call upon you here to assist us. Would you be willing to give us such assistance?"

A double shout of avid agreement rose up to us from voices and minds alike, and either one would have been sufficient to let us know exactly how those women felt. Both together were more commitment than a blood oath would have been, and the men helping Murdock grinned as they began moving down the ramp again. Ashton also grinned as she glanced to me before following the others, and I couldn't help wondering why they were all so pleased. They seemed to have plans that included the armed women of Vediaster, plans that hadn't been mentioned to me.

The crowd moved obligingly back or to either side to give us room to leave the ramp, and then Leelan led one segment of it back to surround Ashton and me. The big blond woman had spent most of her time looking at me, but once she was close enough her gaze went to Ashton.

"I do not doubt that this *wenda* is blood-kin to you, Terril," she said, examining Ashton in a very direct way. "Her mind is of a strength which much resembles yours, and would have been of great assistance to us in our attack against Farian. For what reason did you not make mention of her when we all spoke of those who might be of aid to us in the attack?"

"She failed to speak of me for the reason that she then had no knowledge of me," Ashton said without hesitation, smiling faintly at the *w'wenda* who looked down at her. "It was only when she freed herself from capture that we met, no more than days ago."

"And was it then that you also assumed the burden of giving response to those queries put to *her?*" Leelan asked, her tone dry as the fingers of her left hand toyed with her sword hilt. "Our *Chama* has no need of others to speak for her, nor will such a thing be allowed the while breath remains in my body. Terril, I would know how you truly fare, and would also know if you desire to be freed of the company of this one."

"Such a freeing would indeed be pleasant, Leelan, and yet you must not be disturbed over the matter," I said, the annoyance I'd been feeling disappearing behind amusement at Ashton's sudden annoyance. "I fare as well as I might the while true memory eludes me, and this *wenda* who names herself kin to me has taken it upon herself to guard my every doing. Although I dislike such guarding through having no true need of it, it must yet be admitted that her intentions are for good rather than ill."

"No true need of it," Ashton echoed with a snort while

Leelan and some of the others looked relieved, the mutter putting her fists to her hips. "Our healer foams at the mouth the while she prances all about as she wills, doing rather than resting from her ordeal, and she dares to speak blithely of having no true need of guarding. In truth, what she has the greatest need of is being sat upon. A pity the strength of her mind disallows such a thing."

"And yet there is one greatly eager to see her who has no fear of the strength of her mind," Leelan said, laughing the way too many of the other women were doing over what Ashton had said. "Dallan took himself off to inform him of your arrival even as I hurried here, Terril, therefore shall they soon be with us."

"Dallan?" I said, looking at the big woman as I tried to fight through the mists to a recognition of the name, getting a teasing sense of familiarity and then nothing but blankness. "Am I acquainted with this Dallan? And who is the other who will accompany him?"

"Dallan is my *memabrak* and *drin* of Gerleth, Terril, and you and he are *helid*," Leelan answered, the laughter gone as she glanced in upset to Ashton. "I had not realized to how great an extent— The other, of course, is Tammad, he who is *your memabrak*. Surely you recall the one who occupied your thoughts to the exclusion of all other things?"

"Him again," I muttered in Centran, beginning to be really annoyed. You can get very tired of hearing people tell you how much you care about somebody, but tired doesn't cover it when you can't even remember what the object of your undying love looks like. I was a lot more interested in trying to remember who Dallan was, Leelan's *mamabrak*, the one who had banded her. *Helid* was a very close, nonsexual relationship between two otherwise unrelated people, and I was curious about the man I was supposed to have that sort of relationship with.

"Terril seems unable to recall Tammad, Leelan," Ashton put in when I didn't add to my muttering, her mind spreading out to soothe the agitation of just about everyone in hearing. "We believe that she clung to the memory of him so tightly that our enemies had a great deal of difficulty in taking it, therefore was it more thoroughly erased than other matters. She will surely recover that memory along with the others, and yet will it just as surely find its own time in coming."

"Unfortunately it will likely not be soon enough to spare us the need to calm the fury of a *l'lenda*," another of the women in the crowd said with a sigh, an older woman who wasn't wearing a sword. Relgon, I remembered her name was, and her twin sister was Deegor, a *w'wenda.* Relgon wasn't a woman warrior, but her mind was stronger than Deegor's. "To say it was difficult bearing his worry, is to say one was unable to perceive his mind; when he discovers that his beloved is no longer even familiar with the sound of his name, his need to spill the blood of those responsible will surely take the senses from all in the city with the power."

"His strength is that great?" Ashton asked, her surprise evident. "We were told his mind was discovered to be awakened, yet no mention was made of such . . ."

She broke off in the middle of what she was saying to watch the arrival of more Rimilians, this time an all-male group. The men were a good deal larger than the women, broad-shouldered and wide-chested with body cloths called *haddinn* wrapped around them, barefoot but with swordbelts closed tightly around each set of hips. They all seemed to be moving at a good pace, but there was one out in front leading the pack, larger than most of the others and striding faster than they were. The crowd of women melted away from the path of that relatively calm stampede, which meant there were suddenly no obstructions blocking off sight of me.

The giant of a man seemed to pause between steps as his head came up, the expression on his face more a matter of the relief of ended pain than something to be called a smile. His mind surged powerfully behind a cloud of very thick calm, joyous elation dominating what I could make out through the whirling, and then he was moving forward again, directly toward me. His arms began to rise from his sides as he walked, thickly muscled arms that undoubtedly had no trouble swinging that great bar of a sword which hung at his side, and all of a sudden I noticed something very important about him.

He was blond and blue-eyed, just like Kel-Ten, and a large part of his mind was filled with the same sense of—possession—the First Prime had felt.

I'd had to accept the attitude in the complex, there had been no choice about accepting it, but I was no longer *in* the complex and was no longer turned off. He was still ten or fifteen feet away when I straightened where I stood and let the curtain fall from my mind.

"Terrilian, don't, he's not going to hurt you!" Ashton hissed fast from my right, her hand wrapping itself tightly around my arm.

"Terril, no, that is Tammad there before you!" Leelan blurted from my left, her thoughts completely taken aback.

"Terril, child, there is no battle before you that requires such a gathering of power!" Relgon said hurriedly, and it came to me that her face had gone as pale as those of a number of the women around us. They all had active minds, those women, with Leelan being an odd partial exception, and were therefore all aware of the banishing of my curtain.

The man who had been striding so quickly toward me also had an active mind, and what I'd done had stopped him a second time, bewilderment and confusion pushing away everything else he'd been feeling. There was also something of pain inside him, but the heavy calm he was holding to with both fists didn't let him experience much of it. His face was completely expressionless as he began walking toward me again, this time a good deal more slowly, and when Leelan moved out to stop him about five feet away he seemed only partially aware of her.

"Tammad, those who stole her from us also stole her memories," the big woman told him with a lot of compassion, her hand going to his arm. "She has not given over her love for you, merely has she forgotten it for a time. Those who accompany her say the forgetfulness is not forever, therefore is she certain to come to know you again. Do you hear the words I speak?"

He *did* hear her, that I could tell from the movement of his thoughts, but those very blue eyes hadn't moved an inch from me since the time they'd first found me. I felt as though he were drinking me in, using me the way a man dying of thirst would use a large jug of water, and his thoughts had begun taking on a definite tinge of stubbornness. He'd heard everything said to him, all right, but there wasn't any way on that world he was about to accept it.

"Tammad, my friend, I would have preferred being able to prepare you for this," Murdock said in Centran, materializing out of the crowd to the right, his two helpers trailing behind him. "Is there somewhere we may go to speak privately?"

"As the tongue you speak is understood by very few here, you have already achieved what privacy you desire," the big Rimilian answered, also in Centran, making no attempt to look at the man he addressed. "What words does the Murdock McKenzie imagine would give preparation for so outrageous a doing as *this?*"

"My friend, we none of us knew this would happen," Murdock said in a calm his mind wasn't sharing, almost as though he could feel the growing anger in the other man. "She was taken by those who are enemies to us all, but their flagrant disregard of the honorable commitment made you will now be their downfall. What I wish to speak to you about is the need for patience on your part, obviously for the sake of the woman. She was not treated well by those who took her, and to now expect her to accept a man who is a stranger to her . . ."

"They gave her harm?" the big man growled, his gaze turned to ice as his mind flared crimson with fury and rage, finally moving his head to look at Murdock. Most of those around us flinched at the level of projection he was managing, Ashton drawing her breath in sharply due to the unexpectedness of what she felt, and I quietly retrieved my curtain. The man seemed to be totally untrained but with more raw power than could easily be held off, and protecting myself with the curtain wasn't like blocking everything out with a shield. I could still drop the curtain or even work through it if I had to, something I wasn't convinced I would *not* have to do.

"In what manner did these *mondarayse* give her harm?" the man demanded of Murdock, his big hands fists at his sides, his body held still through sheer will power. "I shall first assure myself that she returns to full health, and then you and I will speak of where I might find those who have beseeched their own deaths. When once my *l'lendaa* and I have done with them, they will no longer even find it possible to look upon the *wendaa* of others."

"You must forgive me, my friend, if I say taking their lives and positions from them is a privilege first due me and mine," Murdock answered, his coldly courteous reply probably the only thing that could have penetrated the rage and fury coming at him. "Far too many have suffered the fate so narrowly escaped by Terrilian, and even more has been done to those who are *ours*. You're certainly welcome to join us if you wish, but you may not take the pleasure for yourself alone. When we leave here, we will rejoin those waiting for us and complete the plans for attack which have already been begun."

Murdock stared up at the giant of a man, his cold gray eyes directly on him, his twisted body in no way flinching back from the promise of violence that was looming over him. The Rimilian could have exploded in anger and killed him, but it wasn't possible to doubt that anything less would affect or move him, not on the subject they had just been discussing. Despite the emotions screaming around inside him the big warrior had no difficulty understanding and accepting that, and after firmly pushing his impatience to one side he nodded his head.

"Then I shall accompany you," he stated, also leaving no doubt that anything would change his mind. "I shall learn from my woman which of them was most responsible for giving her harm, and that one will be mine alone. Is it agreed?"

"With the greatest of pleasure," Murdock assured him, that faint, cold smile reappearing on his face even as he leaned more heavily on his cane. "Since our business here is now taken care of, we can . . ."

"But our business here *isn't* taken care of," I interrupted, knowing that Murdock was about to return to the transfer slip—with his very good friend. "Or, at least *my* business here isn't taken care of. I need to speak to Leelan and the others for a while, and it isn't something that can be put off. Are you going to wait for me, or do I have to make other arrangements to get to my final destination?"

"There aren't any other arrangements you can make," Ashton said in annoyance, matching her brother's response to what I'd said, but managing to get the words out first. "Terrilian, you know how much of a hurry we're in, so why can't your business wait a little while? Now that these *w'wendaa* of Vediaster will be joining us in the attack, we'll be seeing them again very shortly. You can wait until . . . ."

"That's something else that needs to be discussed," I cut in again, glad the point had been brought up. "You maneuvered the *w'wendaa* into wanting to join you, and I expect to hear some damned good reasons as to why it was done. I won't be their *Chama* for very much longer, but that doesn't mean I'll let them be taken advantage of. Do you want to tag along while I hold my discussion with them, or do you want to wait in the slip or the transport?"

"I think you know I'll be right there with you, and there won't be any 'tagging along' to it," Ashton answered, her expression letting me know how much more annoyed she was in case I missed it in her mind. "If whatever you have to say to those people won't wait, then you'll take care of it now, but you'll do it as fast as possible and you'll do it the easy way."

Then, before I could say anything else, she turned to a patiently waiting Leelan.

"Please excuse the rudeness of our having spoken so long in another tongue," she began, undoubtedly sensing how some of the women were holding off feelings of insult. "I have just been informed by Terril that she wishes to speak with you and your sisters, and have in turn informed her that I will accompany you all so that she may be—guarded. May I ask that a place of comfort be chosen for the discussion, so that my task need not be unduly difficult to accomplish?"

Leelan and most of the others chuckled at the way Ashton had invited herself along, their previous insult forgotten behind the satisfaction of knowing their *Chama* was being properly looked after. I didn't consider it nearly as amusing, but before anyone could get to either agreement or argument, an altogether different precinct was heard from.

"From what does my *wenda* need to be guarded?" a voice asked, one that wanted to be more of a growl and would have preferred demanding to asking, but was trying not to take its mad out on those who weren't the cause of it. "I see naught here to menace her, however, should I be mistaken in my beliefs, it will be this *l'lenda* who guards her."

"Be at ease, *l'lenda,* I merely spoke in jest," Ashton said at once, looking up soberly at the very large man who stood so close to her. "In the midst of friends, Terril has need to be guarded only from herself. Our healer wishes her to refrain from exerting herself, therefore have I made it my task to accompany her and see the matter done properly. These *w'wendaa* are already aware of this, and for that reason are undisturbed."

"Yes, the woman is indeed prone to—overlooking the wishes of healers," the big Rimilian answered, not quite feeling annoyed as he glanced at me. "I have only recently learned of her doings here in Vediaster, and will discuss them with her when her memories have completely returned. For now I shall merely accompany her and, as I have said, see to what guarding she requires."

"Your assistance would be most welcome," Ashton said with a grin, glancing at me while enjoying a private joke. "In point of fact if you wish it, *I* shall be most pleased to assist *you,* rather than the other way about. I have learned that Rimilian *l'lendaa* are possessed of a certain—talent—when dealing with their *wendaa*, a talent those raised elsewhere, male and female alike, appear to lack. As Terril has been banded as yours . . ."

"Enough," I said in what was very close to a growl of my own, up to *here* with people who were deeply concerned about me—for reasons of their own. "I belong to none save myself, and grow weary of having strangers and near-strangers speak of what I shall be made to do. What I *shall* do is confer with those I came to speak with, which requires no further discussion on the part of others with reference to me. Have I made my wishes sufficiently clear?"

"Indeed, *Chama*," more than one of the women around me muttered at once, while Leelan and Ashton exchanged highly significant glances. What the glances were supposed to signify I couldn't quite tell, but they were definitely highly significant. The big *w'wenda* and my supposed aunt seemed to be—waiting uncomfortably for the other shoe to drop, is the closest I can come to defining their emotions, not exactly the most technical definition I've ever given, but still more than fitting. They were more wary than nervous, and I didn't understand why they seemed to bracc themselves when the Rimilian Tammad stirred where he stood.

"*Wenda*, those who speak of seeing to your well-being do so because of their love for you," he said, for all the world as though he were gently lecturing a small child, those blue eyes back to memorizing every inch of me. "Though I find it—difficult to accept that you now see me as no more than a stranger, under no circumstances shall I attempt to comport myself as though you were similarly unknown. You are my *hama sadendra*, my most beloved *memabra*, and it pains me to see how thin you have grown beneath that badly chosen item of supposed clothing. You are *my* belonging, and I care little for the state in which others have kept you."

"That's too bad about you," I said in Centran, deciding it might be best to settle things with him then and there. "Whatever—state—I'm in right now is due to the keeping of no one other than myself, and that's the way it's going to stay. Not only don't I belong to you, I don't know you and don't want to know you. I'm sorry if you can't see it the same, but there's nothing either of us can do about it. As far as I'm concerned you *are* a stranger, and I've had too much done to me lately by strangers to want any more. If you try forcing the issue I'll defend myself, and please believe me when I say you won't enjoy that sort of attention from me. Do us both a favor and go find someone else to be your belonging. I'm simply not interested."

I tried to turn away from him to Leelan with that, having found it harder to say the words than I'd thought I would, but his hand came to my arm to keep me from turning. The touch was unbelievably gentle, almost completely unrelated to the knife-sharp pain his mind was trying to both control and ignore, and the oddest look appeared in his eyes.

"You have learned well the proper response to challenge from strangers, *hama*," he said, and damned if he didn't somehow sound—proud. "What remains, however, is for you to learn the sight of one who is no stranger. That, too, will come in its proper time."

His hand moved from my arm to my cheek, the second touch as gentle as the first, and then he turned away to move through the crowd toward where Murdock waited a short distance away, seated in the folding chair one of his assistants had brought along. I thought it probable he was going to tell Murdock he'd changed his mind about coming with us, and the relief I felt over that let me turn back to Leelan with something of a smile. Hurting the man hadn't been pleasant, but at least he would no longer be around to make me do it again.

With all the extraneous nonsense taken care of, the women were finally able to lead me inside the palace to a room where we could talk. On the way inside we passed the group of men who had more or less come along with the one called Tammad, and I was pleasantly surprised to find that I remembered and recognized a number of the faces. Seeing him brought back memory of Dallan, Leelan's *memabrak* and the man with whom I was *helid*, but remembering him also told me I'd be smart to just raise a hand in greeting, smile warmly, and keep on going. The expression on his face said he wanted to talk to me, but I had no time and even less desire to be lectured. I didn't know what the subject of the lecture would be, but I could remember how good Dallan was at never having trouble finding *something*.

The room in the palace chosen for our discussion was large, of white stone draped with gold, white fur carpeting and golden cushions. It had to be one of the rooms meant for the *Chama*'s use, and the arrival of servants with food trays and wine came as no great surprise. The women who had come with me—including Deegor's belated arrival—were the ones who had organized the attack against the palace, and once everyone had tasted the food and drink we got down to cases. I explained that I had come to tell them I could no longer be their *Chama*, and then sat back with the delicious fried meat strips I'd helped myself to and let them get the arguing out of their systems.

They tried every argument they'd used on me the last time we'd discussed the point and then added a few wrinkles, but it all came down to my wanting to give up the honor, and their unwillingness to let me. It went around and around with everyone having their say, Ashton silent but listening carefully from her place beside me, and finally I held up a hand.

"I had thought, from the last time we spoke, that all of you had agreed to understand and comply with the needs which move me," I said, looking around at them. "Your need was for the presence and assistance of one who would find it possible to best Farian, mine was to be gone on my way once that task was seen to. As your needs have been met, I now ask that mine be considered. Am I to be allowed the freedom I yearn for, or am I to be kept chained by imposed demands of duty and responsibility?"

The minds all around me suddenly filled with a lot of upset, the roiling emotions pointed up even more by the complete silence in the room. They all wanted to tell me that I wasn't looking at it right, that being *chama* was a very high, important position and not slavery, but they all knew well enough that freedom and slavery were personal outlooks not seen the same by everyone involved. That I'd helped them when they needed it couldn't be denied; I'd left it to them to say whether or not they would do the same for me.

"Terril, we are all aware of your desire to be elsewhere, and know as well that the desire is no reflection on those of us here or our city," Relgon said slowly after a moment, trying to force some order out of the chaos of her thoughts. "Although it may seem that we have failed to consider your wishes, you must know that we have attempted to find one who may be *Chama* in your place. A part of our difficulty lies in the fact that you, yourself, have no issue, Farian had none, and no female other than Leelan is about as the issue of she who was *Chama* before Farian. Those *l'lendaa* who are brothers to Leelan were driven from Vediaster by Farian, and therefore are not present to band one with the power and legitimatize the seat she takes."

"Even were it possible to find one of sufficient power to be banded," Deegor put in, an exact duplicate of Relgon except for the sword she wore. "Our laws demand that our *Chama* be the one who is possessed of the greatest power, and none we have encountered before or since our first meeting with *you,* Terril, has shown the strength you are capable of. Were we to choose one of lesser strength, our laws would be no more than mockery, and we find ourselves unable to betray our country in such a manner. Perhaps you will find it necessary to leave us with our dilemma, and should that be so we will surely understand. We will continue to lack a solution, yet will we be filled with understanding."

"Filled with understanding," I muttered under my breath, seeing Deegor's calm expression mirrored on more faces than just her sister's. I'd tried making them feel guilty for insisting that I keep the job of *Chama*, and it had worked until Deegor's counterattack. None of them would blame me if I simply picked up and walked out, but that wouldn't solve the problem I'd helped create and was partially responsible for. Whoever they chose would *not* have the strongest mind possible, not as long as I remained among the living, and no matter how many oaths I swore about never coming back, the possibility remained that some day I might. At that point their chosen *Chama* would be nothing more than a sham, sitting her throne only because *I* allowed it by not challenging her. No one could be an effective ruler under circumstances like those, not unless—not unless—

"I believe I have it!" I said, sitting up so suddenly among the cushions that I nearly spilled the golden wine filling the goblet I held. "You here must have a *Chama* with the strongest mind, and yet I must be off and about other doings. How speak your laws upon the point of one who represents an absent *Chama*, one appointed by the *Chama* to rule in her name?"

Everyone began speaking at once, then, some insisting there was no law like that, some saying there *couldn't* be such a law, and some cautiously suggesting there might be a tiny bit of merit to the suggestion. It was impossible separating one voice or mind from the next, and then Deegor held up her arm for silence. She needed Relgon's help to bring everyone down from the ceiling noisewise, but after a minute or two she was able to get to what she wanted to say.

"It brings me surprise that most here have no memory of what is commonly done when the *Chama* travels," the *w'wenda* said, looking around at her countrywomen. "Perhaps Relgon and I, having attained greater age than many of you, are more familiar with such things. When Kirdil, mother of Leelan, chose to travel to neighboring countries, there was ever one appointed by her to sit the throne and speak with her voice. Should such a doing suit our *Chama* Terril, who here has the power to deny her?"

"Sooner should we put the query as to who might have the power to sit for her," came the sour answer supplied by Siitil, a *w'wenda* of Leelan's age who tended to be sour even when she was reasonably happy. "The strongest among us is Relgon, and yet has Relgon ever maintained that she will only advise and never rule. Her delight that the place of *Chama* would not be hers was clearly unfeigned, therefore do we gallop our *seetarr* and yet remain where we began."

"It would scarcely be proper for one such as I to accept any such position," Relgon said as most of the eyes in the room came to rest on her, her sigh doing nothing to cover the unyielding determination in her mind. "Those of my family who have come before have ever been advisors, a position of much pride and responsibility; never were we ones to *be* advised. To usurp a positon neither desired nor earned—to fall before the temptation of the weak and covet a place most properly belonging to others—to consider the thing even for a short while— No, my friends, such a doing is beyond me. No more may I do than advise one who sits the place *rightfully.*''

Siitil held her hands up in a gesture showing she wasn't surprised and a couple of the women began trying to argue with Relgon, but those of us who could feel her mind knew arguing would never move the older woman. It was almost a matter of reverse snobbery, with Relgon feeling, in effect, that to accept a higher position would be lowering herself, and on top of that her attitude was a family tradition. She would advise any legitimate ruler, but the only candidate for *that* spot was—

''And what of you, Leelan?'' I said, remembering well enough how I'd assumed she would take the throne after the battle was won, and how surprised I'd been that no one, including her, considered her qualified. ''As it was you who failed to recall the need to inform me of the great honor awaiting my success in besting Farian, perhaps you will now make amends by becoming my surrogate. As your mother sat the place of *Chama* before Farian, who would there be to say you had not the right?''

''Terril, Leelan has not the *power,*'' Deegor said gently but firmly as Leelan looked down at the goblet in her hands, the minds of everyone else agreeing. ''She, of course, would be ideal, and yet does she lack that which even a surrogate must have. To rule, even in the name of another, requires the presence and use of the power.''

Again most of them began talking at once, all of it suggestions as to who might be strong enough—and trustworthy enough—to be my surrogate, the sudden noise mounting too high for me to have the chance to say that Leelan *did* have the power. Even as I reexamined her embarrassed and self-accusing mind I could see how much power she had, and wondered as I had before why she didn't use more than a small fraction of it. She was able to feel power or the lack of it in the minds around her, but as far as using her own was concerned . . .

My mind-tool of calm control slid into place as my inner sight moved closer and closer to Leelan, the rest of me floating along with no more than faint curiosity to be felt. Most of me was so relaxed I was almost asleep, but one small crew of tiny, invisible workers was briskly busy and getting on with the job in hand in a businesslike way. The job in hand was Leelan's mind, a mind that had somehow seemed strange without my knowing why, and the crew was busy checking into the matter. Her mind was healthy and strong, well adjusted to life in general and her own life in particular, no hidden hang-ups keeping her from doing something she could but didn't believe she could. My inner sight went closer and closer to her, my mind blending and meshing with hers, the two flowing together, breathing together, feeling together—

And then we reached the block, the small, badly constructed block that only did part of its job, crude workmanship that also felt as though it was supposed to be temporary. I suddenly had a very strong suspicion as to what it might be, but understanding it wasn't the important part, removing it was. Leelan had been living with it so long it had almost become a part of her, and I couldn't simply dissolve it without bracing her, or the sudden shock could damage her mind. I brought more of my strength into her mind, then slowly and carefully withdrew to leave her on her own.

I had to blink a couple of times before I saw her face instead of her mind, and then it was another moment before what I was seeing made sense. Leelan sat bolt upright beside the cushion she'd been leaning on, her legs folded stiffly in front of her, an amazed look on her face, wine spilling to the carpet fur past her knee due to the slack hold she had on her goblet. The world had suddenly widened and brightened for her, and it would take a short while before she got used to it.

It was only a matter of seconds before someone noticed Leelan and what she was doing, and then Relgon, Deegor and Siitil, the three other active minds in the group, also noticed her inner difference. There was a small riot as everyone left their places to crowd around the happily grinning *w'wenda* to throw questions at her, or perhaps I should say almost everyone. The sole exception stirred where she sat to my right, as though coming out of a daze, and then her hand touched my shoulder.

"How in hell did you *do* that?" Ashton demanded in

as low a voice as the noise in the room permitted, sounding faintly outraged. "And for that matter, *what* did you do? From where I was sitting it looked like you just—touched her—but touching shouldn't have— What in hell happened?"

"She was blocked," I answered, stretching up straighter where I sat and taking a deep breath as my mind-tool faded back out of control. "All I did was dissolve the block to let her natural ability come through. Building one in Kel-Ten's mind was harder, but in his case I didn't have to brace him."

"You dissolved a block I couldn't even detect," Ashton said, this time speaking flatly and looking at me in an odd way, her hand leaving my shoulder. "Every now and then someone in the community is found to have the ability for such fine inner sight, but that's usually all they can do. I've never heard of a Prime being able to—"

She broke off with the odd look still peering out of her eyes, then shook her head as though to chase it away. When her gaze came back to me it was the faintly impatient, faintly irritated one I was used to, and she raised her hand in a banishing gesture.

"That isn't something to be discussed here, only between the two of us," she said, not far from giving the impression *I* was the one who had brought the subject up and was insisting on talking about it. "Let's just add it to the list for when we get home. But to get back to Leelan, *how* could she have been blocked? Did some enemy of her family decide to try keeping her from becoming *Chama* after her mother?"

"It's possible, but I doubt it," I said, fleetingly wondering how well that list of my abilities would go over with the fine folk back "home." I was supposed to be one of them, but people have been known to turn against an odd bird in the nest even if the bird grew up with them. Which I hadn't.

"My guess is that Leelan was the victim of an unintentional accident," I said, glad that my curtain was still firmly over my mind. "If you stop to think about how powerful her mother had to be to qualify for the place of *Chama*, and then picture a woman trying to concentrate on something important while her baby is broadcasting the way talented babies do— She probably never even noticed wishing there was something she could do to stop the noise just for a *little* while.''

''You mean you think her mother constructed the block without even knowing she was doing it?'' Ashton asked with her brow wrinkled, and then she was slowly nodding her head. ''Something like that would never have occurred to me, but I'll bet you're right. She blocked little Leelan's output to give herself a break, having no idea she was doing it so she couldn't *undo* it. It looks like those who keep insisting we bring all actives into the community as soon as possible are right. If Leelan's mother had been a trained Prime she could have shielded, and then the accident would never have happened.''

I didn't quite know what to say to that, but it turned out to be a good thing I wasn't well prepared to ask Ashton all sorts of carefully calculated questions. The women in the room with us had finally figured out that *I* was the one who had freed Leelan's mind, and their wild delight suddenly came spilling over onto me. Everyone seemed to be laughing and shouting words which were totally incomprehensible, and then Leelan was crouching beside me, her hand reaching for my shoulder.

''Indeed are you one whose like I have never before seen, Terril,'' she said, looking as though she were in the midst of a dream she intended enjoying to the full before waking up. ''Each time you seek to chastise me for having cozened you, you give me more than ever before was mine. It occurs to me I would be wise to anger you again, merely to discover what new marvel you would gift me with.''

''There is a limit to the marvels even *I* am able to produce, Leelan,'' I answered, laughing along with everyone else at what she'd said, feeling how gently but firmly her fingers tightened in thanks. ''Best you concern yourself with learning the use of that which you now possess in full, and leave the angering of me to others. After having spent the time I did among my enemies, giving me anger may well bring gifts few would be eager to have. And now that my surrogate is chosen and accepted, I must be on my way."

Protests and disappointment came from everyone as I got to my feet before finishing the golden wine in my goblet, but none of them was seriously thinking about trying to stop me. They hadn't missed the fact that I'd given Leelan nothing in the way of orders or instructions about ruling, knowing as well as I that if *she* didn't do it right, no one would. They told me sternly that I had to come back to visit the country that was mine on an often, regular basis; I assured them solemnly that if I had any choice in the matter I would do exactly that, and then Leelan made her first decision as my stand-in.

"We cannot allow our *Chama* to walk about in torn outlander clothing as though she had naught save that to wear," she announced, frowning at the light brown uniform which *was* the only thing I had to wear. "Before you leave us, Terril, you must dress as befits your station, else shall those who see you pity our country for being bereft of all *dinga*. Would you have others think of us in such a way?"

All those pairs of eyes in the room were suddenly on me, so I sighed and gave in without an argument. If I didn't want everyone to think Vediaster was penniless, which they would if they saw me, I had to go along with the suggestion. It was hardly an unreasonable request, and wasn't likely to take too long in the seeing to.

Which it didn't. It was only a matter of minutes before I was being led into the *Chama*'s rooms, and seeing it told me immediately what had bothered me so about Kel-Ten's apartment. The large chamber was decorated heavily in gold, just like the First Prime's surroundings, and there was something about the place that depressed me. I couldn't quite remember what the source of the depression was, but that didn't really matter. In another few minutes I would be out of there, and that would take care of the problem.

I was brought an outfit of trousers and shirt and sandals in gold and green, and while I got into it a couple of female servants packed four or five spare outfits—as well as the old stuff I got out of—into leather pouches to take with me. It felt odd having a wardrobe like that, one that belonged to no one but me, one that had been earned through efforts of *mine*. Back on Central I had a much more extensive wardrobe, supposedly earned by my being a Prime, but for some reason it wasn't the same. I tucked the soft green shirt into the tight, clingy, gold cloth trousers, and felt a satisfaction unlike anything I had experienced when dressing on Central.

"Now do you appear much more presentable," Leelan said as she stopped beside me, having come back after inspecting what the servants had packed. "Should your *memabrak* find this clothing less than satisfactory, however, you must gently recall to him that this is the custom of those of Vadiaster. As you are now ours as well as his, he must strive for understanding and acceptance."

"Leelan, I have no *memabrak*," I said, finding a large amount of instant annoyance at the thought that someone else would try telling me what I could and couldn't wear. I'd had enough of that at the complex to last a lifetime, and wouldn't have let it happen again even if I had to get nasty. "You were unable to comprehend a good deal of my conversation with that *l'lenda*, I know, therefore allow me to assure you that he was clearly told of my lack of interest in him. His departure was a considerable relief to me, and it seems highly unlikely that he will approach me ever again."

"Ah, Terril, to be bereft of one's memory is a greater loss than I had ever thought it," she said with a sigh, her blue eyes looking down at me with compassion. "The *l'lenda* Tammad is indeed your *memabrak*, and will not so easily give over what is his. This I tell you as one sister to another, so that upset will not claim you when you discover yourself mistaken. In time shall you recall him and the love that was between you, and then . . ."

"And then shall I likely be too advanced in age to be overly concerned," I finished for her, looking around to see that there was nothing left to do that would keep me there. "You have my thanks for the interest you show on my behalf, sister, and may be certain that the bond between us is a thing I shall never forget. Will you and the others favor me with your accompaniment to the conveyance which awaits me?''

For a moment Leelan looked as though she wanted to add to what she'd already said, but with the other women assuring me that the honor of seeing me off was theirs, she changed her mind and simply added her own agreement. Ashton, who had been standing not far from the door silently watching everyone and glancing around, also seemed to have something to say, but she did the same about joining us in leaving without turning the need vocal.

It was a faintly regretful but well-enough satisfied group that stopped at the foot of the transfer slip's ramp, raising hands in farewell while Ashton and I continued on up. When I turned to wave a final good-bye, I saw that the pouches containing my clothes had been given to one of the transport crewmen standing to either side of the ramp, a man who made no effort to tell the big, armed *w'wenda* who gave him the things that it wasn't part of his job to handle passenger luggage. He'd had the urge to say something like that at first, but then he seemed to remember where he was and who he was about to say that to. The urge was squelched quickly and firmly, and then he and the other were following us up the ramp.

"*You* may think that was funny, but you can bet that crewman isn't taking it any way but seriously,'' Ashton said in a low voice as she led the way into the slip, obviously having seen and felt what I had. "He's never had to face a *w'wenda*, probably never even met one before today, but it didn't take him long to see what most people do: you don't mouth off to one any more than you would to a *l'lenda*. You wanted to know why we were so happy to have the bunch of them agree to be with us when we attack the complex? If what just happened doesn't give you a hint, you'll never know.''

She walked away from me then to find a seat around the outer edge of the circle of the slip, but she hadn't left anything behind that still needed saying. I'd been so close to those women—and they'd been so close to me—that it hadn't occurred to me how others would see them. They *were* warriors, dangerous, deadly fighters you'd have to be insane to want to start up with, and the gentle way they'd treated me didn't change that. I shrugged inside myself, knowing there was another reason Ashton hadn't yet mentioned as to why she and the others wanted the *w'wendaa*, but if no one brought it up in a reasonable amount of time I would simply ask. I had other things to think about right then, and I preferred leaving the subject of the *w'wendaa* of Vediaster for an occasion when I would not be distracted.

Which certainly didn't apply to the time right then. It wasn't until I had taken a seat of my own not far from Ashton's, that I noticed there were only four of us in the slip, not counting the two people flying it. I looked around in a very blank way, then turned to Ashton.

"What happened to Murdock and the others?" I asked, silently congratulating myself for being so observant that I hadn't noticed there were people missing until the slip was already lifting from the ground. "Have they decided to settle in Vediaster, and just forgot to tell me?"

"The slip took them over to the community, then came back for us," she answered without looking at me, a faint amusement turning her lips up in something of a smile. "It's so close to this city we could almost walk—if you could get to the community by walking. My brother will be delighted to hear that you actually missed him enough to ask."

Her eyes moved over to me with that, the laughter in them matching her smile, but her attempt wasn't fooling me in the least. She was trying to distract me from where we would soon be by giving me something to get angry over and argue about, but it hadn't the faintest hope of working. Instead of answering her I left my seat to activate a view port, and tried to think about nothing but looking out.

Ashton was right about how close the community was, and from what I saw was also right about no one being able to walk to it. In a matter of minutes we had passed over the part of Vediaster it had taken days to cover on *seetar*-back, with the valley of Gerleth, Dallan's country, taking its turn sliding by far below us like a handmade miniature nestled in a cup. A large chunk of impassable mountain range came next, its gray and white bleakness chilling me even at that distance, and then we began to slide out of the sky. On the other side of the range was a valley that looked even larger than Gerleth, but where Gerleth had a number of passes leading in and out of it, this second valley didn't seem to have any. It was locked up tight within walls of stone, and flying looked to be the only way in or out.

It really is amazing how fast a transfer slip can reach the ground from very high up, without anyone in the slip feeling the least sense of movement. We landed near what seemed to be a fairly large town, not quite on the scale of the city of Vediaster, but looking a lot like it. The area was unwalled and the surrounding fields were neatly planted, there was forest in the near distance into or out of which a pleasant stream ran, and people could be seen all over the streets of the town, and in the fields, and near the forest. It came as a shock that most of those people seemed to be dark-haired, with blonds only a small percentage; in other places on Rimilia you rarely saw anyone who *wasn't* blond, and . . .

"Don't you think you've been standing next to that port long enough?" Ashton's voice came from behind me, too gentle to be called intrusive. "We're home, Terrilian, and you don't have to be afraid of what you'll find here. Besides, Murdock left me a message with the pilot that you'll be staying at his house for the afternoon. Irin has gone off hunting with Rissim, and they won't be back until later. Once they do get back we'll be lucky if they don't break the door down trying to get to you, but until then we can all have a nice, quiet visit. Come on; Murdock must be wondering what's keeping us."

I think I would have preferred standing by the port a little longer, pretending to be sightseeing instead of admitting I was hiding, but Ashton's arm around my shoulders didn't let me do that. The heavy twisting inside my middle had postponed the knifing instead of giving it up entirely, which meant I might as well go ahead and do what I could before the real attack came. I sighed privately on the inside, wondering where all the hurry I'd felt earlier had gone, and let Ashton urge me out of the slip.

Somehow the air was warmer in that hidden valley than it had been in Vediaster, and we walked from the transfer slip into the town. I carried the pouches of clothes without minding, hugging them to me just a little as I walked and looked around, not really hiding behind them but also not feeling quite as—exposed. No one came rushing over offering undying love and/or friendship—which was a relief—but quite a lot of the people we passed greeted Ashton with their minds, faint curiosity rippling in my direction. The town had dirt streets and one-story houses and shops, stalls clumped together with an occasional one standing alone, people moving through it, kids playing—everything I'd seen before more than once on Rimilia, but at the same time—different.

For one thing, it wasn't just the big blond men who wore *haddinn* and swordbelts. Most of the men on the street were armed, and they seemed to have quite a lot of the—arrogance and untouchability—that I usually associated with *l'lendaa.* The dark-haired warriors were just as big as the blonds they outnumbered, but there was the faintest shadow of deference from dark-haired toward light. As far as the women went there were very few blonds, and quite a number of the dark-haired ones had green eyes.

Which still didn't entirely account for the difference I felt. Letting my senses move out past the curtain I continued to maintain finally showed me what the main difference was: no clamor of uncontrolled minds. Even in Vediaster, where a large number of the women were mentally active, walking or riding through the streets brought that din of minds that had always made it necessary for me to shield in some way. The community had no more than a murmur as a backdrop—with an occasional "shout" from one of the children who briefly paid more attention to the game being played than to mental calm. Everyone else seemed to be—*considering* the people around them, and consciously keeping the noise down.

"This one's Murdock's house," Ashton said with a

touch to my arm before gesturing to a small building on our left. "He's not here often enough or long enough to need more than a few rooms, but those of us who stay enjoy spreading out a little more. Come on inside."

She led the way to the metal-braced wooden door and through it, held it for me, then closed it behind us. It was dim and cool in the small entrance hall we had entered, and Ashton didn't wait for anyone to come out to greet us. She immediately led the way to the left, brushing aside a cloth hanging, into a room that was large enough to hold more than a dozen people easily. It was made of polished dark wood and decorated with bright cloth hangings and carpet fur, had cushions scattered around and a large fireplace with a fire set but unlit, and candle sconces appeared here and there on the walls. Two double doors in two of the walls had been thrown open to provide light and air, and Murdock himself half-reclined on a special chair that didn't rise more than a few inches off the floor. At first glance he seemed to be relaxing among the floor cushions, and I suddenly realized that was exactly the way he wanted it to look.

"Well, we're finally here," Ashton announced unnecessarily, heading straight for the pitcher and goblets that stood on a small table not far from Murdock. "For a minute or two I really believed I'd be bringing an ordinary citizen out of Vediaster with me, but they ganged up on her. She now has a 'surrogate' to handle business while she's not there, but that doesn't change the fact that she's still their *Chama.*"

"It would have surprised me had the matter gone any other way," Murdock answered, his cold, wintry smile standing as poor agent for the warmth of welcome in his mind. "The *w'wendaa* of Vadiaster feel no confusion or hesitancy when it comes to knowing what they want, and what they want is Terrilian as their *Chama.* Since it's quite impossible at this time for them to accept anyone else, they sought for and found a way to keep her. Do have a cup of kimla, child. It was prepared not long ago so it must still be warm."

"What do you mean, they 'ganged up' on me?" I asked from where I'd stopped, addressing both of them even though it had been Ashton who had said it. "They didn't like the idea of me not being *Chama* any longer, but if I'd really insisted they would have had to let me go. What choice would they have had?"

"The same choice they *did* have," Ashton said, straightening away from the small table with a cup in her hand. "Even though they couldn't reach through that curtain to your mind, they knew *you* were reaching through it so they projected belief in their cause almost nonstop. Even the ones who aren't supposed to be actives were doing it, and I could almost see the way your determination to let them work out their own problems became the determination to help them work it out. You need to learn how to tell when you're being pushed around, girl. We'll be glad to take care of it when you start training with us."

I couldn't decide which was more irritating, Ashton's grin or the knowledge that I'd been forced again to do something someone else wanted. That had happened to me too often in the past, suddenly waking up to the realization that someone else's mind was affecting mine without my being aware of it, and I didn't care for the idea even a little. I'd have to do something about it in the very near future, but Ashton's "training" would probably not be the something.

"We really don't intend stealing those clothes until much later, so for right now you'll be safe in putting them down in a corner somewhere," Ashton said, taking a short step forward before sitting on the carpet fur with her cup of kimla. "That's one of the nice things about being in the community—we warn our victims before we strike."

"I think I would really enjoy having someone strike at me right about now," I muttered with a glare for Ashton's grin and Murdock's amusement, then looked around for a place to put the pouches I still held. "The only thing I ever slammed at with full strength was the Hand of Power, but lately I've been getting this *urge*— I never realized it before, but every now and then enemies *do* come in handy."

"One of the purposes of enemies has always been as

an outlet for aggressions,'' Murdock agreed, watching as I put the pouches down near a wall then headed for the pitcher of kimla. ''Life becomes a good deal easier in the living, when one is able to give one's anger to someone other than friends. Are you able yet to discuss what befell you among *our* enemies?''

I waited until I had poured the cup of kimla and had moved around to sit opposite the two before looking at Murdock, and then I merely shrugged in answer to his question. His words had approached the subject as carefully as his mind, and I wasn't being pressured into talking about anything I couldn't. Both he and Ashton had asked during the trip back to Rimilia, and when I'd ignored their gentle inquisitiveness, they hadn't pressed the matter.

''You're going to need the information at some time, so it might as well be now,'' I conceded, raising my cup to sip from it. ''It's—unpleasant to remember, but remembering isn't as painful as living it was. I woke up in a small room, all alone and unable to remember how I got there, and then a woman came to take me to someone who was called the director of the complex. I found out later he wasn't really the head of the place, only someone they used as some sort of figurehead, an obvious incompetent to be looked down on and considered harmless. He—tried to key me into the heavy conditioning and at first it worked, but then he—tried putting his hands on me, and for some reason that broke me out of it.''

''Even adopted Rimilian women know who has and doesn't have the right to touch them,'' Ashton said, her mind refusing to let her hot-glowing anger flare up out of control. ''The first time I visited here I decided Rimilian women were doormats, taking anything their men cared to give, but that isn't true. They were raised in a culture totally different from Central and Central-derived ones, so they accept things we look at as impositions. What they *don't* accept is being touched by any man who doesn't have the right to touch them, and their men back them on that completely. If any man on this world tried suggesting he'd raped a woman because she encouraged him, he'd be maimed and then dead so fast he wouldn't have time to understand his mistake. For Rimilian men *all* women are encouraging and arousing; it's up to the man to control himself until he finds a woman of his own."

"And conditioning of any sort would have difficulty holding a mind like yours for very long," Murdock put in, carefully keeping away from a topic that belonged to women to discuss. "They had no way of knowing that, of course, which made it a stroke of luck for our side. I do, however, find myself curious to know— Were you able to learn the identity of the true head of the complex?"

"As far as I could tell, it was a man named Serdin," I answered, making a face before drinking more of the kimla. "He was the one I used to get me out of the complex, and nothing he said was questioned by anyone. If he doesn't run the thing, the Secs don't know the difference."

"Serdin, of course," Murdock muttered, his mind going as cold as his expression usually was. "He rose through governmental ranks by the simple expedient of quickly showing a talent for knowing when to look the other way, of ruthlessly thrusting others out of his way, and for divining which of those around him were destined for power. He suddenly dropped out of sight a few years ago, and the unofficial explanation was that he had retired because of poor health. It must surely have been Rathmore's idea for him to be behind an incompetent figurehead; Rathmore finds it amusing to let half of those he associates with believe the other half can't be trusted or relied on. It gives them a false sense of security and power he can then take advantage of as he sees fit."

"What did you mean, he was the one you used to get you out of the complex?" Ashton asked, her eyes narrowed as she stared at me. "What could you have done to talk him into it? Threaten to shrink his office by crying all over it?"

"Oh, I didn't have to threaten him," I came back, her manner retrieving all that irritation I'd been feeling only a short while earlier. "He decided he was curious as to what the other men in that place found so attractive about me, so he was going to try me for himself. His interest made it easier getting a grip on him, and after that he thought he was serving his own ends with everything he did. No female—'guest'—had a chance of getting out of that place by herself, but no one tried to keep our 'hosts' from doing anything they pleased.''

"You were able to take over his mind,'' Ashton said, a quiet statement showing very little of the shock she felt. "I know most of us can influence others for a short time, but it's very draining even for those trained in the technique. Just as a guess you had to establish control over him, tell him what you wanted him to do, leave wherever you were with him and wait while he followed your orders, then keep holding him until you were clear of the complex. I would have been burned out halfway through that, even if things happened one after the other with no delays in between. But you weren't anywhere near burned out, were you?''

Her second statement had no backdrop of shock to it, nothing but rising excitement that put the start of a grin on her face. She was sure everything she'd said was true, and that *pleased* her!

"Don't you know how to do anything right?'' I asked, wondering why I was feeling so uncomfortable. "You're not supposed to *like* the idea of what I can do, you're supposed to be afraid of it. What do they teach you people in this place?''

"They teach us that experiment has proven what one of us can do, so can the rest,'' she answered at once, that faint grin growing and widening. "If I see someone who's better at something than I am, I get started right away trying to find out how they do it. Spending time resenting them for managing it before I did is a waste of time, and I'm too busy to have much of it to waste. And now that you mention it, how *did* you develop that much strength?''

"Now that *I* mention it?'' I repeated in outrage, trying to decide how I ought to feel. If they really did welcome those who were different as potential new sources of an increase in their own ability . . . "Ashton, if anyone deserves experiencing what I did in order to develop this kind of strength, you *have* to be the one. Maybe I ought to promise not to let anyone else try it first."

"Somehow that doesn't strike me as being what most consider a generous offer," she responded, immediately suspicious as she studied me. "I don't know the details of everything you went through, but . . ."

"Excuse me, but we're back," a voice broke in from the curtain behind me, drawing Ashton's eyes and interrupting the frown Murdock had begun developing. Even if I'd been completely shielded I would have known who it was, and I mentally kicked myself for not once thinking about who Murdock's agent in my company could have been. There really was only one person it could have been, and I turned where I sat to look up at Lenham Phillips.

"Hi, Terry," Len said with an attractive grin on his handsome face, my brother empath greeting me casually after no more than a short time of us being apart. "They all thought I was crazy not to worry about you more, but somehow I knew you'd get away from those clods. When it comes to picking the winning side, any side *you're* on is the one that gets *my* money."

He stood in front of the curtain that had fallen closed again behind him, not quite as large as a Rimilian but just as blond and blue-eyed. The *haddin* and swordbelt he wore were relatively recent additions, given to him after he had gotten to Rimilia. I knew him better as a coworker in the XenoMediation Bureau back on Central, but I also remembered the last time we'd seen each other—and knew I should never have trusted him.

"You seem to be over your upset now, Len," I remarked, referring back to the time he also had reason to remember. "After we parted company I had the silly idea you might be avoiding me—especially since you didn't show up to say good-bye before I left for Vediaster. I didn't know then that you were probably just too busy making a report to be able to get away, so I spent some time worrying if you were all right. Silly of me, wasn't it?"

"If you're saying I owe you an apology, you're right," he answered, the grin gone but his eyes making no effort to avoid mine. "You scared me badly with that trick you pulled with my shield, but not for the reason you think. And you ought to know why Garth and I weren't there to see you off, we had no choice about it. We both *wanted* to be there, but . . ."

"But you let it slide because letting me know I had *some* friends wasn't an effort important enough to make a fuss over," I finished for him, seeing his flush and feeling the same in his mind. "Making that kind of a stand might have brought you too much in the way of attention, and then you might have had to explain what you were really doing there. Don't worry about it, Len, I understand completely. We all have our priorities, but I can't help wondering what more you would have had to go through in the slave kitchens in Grelana if you and Garth hadn't been two of my higher ones. You probably would have been freed the next day anyway, so it couldn't have been much . . ."

He stared down at me without saying anything, the protest in his mind dying away before it could be vocalized. Only someone who has *been* a slave can know what even one extra day in slavery means, and Len and Garth hadn't had an easy time of it. Len's light eyes were full of pain as he finally understood that his not being there to say good-bye was like my not being there would have been for him and Garth, but I was the one who had been stupid. Only in dreams can you trust other people not to betray you, and even if they do it doesn't matter that much. When I turned my back on Len to show I'd said everything to him I cared to, I could feel the protest being reborn in his mind. It was almost as though I could see the hand he extended toward me, the unspoken attempt to apologize and ask to be forgiven, but his crying mind couldn't find the words. Ashton, frowning, sent comfort past me with her own mind in an effort to ease him, but although I could also feel that she wanted to say something, it wasn't her words that got said first.

"As you recall that much, *wenda*, you must also recall that the fault was neither Lenham's nor Garth's," a deep voice came, calm but faintly disturbed. "It was I who commanded them to keep away, therefore is the responsibility for the doing mine. Should you feel the need to heap accusation and establish guilt, it is I who must be addressed."

"What's he doing here?" I said to Murdock, who was half distracted and half upset, none of which showed on his face. "Why did you bother establishing this community in such an inaccessible place if you drag in every stray who comes along?"

"Terrilian, I'm sure you know by now that Tammad is no stray," Murdock answered, looking and sounding very tired. "You should know as well that Lenham meant you no harm in his role as my agent, and was not permitted to tell you the truth despite his wish to do so. You are understandably upset by all the things you've learned and are about to learn, and are therefore striking out at everyone in reach. Perhaps it would be best if I had you shown to a room where you might rest."

"I'm not in the mood to rest," I denied with a shake of my head, more than eager to be away from all those minds I could feel behind me, but not about to let myself be chased off like a small, helpless animal. "You said you wanted to know what happened to me in the complex, and right now I'm ready to talk about it—which I might not be again. If you're ready to listen, get rid of your pets."

"I will not be dictated to in my own house," he answered, the coldness in his voice and eyes the only indications of the growl in his mind. His twisted body didn't stir in its special chair, but in all other, more important ways, he stood straight and tall. "These people, like you, are my *guests*, and I will not have them insulted. You may either be shown to a room, or you may speak in front of them, and frankly I would prefer that you rested. You have hardly had an easy time of it, and . . ."

"I've already said I'm not in the mood to rest," I repeated, close to a growl of my own. "If you want everyone in the universe to hear this that's your business, but I'm getting it said. After that, don't ask me about it again."

No one said anything else right then, or if they did I

didn't hear it. I was so—twisted tight and whirling inside, just as though there were something wrong with me, which of course there wasn't. I looked down at my hands while Murdock's—guests—brought themselves into the room and found places on the carpet fur, their minds making such a clamor I almost exchanged my curtain for a shield. Two women entered behind them, one with a tray of goblets and one with a pitcher containing *drishnak* rather than kimla. I could smell the spicy Rimilian wine as soon as it was in the room, and even knew the order in which the men were served. First Garth and then Len, then Dallan and Hestin—the healer from Vediaster—and lastly— I found myself wishing I *could* run somewhere and hide, but instead began speaking.

"After the incident with the figurehead director, I was taken to the main part of the complex," I said, still staring at my hands as I took up pretty much from where I'd left off. "Everyone in sight told me what a shame it was that the conditioning hadn't held, but that didn't mean I wasn't expected to do what the other women there did. I was put on display for their exalted male Primes, got chosen by one, but didn't please him as much as I was supposed to. When he put a hand inside my clothes I slapped him, which amused no one at all. They apologized to him for having inflicted me on him, took me to a room where they caused me more pain than I'd thought it was possible to feel, then dressed me up and sent me back to the man I'd insulted. I was being given one more chance to please him, and if I didn't do it I wouldn't be given another."

"Would they have killed you?" Ashton asked very quietly when I paused to sip my kimla. "It doesn't make much sense going to all that trouble to kidnap someone and then simply throw them away if things don't immediately work out. Can they be such fools?"

"They aren't," I answered, only right then realizing I'd shed my curtain for a shield after all. "You seem to forget that it wasn't my mind they needed, but my body. All they had to kill was my mind, my knowledge of self, and then my body would do just as they wanted. I was so terrified at the idea I thought I'd do exactly what they told me to, but I seem to be incapable of acting intelligently in situations like that. When the man humiliated me I insulted him again, this time in front of everyone in the room, and they all went foaming at the mouth. It would have been finished for me right then and there—if the First Prime of the complex hadn't stepped in to claim me.

"Kel-Ten made them all back off, and then he took me to his apartment," I said after a very brief pause. "He wasn't shy about helping himself to my use, but that wasn't the main reason he'd exercised one of the privileges of his position to make me his. When we were in a place where we couldn't be overheard, he told me he wanted to escape from the complex and was offering me the chance to go with him. He needed the help of another Prime he could trust in order to get out of there, and told me that if I agreed to go along with his plans, he'd key me awake.

"I can't say I really trusted Kel-Ten, but he was offering the only option I could accept aside from suicide—which everyone in that place would have done everything they could to prevent. When I agreed he took advantage of the situation to treat me like a slave, using me to ease some of the pressure all those drugs they fed him caused him to feel, but he also kept his promise. He awakened me when he said he would, and I hid the condition behind a shield. The great Primes in the complex don't know how to shield—not through their own choice, anyway—and after that everything should have gone smoothly."

"Only it didn't," Ashton said, still helping me out while I looked at no one at all. "You were all alone in those woods where we found you, so either you two escaped together and then separated, or the man never went with you. From some of the other things you've said, I would guess you escaped alone."

"I wouldn't have left him behind if I'd been certain he *could* go with me," I said in little more than a whisper, closing my eyes against the nagging guilt I continued to feel. "The male Primes all thought they were so free and well-treated, but they were just as conditioned as the women, only in different ways. When I asked Kel-Ten what happened to a First Prime who was defeated, the question never registered in his mind because they didn't want him thinking about that. He told me that at one time he'd tried refusing to cooperate with them, and they'd forced him to change his mind. They knew he still disliked being there so they gave him everything he wanted just to keep him satisfied. It occurred to me that they might have also given him the hope of escape—just to keep him going—but had conditioned him against ever really trying it— I couldn't take the chance, I just couldn't!"

"No, taking a chance like that wouldn't have been very smart," Ashton said with gentle reassurance from very near, and then her arm was around me. I didn't realize until then that I was trembling, but didn't try to pull away even though I had no need of her support.

"It would have been worse than not very smart," I said more calmly, sitting unmoving against the arm around my shoulders, my eyes open again but staring down at the carpet fur. "They have nulls as guards in that place, and one of them decided he wanted me. While Kel-Ten was busy covering the female Primes he'd been assigned to, the null—used the opportunity to enjoy himself. That happened the night before I was awakened, but the next day I found out he planned on doing it again that very day, and my being awakened would have been no use at all. I wouldn't have been able to stop him from hurting me again, so I—ran. I had myself sent to Serdin's office, found out that the null was too important a man to be denied a little thing like—what he'd done to me—and would do again—so I took over Serdin's mind and had him get me out of the complex—and when I got into the woods the Ejects told me I'd be found no matter how well I tried to hide—which meant there was a tracer under my skin somewhere—and then they drove me off to keep me from leading the complex people to them when I *was* found—they get used as targets for the male Primes in their training—and then— I don't remember much after that besides running."

"*Treda*, be calm, you are safe now among friends," a soothing voice said from my right, and I almost told it not to be silly, that I *was* calm, but then I realized how hard I was breathing. It also came to me that my eyes were closed again and that Hestin, the one who had just spoken, had a hand wrapped around my right arm as his other hand stroked my hair. I didn't know how he could have understood what I'd said since I'd been speaking in Centran, but there was no doubt he had because *he* was speaking in Centran. And then there was someone to my left, someone who wasn't Ashton.

"*Hama*, you have my word that I will seek out the ones who gave you pain and will end their lives!" that deep voice said, the tone so full of fury that I nearly cringed to think of what the mind behind it must be like. "Not again shall I allow you to be taken from my side, no matter that in this last instance the choice was not mine. Not again will it be allowed to occur."

The words were almost all growl, the sworn oath behind them so clear even someone without hearing couldn't have missed it. I shuddered without being able to stop it, only beginning to realize how ill I felt, then quickly leaned away from the wide arms that were starting to go around me. I didn't want those arms around me, and when I moved against Hestin his grip on my own arm tightened just a little.

"Tammad, my friend, the woman is not well," he said, surprisingly with a frown in his usually even voice. "Pain lingers in her on too many levels, and for some reason she has done no more than merely begin the healing of herself. Also, she must surely continue to have no memory of you, for the spirit within her retreats in haste from the touch of your hands. Clearly must you exercise patience in regard to . . ."

"What do you mean, 'the healing of herself'?" Ashton suddenly demanded of Hestin, no apology in her tone for having interrupted him. "Is that what you call her use of pain control, or is there something . . ."

"Part of that pain has to be *my* fault," Len said, his voice filled with misery and guilt. "Terry, please, you have to believe I didn't mean to hurt you like . . ."

"Don't let what they did to you bother you any more, Terry," Garth said, sounding utterly savage. "I'll be designing a good number of the attack plans against them, and when I'm through there won't be anything left of . . ."

I sat there staring at the cup of kimla in my hands, surrounded by noise that was climbing higher and higher in its level of strength. Murdock's voice added itself to the others and so did Dallan's, both of them merging into the rising explosion that was making me want to put my hands over my ears and race out of there. In one way or another all those people were trying to make me believe they cared about me, but all I felt like was a rock in a river, something the violently swirling current was forced to go around. I couldn't . . .

"Silence!" a deafening shout suddenly came, a very deep voice that had used sheer lung power to overcome the cacaphony that was about to split the walls. It had come from behind me, in the direction of the door hanging, and quickly got the silence it had demanded. When I realized everyone was looking that way I twisted around to do my own looking, and saw the man and woman who had evidently just come in. The man was in *haddin* and swordbelt and was just as large and blond as all Rimilian *l'lendaa*, but the pretty woman was more my size, with dark hair and light eyes. She wore a long, full skirt that was almost a *caldin* but made of sturdier material, and her long-sleeved blouse was more tunic than *imad.* She also stood in a pair of plain but well-made sandals, and for some reason she was staring directly at me.

"Well, doesn't time fly when you're having fun?" Ashton commented from behind me in a drawl. "Is it sundown already, Irin?"

Irin. The woman didn't answer Ashton but she also didn't stop staring, and suddenly I felt very hollow inside. Those two standing at the door, the man now joining the woman in her stare—they had to be—my real parents—

# 12

"Why does she look so pale?" the woman suddenly demanded, taking a step forward. "What have you all done to her? And why does she think she has to shield *here*, back where she belongs? Damn you, Murdock, if you've made things even worse—!"

"Calm yourself, Irindel," Murdock said from where I couldn't see him, his voice filled with its usual diplomatic smoothness. "Your daughter has been through a trying experience, but felt she needed to relate the episode for our benefit. She would likely have been wiser resting first, but seems to have inherited a good deal of your disposition."

"Then perhaps one of greater wisdom should have seen to deciding the matter in her stead," the man beside the woman Irin said in Centran while she looked indignant, his steady blue gaze now resting beyond me, most likely on Murdock. "One must be in full possesion of one's wits to see the necessary; should the situation be otherwise, those about that one must show sufficient concern to give assistance."

"With all the experience you've had with Irin, Rissim, that's easy for *you* to say," Ashton put in, sounding much too amused for a situation like that. "One of the reasons your daughter tends to shield most of the time is because of the strength of her mind. If you combine that with Irin's stubborness you get someone who isn't that easily 'assisted,' no matter how concerned those around her are. You two may find yourselves glad she's been gone all these years."

"How *dare* you say something like that!" the woman Irin growled, her hands closed to fists as her furious gaze found her sister. "There's nothing that will *ever* make me glad my child was stolen from me, nothing! I'll make you regret that twisted sense of humor of yours, Asha, you wait and see if I don't!"

"Surely, Irindel, there will be better, more appropriate times for recriminations," Murdock said before Ashton could come back with an answer likely to continue the argument. "I, however, would consider it the perfect time for introducing yourself to your daughter, and in turn having her introduced to you. My study is just down the hall; why not use it before returning to your own house?"

Suddenly the woman's eyes were back to me, and none of her previous anger was anywhere to be seen. As a matter of fact she looked more like I felt: completely at a loss with nothing of any sense or importance ready to be said. We stared at each other in silence for what felt like hours, neither of us apparently able to start taking Murdock up on his offer, and the double hesitation proved to be too much for Ashton.

"For pity's sake, do you two intend playing statue for the rest of your lives?" she demanded, the words accompanied by the sound of rising. "Since you're both incapable of taking a hint, let me put it another way: how about moving the reunion into the next room so the rest of us can get back to a conversation with words?"

She must have known her suggestion would do no more good than Murdock's had, and wasn't about to wait around to see it happen. Without warning her hand was suddenly on my arm, and before I knew it the cup of kimla was gone and I was on my feet. The next few minutes were very confusing in that Ashton took charge of me and Rissim began navigating Irindel, both efforts ending us all up in a small room a short distance away from the first. To this day I can't call up a memory from then of how the room was furnished, but at the time it took me no more than seconds to notice that Ashton disappeared immediately without another word. That left just three of us in the room, and at least one of the three decided she probably would have been smarter staying right where she'd originally been.

"Perhaps it would be best, girl, if it were you who

spoke first," Rissim said after a moment, his deep voice very gentle. "It was, after all, we who allowed you to be taken from us, we who permitted the severing of your proper blood ties. Should you wish to voice anger at so vile a doing, the right is surely yours."

I had been standing around on the carpet fur trying to find something to look at, but what Rissim said made me stop and think. How *did* I feel about it all, and if I didn't really believe these strangers were my parents, why couldn't I look at them?

"I don't yet feel any anger," I said after a pause of my own, forcing my eyes back to where the two people stood. "I may decide it's appropriate if I can ever get myself to believe all this on an emotional level, but right now I'm too confused and upset to believe in anything beyond daylight and dark. And if you want to be realistic about it, Ashton made a point that shouldn't simply be dismissed. You've been looking forward to regaining a—member of your family, but how do you know you'll like the woman she's become?"

It took quite a lot for me to get that question out, and while I was under a double light-eyed stare at that. There was no way to ever really know if what I'd missed would have been better and more satisfying for me than what I'd had, and that part of it was gone into the irretrievable past. My point was much more relevant to the time we stood in, and was the one causing most of my upset. At first I saw nothing but two people staring at me, no true expression on either face, and then I realized how wrong I was. Quiet tears were running down Irin's cheeks, and the light of a very warm smile showed in Rissim's eyes.

"Were the question of liking truly at issue, we would now have our answer," Rissim said, the arm he had around his woman gently tightening as the smile spread to his face. "Our love shall always be for the child produced by a union of that love, yet liking, never so easily accomplished, is now the belonging of one who first considers *our* feelings in the matter. In no manner might a daughter such as that be unacceptable."

He seemed to be telling the truth, but the answer he'd given wasn't really the one I'd been looking for. I hadn't asked my question to impress anyone, just to find out something I needed to know, and then it came to me that lowering my shield might be the way to get it. Most of the time it's a good deal easier *not* knowing what others really think of you, but that time I wanted the truth even if it hurt. If all that turned out to be reality rather than a disturbing dream, the truth was something I had to have.

But the condition of my mind wasn't something to be inflicted on those around me, most especially not without warning. Instead of simply dropping my shield I replaced it with my curtain—and the next instant was nearly bowled over. Reaching through the curtain showed that Rissim *had* been telling the truth as he saw it, the vast calm of his mind confirming his words, but Irin—! She wasn't simply feeling agreement she was aching with it, her fiercely burning sense of pride nearly drowning in a flood of loss and guilt. Those reactions immediately made me think she couldn't be trusted, a pointless, mindless thought I thrust away without knowing where it came from, and then I was able to understand why she felt as she did.

I hadn't been told the truth until a few days earlier, but she had lived with it for all the years of my life.

No matter how good the reason, she had allowed her child to be taken from her, to be raised by hated strangers and never told who her real people were.

If her child hated her for it, or worse, simply had no interest in knowing her, there was nothing she would ever be able to do about it. It would come close to killing her, but could never, ever be changed.

I stood there feeling what she felt, understanding her more completely than I had ever done with anyone, realizing almost at once that she didn't know our minds touched. Hers was bright and sharp, not possessing the strength of mine but one of the strongest I'd ever encountered, a loving, self-confident, normally self-satisfied mind that now quaked with terror. The fear I'd felt over not being liked was nothing when compared to her fear of the same thing, a nightmare she'd lived with for so many long, empty years. The passing time had done very little to mar her prettiness, which meant I didn't feel quite so strange when I opened my mind and my arms to her. She was, of course, the elder between us, but she was the one who needed a child's comforting. She sobbed once before rushing to me, and then it was hard to tell whether there was more laughing or crying going on.

It didn't take long before Rissim joined in the hugging with laughter of his own, and before I knew it reality retreated even farther away than it had been before. It felt so *right* to be where I was, exchanging hugs with a woman I'd never seen before, the two of us being hugged by a man I didn't know, all of us touching minds so completely and freely that we'd never be strangers again. That was the way it happened in dreams, with laughter and no sense of worry; something bothered me about that, but it was the only way I could take it.

The strongest emotions are too draining to sustain for very long, so it wasn't more than a few minutes before we all took deep breaths and moved back just a little to look at one another. There's nothing of intrusion involved in really looking at your own, most especially in a dream. Irin had settled into a glowing smile, and after she'd taken a breath she shook her head.

"Asha may have the worst sense of humor I've ever come across, but I can see she wasn't lying," I was told, a hand coming to smooth one side of my hair back. "Your mind *does* have more strength than we've yet encountered, daughter mine, and for the first time in my life I feel like bragging and strutting. Not only do I finally have my firstborn back, and not only is she filled with more compassion than I'd dared hope for, but she also comes back as an excitingly wonderful example. Do you believe most of the people in this valley think our talents have already been developed as far as they can go?"

"If that's true, they may not like finding out they're wrong," I answered, feeling odd and almost comfortable. "People usually don't enjoy having their beliefs torn away."

"You don't understand," she said with a laugh, putting her hand to my arm. "It isn't satisfied conviction your presence will disrupt, it's glum resignation. No one was happy believing we'd stretched to the end, but without anything concrete to give us hope all we could do was accept the conclusion. Now we can accept the truth instead, and as soon as we put paid to the sick plans of Rathmore Hellman and his group, we can throw a celebration feast like you've never seen. After that we'll get to work."

"Perhaps not all those in our valley will wish to begin a similar striving," Rissim said, looking me over with an odd bent to his thoughts, his arms folded easily across his chest. "Our firstborn is truly *sarella wenda*, Irin, and many will be the *l'lendaa* and *varindaa* who come seeking my approval. I shall listen to each with courtesy and patience—and shall see more directly to those who attempt to approach *her* rather than he who is her father. The old ways have not died among us here, nor shall they the while *I* remain among the living."

"Oh, Rissim, no one will try to steal her from you, not with *your* reputation as a *l'lenda*," Irin said with a laugh while I blinked at the big man who stood beside her. "They'll all come to the front door, not try to sneak in through the back, and in any event our little girl is not what I would consider helpless."

She was still grinning when she turned away from him, then laughed again at whatever my expression was like. I hadn't realized how—*protected*—it would feel to have a Rimilian father, and I wasn't sure I liked it. It's really terrible to be all alone and know there's no one there to help you but yourself, but after you do it for awhile you sort of begin getting used to it. I could see from Rissim's mind he expected me to get *unused* to it as fast as possible, and like most Rimilian men wasn't prepared to take no for an answer.

"Now, Terry, don't let your father's overprotectiveness bother you," Irin said as she patted my hand, amusement still clear in her mind. "You're the only daughter I've managed to give him, and although men enjoy having sons they can share manhood with, there's always a small part of them that yearns for a daughter to protect. He only *sounds* as though he means to chase the *l'lendaa* and *varindaa* away. He won't really do it."

"What are *varindaa*?" I asked, mainly to cover the fact that I couldn't think of anything else. Rissim was grinning at me faintly, his mind practically purring, his satisfied thoughts saying more plainly than words that *he'd* be the one to decide what he did and didn't do.

"*Varindaa* are mind warriors," Irin answered, a lot of pride behind the explanation. "They've not only learned the use of a sword, they've also mastered the ability to fight with their minds. It's dishonorable for any of them to accept a challenge from someone who *isn't* a *varinda*, so they never do. Your father is a *l'lenda*, but all your brothers are *varindaa*."

"Which will be of additional aid in seeing properly to my daughter and their sister," Rissim said with even more satisfaction while I felt the word "brothers" echo in my head. I'd used the word many times before, but it had never felt quite so—strange.

"A number of them will be extremely pleased to find they now have a sister," Rissim continued, his mind chuckling. "They have noted that those with sisters are often in the company of *wendaa* it was not necessary to go seeking, for *wendaa* come to visit those sisters. They will likely be less willing to accept suitors than I, for they will not care to be deprived of your presence too quickly."

"Rissim, give the child a chance to breathe before you pair her or don't pair her with a suitor," Irin said with another laugh, her eyes shining. "I for one would like to get to know her first, before she's carried off to . . ."

"I must ask your pardon for this intrusion, yet does honor demand that I speak," a voice said suddenly in Rimilian, a voice I unfortunately had no trouble recognizing. "The woman may not be granted to another, for she has not been freed of *my* bands. This man who stands beside me is my chosen brother, and has come to assure you of the truth voiced by one who is a stranger to you."

"A stranger who intrudes uninvited in family matters," Rissim answered with a frown, looking at the two men who had entered the room behind me. "Should it be truth that my daughter has been banded by you, for what reason does she fail to even turn and look upon you? If your bands are truly upon her, perhaps they should not be."

"Rissim, look, she's shielding again," Irin said as her arms went around me, the glow of happiness gone from her face. "There's something wrong, and you have to find out what it is. I don't care how dishonorable it is to keep a woman from the man who banded her, I won't stand by watching while you give her to him!"

"*Hama*, calm yourself," Rissim said while Irin held me tightly to her, her thoughts having turned downright feral. I wasn't shielded, I was curtained, and because of that knew the woman who held me close would not let me be taken from her without a fight. She had let me go once against her better judgment, and wasn't about to do it again. I put my own arms around her, knowing she needed the reassurance a good deal more than I did.

"Irin, I, too, am able to see that this *l'lenda* believes he speaks the truth," Rissim went on, taking one step forward to put Irin and me somewhat behind him. "I, however, will first have answers to my queries before any decision is made as to what course of action is most honorable. For what reason does our daughter refuse acknowledgment of your very presence, *l'lenda*? For what reason has she withdrawn even her thoughts from you?"

"My brother is no more able to fathom the reason for such behavior than am I," answered a second voice, one I knew as well as the first. "I am Dallan, *drin* of Gerleth, and my chosen brother here beside me is Tammad, *denday* of a great city of the plains, and he who speaks first among those of the Circle of Might. The *wenda* and I are *helid*, so close have we grown through the trials we have faced, yet am I at a loss to explain my chosen sister's actions. It was for Tammad's sake that Terril bested Vediaster's Hand of Power and faced the *Chama* Farian, she who had made Tammad's capture possible. Solely was her concern for him, and mightily did she strive till his freedom was assured, yet now—"

"Perhaps it is as the Murdock McKenzie has said," the first voice put in, sounding the least bit forlorn. "Her love for me was great, I know, as great as mine for her, and for that reason did the enemy find it necessary to bury the memory of me more deeply than the rest. Certainly in time I shall be recalled by her, yet in too long a time many things may occur. Best would be that I remain beside her, to aid in her recollection."

"Best?" I interrupted, finally turning to look at the big Rimilian without letting go of Irin. "Who is that supposed to be best *for?* I've already told you that I don't know you and don't want to know you, so why don't you go back to where you come from? No one has a claim on me, not anyone, and if necessary I'm willing to argue the point. I've had enough of being hurt by men; from now on if there's any hurting to be done, I'm the one who'll do it."

Dallan and the one called Tammad just stood there staring down at me, Dallan's mind whirling with the mix of many emotions, his friend struggling with confusion and anger and loss. It was very clear Dallan had understood every word I'd said even though I'd spoken in Centran, and that told me where he and the others had been during the time Ashton and I had been getting to the valley. Dallan and Hestin had been given the Centran language, and Garth had probably been getting Rimilian, which meant the valley and its furnishings weren't as primitive as they looked from the outside.

"The healer Hestin tells us Terril continues to be in pain," Dallan said after an awkward moment, putting one hand to his friend's shoulder. "I cannot believe Terril would truly harm Tammad even should she recall less than naught of him, yet might it be best were she allowed a time to rest herself. Those who feel pain often strike out with the same, and it would be foolish to provoke an incident. Perhaps we may speak again later."

"A wise suggestion," Rissim agreed, his frown filled with quite a lot of sympathy for the other big blond barbarian who simply stood in silence and stared at me. Even a null would have felt the longing in the man's mind, but I wasn't reacting in the same way. Some people *deserved* to lose things and never get them back, and something told me the man called Tammad was one of those.

Irin and I waited near Murdock's front door while Rissim got my clothes pouches, and then my new-found family took me home. Their house wasn't far from Murdock's but must have been four times the size, all of it spreading wide and easy from the central hallway, left, right, and straight ahead. There were a number of women in the house but no men, and although I expected to be introduced, Irin refused to stop for the amenities. What Dallan had said about my being in pain had upset her, and she lost no time in getting me to a room toward the back of the house. It was a pleasant room with yellow and silver curtains on the windows, yellow and silver cushions on the dark brown floor fur, and yellow and silver silks on the dark pile of bed furs. Just looking at it made me feel comfortable and at home, and when Irin closed the door behind us she immediately pointed to the bed furs.

"That's where I want you as fast as possible, young lady, and then we'll take a closer look at you," she said, her frown in no way aimed at me. "The next time I talk to Murdock, he's going to wish he had no ears! Would it have killed him to tell us right away that you were in pain? Did the imbecile have to wait until we heard it as a comment from a stranger? At the very least, we could have been sitting down while we talked! Do you need help getting out of your clothes?"

"I'm mostly just tired," I answered with a smile for her outrage, walking over to the bed furs to sit down on them. "You have to ignore Dallan and his fussing, or at least not take it very seriously. He's seen me in a really bad way a few times, so now he looks at me and immediately assumes the worst. After I've rested for a while I'll be just fine."

"You certainly will, because *I'll* be here to see to it," she said in a no-arguments tone of voice, her hands on her hips while she studied me. "If I'd known you were here on this world, having trouble, I would have— Well, let's just say there would have been a lot less trouble. Will you open your mind to me again?"

I shrugged and banished my curtain, then lay back on the bed furs when Irin came closer and gestured me into doing it. She sat down beside me and put a hand on my forehead, smiling with a warmth that burned steadily inside her. As close as we were I could see the small lines on her face that said she wasn't a girl any longer, that she wasn't really as close to me in age as a more distant estimate might suggest. I very much wanted to get to know her, and then one day I might even be able to *believe . . .*

Her strong, bright mind reached toward mine, and then I was aware of losing aches and twinges I hadn't even known I was feeling. It was the first time someone else had used pain control on *me,* and wasn't anything like the way it had felt when I'd used it on myself. Very briefly I wondered why I *hadn't* used it on myself again, and then the question faded away behind the soothing influx of someone else's strength, letting me close my eyes and relax.

"Don't fall asleep yet," Irin said after a minute, taking her hand away as her mind separated from mine. "If I know your father, he's right now in the middle of having a meal put together for you, so you might as well wait and get it eaten before settling down to rest. He would have been happy to see you no matter what you looked like, but he'll be even happier once you aren't quite so thin."

"A typical Rimilian-male outlook," I said as I muffled a yawn, feeling very comfortable. "They're so big themselves, they want to make sure the women around them have enough size and strength to accommodate them without falling apart. Please tell him thanks anyway, but he doesn't have to bother. I ate in Vediaster, so I won't be hungry for a while."

"Terry, I feel something—odd—in your mind," she said, the hesitance in her voice drawing my eyes to the faint worry on her face. "When you spoke just now, there was a—strange sort of satisfaction inside you, almost like a gloating. You know enough about Rimilia to know this is Rissim's house where he has the final say on most matters, but you don't have any intentions of going along with that say. Without bearing him any ill will you're just going to refuse to obey him, and I'm willing to bet it's *that* that's bringing you the satisfaction. The fact that you can refuse and make it stick. I don't understand why you feel that way—or am I misinterpreting what I'm getting?"

"You're not misinterpreting," I answered, right then consciously aware of the satisfaction she'd mentioned. "Irin, I spent quite a lot of time on this world, and there was hardly a minute of it when I wasn't feeling like a victim. All the men I encountered forced me to do things their way, *all* the men, but now I no longer have to. I don't have to dress a particular way, I don't have to please them to keep from getting punished, I don't have to eat what I'm given to keep from being force-fed, none of it! If any of them tries to force himself on me I'll take his mind apart and put it back together again inside out, damn me if I don't! I won't ever be a victim again, no matter who tries to make it happen!"

I was startled when I suddenly found myself being held tight by two slender arms, the voice belonging to those arms making comforting, meaningless noises. I hadn't realized I'd sat up on the bed furs, I hadn't realized sights of other places and times had risen in front of my eyes, and I hadn't realized I was trembling. I was feeling more confused than I had in a very long while, but one thing I *wasn't* confused about: what I'd told Irin had been the truth. When you let other people be in control of you you regretted it, one way or the other, but *always.* When you reach a limit on the amount of pain you can accept you either break or start to fight back, and I wasn't about to break.

Irin's mind soothed mine as well, and before I knew it I fell asleep. When I woke again it was full dark, Irin was lighting one of the candles on the wall in my room, and I actually felt rested enough to get up and start doing things. The pouches with my clothes had been brought to the room, so the first thing I did was strip, wash in the room's basin, then dress again in clothes that hadn't been slept in. What was left of the marks on my back bothered Irin, but not so much that she wasted a lot of time making furious and disapproving noises. The evening meal was ready and waiting for us, and disapproval could be voiced at another time.

Food wasn't the only thing waiting for us, something I found out as soon as we entered the paneled, pillowed, and carpet-furred room. Trays held pitchers of *drishnak* and a lighter wine, and various dishes were all ready to begin making the rounds as soon as Irin and I could get started. The others they were going to be making the rounds among were Rissim and his sons, some of whom had women of their own. It was then that I learned I had *eight* brothers, the oldest of whom was less than a year younger than me. Helliar was a *varinda*, as his name showed, and his hug of greeting was a signal for a general rush from everyone else. After that it was impossible separating one from the other even though some were dark-haired like me and Irin, and some were blond like Rissim. *All* of them were big, without doubt *l'lenda* size, and all of them were delightfully crazy—as denizens of a happy dream should be.

By the time the meal was over, there were a lot of plates which had been emptied during unending conversation and laughter. Helliar's woman Keffa had asked me where I'd gotten the beautiful rose and pale gold outfit I had on, and that meant I'd had to tell them I was *Chama* of Vediaster. The revelation brought out delight and curiosity alike, and before I knew it I was telling the story of how I'd become something I'd never wanted to be. Just about every mind there was Prime quality or very close to it, so my story spread out into a general discussion of mind strength which continued until Rissim finished the last of his *drishnak*, then rose to his feet.

"I dislike the need for interrupting so pleasant a time, yet have I just been informed of the arrival of those who asked if they might speak with Terril," he said, looking at all of us fondly. "Those who plan our attack against the enemy are eager to learn what they might of the inner defenses of the places we must enter. Should you be too wearied to speak with them, child, they may be asked to return at another time."

"No, it's all right, I don't mind talking to them," I said, sharing the general air of disappointment that our get-acquainted conversation had to end, but also sharing the eagerness in the minds around me to face our enemy. Once they were defeated the valley could stop being a secret, empaths could stop living half lives—and no more of us would be in danger of being kidnapped and bred like farm animals. I *wanted* to get to the end of planning and the beginning of attacking, and every one of my new-found family agreed with me.

Before going with Rissim I said good night to my two youngest brothers, who were about to leave for their room. In the midst of all the confusion of meeting so many new people I wasn't sure how old they were, but the elder of the two was already as tall as I and the younger almost the same, even though neither of them were young men yet. They were only boys, mere children, but their minds were bright and warm and loving, fiercely glad to welcome me to the family and fiercely determined to see to my future protection. They gave me careful good-night hugs to be certain they didn't hurt me with their already considerable strength, then calmly took themselves off to bed after kissing their parents, quietly discussing their hopes that the attack would wait a little while longer so they would be old enough to join in. They both wore *haddinn* and sword belts like their father and brothers, and although their swords weren't full *l'lenda* size, they were already good with the weapons.

I was so wrapped up in deep, pleasant thoughts that I followed Rissim through the house without paying much attention to where we were going. I'd never known anything could be as good as that meal I'd just been a part of, the full and complete sharing of people who were just like me, knew me for what I was, and still very much wanted me to be one of them. I wondered briefly what it would have been like actually growing up in that atmosphere of love and caring and sharing, and suddenly felt very cheated. I hadn't been allowed to stay with my own, had been forced instead to spend my time among cold, crippled strangers, but it wasn't Irin and Rissim's fault and it wasn't Murdock McKenzie's. It was the fault of those—*people* we had to face and defeat, those filthy animals who had made my exile necessary.

"I hope that expression isn't meant for one of us," a voice said suddenly, bringing me out of the dark red cloud that had come into being around me. "All we came for was to ask a few questions, but we didn't intend asking them with swords. Are we going to have to defend ourselves?''

I looked up in surprise at seeing Garth, realized his question had only been half-joking, then glanced around at the weapons-hung meeting room Rissim and I had entered. Six or seven men stood on the far side of it with Rissim, five of them studying me with one degree or another of concern. I understood then that I hadn't shielded or curtained my mind in hours, and what I'd been feeling toward the people on New Dawn must have been painful for those who could feel it. As a matter of fact there was a light sheen of sweat on Garth's forehead, which probably meant I'd gotten through to the untalented as well. I could see there was still a lot I had to learn about controlling myself, and if I didn't learn fast I'd end up as cut off from the people around me as I would be unawakened.

''Gentlemen, I'm sorry,'' I said quickly, trying to make them know I really meant it. ''I've grown too used to having no one but myself able to feel my emotions, the results of living my life behind a curtain. Please let *me* be the one to shield, at least until I learn to pay attention to what I'm projecting.''

''No, *wenda*, such shielding would be neither pleasant nor necessary,'' one of the group around Rissim said, a faint smile on his face as he held up one hand. ''We are none of us harmed by the magnificent strength of your mind, and anger shared is anger eased. We ask only that you take a moment to compose yourself, and then we may begin our discussion.''

The blond man, wearing a long robe over his *haddin* and no swordbelt, bowed toward me before turning to the men with him, and beside me Garth shook his head.

''The magnificent strength of your mind,'' he repeated, his smile on the wry side. ''If even *I* felt it, magnificent is too pale a word. I hope you know how much I appreciate your having spared me that until now.''

''Not as much as you'll appreciate being spared from now on,'' I came back, looking up into his gray eyes. ''If I don't learn to watch myself, I'll deserve being locked up alone in my head. I see you had no trouble understanding what the man said in Rimilian, so you *were* given the language. The only thing I don't understand is what you're doing here.''

''I'm here as a member of the attack-planning team,'' he said, faint surprise in his mind. ''As soon as they found out I was Tammad's intended tactician, they drafted me for their own effort. Didn't you hear me when I told you that earlier?''

''I suppose I heard it, but too much has happened in between for me to have remembered,'' I answered, taking a deep breath. ''I'm trying to believe them, Garth, I'm really trying to believe I belong here, but sometimes I feel like I'm digging under a wall that extends down into the ground. If I keep digging I might find the bottom, but I also might find nothing but more wall.''

''Don't be afraid to believe, Terry,'' he said, the sober words soft as he put a hand on my arm. ''I know how much hurt there is in believing the wrong thing, but there are times when you have to trust your instincts and take the risk. I knew I belonged on this world as soon as I got here, and now you have the chance of finding out the same thing. Just remember who told you that first, way back at the beginning.''

His faint smile was warm and friendly, but remembering when he and Len had tried to get me to commit myself to the Rimilian cause didn't make me feel the way he did. It made me feel strangely—empty instead, which meant it was time for a change of subject.

''Well, I'm ready to get started,'' I said, looking around toward where the others stood. ''Anybody else in the mood to discuss our enemy?''

The immediate agreement I got showed just how much in the mood they were, so we all sat down on the floor fur with cushions handy, getting comfortable before getting down to it. I saw Rissim where he stood to one side of the room, his arms folded and his mind concerned despite the firm hold he had on his emotions, and was surprised that he wasn't joining us. It almost seemed as though he were standing guard against something while the rest of us worked, but what he might be guarding against I couldn't imagine.

The man who had first spoken to me was Lamdon, and he was the one who chaired—or floored—the discussion. He questioned me about the complex, and saw to it that the others took turns with the questions *they* had instead of all talking at once and drowning each other out. Those men were *avid* for anything and everything I could tell them, knowing that each bit of information put them closer to the doing and farther from the waiting. They'd waited long enough, and now they wanted to *do*.

"And the guards, you say, were unarmed," Garth recapped when it was his turn, his expression all frown, his mind not far different. "How can they be considered guards, if they don't even have so much as a calm-down spreader? Or could they have been carrying spreaders without your knowing it? Do you know what a spreader looks like?"

"I would venture to say they indeed carried naught," Lamdon put in before I could admit I wouldn't have known a spreader if it had been dropped in my lap. "You must recall, friend Garth, that those who must most be guarded against are within rather than without, and those within may not be allowed close proximity to weapons. With sufficient mind strength one may gain such a weapon for oneself, a happening those of the complex would scarcely be eager to allow. The *wenda* has told us that those without the dwellings bore weapons, while those within did not. From this we must allow for the possibility of hidden weapons within, weapons which would quell an outbreak of strength, yet do naught of permanent harm to those they touched. Does this seem likely to you?"

"Very likely," Garth answered, nodding slowly as his mind worked furiously. "Within those parameters there are only a small number of devices they might possibly have in use, and they're not hard to guard against if you know they're there. We'll have to take precautions just in case they also have actual weapons, but crash teams going in first should be able to handle the possibility. We neutralize the outer defenses, hold the entrances while the crash teams go in and knock out their central monitoring stations, then we take the place down one section at a time. Those inside guards have to be specialists in hand-to-hand, they'd be useless decorations if they weren't, so we'd better make sure we don't forget the point."

"I think they *are* better than average with their hands," I put in, fascinated with the way everyone spoke the language he felt most comfortable with, then listened in whatever language was being spoken *to* him. "One of their nulls made a comment about not being afraid of what Kel-Ten might do to him with his hands, saying there would be nothing he *could* do. Kel-Ten is too big to dismiss that lightly, even by someone the null's size, unless there's more involved than size."

I still felt a shiver pass through me at thought of that null Adjin, a touch of terror I couldn't seem to shake even though I knew I'd never see him again. I fought with the feeling while everyone considered what I'd said, then let myself be distracted when Lamdon stirred where he sat and smiled at me.

"Such information as that is precisely what we seek, and yet was it nearly unmentioned by cause of your not having sooner realized its value," he said, making a comment which was in no way a condemnation, his light eyes mild. "I wonder if we might ask a favor of you, *wenda,* one which would benefit us a great deal. Should you agree, I have the ability to merge minds with you in a manner which is likely unfamiliar to you. You would have little or no knowledge of that which was said by you, for I alone would direct the path of your memory, touching all things in detail or merely in passing. Naught would be forgotten nor overlooked, and still you would have no need to relive that which continues to bring you pain. Would you permit a merging such as that?"

Every man there sat quietly waiting for my answer, and only then did I understand that they hadn't missed what discussing the complex made me feel. Being completely unshielded had its drawbacks as well as its benefits, and I nearly called up my curtain before realizing that hiding would not help. If I was ever going to be one of those people I had to be one of them without anything to hide behind, and forcing myself to cooperate right then might make it easier the next time I had to do it. My first, most immediate reaction would have been to refuse, but I pushed the refusal away with a shrug.

"If I can help without having to scratch at wounds which haven't yet healed, of course I'll do it," I said, trying for an encouraging smile to give all those gentle, worrying minds. "I want to get those people at the complex at least as badly as you do, so we can at least try this mind merging. Will my not being familiar with it make it harder to do?"

"No, *wenda*, only I need know what must be done," Lamdon said, his voice as soothing as his smile. "Also would I have you realize that it shall not be we alone who benefit from the effort. You, too, will have an easing for your striving, an easing which should have been given you many days earlier. A pity there were none with Murdock McKenzie who possessed the ability, a great pity, a great pity, a great pity, a great . . ."

His voice droned on and on without meaning, his lovely blue eyes growing larger and larger as his gentle mind came closer to mine. I had never seen eyes grow that big before, and before I knew it I was bathing in them, bathing in them, bathing . . .

And then I was taking a deep breath and blinking, needing to stretch a little where I sat on the carpet fur, but otherwise feeling better than I had in quite a while. I had an immediate sense of time having passed from the minds around me, so that meant whatever had been tried had worked even if I didn't remember it. Lamdon wasn't within inches of me as I seemed to remember him being so I was able to look around at the other men, but once I did the smile I had begun faded to nothing. The people in the room weren't the same ones who had been there before that—merging, and I didn't much care for most of the substitutions.

"Please don't be angry, Terry," Irin said as she moved closer to me, her long skirt making the shift awkward. "You have a problem that needs to be solved for everyone's sake, most especially yours. Lamdon helped us all understand what it was, and now we have to make you understand. Will you let us do that?"

Her mind and eyes were filled with compassion and a very great need to help, but it was still all I could do to keep my anger from reaching out to her and everyone in the room. They were *all* desperate to help—Irin and Rissim and Lamdon and Garth and Len and Dallan and Hestin and that one called Tammad—whether or not I wanted to be helped. I sat silently for a moment, working to control myself, then nodded curtly.

"All right, you all feel I have a terrible problem and you're determined to help me solve it," I said, making no effort to have them think I was feeling in the least friendly. "Since I can see you're going to keep bothering me until I agree to listen I'll do it, but don't expect to be satisfied with the way the discussion turns out. I'm promising to listen, but that's all I'm promising."

"The stubbornness of stone has ever been one of your virtues, *wenda,*" the one called Tammad commented, his tone dry and his mind annoyed. "The wrong done to you has been more than great, a wrong I shall right with the edge of my blade, yet have I, too, been wronged. As you alone may right this second wrong, perhaps you will consider acquiring a like determination."

"I feel sure, *denday* Tammad, that my daughter will approach this matter with reason and understanding," Rissim said from his place to Irin's right in the circle our group formed on the floor fur, his voice calm and his mind the same. "Although in one sense she has not long been a daughter to me, she is, in fine, no other thing and has never been other than that. She is blood of my blood, and will surely conduct herself as such."

His light blue eyes came to me at that point, nothing in them but the easy conviction that everything he'd said was true. I hadn't much liked what that Tammad had said, but suddenly I was wondering if I liked Rissim's speech any better. There was no doubt in his mind that I *was* his daughter, and I'd been wasting my time worrying about whether or not I'd be accepted. Acceptance was inarguable and automatic, mine simply by virtue of my being there, but what I *did* did not fall into the same category.

"I'm sure we'd all like this to be over and done with,"

Irin said hastily, her arm suddenly around me, most likely in response to what she could feel in my mind. "Since going over the problem should settle it, let's start going over it. Len, you said you could do it best?"

"I think so, but first there's another misunderstanding to straighten out," Len answered with a nod from where he sat between Garth and Tammad, his sober gaze resting on me. "Terry, when I saw all the things you were becoming able to do with your mind I *did* run scared, but not for the reason you think. I wasn't afraid of you, and I didn't mistrust you; except for being the one to accomplish all you did, you really had nothing to do with it at all."

He paused then, to give me a chance to comment if I wanted to, but he was the one with all the explanations. When he saw I had nothing to say, he sighed inwardly and plowed on.

"You have to understand one very important point before any of the rest of it will make sense," he said, his eyes now trying to send belief, his mind deliberately refusing to do the same. "The Amalgamation differentiates between Primes and ordinary empaths, but Terry—our people here have found that the only difference between the two is this: Primes are born with the greater strength, and other empaths have to work for it. Prime strength can be achieved by *any* empath if they're properly trained, so every one of us is a potential Prime."

This time I didn't say anything because my mind was too shocked, not to mention too busy racing around trying to digest that unbelievable statement. All the valley people present were confirming what had been said with their calm acceptance of the matter, leaving me no choice but to believe the unbelievable. All empaths were potential Primes, and where you get has always been more important than where you start from. The same strength was available to all of us, but the Amalgamation didn't know that!

"Good grief, Len, they've been throwing their ordinary empaths away!" I blurted, suddenly even more shocked. "They keep the born Primes, and all the rest are called Ejects and simply kicked out to live as they can or die if they can't! They've had just the numbers they wanted right in their hands, and all they did with them was throw them away!''

''Which is *my* idea of proper justice,'' Len said in agreement, sharing the grim pleasure the other valley people felt. ''I hurt for the pain given my brothers and sisters, but at least they were spared the need to find themselves working to further the aims of their enemies. Once we defeat that garbage, our people will be rescued and helped to live normal lives.

''Considering what I've just told you, I now have to explain why *I'm* not Prime strength yet,'' he went on after taking a deep breath to calm himself. ''I've visited here often enough to have gotten the training, but the day I reached Prime strength would have been the day I had to stay here permanently. I'm not *supposed* to be a Prime, and if I went back to work for Central and someone accidentally discovered I was, my usefulness and freedom would have been over together. Not to mention the fact that they would then have known a lot more than we wanted them to.''

''Okay, I can understand that,'' I conceded, finding it just about the *only* point not wrapped a mile deep in confusion. ''What I can't understand is what that can possibly have to do with your being afraid. Since you know so much more about it, you shouldn't . . .''

''Terry, the fact that I know so much more about it *is* the point,'' he interrupted, more upset with himself than with me. ''I'd thought, just like everyone else, that there was a limit to what Primes can do, and then there *you* were, so far beyond our best that it was frightening. And not only that, but it was clear you were still growing! If I'd thought those sorts of abilities were beyond me I wouldn't have minded, but what one of us can do, so can the rest! But we'd tried, hard and often, and had discovered that ordinary practice couldn't advance us to your level. That meant we'd have to go through what *you* went through—all that pain and terror—once I reached Prime strength I'd *have* to try for it, my nature would refuse to let me do anything else. I don't think I've ever been so frightened in my life—''

He sat trembling with his hand over his eyes, his mind reaching out for and clinging to the comfort being sent to him by just about everyone in the room, the fear he'd spoken of a very odd thing. It wasn't the sort of fear most people feel, the kind that sends panic racing through you and you racing through anything in your path to getting away. Len's fear was the terrible sort that's felt when the last thing you want to do is what you intend, but you know you *will* do it because you have to. No matter what. No matter how much it hurts. That kind of fear just sits on you and digs in, spreading out and using its claws and teeth, turning your life into a waking nightmare. I would have known how Len felt even if I couldn't read his emotions so clearly, and from that I knew the comforting the others were giving him was no more than wasted effort.

"I think I've found another difference between Primes and ordinary empaths," I said after a moment, putting an insulting drawl into the words. "Primes learn to think, an ability that seems to be beyond some of the ordinary."

The minds around me immediately began registering offended outrage and disapproval on Len's behalf, but Len was the one I was watching most carefully, and his sense of insult died almost before it was born. He pulled his hand from his eyes so he could look at me with all the suspicion he felt, knowing I'd said what I had on purpose even though he couldn't see the purpose, so I shook my head at him.

"You know, Len, I really admire the courage of people who get their exercise from jumping to conclusions," I said, feeling how my continued drawl was adding to his annoyance. "I don't think much of their intelligence, but I do admire their courage in making assumptions and then living their lives to suit the conclusions. Doing it that way means they never know *what* will happen, but that doesn't stop them from plowing through life both deaf and blind."

"All right, Terry, why don't you just say what you have to straight out," he came back, the annoyance turning his voice into the next thing to a growl. Before all the time he'd spent on Rimilia, he would have reddened; right then he was more angry than embarrassed. "I know you're dyng to show me how wrong I am, so why don't you just do it."

"After a lovely invitation like that, I'll be glad to," I responded, leaning down to a red cushion as I grinned at him. "You've already said you know what *I* had to go through to develop strength and extra abilities, but there's one thing you haven't said. How do you know everyone else will have to go through the same?"

"Why—it stands to reason," he answered, but more defensively and hesitantly as he frowned. "The people here have tried to go farther ahead, and haven't been able to do it. You did it, but only after going through the outlying districts of hell. What other conclusion is it possible to draw?"

"Len, when people first started flying, they did more crashing into the ground than staying in the air," I told him gently, feeling the attentiveness that now surrounded me—and from him as well, which was what I'd been trying for. "Just because the pioneers crashed doesn't mean we have to accept crashing on a regular basis if we want to fly, all it means is that we have their pain to thank for our present comfort in traveling. I happen to believe that if you crash you're not doing it right, and history tends to be on my side. When you know something is possible but dangerous you look around for a way to make it safe, and that's called *progress*."

"I think you almost have me convinced," he grudged, his mind a good deal happier and freer than his tone, and then his eyes were directly on me again. "I still don't like the way you got me to listen, but I suppose stubbornness is another thing Primes and ordinary empaths have in common. And now, I'm happy to say, it's my turn to give *you* a hand."

"I've had a hand from you before," I told his grin as I straightened off the cushion again, remembering all too clearly the times he'd touched me when I hadn't wanted him to. "Since I don't expect this time to be any better than the others, just do it so I can get back to my room."

"Terry, you're not about to be heartlessly violated," he said, the words strong and direct without any pity or overgentleness to them, his eyes and mind the same.

"You're confused and very hurt over what happened to you, and all we're going to do is clear the confusion away. Lamdon has already helped by making sure talking about it will be a little easier for you, so let's get started. This First Prime named Kel-Ten, the man who claimed you; what kind of man was he, and what did he look like?"

"He didn't look any different than anyone else," I answered, taking my turn at frowning. "He was a fairly big man, and few of the others were able to match his size. He had blond hair and blue eyes, I suppose you would call him handsome. He had a lot of women to take care of due to his being First Prime, but he seemed to be more interested in me than in them, and not only because we were planning to escape together. I don't know, there was something about the way he looked at me, especially after they told him he would be the first to—to—"

I couldn't quite bring myself to talk about being bred like an animal, not even when it was fury I was beginning to feel at the thought instead of the desperate sickness I'd felt at the time. I looked away from Len while I tried to think of a more graceful way to get out of going on than simply stopping, but he saved me the trouble. He'd asked his question for a reason, and what answer I'd given was apparently enough.

"So the man was big, blond and blue-eyed, important, and claimed you because he wanted you," Len summed up, ignoring the ragged ending I'd given him. "You remember everything about him, especially not liking him and not trusting him at all. What you claim you don't remember is anything about Tammad, even though the rest of us can feel your hostility toward him without half trying. Terry: is it really true that you don't remember Tammad—or are you remembering him with Kel-Ten imposed on top? Is it really Tammad you don't want to know—or is it Kel-Ten you're rejecting in his place?"

By that time I was back to looking at Len, the soberly intense questions he'd asked making me feel even more confused than I had moments earlier. I didn't even glance at the big Rimilian to his left, but suddenly I became aware of a cloud of calm that was thinning around the edges. Underneath was a thick conglomeration of most of the more violent emotions—rage, fury, the need for vengeance, bloodlust, hatred—but somehow I knew none of that was aimed at me. What *was* aimed at me was something I had no interest in, something I didn't even want to try to read.

"Terry, you're backing away again," Len said, a faint sound of warning in his voice. "If anyone should know you can't solve a problem by running away, I'm it. Think about what I'm saying, and consider the possibility that it's true: you're blaming Tammad for something Kel-Ten did, but you aren't doing it consciously. They must have put you through extra conditioning to erase Tammad from your memory, so you're having a harder time bringing back the truth of him. With just about all of the rest of your memories restored you think you should be remembering him too, but you aren't. What you're doing is filling in the gaps with Kel-Ten, reconciling what's missing that way. You *do* remember Tammad, but the Tammad you remember isn't what you should be remembering. Won't you admit that what I just said makes sense?"

Len's voice had taken on a coaxing, urging quality, his effort to get me to admit the possibility shared by most of the minds around us. They all believed he was right and wanted me to believe it with them, but my mind had developed a sort of—transparent buffer that let me see the emotions being sent at me even as they were shunted past me. It was almost like what I'd seen that trainer do back in the complex, a trick I seemed to have borrowed to take care of the way other people's minds influenced mine without my being aware of it. That was a problem Ashton had mentioned to me, one that was now settled. Another was that I *was* seeing Kel-Ten when I looked at Tammad, but only because they were two of a kind.

"What you said makes a lot of sense, Len," I conceded, giving no indication that I saw the flash of triumph in his mind. "The only problem I have with it is—it isn't entirely true. I'll admit I was lying when I said I didn't remember Tammad; after seeing him a couple of times it all came back in a rush. Insisting I didn't remember seemed the easiest way of getting everyone to stop pestering me about him, but since it isn't working I might as well tell you all the truth. I remember everything about him, but I *still* don't want to know him. Can I go back to my room now?"

A deafening uproar doesn't necessarily have to be verbal, not when it's a bunch of empaths you're sitting among. The silent torrent of shock and protest and confusion would have come close to drowning me if that buffer hadn't still been in place, and then the flood was distracted by the expected someone, who managed to put his thoughts into words first—as usual.

"*Wenda,* I cannot find meaning in what you have said," Tammad told me, his voice soft and even despite the raging hurt and disappointment boiling around behind his cloud of calm. "You would have me believe you recall the life we had begun together, the deep, full love we shared, and still you wish to know naught further of me? Surely must there continue to be confusion within you, a lack of true memory and the sight of another in my place. It cannot . . ."

"You don't believe it's you I'm remembering?" I interrupted, finally looking straight at him instead of avoiding it the way I'd been doing. "You still think it's only Kel-Ten? Well, try this: He saw me and decided he wanted me, and I had no say in the matter. He really enjoyed taking me to bed, but the thought of sharing me with others of the Primes didn't bother him at all. He forced me to obey him, dressed me the way he pleased, humiliated me any time the mood struck him, and never once doubted he had the right. Does any of that sound familiar to you, *l'lenda?* Can you never remember being amused over something that shamed me, was there never a time when what *I* wanted was immediately and absolutely dismissed from your consideration? If that's your definition of love, I'd rather be hated. Or beaten, which is something else I'm sure you can't remember ever having done to me. I really would like you to find someone else to love. I'm too tired to go through any more of that."

I didn't need Irin's arm tightening around me to know how ragged my emotions had grown, a condition that cut me off from the man I'd been looking at. Only one small part of me refused to admit I didn't want him near me any longer, but that one part probably enjoyed the pain I'd been given. The rest of me *didn't* want him any longer, or the pain either.

"Is it possible my daughter speaks the truth, *denday* Tammad?" Rissim asked in the ragged silence while Irin urged me to put my head down on her shoulder. "Most of those seated with us feel appalled, yet do I hear naught of protest even from you. Can it be this lack of words speaks more clearly than a score of voices?"

"No!" Tammad denied immediately, his emotions trying to rampage out of his control of them. "I am *l'lenda*, and when I came upon an unbanded woman I desired, I took her for my own! The price I gave for her possession was more than *dinga*, yet did I give it gladly! My heart was hers nearly from the first moment I beheld her, yet was it necessary that I labor long and strenuously before hers was mine as well. Was there never a time we quarreled, never a time when despair drove me to offering her pain rather than due punishment? Most certainly there were such times, yet not beyond the moment we truly looked upon one another. Are you able to deny there was a time such as that, woman? Did we not come to terms with our differences, and find happiness in each other's arms?"

"How much happiness did we find when I told you I didn't want to go with you to the *Chama*'s palace in Vediaster, but you forced me to go anyway?" I countered, closing my eyes to help keep my voice steady. "I asked you to let me go with Dallan instead, but you decided it would be foolish to pamper a woman's groundless fears. Didn't that happen *after* that coming-to-terms time? Have you any idea what was done to me because you were too high and mighty a *l'lenda* to listen to a lowly *wenda?*"

"In my own capture I was fully informed of what had become of you," he answered in the newest, deepest silence, his voice now dead, his mind overflowing with self-condemnation. "I—begged—to have the agony of such torture given instead to me, yet such as those who held us take what they wish and give naught in return. So now we have come to the true reason you no longer wish knowledge of me, and I find myself suddenly bereft of the ability to seek argument against your choice. You have cause to feel disgust in my presence, *hama sadendra,* a fact which *I* cannot deny."

Even without opening my eyes I knew that his head was bowed low, the mighty *l'lenda* who was never ashamed to shed tears when the pain he felt was great enough. I knew exactly how much pain he felt; I could reach it even through the cloud of calm he used in place of a shield. He'd sworn to protect me and had instead been the cause of my capture and torture, and that was something he would never be able to forgive himself for. I pressed my cheek into Irin's shoulder, fighting to keep myself from soothing away that guilt, struggling to show nothing of what was really inside me. If I could just hold out long enough it would all be over, and neither one of us would ever have to cry again.

"And yet, Tammad, it was fear for your safety and the need for your freedom which filled her thoughts at all times," Dallan said suddenly out of the blue, sounding as though he were doing no more than thinking aloud. "When she first awoke in Leelan's house, she would have immediately gone seeking you in the palace had she found herself able to stand. Hestin and I together were unable to hold off her determination past the time she *was* able to stand. Had it proven necessary, she would surely have gone to the palace alone rather than in the company of *w'wendaa,* with others poised without the walls awaiting the time to strike. Can those be the actions of one who condemns her *memabrak* for having placed her in jeopardy?"

There were no comments made aloud to that, but Hestin's firm agreement couldn't be missed any more than Tammad's sudden confusion. I was so tired I wanted to give it all up and run, but Len had been right about the futility of running. I'd been trying to make sure there would be no pursuit when I finally took to my heels, but it wasn't working out at all the way I'd wanted it to.

"Also do I now recall a comment which was made at the time," Dallan went on, warming to his subject apparently without noticing everyone's reaction to what he was saying. "It was pointed out by my sister Terril that although she had somehow known danger lay in wait for her and the others, she had failed to realize that it was her dark hair and green eyes which would betray them to their enemies. Had this understanding come to her soon enough for her to speak to you of it, brother, would you have continued refusing to give heed to her insistences? Somehow I think not."

"It is among my own recollections that this *treda* longed for you even when asleep, Tammad," Hestin said, speaking as comfortably as Dallan had. "There was fury in her for none save those responsible for many outrages, naught of anger for those who fell victim to them. I feel that the sharpness of her recent words have as their source part of the pain which continues to hold her so tightly, a pain which I cannot read save for knowing of its presence. There is more here than meets the eye, my friend, and I believe we would be wise to delve more deeply into it."

"*Hama,* what words are these that they speak to me?" Tammad asked, still feeling confused but with his head no longer down. I could see him so clearly even with my eyes closed, just as I had always been able to do, but what difference did that make? Back to the beginning of time people had been able to see clearly the far horizon and long for it, but that didn't mean they were ever able to reach it and make it theirs.

"Daughter, you too must speak to us in explanation," Rissim said, his tone very gentle but not one that would let itself be ignored. "No more than truth has been uttered by you thus far, yet is it a strange truth seen from a view others fail to share. Should you remain mute, I will have little choice save to return you to the bands of this man who is your *memabrak.*"

"You can't return me to him because he *isn't* my *memabrak,*" I said, beginning to feel dizzy and even more tired despite the loving support being sent me by Irin. "When he heard they wanted me to be *Chama* of Vediaster he decided to give me up for the sake of those who claimed to need me so badly, sacrificing his own claim for the sake of a city full of people. That wasn't the first time he decided to give me up and it looks like he changed his mind again, but this time I'm not going to let him change it back. This time he's going to go through with it."

If the earlier noise in the room was mental, what broke out right then was mostly physical. Rissim rumbled something in outrage, Len and Garth immediately began throwing questions around, and Tammad's own words were buried under everyone else's. Emotions flew behind the gabble like attacking ghosts, every feeling ready to go for the throat of all the others, and I don't know how long it would have continued if thick, heavy serenity and calm didn't suddenly appear in the middle of it all to force its way outward. I opened my eyes as the raging riot settled down then faded to nothing, and so was able to see the faint smile on the face of Lamdon.

"For all to speak at once is possible, yet only among those with no interest in listening," he said, looking around to make sure everyone understood it was he who had quieted the room. "As the girl's words have clearly caused a great deal of agitation, best would be to speak in turn so that all may hear what is being said. Which of you will begin the thing?"

"*I* will begin," Tammad jumped in before any of the others could, anger flashing from his light blue eyes. "I have no understanding of the reason which would cause so patently false an accusation to be leveled at me! The girl has been through much, I know, yet to lower herself to such absurd . . ."

"Absurd?" Len interrupted with a snort, so coldly angry and aggressive that I almost didn't recognize him. "How many times is she supposed to go through the same thing with you before her refusal to do it again *isn't* absurd? Are you trying to claim you never did decide to give her up and then changed your mind, or are you saying two or three times isn't enough to complain about? I agreed to follow you, Tammad, so why don't you make the effort to show one of your followers just how honorable you are?"

Len was staring at Tammad with Garth to Len's right wearing the exact same expression, two minds filled with bitter disappointment over seeing their idol crumble. The big barbarian returned their stare with the anger fading inside him, having no trouble understanding that the two weren't challenging him. They both knew he could draw his sword and end them without either of them being able to stop him, but they didn't particularly care if he did just that. They were too full of hurt and bewilderment to care, but all Tammad felt himself was confused.

"It did indeed seem, on more than one occasion, that best for the woman would be my unbanding of her," he allowed, trying to be gentle with the two men despite his own upset. "Each time I found that life without her would be no more than death in truth, therefore did I strive to give her understanding rather than unbanding. This last instance, however, did not occur, for I would not have . . ."

"Tammad, my friend, the incident was spoken of to me at the time," Dallan interrupted in embarrassment, obviously trying to keep his chosen brother from outright lying. "The woman cannot be accused of speaking falsely, for I saw with my own eyes the shattered bones of her contentment, the meaninglessness her victory had become. She walked and breathed, yet true life was no longer within her."

"Dallan, it cannot be so," Tammad protested, even more confused than he had been, his eyes now resting on the man who looked back at him in discomfort. "If such a thing was told you, why was the matter never spoken of to me? Is a man to stand condemned through accusation alone, in no manner permitted to speak upon his own behalf?"

"I would certainly have discussed the matter with you, had Terril's disappearance not driven us all to distraction," Dallan answered, no more than the faintest hint of defensiveness in his tone as he straightened just a little where he sat to my left. "As you may recall you spent much of the time wrapped in the sleep of healing given you by Hestin, and when you awoke there was occasion to speak of naught save the disappearance. We all of us were so fully engaged with that, the earlier matter simply slipped from my memory."

"There cannot have *been* an earlier matter such as that," the barbarian insisted, vexation now flaring from his mind as his eyes shifted to me. "It cannot be, *wenda*, it simply cannot be! You must surely have mistaken whatever words were spoken to you, giving them meaning they were not to have."

"You said, 'I may not have you,' " I quoted without letting the memory tear me the way it wanted to, leaning on Irin and my mind-tool of strength alike. " 'There are others who now need you more,' you said, 'and such things must be understood and accepted.' That's word for word what you told me, and I'd like to know how else it was supposed to be interpreted. I have no idea why you changed your mind again, but more to the point is the fact that I don't care. Those few words hurt me more than anything Farian's people would ever have found it possible to do, and I'll never let myself be hurt that way again. As far as I'm concerned I don't know you, and anyone who tries to change that will be in line for hurting of his or her own."

I let my eyes close again to cut off sight of his stunned, almost open-mouthed expression, the newest silence in the room feeling really good. Most of the minds around me were maintaining a matching silence, too shocked to think or feel, Irin being the only exception. The woman who held me so tightly to her was fiercely glad I'd done as I had, and was more than ready to help me argue with anyone who disagreed.

"*Treda*, there is a point here which eludes my understanding," Hestin said after a minute, faint confusion even in *his* voice. "These words which were spoken to you by your *memabrak*, words I have no doubt you truly heard—in what place and time were they uttered? Are you able to recall that?"

"It was right after I defeated Farian," I said, too tired to try refusing him an answer on a dead issue. I, too, felt the next thing to dead, and all I wanted was a final end to the episode. "You should remember the time yourself, Hestin. It wasn't long after that that you showed up and took him somewhere else. You and Dallan put him to bed, I think."

"Yes, I do indeed recall the time," the healer said, his usually calm voice now back to normal. "I had thought that the time you referred to, yet was it necessary that I be certain. *Treda*—you must hear the words I speak, and also must you find belief in them. It was not possible for your *memabrak* to have chosen to unband you just then, for it was not possible for him to utter choices of any sort. His mind and sense of self were—elsewhere due to the urgings of the potion within him, the same potion which had held him as slave for so long. It was not *possible* for him to do other than accept the will of those about him."

"And—possibly the words of others as well," Dallan said in a tone of slow revelation as I opened my eyes in shocked disbelief to stare at Hestin. Dallan sat between us to my left, and I could see his elated expression even though I wasn't looking directly at him. "I had not earlier thought upon the point, yet now I do recall how odd Tammad seemed when we freed him. What was said to him was not commented upon by him but repeated back, as though there were no thoughts of his own filling his head. When he awoke he had no clear memory of what had occurred after his release, therefore was it certainly not by his own choice that he spoke. Likely was *he* spoken to in such a manner earlier, and then merely echoed what he was able to recall of it."

Dallan's triumphant summation caused a burst of low-voiced comments to be exchanged between Len and Garth, but I had no idea what they were saying to each other. I straightened away from Irin in deep shock, remembering all too clearly how that slave drug worked from my own experience with it. It had only been possible to resist it a little when its hold began weakening, not at all when it was fully in control. That one swallow Tammad had had of it before I could interfere—it must have combined with the residue of drug in his system to throw him right back under its full control—without my noticing it more than marginally—and hadn't Deegor said something to him not long before—

"I see, *hama*, that we both voiced the truth," Tammad said with joyful gladness, drawing my gaze to a face covered with loving happiness. "You did indeed hear what was in no manner said by me, and now there is naught further to stand between us. Come to my arms, *sadendra* mine, and share my vow that we will never again be parted."

He opened his arms to me in the way he had always done, his love and desire rolling at me in waves, adding terribly to the whirling dizziness trying to push its way out of my head. I felt hot and cold both at the same time, queasiness twisting at me along with the dizziness, and there was no way in hell I could stand it any more.

"No," I denied, trying to get my feet under me so I could stand. "I won't put myself in a position where it can ever happen again, real or not. Leave me alone. I'm going to my room. I'm going."

What I managed was to get halfway to my feet before the dizziness took to swinging the room around, and after that reached nothing but blackness.

# 13

I awoke in the bed furs of my pleasant little room, the warmth of the sunshine coming through the windows telling me a new day had been started before I'd been conscious enough to notice. The dizziness that had gotten the better of me the night before was gone, but every bit of the oddness and depression I'd felt was back and hanging on. I'd remembered everything the instant I'd opened my eyes, and didn't have to move from where I lay on my right side to know why the depression had flowered again so quickly. I wasn't alone in that pleasant little room, and my companion was the reason I'd gotten depressed in the first place.

"I see, *hama*, that you are awake and aware of me," Tammad said from the bed furs behind me, using the word "see" when what he really meant was "feel." "You will spend this day taking your ease and doing no other thing than eating well, for I will not have you fall swooning in such a manner again."

"You have a different manner of swooning you'd rather see?" I asked without turning, not in the least surprised to find him there and back to giving orders. "Why don't you sit down somewhere and make a list of your preferences, and later on I can memorize the list."

"*Hama*, though for some reason you feel you must do so, you cannot simply refuse to be mine," he said with a sigh, thick patience plastered firmly all over the inside of his mind. "We continue to be upon *my* world, which has proven to truly be your world as well. Even Rissim, he who is actual father to you, has agreed that my bands are upon you, therefore are you unquestionably mine.

Speak to me of what disturbs you, and we will together find an answer to the difficulty.''

''What disturbs me is very simple,'' I said with a sigh of my own as I turned to my back so that I might look at him. ''I was so—shattered, to use Dallan's word—when I thought you were giving me up as a matter of honor, that all I wanted was to die. That's what I was doing outside the city that day I was taken by my enemies, looking for a way to die. It doesn't really matter that I was wrong about your wanting to give me up, all that matters is that I believed you would. I *know* honor is more important to you than I am, so I continue to believe and always will. If it comes down to a choice between me and honor I know I'll lose, so I won't let myself be put back in a position where the question might some day arise. I'd rather not have you than take the chance of losing you, and *you'd* better believe what I say. If you don't leave right now, there won't be any argument about what happens.''

''Indeed shall there be no further argument between us,'' he said very gently, his eyes and mind both showing how he hurt for the hurt *I'd* had in the look he sent down to me. ''You need not fear that I shall ever give you up for I shall not, most especially as honor might in no way be entangled. My love for you and my love of honor have no meeting point, *hama,* therefore shall we put the matter from our minds and concern ourselves with more pleasant things.''

The hum in his mind broke out from under the patience that had muffled it for a while, and he began to put one of those ridiculously well-muscled arms around me to pull me closer. He was already under the top bed fur with me, and if he wasn't as naked as I, it wouldn't take him long to get that way. Instead of returning his smile or letting the humming reach me or trying to struggle the way I used to, I put one hand up to intercept that giant arm—at the same time reaching out with my mind. The mighty *l'lenda* was amused to see me trying to stop him—until his arm touched my hand and he had to jerk back with a hiss. Cold can be as painful to touch as heat, and

Tammad *denday* hadn't remembered what I'd done to him that day on the trail to Vediaster.

"My decision has already been made, *l'lenda,* and I advise you to abide by it," I said as he sat up to rub at his arm and glare at me with low-browed disapproval. "I've finally learned the proper way of answering a challenge, which means I never have to be a victim again. Since I'm stronger than you it's only fair that I warn you one more time: don't try to fight me on this, you'll only lose. There's nothing you can say or do to make me change my mind."

"Can I not, *wenda?*" he returned, deadly anger flowing swift and menacing out of his mind as he stared at me with narrowed eyes. I recognized the emotion as soon as I felt the edges of it, that same emotion he'd always used to send me shivering back away from him, but this time it didn't reach me. It was shunted past without affecting me in the least, and all I could do in return was sigh and keep my word.

"Rimilia is your beloved world, Tammad *denday,*" I said as I reached to his mind again, thrusting aside all attempts to stop me. "Protecting the peoples of this world from the *mondarayse* is your privilege and responsibility, *l'lenda,* yet do you do no more than lie about in the furs dallying with a female. Is this the manner in which you discharge your responsibilities, the manner in which you see to them with honor?"

"No," he answered in a whisper, a faint frown on his face to show his self-disapproval, his gaze more inward than it had been. Despite his stronger mind he'd been easier to take than Dallan had been in Vediaster, and rather than using a brother as I'd done with Dallan, it was the entire world Tammad was wrapped up in worrying about. He *knew* that his people were doomed if he didn't do something to protect them, *believed* that if he stopped trying there would be no one to take his place, and was *determined* not to waste any time, which is all bed-play with a woman was. Time enough to do as he liked with her once more important business was taken care of. I could almost see him thinking like that as he got out of the bed furs and headed for his *haddin* and swordbelt, his mind busy with plans and stratagems. He'd completely forgotten his efforts weren't needed any longer, and was *determined* to do what he *knew* and *believed* was required of him. I lay there holding his mind with almost no effort at all, wishing he hadn't forced me to do that to him, but a wish like that was a waste of time. *L'lendaa* were too thick-headed and stubborn to listen to reason, so they had to be shown what was right in other ways.

As soon as he was dressed he left the room, too preoccupied to remember I was there—as long as I helped the preoccupation along. I set my mind to follow and hold his as long as possible, wondered whether I could really do that, then shrugged the question aside and got out of bed. Lately my mind had taken to finding ways of doing the things I decided needed doing, and it really didn't matter whether this newest thing worked. As soon as Tammad went beyond the limits of my range he would be free, and not long after that he would understand what had been done to him. At that point he would probably come raging back, not realizing that I intended doing it again and again until he gave it up and stayed away. It was the only thing I *could* do, after all; what else is there, when you know no one in the real world can be trusted?

I was still too depressed to pay much attention to something like dressing, so I was out of the room and wandering the halls before I knew it. What I wanted was to go outside and take a long walk all alone, but what I ended up with was something else entirely. I suddenly found myself face to face with an Irin who had been looking for me, and not long after that I was being forced down among cushions in a private corner just beyond the kitchen. Three or four different dishes had apparently been kept warm for me, but the pitcher of fresh kimla brought over first was all I could raise any interest in. I poured a cup and sipped from it, then sat staring at it until Irin settled herself among cushions of her own.

"Don't take too long getting started on that food, or it'll be ice cold before you finish," she said while pouring a second cup of kimla, using her chin to gesture toward the small table on my left. "The other girls and I aren't bad when it comes to making things tasty, but cold can turn even the best of meals to glop."

"That's exactly what the best of meals would taste like to me right now," I answered, mostly still staring at the kimla. "I must be working on minus hunger at this point, so please don't be insulted if the food ends up untouched. I'm going out for a walk in a little while, which just might stimulate an appetite for later."

"If I were you, young lady, I'd try to find that appetite right now," she said, a wry amusement in the way she looked at me. "Your father is absolutely delighted to have back the daughter he's missed for so long, but I guarantee his delight will fade very quickly if he finds out she isn't eating the way every healer in the valley wants her to. And don't think being banded will save you. As long as you're under his roof, you'll still— Terry, what *are* you doing?"

"Just disentangling from something," I said with a faint smile, reeling in, so to speak, the contact I'd had with Tammad's mind. It had taken him a while to move out of my range, but when it had happened even Irin had felt it. A few minutes more and he would be back to himself, and then— "Just to set things straight, you ought to know I am *not* banded. It doesn't matter what anyone else says on the point, only my opinion counts. If that sounds too self-centered for a dream-place like this I'll leave, but I won't stop insisting on it."

"What you can stop saying is anything about leaving," she answered with a frown, the candlelight around us in our corner making her eyes glow green. "I couldn't follow what you were just doing with your mind, but I know you were doing *something*. Terry, Tammad took you to your room last night with every intention of staying with you from then on. When I felt you moving around the house it didn't occur to me to wonder where he was, and now you're insisting again that you aren't banded. Would you like to tell me what in freedom's name you've done with him?"

Irin was trying so hard not to be outraged or worried or any of a dozen other things that I couldn't keep from finding it funny; watching a Prime-level mind skittering around like that was like seeing a talented wire-walker trip over a shadow on the ground. She'd been too busy trying to poke at my mind to pay complete attention to what she was feeling, so it had almost gotten away from her. And she hadn't even been able to get anything from me; what had happened had occurred too far out of her range, and there was nothing else for her to find.

"I convinced Tammad he had more important things to do than hang around with me," I said before sipping again at the kimla, glad Irin hadn't felt me laughing at her involuntary antics. The urge for laughter had faded almost as soon as it had started, leaving me just as depressed as I'd been. "He isn't nearly as hard to handle as he thinks he is, but it's going to take a little while before he's permanently convinced. If shouting at roof-raising level bothers you, you might want to find somewhere else for me to stay until it's all over."

"If shouting at roof-raising level bothered me, I'd never have stayed with Rissim as long as I have," she countered with a snort, gesturing the point aside. "Are you saying you—did something to Tammad to make him leave you, and if he comes back you'll do it again? Terry, it isn't fair to take advantage of someone who doesn't have your strength."

"He was the one who came to me," I answered with a shrug, feeling nothing of guilt but another ton or two of depression. "I told him I'd rather not have him than take the chance of one day losing him, but he refused to listen just the way he usually does. I also gave him clear warning that I intended defending myself, but he's too used to winning against me. After another few tastes of being shoved into unreality, his opinions ought to start changing."

"I'm beginning to wish all my children after you weren't just boys," she said with the strangest look on her face and a sigh in her mind, her hand reaching out to touch mine. "Girls don't seem to have the same problems—or at least they don't look at them in the same way—maybe it would be best if I simply said this straight out. Terry, you're doing something that isn't very bright, and even *you* know it. You just refuse to admit it."

"I'm only doing what *has* to be done," I came back, having no idea what she was talking about. "I think it's fairly clear I'm not enjoying it, but that doesn't mean I can stop. Tammad and I have no future together, not when I'm afraid to trust his love, so all I can do is walk away from him. Or, as it's working out, make him walk away from me."

"That explanation sounds so cool and logical," she observed, leaning back with her cup of kimla as she studied me. "Anyone listening to you couldn't help but admire how well you're handling it all, this thing with Tammad, suddenly finding out you're part of a family you never knew existed, the fact that you were used by your own blood-kin for purposes even they don't fully understand—all of it. Being in that complex shook you up, but ever since then you haven't had trouble coping with anything."

"I'm not an infant," I pointed out, finding her inspection the least bit uncomfortable. "I'm a grown woman, and grown-ups are *supposed* to be able to cope. Would you be happier if all I did was sit around crying and wringing my hands, complaining that I didn't know what to do?"

"Actually, I would," she said with a judicious nod, still keeping her eyes on me. "You know, getting close to your mind is difficult, but with a little practice it can be done. It's not quite like looking at the sun with unprotected eyes, more like looking at a very bright torch, and if you manage to filter just a little you can see everything you have to. Would you like to know what *I'm* seeing?"

"Why not?" I responded, just stopping myself from snapping closed my strongest shield. I couldn't understand where that conversation was coming from or going, but hiding behind a shield wasn't necessary any longer. I finally had everything worked out, and never had to be a victim again. The kimla I swallowed at was beginning to cool, but it still did the job of wetting my mouth and throat.

"Terry, listen to me," she said as she put her hand on my arm, and I looked up to see that she was leaning toward me with urgency in her eyes. "What you're doing *has* helped to keep you sane until now, but if you keep on doing it, all you'll find is madness. You said you're coping with things, but that's just the point, you're *not* coping with them. Murdock told you *he* was responsible for taking you away from people who loved you to leave you with strangers, and you weren't even angry with him. Rissim and I welcomed you to our home as our daughter, and you simply smiled and moved in. Terry, you're looking at everything that's happening as though it isn't real, treating it all as a dream that can be experienced and enjoyed, but isn't anything to get excited over. Carried far enough, an attitude like that can cause complete withdrawal, so you have to stop it *now.*"

"I don't know what you're talking about," I said, holding tight to my cup of kimla as I wished she would let my arm go and stop staring at me like that. "Just because I'm finally learning how to control my emotions doesn't mean I'm not in touch with reality. You have to admit everything I've been told lately *is* just a little beyond the bounds of normal belief, so if you're getting an echo of the unreal from my mind, that must be the reason. After everything settles down, I'll be just—fine."

"Will you," she said, finally leaning back a little but still holding my arm, those green eyes glowing. "Is that why you're so determined to rid yourself of Tammad? You don't *want* to be rid of him, all you want to do is believe everything he tells you, but he has no place in the dream world you're building except as a painful, once-beloved memory. When he's gone you can relive the good times with him without risk, knowing he'll never be any less yours, knowing he'll never do anything to force you back to something you don't believe you can deal with. You've just been through a lot of hurt, my darling, but you mustn't believe that's all life holds for you. You're not alone any longer, and we're going to see to it that you're never alone again."

Never alone again. I stared at her as I let that phrase repeat itself over and over in my mind, feeling exactly what it meant to me. When you set people into place in your mind and then let yourself join them, they always say and do just what you like and never exclude you from their company. You have the best time you've ever had, you know you're loved and even liked, and all you have to do is be yourself to be witty, charming and completely accepted. Mistakes aren't important, because if they happen you just wipe everything out and start again, this time doing it right. Ordinary people can hurt you at any time no matter how often they swear they won't, but those who keep you company in your mind . . .

"It's trust, isn't it?" she said softly, sharing compassion with me. "All trusting people has gotten you so far is betrayal, and you're really afraid to try it again. Well, you don't have to, you know, at least not right away. We're willing to let you sit back and wait until we prove we can be trusted, we don't mind. After everything that's happened, it's the least we can do."

Her smile was friendly and warm and *real,* as real as the offer she'd made and just as sincere. It was also one of the oddest things I'd ever been told, and I got some idea of what my expression was like when her smile changed to a grin.

"With the rest of us taken care of, at least for a while, all you need to think about now is Tammad," she said, the conversation immediately changing from serious to amused along with her mood. "You can pretend the rest of us are unreal as much as you like, but *l'lendaa* have a habit of not letting themselves be treated that way. What will you do if the next time he shows up he's shielded?"

"He doesn't know how to shield," I said, making a face before finishing up the kimla in my cup. "And even if he happens to learn, didn't you hear what Len said? I've developed the ability to get *through* shields, which is what I had to do to win against Farian and become *Chama*. I don't expect to have any trouble with Tammad."

"Ouch, there goes that depression again," she said, making a face of her own. "With him it's not just a matter of trust, is it? You really are afraid to take him back because you might lose him again, but in the strangest way you're acting as if you already *have* lost him. I can feel disappointment, but you also seem to be blaming yourself as the cause of the disappointment. You're disappointed in him, but whatever he's done it isn't his fault. Hmmm."

Her sight went unfocused as her mind went into high gear, leaving me to reach for the kimla pitcher in an effort to keep my annoyance down. In a way Irin was behaving just the way Rissim had the night before, calmly deciding she had the right to mix into my life without once asking whether or not I minded. Considering the way Rimilian men were, his doing it wasn't very surprising, but what gave *her* the right to . . .

"Aha, I think I have it!" she said with a small laugh, her self-satisfaction very clear. "I'm usually not all that good at figuring these things out, but this time it was almost easy. The key was in what you said about not expecting to have any trouble with *l'lendaa*, and also in your comment that Tammad was used to winning against you. You liked the idea of his being able to stand up to you, but now that you've come to terms with your mind strength you don't think he'll be able to do it any longer. That's also why you're not very worried at the thought of your father being annoyed with you, but where Tammad's concerned you're disappointed rather than unworried. You didn't *want* to grow beyond him, but that didn't stop it from happening."

"He's the sort of man who has to be in charge, and with me around he can't be," I said with a shrug, finding her guess close enough to the mark to make correction unnecessary. "He once admitted he'd always had trouble coping with me, and the way I am now he'd have more than trouble. I can't trust him not to give me up one day for the sake of an ideal, and although he doesn't realize it yet, he can't trust me not to do things that will make him feel like less of a man. If it was just me I might take the chance, but knowing what it will do to him . . . What was that you said about reality being better than a dream world?"

"It *is* better, and you've got to believe that!" she said with intensity, no longer amused, her hand on my arm again. "Every time something like this happens you put up another layer of glass between you and the rest of us, but it's not shutting us out, it's locking *you* in! I'll bet that even when you cry the tears aren't real, not with the way you're refusing to feel anything. If you keep going on like this you'll be *made* of nothing but glass, and I don't think you need to be told what usually happens to things made of glass."

"For one, they seldom find themselves held in the arms of a man," another voice said, one I really hadn't been expecting. He shouldn't have come back calm and under control, he should have been mad as hell! "All *wendaa* deserve to be held in the arms of the men who love them, so that together they may find a solution to their troubles."

"Tammad, do sit down and have some kimla with us," Irin said in delight, really enjoying playing the gracious hostess in the middle of a primitive world. "Did you sleep well last night?"

"Your hospitality was most appreciated," the barbarian answered courteously as he came forward to sit cross-legged on my left, paying no attention to the fact that I wasn't even looking at him. "What oddness I faced this morning stemmed from a source beyond the control of you and the *l'lenda* Rissim, and I must therefore apologize for having taken my leave without first having given you thanks for your courtesy."

"Considering the fact that she *is* our daughter, apologies on your part are totally unnecessary," Irin came back, giving him a commiserating smile. "If she weren't already banded as yours, we would be the ones who needed to apologize. How much of our conversation did you hear?"

"Enough," he said, a turn of his head letting me have the weight of his eyes. "I felt much the fool, to discover myself busily out and about a doing which was no longer mine alone. It was not difficult knowing my *wenda* was to blame, for Dallan had told me of the thrall under which he had been kept in Vediaster. To say my anger was great is to say one is mildly pleased when one is victorious in battle."

"But you don't seem angry now," Irin pointed out, reaching the pitcher of kimla over to fill the cup her guest had picked up. "Did you change your mind along the way, or did you first have to hear what we were saying?"

"The condition of my anger has not changed," he said, the calm in his mind swirling as thickly as ever. "I had no wish to warn the woman of my approach, therefore did I cover what I felt before returning here. There will be punishment for what was done by her, yet now do I see the necessity for first assisting in returning her to that which she was. No man joys in having a woman without feeling."

"I love the way *l'lendaa* never give up on anything they really want," Irin said comfortably, amusement in her glance to me as she brought the pitcher back. "Rissim was like that when he first decided I was the one he wanted to band, and you can take my word for the fact that he didn't have an easy time of it. And it never bothered him that my mind was stronger than his. How much does Terry's strength bother *you?*"

She really was very pleased with herself when she turned a bright smile on Tammad and waited for his answer, but the smile faded when she saw the unfocused look in his eyes. He sat very still for a moment, head cocked as though listening intently, then dropped his cup of kimla, surged instantly and gracefully to his feet, and raced out of the private area he'd earlier barged into. He didn't make enough noise for us to follow his progress through the house by ear, but Irin wasn't listening by ear. I could feel her trying to reach his mind, but she'd really started too late. Before she could do anything at all he was out of her range, which let her turn her furious face to me.

"What have you done to him *now?*" she demanded, her annoyance and frustration so strong I was surprised she wasn't throwing things. "We had it all out in the open and he didn't *want* to leave, and all you needed to do was let him help! And just look at that mess you caused! What did you do to make him run out like that?"

"He thinks he hears his beloved calling out to him for his help," I said, then drained my cup of kimla before putting it aside. I hadn't known I could do that without using words to suggest the state of mind I wanted, but there had been too many surprises lately for me to spend much time oohing and aahing over another. "He's out there right now trying to find her, but all he'll find is the hard fact that his help isn't wanted. I appreciate the hospitality you've shown me, Irin, I thank you for your concern, and I hope you'll pass on my thanks to Rissim as well. As soon as I find a place to stay, I'll send for my clothes."

"Terrilian, you can't move out of the house!" she cried, climbing to her feet as I got to mine. "Do you think if you're not here that will stop me from trying to help you? Nothing will stop me, and you can bet everything you own on that!"

"You aren't helping, you're interfering!" I snapped back, conceding then that a polite leave-taking wasn't going to be possible. "You have no right encouraging a man I don't want anywhere near me, especially not after I told you *why* I don't want him. If that's your idea of making someone feel like part of a family, I'd rather be alone."

"That's exactly what your whole trouble is, too much of being alone!" she fumed back, fists now on hips. "That and being brought up to believe your opinion counts more than anyone else's. Do you have any idea how much arrogance it takes to decide you're not going to let someone make a sacrifice for you without even knowing whether or not *they* consider it a sacrifice? *You're* deciding what's best for *him* without making any effort to consult *his* wishes!"

"He's too stubborn to know what's good for him, so why would I waste the time?" I retorted, finding it more than clear that the discussion I was then in fell into the same category. "And if it's arrogance to want to direct your own life in your own way, then go right ahead and call me arrogant. Just as long as you do it from a distance, something *I'll* take care of, I don't mind in the least."

"Once that life you just mentioned becomes entwined with those of other people, you have to think of them as well as yourself," she said, refusing to give it up even as I began turning away. "It's *our* fault you never learned that, so your father and I will have to be the ones to do something about the lack. You're not finished with us, young lady, you're only starting, and that goes for whether *you* like it or not!"

Instead of answering I just kept going, making my way up the hall to the front door and then out. I was so annoyed it was all I could do to control the emotion, and actually had to stop for a minute once I was outside in the sunshine to get a better grip on myself. That woman had more nerve than anyone I had met in my entire life, and I was delighted I would *not* be living in her house any longer. It was hard to believe she would actually suggest I was *forcing* Tammad to do things my way. *He* was the one who went in for forcing, not me, and if she hadn't been so interested in her own interpretation of things she would know that. I stood squinting into the sunlight until I was calm enough to unclench my fists, then went looking for someone to tell me how to find the place I wanted to go.

Getting directions turned out to be simple. The first person I stopped knew exactly where the attack-planning group was meeting, and cheerfully gave me directions to a house not far from Murdock's. It hadn't occurred to me sooner, but in a situation like that everyone in the community could be expected to know what was going on because they all had a part in it. If they weren't planning they were part of the plan, so there was nothing more natural than that they know. A man who seemed to be a head servant let me into the house and politely asked me to wait, then went looking for someone to tell I was there. I waited with a patience I wasn't really feeling, but the wait turned out to be extremely short. I hadn't shifted in place more than once before a very familiar face came out from behind the hanging the servant had gone through.

"Terry, this is a pleasant surprise," Garth said, the warm greeting in his mind making me feel a little better. "Are you sure you're well enough to be here? Last night Tammad and Rissim agreed you'd be spending the day today taking it easy."

"I *am* taking it easy," I pointed out, seeing no need

for going into the question any further. "I just thought I'd check to see how far along you people are, to get some idea of when the attack is planned for. I had the impression you don't intend wasting much time before striking."

"We *can't* waste much time," he said, beginning to lead me back in the direction he'd come from, enthusiasm lighting his eyes. "Getting an attack off the planning board and onto the battlefield is usually a time-consuming process because of how careful you have to be with the lives of your people, but in our situation we have to move as fast as possible. We have someone with a supposedly faulty transponder set on your frequency leading their searchers around now, making sure the transponder goes out at the critical time to keep the complex people from catching him, but we can't keep that up forever. It won't be long before they either catch our man or come to the conclusion they're being had, and once that happens they'll be warned. We want to attack *before* they're ready for us, but there are nitty little points we're being tangled up in, which is why we'll all be glad you're here. You can answer what questions we have as we go along, and in between those times you can relax. Help yourself to something to drink, then make yourself comfortable."

By that time we had reached the large room the planning group was using, and Garth left me to go back to the circle of men and women who were busy arguing out two or three points at a time. They were at the end of the room closest to the unlit fireplace, between two of the four opened terrace doors in the long wall straight ahead, and I didn't have to ask if they'd mind having someone listening in. They already had an audience of one, and when Ashton saw me she grinned.

"Well, fancy meeting you here," she said from her place among the cushions on the near side of the room, saluting me with the cup she held. "Do you mean Irin's actually letting you out alone *this* soon? She must be sick or something."

"I'm a real, live grown-up, and as such I go and do as I please," I answered sourly, stopping near a small table to pour myself what felt like my twentieth cup of kimla.

"Let us also not forget that right now I have the strongest mind in the community, a mind I'm not at all reluctant to use. With that in view we might want to watch what we say to me, just to be certain we don't find out first-hand exactly how much getting smacked can hurt."

"My, my, aren't *we* touchy this morning," Ashton observed with only a little of her grin gone, watching as I sat down not far from her. "I can empathize with the position you're in, but you really do have to remember how long my little sister has been waiting to get you back. No one is going to be able to stop her from treating you like a backward infant for a while, but it won't be forever so you might as well just relax and enjoy it. Once she gets used to having you around she'll be handing you chores the way she does with the other women in the household, so you'll be best off making the lazy time last as long as possible."

"I'm afraid I won't be around long enough for either familiarity or chores," I said, sipping at my kimla while staring out the nearest open terrace door at a very pleasant private garden. "I intend being part of the attack force and afterward will spend some time trying to help the rest of you get past the plateau you're stopped at, but after that I'm leaving. I really do prefer more civilized surroundings, and with our war won I'll be able to go back to them."

I was able to enjoy the sight of pretty flowers in golden sunshine for a minute or so in silence, but I'd already learned that where Ashton is concerned, silence doesn't have much of a life span.

"There's more than simple fussing wrong between you and Irin," she stated, all amusement gone out of her voice. "I would have detected it sooner, but I didn't want to— Terry, you can't seriously mean that you *want* to leave all this, that you'd rather live with people who haven't the faintest idea what it is to share themselves with others? I've lived that life so I know what it's like, how narrow and individual and unsatisfying it is! You know you're one of us and that you belong with us, so how can you talk about leaving?"

"I open my mouth and move my tongue, that's how I

can talk about it,'' I said, still looking at the garden. ''If I want to live somewhere other than here that's *my* business, and I don't need anyone's permission to do it. If I get tired of the civilized life among the unawakened I can always visit Vediaster for a while, but I don't have to stay locked up here.''

''Locked up,'' she echoed, her mind disturbed and seriously concerned. ''And used together with 'have to.' I hate to imagine what went on to bring you to a point like that so soon after your being scared to death no one would accept you. I think it's time your aunt Asha had a long talk with her sister and your mother, just to . . .''

''Do me a favor and do your first talking to your brother,'' I interrupted, again finding myself unsurprised that Ashton intended getting on with her own quota of meddling. ''Since Murdock's the one responsible for bringing me here, he can also be responsible for finding me some place quiet and private to stay. If he doesn't manage to do it by sundown, he'll find me camping in his entrance hall.''

''Murdock's up to his ears right now arranging transports and coordinating the calling up of all our fighting forces, but I'll see what I can do,'' Ashton grudged, not happy about having to make the promise. ''If it comes right down to it, you can always stay with me. All right, all right, stop trying to kill me with a stare. You're not interested in sharing quarters with family, and that's all there is to it. But what about that gorgeous hunk of a man you've been avoiding? If you need a place to sleep, I'm sure he'd be more than happy to . . .''

Since I was already up on my feet and walking away from her I managed to avoid the rest of her clever comment, and happily she knew better than to pursue it by coming after me. I had more interest in what the planning group was up to than in anything Ashton could find to say, and it wasn't hard shifting my attention to them. Time went by while they argued, agreed, argued then agreed again, and some time during that period Tammad moved out of my range again. As soon as he did I called up my curtain, then went back to paying attention to what the planners were saying and doing.

I didn't have much experience watching strategists at work, but if that group was what they were normally like, I was really impressed. The going had seemed somewhat slow to begin with, but after a little while they really began rolling. Problems were brought up and solved one after the other, and during that time I discovered Ashton wasn't there just because she had nothing better to do with her time. After she answered the fifth or sixth question thrown at her it was possible to believe she had all the coordinating data there was, every bit of it filed carefully in her head. The first question she'd been asked had had to be repeated before she was drawn out of distraction, but that was understandable. I'd given her something not terribly pleasant to think about, and that was obviously what she'd been doing.

Garth had given me a smile when I'd first walked over to the group, but aside from that no one paid any attention to me unless they had a question about the complex. Perversely enough it felt good being that unpopular, and after a while I was able to simply listen without having to fight off thoughts of my own that were trying to distract me. A lot of kimla went down my throat during that time, and I was just thinking about refilling my cup when the strategists stirred and stretched and began talking about having a meal instead of how to get past enemy firepower. I thought briefly about joining them, decided against it when I found I still didn't have much of an appetite, so I got to my feet to leave. Where I intended going I wasn't quite sure, but when I turned to walk away I found Rissim directly in my path.

"I believe you were told, *treda* mine, that you were to remain at home this day so that you might be cared for," he said, looking down at me the way Rimilian men do when they're not very happy with you. "I returned to see how you fared, only to find that you had disobeyed and departed. I had hoped the time would be longer before you required guidance from he who fathered you, yet such is not to be. You will return home with me now, and for a short while we will talk."

He stood like a broad, tanned, immovable object, arms folded across his chest, light eyes pinning me where I stood. I had no idea how he'd found me—unless he'd been extremely clever about it and had asked the people in the shops around his house if they'd seen me—but I did know I wasn't going with him. I'd had more than enough "help" for one day, and "talk" was the next item on the same list.

"Rissim, I appreciate your concern, but I'm not going back," I said gently, trying not to hurt and disappoint him any more than I absolutely had to. "I came here to find out how soon we'll be attacking, because not long after we've won I'll be leaving Rimilia. I—miss my house and friends on Central, and after being away for so long I really need to go back. It has nothing to do with you and Irin, it's just a case of homesickness, so . . ."

"So we need only step aside and allow you to return to the solitude and loneliness which have ever been yours," he said, giving me no chance to finish the fine-sounding excuse I'd been weaving. "To believe that your mother and I would abandon you again is great foolishness, *wenda*, for such a thing will not be. And should you truly wish to be allowed to join in the attack you must practice obedience, for unless you have returned to adequate health you will merely watch others engaged in the effort. Come now, and we will see to your feeding before you sleep for a time."

"I said, I'm not going with you," I repeated with less gentleness, trying to keep from getting *too* annoyed. "I don't need anyone's permission to do anything, and I'll eat and sleep when *I* want to eat and sleep. If you people don't have enough to keep you busy with running your own lives, find someone else to take over and direct. I've had enough of being told what to do to last me till I'm old and gray."

If there were any chance of my living that long, I added to myself as I began to step around him, beginning to be aware of that deep weariness inside me again. Enough is enough is too much, and I seemed to have passed even the too much stage quite a while back. I had actually already dismissed Rissim from my thoughts when a big hand closed carefully around my arm, and I was no longer walking out of the room.

"You must learn, *treda* mine, that there is a great difference between those who direct you for their sake, and those who direct you for your own," I was told, the deep voice just as calm and patient as it had been. "Those who command you from love do so till you, yourself, are able to do the thing, till confusion and uncertainty have gone from you. When such completeness has returned to you, you will again be prepared to seek your fate. For now, you will merely obey."

"The hell I will," I answered, banishing my curtain as I looked up at him. "When I said I'd never be a victim again, I meant i—"

My words cut off in midsentence as my mind reached his—or, to be more precise, stopped as close to his as it could get. I hadn't noticed sooner but Rissim was shielded, and not with the sort of shiny round shield it was so easy to get through. His mind was tightly enclosed in the small, thick shield I also had, the kind I had to work *around* in order to get through. In desperation I crashed my mind against that shield, willing to work blind if I could just get around it, but there wasn't enough room to go around. From the inside there was plenty of room, but from the outside—

"You can't do this to me!" I shouted, trying to pull my arm loose from his grip, dropping the empty cup I held to free the hand for beating at him, but it all did as much good as it ever does with Rimilians. He paid no attention whatsoever to my struggling, acting as though I were standing still.

"For what reason can I not?" he asked, his continuing mildness and gentleness infuriating. "Are you not flesh of my flesh, and is it not the duty of a father to see to his offspring? In truth this duty should have been another's, yet am I told that you have declared yourself unbanded, and he who laid claim to you is no longer about. In view of these things we shall now return home."

He turned and began to make his way out of the house, and with his hand still around my arm there was no question about whether or not I went with him. Ashton and the others made no attempt to interfere, and neither did anyone on the street. I was gently and carefully dragged all the way back to his house, up the hall, and into my room. The open windows were no longer open, at least not down where I could reach them; above the regular windows, near the ceiling, were two-foot squares that let some light and air in through screening. I would have bet quite a lot that I'd find the lower windows locked in some way when I checked them, and Rissim's finally releasing my arm seemed to confirm that.

"Your mother will soon appear with a meal for you, *wenda,*" he said as he closed the door, then turned to look down at me. "She and I care for you very deeply, and have no wish to see you fade away before our eyes from lack of nourishment. You have said you wish to be a part of the attack force; should this continue to be so, you will obey us in an effort to grow strong again."

"If I wasn't already strong enough, you wouldn't be so closely shielded," I said, folding my arms as I looked up at him. "How long do you think you can keep me here like this?"

"As long as necessary," he returned with a shrug, folding his own arms. "Would you care to speak of what disturbs you, and afterward be given my views of the matter? Too often are we able to see no other than a single side of a difficulty, when sight of two sides is required for a solution."

"I have all the views of my troubles that I need," I came back, really hating all that patience and understanding. "I'll get out of here, you know, just the way I've gotten out of every other prison trying to hold me. No matter what you do to me, you won't stop me from succeeding."

"Should you wish to be released from here, you need only obey me a short while," he said, a gleam of—pride?—in his eyes. "Your imprisonment here is not imprisonment but punishment, a child's punishment for the behavior of a child. To endanger one's health and well-being is foolishness, *treda* mine, and to see those who attempt to aid you as enemies and captors more foolish still. When your behavior shows you to be no longer a child, you will have no need to seek escape. You will walk from here to freedom as does any adult."

"You're lying just to confuse me!" I shouted, my head whirling almost as badly as it had the night before. I'd fought so hard against enemies pretending to be friends, and now he was calling me a fool for keeping on with it! Everyone was *always* after me for something, Aesnil in Grelana, Farian in Vediaster, those people at the complex. I *couldn't* let my guard down and believe someone was doing something for *me*, I just couldn't! I began to turn away from him with my fists in my hair, but the return of his hand to my arm stopped me.

"You may not give insult to those about you without adding to your punishment," he said, looking more hurt than angry. "As you continue to show the actions of a child so will you be treated, and perhaps such a doing will be best. One must be a child before one is able to grow to adulthood."

I had begun feeling again as though I were walking through a dream, and what happened after that just made the feeling worse. Rissim sat down and put me over his knee, then spanked me as though I *were* a child. There was no doubt about whether or not it hurt, but it didn't hurt like torture, only like punishment. By the time it was over Irin was there, shielded just the way he was, but with commiseration and compassion still flowing thick enough to fill a river. She spent a short time comforting me and a longer time getting me to eat some of the food she'd brought, and then she got me out of my clothes and into bed. She and Rissim were still there in the room, but I fell asleep just as though I had nothing to worry about.

When I woke again it was dark outside with a single candle burning in the room, and I was so confused I didn't know why I wasn't dizzy. At first it had been pleasant fantasizing those people as my parents, but now things were getting complicated. I *knew* they wanted something from me, but I hadn't yet been able to find out what it was. The longer it took the less sure I became, and I didn't like not being sure. I lay belly down with my cheek to the furs under me, thinking about all that not-knowing, and suddenly it came to me to wonder if there really was something wrong with me. Confusion seemed to be the only emotion I was able to feel any more, that and suspicion. I hadn't been feeling really right since I escaped from the complex, and having no true desire for food was only a small part of it. Most of the time it seemed that everyone else was at fault, but if I held very still and thought about it—

I cursed under my breath as I leaned up on my elbows, feeling the truth of the thought I'd begun. There *was* something wrong, no doubt about it, but getting rid of it wasn't going to be easy. If I didn't even want to think about it—and the way my mind was avoiding the issue showed exactly that—how was I supposed to figure out what was wrong and fix it? I certainly couldn't trust anyone to *help* me find it—

"Hell and damnation!" I growled, knowing it was working on me again but helpless to stop it. Layers of glass between you and the world, Irin had said, layers that just got thicker and thicker. You on the inside, she said, and you'll never get out. Me on the inside with whatever was wrong, and how the hell was anything supposed to reach—

I had started shifting around in annoyance, but a twinge of pain in my back brought me up short. My back still wasn't in very good shape, because it wasn't healing more than slowly. I'd used pain control a couple of times, but not once since I'd gotten back to Rimilia had I tried to use the deep-healing aspect of pain control. I'd used it before so it didn't make any sense—and then I could feel the urge to try it beginning to fade—

"Something is making you not want to use it, so you've got to do it anyway," I whispered to myself, trying to sound and feel determined. I really didn't want to do it so that meant I had to, to keep from being forced into anything. Even that thought confused me, more than I felt I could stand, but maybe the inner healing *would* work. Without floundering around the question any longer, a question I would soon drown in, I got a two-hand grip of the fur under me, bent my head, then turned my attention inward.

The first time I'd tried deep self-healing I hadn't been

aware of the passage of time, and my second effort was just like the first. I came out of it wondering if I'd accomplished anything, turned over under the cover fur to sit up, then rubbed at my eyes with my hands. I'd been surrounded by people I couldn't trust, people who only wanted to make me a victim and use me for their own purposes—but the strong suspicion as well as the conviction was already fading. It looked like the first half of the irrational conviction had been a mental disorder, probably set in place by conditioning, most likely to keep me from trusting anyone at the complex. If those who were aware of what was going on didn't trust anyone there, they wouldn't plot with them against those who ran the complex. Then something had happened to make the distrust begin coloring everything else I was feeling, putting a veneer of the complex on Rimilia and binding them inseparably together. I could see that now, also remembering I'd wanted to die in both places, and the reinforced feeling had convinced me not to heal myself any farther. If I'd just left it all alone my problems would soon have been solved, and I'd simply have slipped from dreams to death without once having to touch reality. It would have been the easy way, the pleasant way, but I'd always been too thickheaded to take one of those paths . . .

"Oh, good, you're awake," Irin's voice came suddenly and I dropped my hands to see her standing in the now open doorway. "Are you feeling better after your nap?"

"I'm feeling better after something a little more effective than a nap," I said, watching her walk closer to the bed I sat in. "Irin, about the way I've been behaving . . ."

"Now, don't you let that worry you even for a minute," she interrupted, giving me a smile as she put a hand to my cheek. "Every time so far you've been better after getting your rest, so I'm going to see to it that you get all the rest you need. You'll stay in that bed until you're completely better, which will happen in no time at all. Are you ready to eat again?"

"No, I'm not ready to eat again," I answered, trying

to keep the annoyance out of my voice. "What I'm ready to do is explain why . . ."

"Terry, you don't want your father to hear you refusing again, do you?" she asked, suddenly being very conspiratorily serious. "It hurt me to see him spank you like that and I know it hurt him as well, but he'll do it again if he has to. He wants to know you're eating well, and he won't like what you just said. Do you want me to tell him?"

"Good lord, no," I muttered, wondering how she had the nerve to say it had hurt *them.* "Irin, listen to me, there's something I have to expl—"

"Then he won't be told," she plowed on, beaming at me over the secret we were going to keep together. "As long as you're a good girl and do as you're supposed to, you won't have to be punished. I'll be right back with your food."

I watched her walk out and close the door again, then let myself fall back flat onto the bed furs. It was upsetting to realize Irin had been treating me like a very small child, just the way Rissim had decided I needed to be treated, and I hadn't been able to get through her wall of make-believe any more than I'd been able to get through her shield. As soon as I explained why I'd been acting so strangely they'd let me out of there, but first I had to get more than three words in edgewise—*without* sending her running for Rissim. That spanking had hurt even through my trousers, and I didn't want to have to try explaining things during a second dose of it. I'd have to get through to Irin while I was eating, and then I could take some time off to do a little thinking.

Irin and the food came back, but getting through to her wasn't on the menu. She chattered away happily while she sat at the side of the bed-furs feeding me, and it was Rissim himself who stood beside the doorway watching. Every time *I* tried to say something he got that look in his eyes, and then Irin was shoveling in more food. I wasn't reluctant to eat any longer, not after the healing had finally let me know how much I needed it, but my capacity was way down and I was getting more and more desperate to explain something they didn't want to hear.

It was *not* what might be considered a fun time, and when Irin finally let me off the hook, Rissim took his turn.

"There are those who would speak with you now, *wenda,*" he said, giving me that well-known Rimilian-male-light-eyed-stare. "As I will not have one of mine giving insult to guests beneath my roof, you will speak yourself only when spoken to, and then will reply politely and to the point. At all other times you will remain silent, else shall you be given a reason for raising your voice. Is my meaning clear to you?"

I nodded glumly as I leaned against the cushions Irin had put behind my back, understanding I had to acknowledge temporary defeat. Rissim didn't want me insulting whoever his visitors were, so I either kept quiet or got put over his knee again. I'd have to wait until they left before taking the chance of insisting on speaking my piece, but that would be a time when Rissim would be more likely to listen. First I'd wait, and then I'd take the chance.

Irin took the food away, and then came back leading a group of men and women who were mixed part Rimilian and part Centran, just like the group of strategists I'd spent the morning listening to. They were introduced as a group rather than individually—to keep from tiring me with unnecessary introductions, I was told—and the group they were was the one concerned with mental abilities. They'd come to find out just how far I'd gotten, and even beyond that, how I'd managed to get that far.

I told them what I could about the progression of my abilities, mentioned all the new things I'd started finding after almost being burned out, and then I was told something I hadn't expected to hear. I'd finished answering questions about my fight with the intruder in the resting place of the Sword of Gerleth, having related everything about it just to be sure I didn't leave out something important, and for a moment there was a very heavy silence. I could feel the group's roiling emotions despite the excellent control every one of them had, and then one of the women sighed.

"I'm—afraid the—experience you had was—in a

roundabout way—the fault of this community,'' she said, forcing the words out past a very great reluctance, her eyes having difficulty staying on my face. ''That—intruder who did so much to hurt you and the others. It pains me to admit it, but he was one of ours.''

''Yours?'' I echoed, shocked to hear her say something like that. ''But he wasn't an empath! How could he be one of yours?''

''He was a strange-birth, a result of the mixing of Rimilian and Centran blood that happily occurs only very, very rarely,'' she answered, still dragging the words out. ''He was born without a trace of the least amount of mental ability, and to make matters worse was larger even than native-born Rimilians despite his dark hair. He was—very delicately balanced even as a child, and the older he got the worse the instability became. When he changed from a boy to a man, he tried to get the girls interested in him, but they were all empaths and wanted nothing to do with an untalented no matter how physically attractive he was. He tried for a long while before he gave up, and then he retreated into a fantasy world.''

''One in which everyone was like him, and everyone conformed to the rules he had devised,'' I said, shivering a little as I remembered how he'd insisted *I* was from his secret community. I'd thought he was insane and he certainly had been, but he really hadn't been wrong. ''No wonder the girls of his world weren't allowed to pair with men until they were 'fully grown.' That was the reason none of them had paired with *him*. . . .''

''Yes,'' the woman agreed in a pitying whisper, adding something about his disappearing one day and never coming back. He must have found some secret way into the mountain, and then had discovered the resting place of the Sword. There was another silence, this one filled with the emotions of farewell, and then they were all on their feet and heading out the door. My memories of the time had caught and held me for a short while, and they'd known without being told that I had no real desire to continue the discussion. Irin had given me a hug and a kiss good night, had blown out the candle, and was already gone with the door closed behind her before I remembered I'd wanted to talk to Rissim. He had left with her, of course, which meant I would have to wait until the next day before I could get another chance at him. I spent a long number of minutes cursing just loud enough for me to hear, then spent even more time trying to fall asleep.

The next morning I wasn't awake long before Irin and one of the house servants showed up with breakfast, and when I was forced into trying to shout down her endless, cheering chatter, she refused to let me do it. She had decided to give me no chance to say anything at all in order to keep from getting into another argument with me, and very nearly got into an argument with me trying to stick to her decision. When she insisted that all she wanted to hear was whether or not I was going to eat breakfast, I lost my temper completely and told her what she might do with that breakfast. The serving woman gasped and turned red then hurried out of the room, leaving Irin to work briefly at keeping herself from exploding before she turned and stomped out after her. Once the door was slammed closed I was all alone again, but I knew it wouldn't be for long. As soon as Irin spoke to Rissim I'd have company, but not in the mood that would do me much good.

Rissim must have been out of the house, as I had enough time to dress and do some long-distance looking around before he showed up. I'd discovered that everyone in the house was shielded, and had been spending quite a while picking away at one or two of those shields when the door to my room was opened. I blinked away from what I was doing to see Rissim standing there and staring down at me, and his meaningful silence at least let me have the chance to speak first.

"Before you start lecturing me, I'd appreciate it if you would listen to me for a minute," I told him, sitting up and folding one leg under me. "I've been trying since yesterday to tell Irin I found out what was wrong with me, but she refuses to stop talking long enough to hear it. Some of the conditioning they'd put me through was still affecting me, but I managed to neutralize it and now it's all gone."

"Indeed," he said in much too neutral a way, folding his arms and leaning one broad shoulder against the door jamb. "I am to understand that what ailed you previously is now no more, and therefore should you be released from this punishment?"

"Well, you did say it was only a temporary measure," I muttered, having no need to touch his mind to know he wasn't believing a word I said. "You were absolutely right about how childish I was being, and if you'll drop your shield you'll be able to see for yourself that that's all over with."

"So, I am to release my shield and touch your mind, and then I will know the full truth of the matter," he said, nodding slowly as he kept those eyes on me. "I am to put from my thoughts your ability to seize an unprotected mind, and seek the truth in the manner you suggest. You must forgive me should I appear skeptical, *wenda*, and also forgive my observation that there is another manner in which the truth might be learned."

"What other way?" I asked with a sinking feeling, knowing beyond doubt that our conversation was *not* destined to turn out well. Rissim had already made up his mind about what he was going to do, and only had to explain it to me before he got on with it.

"To see truth, very often one need do no more than look about oneself,"he said, that horrible calm and patience sickeningly clear. "My girl child was told what was required of her, and also was she given punishment for offering insult to a parent, yet what did I discover this day upon my return to my house? I discovered that this selfsame child was no longer in the bed furs where she was to remain, she had once again refused nourishment, and had given her mother insult in the hearing of a servant. Now I am to believe that my child no longer suffers from what previously ailed her? I am to withhold additional punishment, for I have not been told what truly occurred? Speak to me, *treda* mine, and assure me that these things are not what they seem."

"But they're not!" I protested, trying to hold my voice

steady as I got to my feet. "Yes, I argued with Irin, and yes I insulted her after refusing to eat, but I was provoked into doing all that! I really did find out what was wrong with me and fix it, but none of you will believe me! Do you know how frustrating it is when people won't listen to you? I suppose I shouldn't have lost my temper, but I'm not a child and I don't do well being treated like one. You said you would treat me like an adult when I behaved like one, so I'm going to hold you to that. I stand as an adult before you, and now I want to be let out of here."

"To speak of oneself as an adult is not to be that thing," he came back, completely unconvinced. "At all times do one's actions speak more clearly than one's words, and what actions we have had from you are veritable shouts. I fear I must do my duty as I see it, and punish the disobedience of a child."

"But that's what I always act like," I mumbled with that sinking feeling back as he unfolded his arms and leaned off the door jamb. This time I knew he would spank me harder, and I really didn't want to experience that. I was trying desperately to decide if there was any place for me to run when he moved partway out of the doorway, giving me the chance to see beyond him, and for a moment I didn't believe what I saw. Folded into an easy crouch not five feet from the door was Tammad, and as soon as my eyes touched him I found that he was also looking at me. For an instant my heart leaped as my lips parted and I began reaching a hand out to him, knowing that he would protect me and keep Rissim from doing what he intended, but then I was yanked back to the real world. Even if I hadn't done what I had to Tammad, I still couldn't have asked him to interfere, not when there was nothing left for us to share. It simply wouldn't have been fair, and the least I owed him was fairness. I closed my lips as my hand fell, then let my gaze do the same.

"On second thought, I undoubtedly deserve whatever you do to me," I said to Rissim in an unliving voice as I stared down at the carpet fur. "And when you stop to think about it, it doesn't even matter."

My eyes closed all the way then, all the thoughts I had about Tammad trying to crowd at once into my mind. I'd never love anyone the way I loved him, but the reasons for our separating hadn't changed at all. I'd rather die than hurt him, but if I stayed with him hurt was all he would be. Right then I really regretted the loss of that leftover conditioning, the mind sickness that had let me do what was necessary without once thinking about my feelings for him. I'd been able to blame him for everything he'd ever done to me without trying to understand any of it, the whole thing simply showing me more clearly how untrustworthy he was. Him, my beloved, untrustworthy. I turned blindly away from the door and hurried to a pile of cushions on the carpet fur, sinking down to wait there for what Rissim would do.

It wasn't long before I heard my door being closed, and the faint sound of bare feet moving across the carpet fur. At that point I really didn't care what happened to me, but when a big hand touched my hair gently I couldn't keep from shivering. So many times it had been *he* who had touched me that way, but this time it wouldn't be the same. I needed so desperately to be held that I wrapped my arms around myself, my eyes still closed tight against sight of the real world I had come to hate. I had no choice about being in that world but I did have a choice about looking at it, and then all the confusion I had thought resolved came rushing back. Two wide, powerful arms circled me to hold me to a broad, well-muscled chest, but the gesture wasn't one of a father comforting his daughter, and the hum in the mind above my head confirmed that. Shocked, I began to struggle in protest, and only then did I realize who the hum belonged to.

"Yes, *wenda*, once again it is I," Tammad said, looking down at me with those beautiful blue eyes while I gaped up at him in disbelief. "To rid oneself of a *l'lenda* is not quite as easily done as some apparently believe."

Without even stopping to think about it I squirmed higher in his arms, threw my own arms around his neck, then kissed him with all the longing in the universe. I know it wasn't right and certainly wasn't fair, but I'd missed him so much and it was only a kiss. He contributed more than his own share to the meeting of our lips and souls, but when I felt the hum in his mind begin changing to a growl I gently pulled away.

"I'm sorry," I said, touching his face with my fingertips as I drew away a little more. "I had no right doing that, but I—couldn't seem to stop myself. And I'd also like to apologize for what I did to you yesterday. There was something wrong with me, and I didn't care what I did to anyone as long as doing it accomplished what I wanted. The same thing still needs doing, but I can see to it without hurting or humiliating you."

"You cannot be saying you mean to continue with this foolishness," he stated, the look in his eyes beginning to harden. "Have you not just this moment proven that your love for me is as great as ever it was? Have you forgotten my vow that I will allow none to take my woman from me? Think you that vow precludes the doings of the woman herself?"

"It's not foolishness, and keeping on with it is exactly what I intend," I told him, deliberately ignoring everything else he'd said as I sat back down on the carpet fur. "I wasn't lying when I said I'd rather not have you than take the chance of losing you, and you've got to understand that."

"*Wenda*, how is it *possible* to understand such a thing?" he demanded, automatically moving his sword out of the way as he shifted to sitting cross-legged opposite me. "To *give up* a thing is to *lose* it, more quickly and more definitely than with an as-yet unrealized possibility which may or may not lie ahead! To commit an actual doing out of fear that a *possible* doing may occur, is the act of one who is likely age-addled!"

"Since you're older than I am, if I were you I would watch who I called senile," I retorted, almost wishing a talk between us wasn't necessary. "I can't help it if you don't follow simple logic, but I would prefer if you did understand. Look, it's really easy: if I give you up now it's all over and done with, nothing left to spend my life dreading, nothing to lie awake nights worrying about. Knowing it's all over with hurts, but not as much as sitting around waiting for it to happen. Do you understand now?"

"In no manner," he said very positively, still looking at me as if I were crazy, and then he sighed. "Clearly is this a view seen only by those who are *wendaa*, a landscape forbidden to the sight of men. As I am unable to find understanding in *your* words, *hama*, perhaps you will have greater success with mine. You fear that one day a facet of the demands of honor will cause me to turn from you, and I say that such a consideration shows only that you have not yet grasped the place where the heart of honor lies."

I parted my lips to tell him that wasn't so, that I knew more of honor than I wanted to, but he shook his head to silence me and took my hand in both of his.

"Most certainly is it true that the demands of honor are undeniable to one who is bound to them," he said, his expression sober and calm, his eyes looking into mine. "Honor is—a thing of fitness, a thing of right, a manner of being which allows one to see what must be done so that the weak may find happiness as easily as the strong. It is these and many other things—yet is it above all fitting. For a man to give his life to honor would be fitting—yet not so were he to give the life or happiness of one who feels love for him. Such would be a great *dis*honor, to feed one's pride with another's pain. That one is most honorable who knows and acknowledges the *limits* of honor."

"I—don't think I understand what you're saying either," I admitted when he fell silent, obviously giving me a chance to comment. "All I know is that I thought I'd lost you, and I didn't want to live any more. But that isn't the only side of this, or even the most important. You can't say you've forgotten what I did to you yesterday, and I can't say I won't ever do it again. I don't *want* to ever do it again, but that doesn't mean I won't. If you think I'll hang around waiting until the next time I end up making you feel like a fool, *you're* the one who's senile."

"But that, too, is a problem with its solution," he said, grinning faintly as he stroked one of his hands just a little higher up my arm. "When I was able to know I had been taken a second time, I gave over the foolishness of believing I might best a blood-mad *fazee* with my hands alone, and sought out the aid of the Murdock McKenzie. He it was who sent me the man Lamdon, and with that one's assistance was I able to fashion the thing I required. When I came upon Rissim early this day, instructing the young in the use of a sword, I informed him of my intention to approach you yet again, and he asked the favor that I await the time he might accompany me. For that reason was I there, where you saw me, allowing him the opportunity of speaking first with you. Now would I have you attempt to make my thoughts yours again."

"But I really don't want to," I told him, paying only partial attention to what was being said. His fingers stroking my arm had riveted the major portion of my attention to him, so much so that I just *had* to use my free hand to touch his own arm. So tanned and warm it was, so hard and yet so delicious to feel, so much a part of him . . .

"And yet you must," he insisted mildly, the strength in his fingers now gently kneading my flesh. "How else are we to know whether my precautions are adequate? Strike swiftly and with skill, and then shall we know."

"Swiftly and with skill," I repeated as his hand made its way up to my shoulder, then I swallowed and muttered a what-the-hell. If he wanted me to do it again, then I would do it again, and maybe there would be something afterward I would have to order him to forget. I began to approach his mind, not as ruthlessly as I had the other times but well enough—and then I pulled back in surprise. Instead of the cloud of calm he had always used as a shield there was suddenly an actual shield, but not like mine or Rissim's or Irin's. Tammad had learned to generate a shifting diagonal shield like Farian's, but its rate of motion was so much faster it was nearly a blur.

"Now do you see the fruits of my efforts," he murmured, circling me with one arm to draw me close to him again. "You may not touch me should I disallow it, no matter the greater strength of your mind."

"But that doesn't mean anything," I protested weakly, trying to get him to stop kissing me in between words.

"You can't stay shielded forever, and once you release the shield you're vulnerable again. And what if I solve your shield, the way I did with Farian's?"

"Your time must be taken up with other things, so that you have none to spend on worrying and solvings," he said, putting me to the carpeting before sending his hands to my clothing. "It has been far too long since last we shared our love, *hama,* and no longer am I able to keep my hands from you. I will see you well occupied, my beloved, and so well loved that never again will you doubt the wisdom of our sharing each other's lives. You are mine, and never will I release you."

My clothes were gone so fast I barely saw them go, and no more than an instant later his swordbelt and *haddin* were down with the rest. It was so mindlessly wonderful to be held and loved by him again, so achingly good to touch him all over, but along with the pleasure there also came something I hadn't wanted and certainly hadn't been looking for. By the time we had satisfied ourselves physically I was mentally at a new low, and not only because Tammad had proven one of my points for me. His excitement had been too high to let him keep his new shield in place very long, and he had ended as deeply inside my mind as he was in my body. Something very definitely had to be done, so I sighed and got started.

When we walked into the kitchens Irin was there with a number of the house women, but Tammad didn't even glance at them. He went immediately to one corner of the room and began rummaging around, having no idea how many people were staring at him. Everyone was puzzled but then Irin got it, and a moment later she was over staring at me instead.

"How could you do that to him *again?*" she demanded, more upset than angry. "He loves you, and look what you're making him do!"

"He *said* he wanted me to try again," I evaded, trying to gather my courage, then said to hell with it and simply plunged in. "Irin—I'd like to apologize for what I said to you this morning. I shouldn't have lost my temper with someone who was just trying to help—and certainly not when that someone was you. I'm really not quite *that* bad, at least not any more."

She stared at me intently for a minute, trying to decide if I were lying, most likely, and then she realized that with Tammad under my control I had no reason to lie and could simply have left without saying a word. Her face softened and she came closer to hug me, and after I'd hugged her back she used one hand to smooth my hair.

"You don't have to apologize to me, not with the way I was treating you," she said, a lot of relief along with the amusement she showed. "If anyone had treated *me* like that, I probably would have thrown plates instead of insults. But I don't understand what's going on. Your father told me you and Tammad were back together again, just the way he'd hoped you would be. Why are you controlling him again?"

"To make a point and because I have a problem," I answered glumly, letting pass what she'd told me about Rissim's plans. He'd pretended he was going to spank me, trying to force me to run to Tammad for protection, but it hadn't worked out quite the way he'd wanted. "Irin, Tammad says he'll never let me go, but a little while ago I realized why I've been so convinced that Tammad and I are through. With all the confusion and such cleared away I can recognize the feeling I have, a kind of feeling I've had before. It tells me I'll never belong to him, and every time so far that feeling's been right. I have to tell him it's over between us no matter how hard he tries to fight it, but I don't know how to make him believe me. Do *you* have any ideas?"

"You have a 'feeling'?" she asked, frowning at me but not in disbelief. She'd let her shield dissolve, and her mind was also trying to stare at mine. "I don't like the sound of that, and I think we'd all better sit down and talk about it. Is this feeling the same thing you called a conviction when you spoke to the searchers last night?"

I nodded as she called one of the women over and sent her to get Rissim, then we waited until he showed up. Tammad kept busy searching the kitchen methodically, and Irin almost choked when she asked what he was looking for and I told her. The mighty *l'lenda* was looking for the shield that was going to protect him from me which he *knew* was hidden somewhere in the room, and he was *determined* to find it. She shook her head at me in forced disapproval, trying to swallow down laughter from inside, and made sure not to mention the point to Rissim.

Once he was there and had been told what was going on, I was able to release Tammad. After the couple of minutes necessary for his head to clear it was Rissim I had to hide behind, but the older *l'lenda* was able to calm the younger, and then we all went to a small, pleasant room to talk.

"I see no call for discussing a matter which need not even be considered," Tammad growled when we were all seated among the cushions, his new shield tight around his mind. "The woman merely seeks to justify the stand she has taken, for stubbornness brings her naught when offered to me."

"Tammad, we *do* have to discuss it," Irin said with commiseration plain on her face, knowing he couldn't get it from her mind. "Terry isn't trying to be stubborn, she's being told something, the same sort of something Murdock was told when he took her from us. Precognition seems to be a family trait, and she's inherited it."

"To refuse to give ear to a warning is not the doing of a brave man," Rissim said, seeing along with the rest of us the way Tammad's jaw set. "Instead is it the doing of a fool, for with sufficient warning a man may take victory from the grasp of his enemies. Tell us again of what has come to you, daughter."

"I just suddenly *knew* I would never belong to him," I answered, looking at Rissim rather than at the man I spoke about. "I've learned that it doesn't matter whether or not I want it to be like that, it will happen anyway. Trying to talk me out of believing it won't do any good, no more than forcing me to ignore it. We've already tried those things, and they didn't work."

Out of the corner of my eye I saw Tammad straighten where he sat, remembering in spite of himself the previous warnings I'd tried to give him. I'd asked to be taught how to use a sword and he'd laughed at me, but he hadn't had any laughter left when I lost him to Roodar because I *couldn't* use a sword. I'd asked not to be taken to Vediaster and especially not into the palace, and he'd ignored me—causing us all to be captured and enslaved. His anger backed down a little, letting him join us in talking about the problem, but we talked for the rest of the day without finding any answers we could all live with.

We could have continued talking about it the next day, but the next day we all left to attack the complex on New Dawn.

# 14

I've never found wilderness particularly attractive, but there was something very satisfying in being in the wilderness on New Dawn. We who had gotten there on five large transports had set up a temporary camp just out of detection range of the complex, and it wouldn't be long before we got the attack under way. I was wandering around alone for once, Tammad, Irin and Rissim all being occupied with other things, and I made excellent use of the thinking time. I couldn't say I was particularly happy with one of the decisions I'd made, but another of them made up for it as far as it could ever be made up for. In a small way it even brightened the cloudy skies above me, and made me fairly eager to be finished with what we were doing so I could get started. . . .

"Well, fancy meeting you here," a voice drawled, and I looked up to see Ashton giving me her usual grin. "Did you escape, or are you out on parole?"

"The rest of them are busy," I answered, amused in spite of myself. "And I'm not being held prisoner, we're just trying to work out a problem together. It only looks and feels as though I'm being held prisoner."

"Well, Murdock and I have missed you these last days," she said, putting an arm around my shoulders to aim me toward one of the tents. "Why don't you visit with us for a few minutes during what will probably be our last lull, and tell us what's been happening with you?"

Having nothing better to do I shrugged and agreed, and a moment later Murdock was adding his welcoming words to Ashton's. He looked really tired and so did she, but that was only to be expected.

"Nothing very much has been happening," I said when Ashton repeated her question, sipping from the cup of kimla I'd been given. "There's something Tammad and I can't agree on, and even with Irin's and Rissim's help we aren't finding it possible to settle. I'm more than willing to keep trying, but I'm afraid that very soon he and I will be going our separate ways."

I thought about what I'd be losing as I sipped at my kimla, and about all those glorious nights and satisfying days I'd been spending with Tammad. That first night on Rimilia I'd been more than ready to give him up, furious that the beast had kept himself shielded and then had given me the spanking I'd missed getting from Rissim. He'd punished me for controlling him and had pointed out that he would and could do it again if I ever tried controlling him again, and then he'd taken me in his arms and had made love to me. After that things were somehow different between us, just as though I was no longer simply a *wenda* in his mind, more like he thought of me as *w'wenda*. It was an acceptance above and beyond the love he felt, and I'd never known anything could be that good.

"What plans have you made for after the attack is done?" Murdock asked suddenly, as though something had just come to him. "Am I mistaken in believing you mean to remain on Rimilia a short while to assist in investigating the source of your strength and abilities?"

"I have something to do first, but after that I'll be back on Rimilia to help," I answered with a smile, again feeling that sense of excited anticipation. "I'm very glad there's a coordinated attack being launched at Rathmore and his group while we're seeing to this one, because I really do need to go to Central for a short time. I—left something there a while ago, something that doesn't entirely belong to me, and I'd like to get it back and give it to its rightful owner. It's all I can do, Murdock, and maybe it will help a little."

"The child you left in stasis," Murdock said with no expression on his face, surprising me by knowing about it. "You intend having the fetus reimplanted, bearing the child, and then giving it to Tammad. To make up for your not being able to remain beside him.''

"Why, yes,'' I said, flustered over seeing what had to be his talent at work, not understanding why his eyes and mind were as dead as his voice. "The child is his and mine, and I've never wanted anything more than I want to give my beloved our child. I know I won't be able to stay with him, so this is the only way to do it.''

"Terrilian—my dear child—how do I say this?'' Murdock whispered, the tortured pain in him so heavy that Ashton was as shocked as I. "They—knew about the child, just as they know everything about the Primes they're so concerned with. They couldn't—allow a 'tainted' mixture of blood to remain where it might have—embarrassed them. They—they—''

He raised a trembling hand as he found it impossible to go on, his eyes trying to tell me how much he hurt for me, but all I could do was stand up while letting the cup of kimla fall to the tent floor. They'd taken my baby from where I'd left it and they'd killed it, throwing it away as though it were so much disgusting garbage. Ashton's mind was crying as she tried to reach for me, but I thrust her away with more strength than my arms had ever had and ran out of the tent. I had to get away from there, away from the place I'd been told something so terrible I couldn't bear it, and running was the only way to do it. I ran and I ran, out of the camp, into the forest and beyond, trying not to think, using the power of my mind to keep anyone from following me. I had to get away, and it didn't matter to where.

Running hard and wild does help to keep you from thinking, especially when you're crying and raveningly furious and totally shattered, all at the same time. I ran on for what felt like hours, picking myself up and going on again when I fell, not caring where I was going or how scratched and bruised I was getting. There were no predators in the area to threaten me, none would have dared even if they'd been there, so I just kept going. I had to find some place that agony couldn't reach me, some place I could scream out loud and no one would hear it, but when I was finally forced to stop for a while

I still hadn't gotten there. Sweat streamed down my face and mixed with the dirt on it while I stood panting and gasping for breath, but I still wasn't where I wanted to be. We had scouts out in the woods, I remembered, and I had to avoid them or I'd never find the place I needed.

I wiped my torn palms on the brown uniform I wore, the same uniform I'd been wearing when I escaped from the complex, the uniform I'd somehow felt I *had* to wear even though Tammad had hated the idea. It seemed to be coming in handy after all, getting even more torn and ruined than it had been, saving good clothes from being treated like that. I started to laugh at myself for thinking about clothes at a time like that, but it immediately turned to sobbing, that forced me to put a hand over my mouth, and then I began running again.

I *began* running, but suddenly something sharp pinched my left arm, and I looked over to see the dart, and then I didn't see anything—

I woke up feeling lethargic, but it only took me a minute to understand what had happened and where I was. I was still in the filthy, sweat-covered uniform, and my left arm hurt a little where the dart had hit me. I must have known I'd run into some of the people from the complex even before the knockout drug had taken effect, and looking around at the small room I lay in confirmed that. I was on a narrow, padded couch of brown leather in a neatly dark-paneled room with a tiny, spotless desk, and the Sec staring at me just completed the picture. I took my time getting around to examining her face, but when I did she smiled faintly.

"In case you don't remember, the name's Finner," she said, studying me from the chair she sat in. She was a big woman with blond hair and gray eyes, and I recalled her as the Sec in the dorm room who had tried to talk me into cooperating.

"I remember," I said, examining her mind to find what I thought I would. She was a null, even if she did show more emotion than the rest of the breed. "Do they really think hiding behind you will do them any good?"

"They know it will," she answered with a wider smile,

crossing her legs as she relaxed back in the chair. "You did a good job of keeping out of the way of searchers for a lot of days, but your luck ran out when you stumbled over that team looking for targets to bring back. You really couldn't have expected to stay loose much longer, and now that we have you again you might as well be reasonable."

I sat up on the couch to cover my surprise, only right then understanding that those people still didn't know I'd been rescued. That meant they also didn't know about the attack ready to happen, and I intended keeping it that way.

"What is it you expect me to be reasonable about?" I asked as I ran my hands through my hair, finally understanding why I had felt it necessary to wear that brown uniform. "If you remember me all that well, you might also remember my opinions about cooperating."

"Look, honey, there's only one reason you and I are holding this conversation," she said, her gray eyes directly on me. "If any other girl had given them the trouble you did, right now she'd be finding it tough to understand the wall she was staring at. They didn't take your mind because they want to find out about it first, and they don't much care how they accomplish that. Once they have everything they need, you're off the hook. You'll go quietly to sleep, and when you wake up again you won't mind making babies or anything else."

Straight out, without trying to fool me; the only thing I had to look forward to was pain if I didn't cooperate, a final end to all the trouble if I did. It was the closest they were willing to let me come to freedom or death, and were offering it as a prize for my cooperation. I didn't want to shiver, but not wanting to didn't stop it.

"I really do have to remember to thank them for their generosity," I said, letting my mind reach out as I looked away from her. "Just what kind of answers do they think they can get from me, and what good do they expect it to do them?"

"They want to know what you did to Serdin," she answered willingly enough, still sounding mostly unconcerned. "They also want to know if you can do anything else, and if so, what."

My searching mind had had some difficulty getting through the—tension—of some sort that seemed to surround the room, but once through I was aware of all the minds available to be reached. Most of them were rather far, but a group of five plus three null minds couldn't have been more than a room or two away. They were also listening to what was going on in *my* room, that was almost as clear as words, and suddenly I knew how I wanted to respond to their questions—and incidently divert them from looking outside for a while.

"I can't explain what I did to Serdin," I said, bringing my eyes back to her while giving no indication that I knew anyone else was listening. "I don't understand myself how it works, all I know is how to do it. As far as the rest of it goes—what I *can* do is beat any Prime in this place. If none of them have ever gotten out the way I did they can't be much, which is exactly what I think of this whole operation. Half-baked normals puffing up the pride of a bunch of so-called Primes, all of them trying to hide how incompetent they are by telling each other how great they are. But they *are* men, Finner, so I never expected any more."

"Is that supposed to be between you and me?" she asked, fractionally more amused. "Did you check a mind or two on your way out, and that's how you know what they're like? And while we're near the subject, just exactly how did you get reawakened in the first place?"

"How I got to be awake is a piece of information I'll be keeping to myself for a while," I said, making it sound as though I intended bargaining with the point at a later time. "You can tell or not tell what I said about their operation, I couldn't care less, but I don't think they'll really enjoy hearing it. And no, I didn't check any minds on my way out, but I didn't have to. As great as Kel-Ten thought he was, he was still *here*. By getting out, I proved I'm better."

"I see," she said, stirring in the chair before getting to her feet. "For some reason they don't want any men around you, so you and I will be spending some time together. I'll let them know you're awake and somewhat willing to be reasonable, and then I'll be back. Want anything to eat or drink?"

"You've got to be kidding," I said with a snort, folding one leg under me on the leather couch. "What I found in the woods and got from the Ejects was no banquet, but at least it wasn't added to. I'd rather starve than find myself drugged up again."

"So it *was* the Ejects who helped you," she said, nodding at the confirmation she'd gotten out of me. "We thought so, but didn't know for sure. They'll end up teaching them not to do that again, especially after they thought they knew better than to interfere with one of ours to begin with. I'll be back in a couple of minutes."

She went out and closed the door behind her, leaving the room a little darker without the presence of her white uniform. I kept my face expressionless and my mind curtained, but I wanted to bare my teeth at what they thought they'd be doing to those "Ejects" who had helped me. I couldn't wait until they really were mixing it up with those who had helped me, but I had to stall for time until everything was ready. That was why I'd insulted them and their precious Primes, pretending at the same time that I knew nothing about the level of mind power I'd be going up against. Injured pride very often makes people act like fools, especially if they believe they can get the answers they want along with a good deal of satisfaction. If they let me challenge their people they could have me watched while I did it, and then they could find out about my abilities before I was flattened. That was the way I was hoping it would work, but I still kept my fingers crossed out of sight while I waited.

It was longer than the couple of minutes Finner had mentioned before she got back, and she certainly hadn't been reporting anything to anyone. She'd gone to the room her bosses were in and had waited while they argued about what to do, and I thought I knew how it had worked out. If Serdin hadn't been one of the ones listening my planning probably would have ended up down the drain, but he *had* been one of them, and what *he* wanted was revenge. The others had argued with him but he'd shouted them down, and then he'd given instructions to Finner.

"You were right about them not liking the way you looked down your nose at their Primes," she said as she closed the door behind her before going back to her chair. "They decided that if you're all that good, you won't mind answering a challenge or two from their men. I told them I doubted if you'd mind at all."

"Of course I wouldn't mind," I blustered, trying to sound nervous and unsure but too stubborn to back down. "I know they can't be anything much, so why would I mind?"

"You wouldn't, so you'll be glad to know they're setting it up now," she said, getting some amusement out of my discomfort. "As soon as everything's ready they'll send for us, so we can relax until they do. And in case you were wondering, this room *is* in the middle of the complex, but don't expect to pick up anything through the walls. The room is shielded, so you won't be able to get through."

"Oh," I said in a wilted way, hoping I looked completely chastened instead of ready to stick my tongue out and make a rude noise. So that was what that strange tension around the room was supposed to be, shielding, and didn't Serdin and his friends feel safe behind it. I made myself more comfortable on the couch while I hoped they felt very safe—right up to the minute I reached through it to get them, and then gave them my thanks for what they'd done to me and the child I would now never know.

It took me a couple of minutes to back my rage down to a manageable level, but once it was done I found I had nothing to occupy me enough to *keep* it down. I needed a distraction until my challenge was arranged, but friendly conversation with Finner was out; the less I said the less chance there would be of my saying the wrong thing, and I didn't particularly *want* to get friendly with Finner. That left nothing but her mind to occupy me, a mind I couldn't touch because she was a null. I'd never really been that close to a null before with nothing else happening, and I had nothing better to do anyway. . . .

Twenty minutes later that was all I had out of my efforts: a whole lot of nothing. Finner sat relaxed in her chair while I shifted on my couch, trying to figure out where she could be feeling whatever it was she did feel. I'd done a little gentle sending just as a test, but the big blond Sec hadn't felt a thing. I knew she was there and alive, I could see that even if I couldn't prove it with my mind, but where the hell were her emotions? They had to be *some* place if she was feeling things, and the amusement she'd shown meant she *was* feeling them. Were they working on a different frequency, hidden in another dimension, what? Where in hell could they possibly—

"Okay, they're ready for her now," a voice came from the doorway, making me jump and look up. Another null female Sec stood there, and she was talking to Finner.

"Okay, honey, now's the time you get to show everybody what you can do," Finner said, getting out of her chair. "You follow her, and I'll follow you."

I stood up slowly, still playing scared but stubborn, and went toward the newcomer Sec. She waited until I reached her before turning and leading the way, and once I was out in the hall I understood where I was in relation to the part of the complex I knew. We were walking through the area on the inner side of the executive offices, and the women's Medical section was just ahead. After just a few steps we were passing their lines, and they still didn't look around in curiosity.

I was escorted through the women's dormitory and the low dining room into the men's area, and from there to the part of the building where all the exercising and training was done. When we moved out of the lift area we could see a small crowd of people waiting around the assignment board, mostly male with a couple of female executive types among them, and I didn't realize the welcoming committee wasn't official until Finner moved up to walk to my right instead of following along behind.

"I hope you'll excuse our not stopping, but we have people waiting for us," she said to the group in general, keeping it polite but also making it firm. "Since you were all invited, why don't you just come along with us?"

"We prefer voicing an opinion or two ahead of the rest," the lazy answer came as one man stepped out in front of the others, his grin full of anticipation. I didn't have to look twice to know Jer-Mar, the very first Prime I'd met in that place, and when his blue eyes came to me I also had no trouble remembering the vicious delight they usually showed. "Well, well, sweet thing, so you've returned to us in ignominy. They won't be letting Kel-Ten keep you all to himself any longer, you know, which means you'll be available to the rest of us again. They intend seeing how well you do being tied down in a room with an open door, I hear, so I've already volunteered to be first. And tenth. And fiftieth. You have no idea how much I'm looking forward to that."

He had moved up to stop in front of me by then, deliberately blocking our path, his mind positively writhing with delight. Finner put a hand to my arm, obviously intending to guide me around him, but the slime wasn't finished. Once he'd said the words meant to send me cowering to the floor at his feet, he reached a hand out and closed his fingers hard on my left breast.

Any competent tactician would know that the worst thing you can do is show your surprise reserve before the battle starts, but it wasn't a tactician who had had so much done to her by that lower life form, it was me. Without even stopping to think about it I reached through my curtain to Jer-Mar's mind, and then it was him doing the screaming, his face twisted in shock at the pain he felt. He went to his knees clutching his groin, his screams echoing in the otherwise silent area, and the faces of his cronies were gray with suddenly-departed gloating.

"So now we know one of the things you can do," Finner observed calmly, looking down at the writhing Prime. "Would you like to tell me what it is for the sake of my next report?"

To possibly keep them off your back for a little longer, was the suggestion, which might or might not have been true. At that point it hopefully didn't matter that much, so all I did was shrug.

"He thinks he's feeling very sensitive parts of him being squeezed in a strong, angry fist," I answered, watching Jer-Mar collapse completely to the floor as I released him. "I'm sure you know it isn't the pain we're given but the pain we think we feel that hurts, so I didn't have to touch him to do that. All I had to do was give him the proper sensations."

"All," the other Sec said in a mutter from my left, still staring at Jer-Mar. Finner did no more than nod, and then we continued on our way. Behind us we left a number of very upset males, and two equally disturbed females in yellow uniforms. Quatry and her loyal assistant still hated me, but now they feared me as well.

Our final destination turned out to be one of the bigger training rooms, and there were quite a lot of people in it. Aside from white-clad Secs and black-clad trainers there were dozens of Primes dressed in their short exercise clothes, most of their minds filled with outrage and indignation. I'd been told how touchy they were when it came to being challenged, but that was just too bad about them. You didn't have to be special to challenge someone, you just had to be good—or ready to fall. As I felt my curtain thickening against the noise I knew I wasn't ready to fall, and wouldn't be if I had the choice. Through the windows we'd passed I'd been able to see it was almost full dark, not far from the time the attack was scheduled for.

I was led through the big room to the back of it, away from the doors to the hall where the major portion of the crowd was. There were two men in black waiting for me there, giving off the air of being in charge, but I already knew they weren't. We were being watched and monitored from very near, from a place that was safely behind shielded walls, where those in the room could remain untouched.

"So this is the ring who thinks she can face up to Primes," one of the trainers said as we came up, his voice dripping contempt as his mind probed toward mine. "It's too bad we were all dragged away from what we were doing for nothing. Her mind power is so weak, I can barely detect it."

"That makes *you* weak, not me," I countered as I stopped a couple of feet in front of him, refusing to get flustered or angry or embarrassed the way he wanted me to. "If you were all that good you'd be showing off your knees like the rest of them, not wearing black from head to toe. If we're supposed to be here for a reason, why don't we skip the conversation and get on with it."

The man's face flushed as his mind filled with insult, but he realized very quickly I was just giving back what I had gotten. He didn't seem to think I had the right to do that, but he wasn't too thickheaded to remember I *was* a Prime, and one who could do things no one knew much about. He would have preferred continuing the argument, but he gritted his teeth and got on with the show instead.

"If you're in that much of a hurry to lose, I think we can oblige you," he said, still stiff with affront but also pleased at the thought of what he knew would be done to me. "Step right out here and we'll get started."

He gestured toward one of the lines on the floor before beginning to head for it, and my two Sec companions moved toward the back wall when I followed the man. They were the only other women in the room, and even though their faces were expressionless I had the strangest feeling they were hoping I *wouldn't* lose. The men in that place were arrogant beyond standard for the breed, and even though female Secs would not be given the disdain used on female Primes, they must have had *something* they would have enjoyed getting even for. I smiled to myself just a little at that, taking it as a confirmation that nulls did feel things like everyone else after all.

"There's no sense in having one of our absolute best waste his time on you," the man in black announced more to the audience than to me when I joined him on the line, a smirk creasing his face. "After this is over you'll have their attention, but not now. Prime Ind-Fam will begin, and will probably also finish. Just face him, he'll take care of the rest."

The man stepped away from me to the accompaniment of laughter from the watching Primes, all of them really enjoying themselves. The one who seemed happiest, though, was the brown-haired, brown-eyed man who stood facing me on a line of his own, twenty feet away if the distance indicators were accurate. That had to be

Ind-Fam, of course, and he didn't waste a minute beyond the time it took for the trainer to get out of range.

"You don't *have* to be afraid of me," he called while projecting heavy fear, his mind steady and confident. "You'd be very wise if you were, but you don't have to."

The man had moderate strength in his range, but just as the trainer had said, he wasn't one of the best. I shunted the spread-out fear past me, then sent back a little gift of my own.

"You don't have to be sorry for what you did, but somehow I think you are," I called back, playing the game while I sent him grief instead of sorrow. His mind blotted up the emotion like a dry towel dropped in a puddle, his frantic efforts to resist proving absolutely worthless. His eyes widened as he began to tremble, and then he was on his knees sobbing with heartbreak, his face buried in his hands. There was shock in the minds behind him, and then two of his friends came forward to help, while that second trainer I'd seen moved out of the crowd and came forward. By then the first one in black was standing beside me again, and he was the one the second trainer spoke to.

"Nothing," he said as he came up, his face on the pale side. "If there was any spread I couldn't detect it, and neither could the Primes in front of me. I was watching them at the same time."

"Why should there have been any spread?" I asked innocently, just as though I didn't know what the problem was. "I was taught to keep my projections tight. Weren't the rest of you taught the same?"

The two men stared at me without answering, knowing damned well that *everyone's* projections spread at least a little at the edge of their range. Since twenty feet should have been close to my limit they didn't understand what was happening, but standing there guessing wasn't getting them anywhere.

"We'll go on to the next one," the first trainer who was obviously in charge decided, ignoring me in favor of his coworker. "Get back in position."

The second man nodded then turned and trotted back to where he'd been, passing another great Prime who had stepped out of the crowd to claim a line. This one wasn't laughing or making clever comments, and the line he stood on was thirty feet away. As soon as I was alone again he launched his attack, which proved to be a little stronger than the previous one. Increasing your range also increases your strength, of course, and the scathing, belittling contempt should have sent me shuddering back in shame and inadequacy, firmly believing I had no chance against him. He also held the projection longer, which meant I had to work around what he was sending in order to reach him, but reach him I did. His projection began wavering when the insecurity touched him, and only seconds later he was also down on hands and knees, but not crying like his predecessor. His problem was that he was so unsure of himself he didn't dare trust himself to stand without falling, and wasn't even certain he could keep the floor under him with the help of his hands. This time there was a thick, faintly frightened silence before anyone came forward to help him, and after that the muttering began.

"You're playing some kind of game with us, aren't you?" the first trainer said from his place to my left, having already gotten a headshake from his second in command in the crowd. "You're showing nothing like enough power to do all that, but you're still doing it. Who the hell are you, or better yet, *what* are you?"

"I'm a Prime of the Centran Amalgamation," I answered, turning my head to look him in the eye. "Did you think they gave that calling just to superior men, and simply let the women use it to soothe their delicate little egos? Did it never occur to you that you might have done better training the girls?"

Again he simply stared at me, trying not to believe I was telling him women were potentially more powerful than men, an outright lie I was hoping they would all start to believe. They deserved to be driven wild for what they'd done to the women in that place, even if that wildness lasted only a little while. The ones who survived would learn the truth—but first they had to survive.

"You're still playing games," he said flatly after a moment, not really believing his supposed decision. "I don't know what you're after, but whatever it is, you won't be getting it. Those who win their challenges also win the right to face the best, and that's where you've managed to get yourself. They've already been sent for, so why don't you spend the next five minutes getting your strength back?''

He gave me a very small, very cold smile and turned away, leaving me to stand on my line all alone. He couldn't get through my curtain to really touch my mind, but after facing two challenges he knew I *had* to be very tired and almost to the end of my strength. If I had been tired five minutes wouldn't have been long enough to rest even if I used trance, especially not with the big guns coming. Happily for me I hadn't expended much in the way of strength so I didn't have to rest, but there was no sense in sharing that piece of information, even though it would have made them all feel worse. Let them think I was tired but stubbornly refusing to admit it; their eventual enlightening and disappointment would only be that much sharper.

Anyone watching me should have concluded I was waiting deep in worried thought, but instead of worrying I was looking around for some indication that the attack was starting. The crash teams were scheduled to come in first and disable the outer defense weapons, and then they were to do the same with the inner ones if they could. No one wanted them setting off alarms or cutting off the lighting system to warn the inhabitants our fighters were on the way, but once those fighters were inside, the defenses would go no matter what went with them. Our fighting force consisted of those of Central stock with sophisticated hand weapons, those of Rimilian stock with swords, and everyone with a mind shield for defense and Prime strength for offense. The *w'wendaa* with us hadn't been trained to community-level ability, but they'd been paired with mind warriors as a protection, and also to give them a chance to see what it was possible to accomplish. The community had a large number of *l'lendaa* but only a few *w'wendaa*, and they'd been invited to join the attack in an effort to recruit some of them. The community wanted them to join and train, but believed more in enticement than in coercion.

I touched a number of minds around the building, finding nothing out of the ordinary, and then I caught just a trace of extreme pain before the mind winked out. Unconscious or dead I couldn't tell, but I was definitely able to detect a number of shields around the place that mind had turned off in. It had to mean at least one of the crash teams had made it inside the building, which also meant it would only be a matter of minutes before everyone else joined them. I found myself flooded with vast relief even as I pulled my mind back, finally able to admit I'd been starting to feel very alone again. Just being in the complex made my hands want to shake, but knowing I would soon have my own there helped to keep them as steady as I needed them to be.

"Rest time is over, girl," the trainer's voice came suddenly, a lot of satisfaction in it. "Open your eyes and turn around, you have very special visitors waiting to get a look at their challenger."

I opened my eyes and turned as he'd suggested, but the newcomers weren't in any way surprising. The crowd had separated and moved left and right in the room, leaving a broad aisle that framed three men who stood at the other end. Two were in red shorts and top, one of them Ank-Soh and the other most probably his co-holder of second place, they two in turn framing the man who stood between them. That one was dressed in the gold he alone was permitted to wear, and even at that distance I could tell his eyes were on me. His emotions were being held rigidly in check, and someone who didn't know better would think Kel-Ten was only faintly interested in answering my challenge.

"When they told him you were gone, they had to drug him to bring him down out of the rage," the man beside me murmured, knowing well enough who I was looking at. "He's not used to having rings turn their back on him unless they're on hands and knees, and he's sure as hell not used to having them turn around and challenge him after he's dipped them good. He wants more than a small piece of you, girl, he wants what he's been promised when he wins: enough hours with you to take the bad taste out of his mouth."

With me still completely aware while it was happening, the dirty laugh in his mind told me, something he couldn't say out loud in case I didn't yet know what my final fate was to be. I closed my hands to fists at my sides to help keep them steady, all the while continuing to stare at Kel-Ten. As far as he knew I'd run out on him after he'd taken the risk of awakening me, not caring that I was leaving him behind as long as *I* got out. He didn't know he would soon be free and maybe wouldn't have cared even if he'd known; what I was searching for was some vestige of tender feeling inside *me* for *him*. He was the one who had made my escape possible, the one who had saved me from Jer-Mar and the women in yellow, the one I had spent so much time with. I should have been feeling *something* for him besides the deep-burning anger and almost-hatred I did feel. I'd forgiven Tammad for what he'd done to me; why couldn't I forgive Kel-Ten?

"Are you starting to feel nervous, girl?" the trainer asked with the dirty laugh now showing up on the outside, clearly misinterpreting my reactions. I was starting to worry, all right, but not in the way he thought. Considering the fact that I owed Kel-Ten quite a lot it wouldn't have been fair to hurt him, but that was exactly what I wanted more and more to do. I kept remembering being ordered to my belly, and being dressed in a tight gold shirt that was then torn almost to my waist. I remembered being treated as though I were nothing, used to satisfy *his* needs, ignored when it came to my own. He'd awakened me, all right, to make sure that *he* was able to escape, but I *had* to keep telling myself I owed him. . . .

"I think they're just about ready for you," the man beside me said, his gloating anticipation very strong. "As luck would have it, all three of them have had a really easy day; they're as fresh and rested as if they just got up from a good night's sleep. And since you like games so much, we've decided we've got one for *you.*"

"What are you talking about?" I asked without looking at him, still trying to soothe the growl out of my mind. If I had to fight Kel-Ten in my current mood I'd end up really hurting him, and the worst part of the problem I faced was that most of me *liked* the idea. I *wanted* to hurt him, wanted it very much because I hated him, and couldn't find the faintest trace of guilt in me to make the hate go away. The only thing I had going for me just then was that Ank-Soh and his partner would need to be faced before it was Kel-Ten's turn, and being number three on the list just might save him.

"I'm talking about the new game we just made up," the trainer said, really enjoying himself. "Until now you've done it just the way it's usually done, one challenger and one defender, winner going on to face the next higher defender. Maybe if you weren't a—'Prime of the Centran Amalgamation' we would have continued doing it that way, but seeing you're so important we decided you deserved something special. Instead of facing them one at a time, they'll be coming against you together—unless you'd like to answer the question of where you learned to do what you're doing. That will get you two on one, and to bring it down all the way you tell us exactly what your range and capabilities are. You can have thirty seconds to think it over."

I finally turned my head to look at him, but he was too busy checking the time to return the look, and I might not have noticed even if he had. My thoughts were thundering around inside my head, and I couldn't decide whether I felt suffocated or chilled. I couldn't answer the questions they'd asked, not even if I *wanted* to tell the truth, but I also couldn't face all three of those men together. I *knew* I couldn't best all three unless I killed them the way I'd killed that Hand of Power, and for all the hate I felt I didn't even want to see Kel-Ten dead. Hurt for the way he'd hurt me, yes, but not dead!

"You can't expect me to take this seriously," I said to the man counting time, finding it was definitely chill that was all around me. "If those three together manage to stomp me flat, you won't have your answers and you won't have me. Besides, I thought Kel-Ten was promised something."

"He was," the trainer said without raising his head, the smile visible only in his mind. "That's why the three of them won't *be* stomping you flat, only making you wish they had. Have you ever had three male Primes playing your mind the way they would play your body if you were theirs to keep? Until now they've only practiced on female targets, keeping it relatively short and simple. With you it won't be either, and if you expect the screaming to bother them you're kidding yourself. Your thirty seconds are up."

His eyes came up to me then, clearly hoping I would still refuse to cooperate, and there was nothing I could do but oblige him. His mind had confirmed the truth of everything he'd said, but there was still nothing I could tell him that would do anyone any good. I'd have to face the three—but then it came to me that maybe there was something I could *show* them.

"So you're curious about what my range is," I said, as flatly as he'd spoken earlier. "I think I *will* let you know that—in my own special way."

I turned from his newborn frown to walk two steps forward, knowing I wasn't about to give anything away. If I had to face three strong, trained minds I couldn't do it with my curtain in place and possibly getting in the way, so I had to banish it. Doing it with a flair might not get me anything that would help, but there was a chance it could and none that it would hurt.

"Brothers, there's something you have to know," I called to the three men at the far end of the room, using the opportunity to try reminding them that we were, after all, the same kind. "The people running this place want you to face me, but they're using you just like they always have, this time to see if you can succeed where others have failed. I know your minds but you don't know mine, so why don't I show it to you before you decide whether or not to let them use you again."

There was just enough time for a startled mutter to break out in the crowd of watchers to either side of the room, and then it turned into a concerted gasp to greet the banishing of my curtain. The strongest mind those men had ever seen was Kel-Ten's, and I could feel the shock in every one of them when they were able to reach mine. From where they all stood they shouldn't have been *able* to reach me; the fact that they could told them *I* was the one doing the reaching, and that in itself turned them very shaken.

"I see Ank-Soh and his level-brother are uncertain," I said, pressing my small advantage while at the same time sending a strong "patience!" to Kel-Ten. I wanted him to know the game we'd played wasn't over yet, that there was still a chance for him to have what we'd plotted for, but I couldn't quite get how he took it in the midst of all the new mental noise flying around. "Yes, I *can* read you from this distance, but more to the point I can also touch you. Are you going to let them send you against me, forcing me to destroy you, just so they can find out what I'm capable of? In range and together you three may well be stronger than I am, but let me show you another thing I can do."

I called up the light shield to cover my mind and immediately reached through it, but almost didn't have to bother. The crowd of watching Primes was going wild, knowing I was right then untouchable to each and every one of them, something they'd never seen anyone do on their own before. Things seemed to be going well enough to let me feel encouraged, but at times like that there must be a law that causes *someone* to come along and spoil it.

"Be quiet!" the man in black shouted as he came up beside me, his face red as he raised both arms to command the silence he'd demanded. "Shut up and listen to me! You're all acting like a bunch of tight-assed virgins, listening to this ring and taking her seriously! Didn't any of you ever face a challenge before? Did you let your opponent *talk* a win out of you? If she didn't know damned well she would lose, wouldn't she be fighting instead of flapping her mouth? Are you men and Primes, or are you shivering rings yourselves? Get over here and make her drop this shield, then teach her what you do to females who try getting out of the place they belong!"

He shoved me forward a few steps then, deeper into the new mutter rising to both sides of the room, but worse than that closer to the three he'd mainly been addressing. They'd all been staring at me during his harangue, their minds too far away to reach easily through the shield, and after a very brief hesitation Kel-Ten started forward! All I could think of was the time Len had used his mind to make my body react, the times Tammad had done the same, all those times other Rimilian males had unknowingly coerced me into doing what pleased them. If Kel-Ten and the others got control of me I'd do anything they said, answer any questions they asked, and being done like that frightened me more than even the thought of death could. If I stayed shielded they couldn't touch my mind—but the trainer had said it was possible to *force* a shield open! To keep them away from me I'd have to kill them, but I didn't *want* to kill them! I was very much afraid it wasn't possible to kill with your mind when you didn't want to, which left me with nothing at all to do to protect myself. I stood in the middle of the floor as Kel-Ten, leading the other two, slowly got nearer, helpless to keep myself from trembling and not far from a whimper.

"The girl isn't the only one who had a lot to say," Kel-Ten announced suddenly, stopping just as abruptly with the other two behind him. "You did a lot of talking yourself, Master Trainer, but I somehow missed the part where you proved she was lying when she said you were using us. Did you miss the fact that we could feel her mind all the way over on the other side of the room? Would you like to know how little spread there was even at that distance? We were told we were being rewarded by being allowed to go after her together to teach her a lesson. We could do anything we liked as long as we didn't hurt her permanently, they said. Facing a mind like that is a reward? Without being told we *have* to work together, otherwise we'll end up losing? Would you like to tell us how many of us you expect to lose anyway? Would you?"

By that time Kel-Ten was shouting, his fury so strong it blazed out of him in all directions. Even through my shield I could feel that Ank-Soh and the other Prime in red were linking their own fury and sending it out with his, spreading it to every Prime in the room. The man in black beside me had gone pale, and then he was staggering under the storm of rage echoing throughout the room.

"Get them all!" Kel-Ten screamed with teeth bared,

and without an instant's hesitation the Primes in the room turned on every white or black-clad figure, using their minds against the black and their fists and feet against the white, those two colors going down beneath whichever torrent overwhelmed it. There's a limit to the amount of power you can shunt aside when it comes at you, and every trainer in the room was well beyond that limit.

I stood in the only sane three-foot square in the room, watching in shock as the Primes raged and ravened all over the rest of it, attacking the paneling on the walls when there were no more living enemies to go after. Every shred of resentment and anger they'd ever felt had been triggered at once, turning them into deadly, unreasoning animals, not caring what they did or who saw it.

Saw it! I realized with another shock that they didn't know we were being watched by what was probably every higher-up in the complex, who *had* to have some way of stopping riots like that. I knew I had to do something to stop *them*, but it wasn't possible to work through the boiling sea of insanity the room had become. I had to get out of there, and then I would do what I could.

I actually glanced over my shoulder to see whether or not I was being watched by the two Secs who had brought me there, then looked quickly away again before starting to make my way out of the room. I would have felt stupid for not realizing that a white uniform is a white uniform no matter who's wearing it—if I hadn't felt so sickened instead. That they were women had made no difference to the Primes, all that had mattered was that they were Secs. I would have closed my eyes and emptied my insides at that horrible example of total equality, but I simply didn't have the time.

It didn't take me as long as I thought it would to get out of the room. I was worried about the brown uniform I had on, but wrapping myself in a strong projection of unimportance had let me move through the riot without anyone paying any attention to me. I stopped out in the hall and took a deep breath, but didn't have any more time to lose than that. Once the training room was completely demolished the riot would spill out into the rest of the building, and I had to be away after the people I was looking for well before that. Glad that the shielding on the room was still intact I sent my mind out, and found what I was looking for almost immediately. Those very important people were very close, and all of them seemed to be in a panic. I saw where they were in relation to the room I had just left, and quickly headed that way.

Down the hall and around one turn brought me to a door marked, "Do not enter," and I had no doubt the command was usually obeyed. That time, though, it was ignored completely as I turned the knob and quietly entered, the noise in the room hitting at me as soon as I opened the door. The room was very tastefully and comfortably decorated around the half dozen viewing screens it held, but the men occupying it weren't enjoying what it offered or taking advantage of the viewing it afforded. They were arguing bitterly, and Serdin seemed to be one against all the others.

"I don't *know* why the pacifiers aren't working!" he was shouting, his gray uniform looking rumpled rather than neat and cool. "That's why I sent a repair crew to central control! What more do you want me to do?"

"We want you to get this stopped!" one of the men came back in a hiss, a heavy man also in gray who had very long brown hair and rings on nearly all of his fingers. "If this is an example of the way you've been running this complex, I'm surprised it's still standing! You can be sure Rathmore will hear all about the way you entertain important guests, you certainly can be sure!"

"Krover, you've already been told this has never happened before," Serdin growled, then gestured toward another man in yellow. "Your own spy there told you that, and if you're not going to believe him, why did you bother sending him here to be my assistant? You and your associates will be just as safe in this room as I am, and once we get them quieted down you can even help me decide what to do to them for this outrage. Something like that should brighten your visit considerably."

"I'd rather do something to darken it," I said as the fat man began to appear mollified, stepping forward to let the door swing closed behind me. Every head in the room turned in my direction, most of them showing expressions of shock, but Serdin looked furious.

"You!" he spat, taking one step toward me, his hands closed to fists at his sides. "You have the nerve to walk in *here* after everything you've done?"

"Why not?" I asked mildly, letting him see nothing of what was growing in my mind—or letting him know I'd dropped my shield. "You don't have your nulls with you any longer, so what was there to keep me from paying you a visit?"

"You can ask that when there are five of us?" he blustered, his mind suddenly cold with worry. "We saw you fighting to get out of facing three men, so what could you possibly do against five?"

"Those weren't three men, they were three Primes," said, still keeping the words to a drawl. "Don't you know the difference yet between the two? Here, let me show you."

I took Serdin's mind with mine and froze him in place, then reached out to the fat man who stood quivering with fear. I replaced his fear with infuriated outrage aimed at Serdin, then watched as the man fronted Serdin, spit at him, then slapped him hard across the face. At that point I released them both, then smiled faintly.

"See what it means to be a Prime?" I asked, feeling their minds clang with shock while the other three men whimpered and backed away. "I couldn't have done that to *them,* not without half crippling them, but I can do anything I like with the untalented."

My two victims stared at me in horror, their eyes wide as they remembered every fairy tale they'd every heard about why it wasn't safe to have awakened empaths around. Serdin's mind stumbled across an idea and seized on it, and he laughed harshly even as he wiped a hand across his mouth.

"You can do anything you like while you're *awake!*" he spat at me, vindictive delight coursing through him. "The only thing I have to say to a Prime is—"

The word he spoke registered in my mind even though I couldn't quite hear and retain it, but nothing happened. I realized then that he'd tried to turn me off, but I'd been right about two "offs" being unworkable. I'd broken out of the last "off" and had never been turned "on" again, and that made whatever word I was keyed to absolutely worthless. The fat man was staring at me with the same hope-for-vengeance Serdin showed, and wasn't it a pity I had to disappoint them.

"Would you care to repeat what you just said?" I asked, stabbing into each of their minds with a pinpoint of pain. "I'm afraid I didn't quite hear it."

The two men screamed with pain and fear, making the other three cower even harder against the wall they'd backed to, and suddenly I was no longer in the mood for games.

"You take people and do whatever you please to them, and don't give a damn as long as *you're* as well off as you want to be," I said, beginning to walk slowly forward. "You kidnapped me and drugged me and took away my memories and had me savaged, and all the while you laughed and enjoyed what you were watching. That was bad enough, worse than bad enough, but then I found out you had *even killed my baby!* Do you know what that means I'm going to do to you now? Have you any idea how bad agony can get?"

The two I was screaming at were on the floor trying to crawl away, slobbering and mewling at what they felt from the leakage of my mind. I wasn't projecting at them yet, only screaming, but the force inside me had been building ever since Murdock had told me what they'd done.

"You're equally guilty, both of you, and what I give you will be only a taste of what Rathmore will get if I ever find myself in reach of him!" I screamed. "You were worried about being safe, both of you wanted to be safe! Well, I'm going to make you just as safe as my baby was!"

I projected at them then, so insanely furious that I was aware of nothing but punishing them. Faintly I heard agonized and terrified screams, as though from far away, but nothing reached through the madness controlling me. I just kept on projecting, until suddenly there was nothing but black.

* * *

I stirred where I lay and took a deep breath, feeling a little tired but very satisfied. I opened my eyes to find out where I was, saw a large room decorated in red and black and cobalt blue, and didn't understand. The room was a very large bedroom, specifically shown by the wide bed I lay on, but I'd never seen it before and couldn't imagine where it was. For that matter I couldn't quite remember where I'd *been*, but as I sat up with my hand to my head I got all the answers in a way I would have preferred never having encountered.

"Well, now, I'm glad to see you awake again," a voice said from my right and somewhat behind, a voice that chilled me to the bone. "It's a good thing I had the foresight to bring you here rather than leave you where I found you. Here we won't be disturbed."

I didn't even want to breathe let alone turn around, but a fascination for horror must be part of all of us. Still sitting on the bed I twisted to the right, to see there was no headboard or wall behind me. Instead, the room extended back almost as far as it did ahead, and sitting in a chair watching me, still in his white uniform, was the null Sec Adjin. Sight of his dark hair and eyes started me trembling, which in turn brought him a smile.

"You killed all five of them, you know," he said, uncrossing his legs to get out of the chair. "If I didn't know better I would have sworn they suffocated, there in a room with all the air they needed. You were screaming something about that being the way to kill an unborn baby, to deprive it of what it needs to live. I watched you waiting until they stopped moving, and then I watched you collapse."

He walked up to the bed and then started moving around it, obviously coming to the side where I sat. I wanted to run farther and faster than I ever had in my life, but his dark eyes kept me frozen where I was even as he strolled nearer.

"Those people are all over the complex by now, did you know that?" he asked, the calm conversation making it seem like a nightmare for me. "Before any of us were aware of it they were inside, and somehow most of our defensive and pacification systems were out. I went back to tell Serdin what was happening, and found that Serdin had no more interest in knowing. That was where I also found *you.*"

"Those people are friends of mine," I whispered, so petrified that all I could do was shake as he sat down beside me to the left. "They know I'm here, so they won't stop looking until they find me. You can't keep me . . ."

"But I *can* keep you," he contradicted over my gasp of pain, the fingers of his right hand closed tight in my hair as they forced my head back. "I've brought you to a special room of mine, and your friends will be far too busy with the inmates of the complex to find this room for quite a while. By the time they do we'll be gone from it, and already started on our new life together."

I cried out and tried to fight free of his grip, but all he did was tighten it as he laughed. I'd also been trying to hammer at his mind, and for some reason I believed he knew it.

"I'm really going to enjoy owning you," he said, bringing his face down so close to mine that I thought I'd be sick. "Not only will I have your body to use, but I'll also have the use of your mind—in the way I train you to use it. Those friends of yours must have gone after Rathmore Hellman on Central too, but what they don't know is that they're just clearing the way for *me.* Before they turn around I'll have all the reins in my hands, and then they'll find it's too late to stop me. I'll see to the removal of the unimportant, those whose deaths won't stir up a fuss, and you—you'll take care of the ones who'll be best dead without a mark on them. You'll also be able to reach the ones hiding behind doors and guards, the ones who think they're safe. You *will* do it for me, sweet thing, because you won't dare not to."

Again I tried struggling as his lips lowered to mine, but I simply couldn't force him away from me. I was terrified of him, terrified of what he would do, but I couldn't get away! Deep inside, my mind was crying, a terrible small-child wail that acknowledged the fact of my being lost forever. I'd killed those who had killed my baby, and maybe that was why it was happening, as punishment. I would have done it again even if I knew the price I would be paying, but that didn't change the fact that I would be owned by a man I both loathed and feared horribly, a man who would give me nothing but pain for the rest of my life. That had to be why I couldn't belong to the man I loved, the reason why this null who held me had terrified me from the first moment I saw him. Some part of me had known he would own me, and there was nothing I'd ever be able to do to get free again!

# 15

I sat on the bed with the top of my brown uniform open and the cloth shoved down to the middle of my arms, bared to the sight and touch of the null. His left hand fondled my breast just as any man's hand would, but he wasn't just any man. He'd already hurt me once for being too slow in getting the uniform open, and my flesh still ached under the hand that now gently stroked and caressed it. He was deliberately giving himself enjoyment without giving any to me, and I didn't know how long I could take being treated like that without going insane.

"Most people would have trouble believing how really easy it is to train a woman," he said as he touched me, the words not only casual but downright lazy. "First thing you do is teach her what pain is, and then, once she learns, you give her a very small amount of pleasure or even kindness. After a while you find she'll do anything to get that small amount of pleasure, anything to get even one kind word. At that point she's completely yours, and you'll never have trouble with her again."

Or you can give her all the love and understanding you have, and give her pain only when she forces you to it, I thought. That's the way Tammad had done it, and his way had also made me completely his. That was the difference between Tammad and Kel-Ten, I realized, the difference that had brought me to love one while I hated the other. Tammad had done what he had for *my* sake rather than his own, and would never have done even half of it if I hadn't forced him to it. I'd tried to reach the mind of my beloved for one last touch, but even though the room wasn't shielded I hadn't been able to find him. I hadn't, in fact, been able to reach anyone in twenty minutes of trying, which had told me I really was lost for good.

"You know, if I didn't know better I'd think you were ignoring me," the null said, the gentleness of his stroking unchanged. "Are you telling yourself that if you close your eyes I'll just go away?"

I shook my head and then did close my eyes, finding the truth of what he'd once said to a doctor in that place. With my eyes closed he wasn't there even if I did still feel his hand, a hand without a mind behind it and of someone who wasn't there. But of course he was there, I knew he was there, I just couldn't see him with my mind. He was hidden away and out of sight somewhere, on another frequency or in another dimension. . . .

"Don't!" I screamed, trying to bend forward with the pain his fingers were giving me, his hands keeping me from pulling away. "Don't hurt me like that!"

"In what way would you like me to hurt you?" he asked in the same lazy tone, not easing up at all. "You won't ever be allowed to ignore me, you know, and closing your eyes will never make me go away. You can't see me any more than those imbeciles could see you were awake, but that only means you'll never be able to touch me. I'm the one who'll do the touching, and you're the one who'll feel it."

I cried out again as his fingers twisted harder, but part of the scream held the possibility of triumph rather than the ring of pain. He'd been trying to torture me with how impossible it was to reach him, but instead he just might have given me the key to where he was! I struggled my arms up despite the uniform holding them down and beat at his face in an effort to make him let me go, knowing my mind-tool would help me do what I had to if I could just stop the pain long enough to reach it. He cursed at me as he blocked my fists, and then the room was spinning and clanging from the slap he gave me, my cheek flaming to fire as I went over sideways on the bed. The next instant his fingers were twisted in my hair again, and I was pulled to my back to see him looming over me.

"You're not picking up on this very well, pretty girl,"

he said hoarsely, the look in his dark eyes so cold I shivered. "*I'm* the one who does the hitting, *you're* the one who does the getting hit. Here, let me show you again how it goes."

He raised his left fist angled back and down, giving me more than enough time to see where he was aiming. He was going to hit me in the stomach, probably to keep the bruises from annoying him by showing, caring nothing at all about what damage he might do. I needed time to try the idea I'd had, but he wasn't giving me time—and then I nearly screamed again at the sound of the door shattering. He let me go instantly and threw himself from the bed, and when I managed to struggle half erect I saw—

Tammad, standing in the room with pieces of door scattered on the floor behind him, that giant sword in his fist, kill-lust in his mind. He'd seen what Adjin had been about to do to me and knew what had already been done, and all he wanted was to end the life of the man he stared at. I couldn't believe he was there, couldn't believe he had found me, couldn't believe it was all over—

"Don't come any closer, savage," Adjin said in a very cool, very unexcited voice, obviously talking to my beloved. When I turned my head furiously to look at him, the words I would have said froze on my tongue. Adjin had something small and round pointed at me, and the faint smile on his face was no bluff.

"If you so much as think about taking another step, I'll kill her," the null said, his hand absolutely steady on the weapon. "Then you'll be able to kill *me*, but she'll still be dead. If you don't want it to happen, put that sticker back in its nest, then get rid of the whole belt."

"Don't listen to him!" I shouted as quickly as I could, looking at the barbarian, but I was already too late. Knowing men and what they were capable of far better than I ever would, Tammad was wasting no time following instructions. His light, furious eyes were locked to the dark ones watching him, his teeth showed in a silent snarl, but his hands were already empty and reaching for his swordbelt. I'm sure he knew he would be dead at most only minutes after he disarmed himself, but that didn't matter to him as long as *I* lived.

Well, congratulations, Terry, you managed to get rescued, a voice inside me said, sounding sickeningly sweet. Now that Tammad's started the ball rolling, do you think you might make the effort to give him a hand?

"Damn!" I said under my breath, immediately reaching for my mind tool. Talk about your softheaded, helpless females! The big hero arrives, and she just sits there and watches him die. *That* could have been the meaning of the conviction I'd had, that I'd never belong to Tammad because he would soon die, but if it happened it would not be because I just sat there!

Putting my mind-tool into use always seems to make time stretch, as though everyone but me has slowed to a crawl. That time I really needed the edge, as I had no true idea of what to do to make my guess work. Adjin had said something about me not being able to see his mind any more than the complex people had been able to see I was awake, and that had to be the answer. No one had known I was awake because I'd been *shielded,* that being the only way to keep an empath from a living mind. It had suddenly come to me to wonder if it were possible that nulls were *born* shielded, and not being empaths had no way of ever banishing that shield. If that proved true then their emotions were right where they could be easily reached—by someone who knew how to get through a shield.

But I'd had the time to examine Finner's mind closely, and hadn't been able to detect the gaps an ordinary shield contained! If my theory was true, then it had to be an impenetrable shield that enclosed their minds, and there *was* no way to get through one of those. All it was possible to do was go *around* it, and I hadn't been able to get around Rissim's shield or Irin's—

But you also didn't want to hurt Rissim or Irin by experimenting, that inner voice reminded me, the mind-tool immediately calming my upset which had begun growing. You may *not* have the room to get around the null's shield, but if you hurt him will you really care?

Yes, I admitted with the calm I was being made to feel,

but I'll do it anyway. I *have* to do it, or he'll just go on hurting more and more innocents.

"That's exactly what I wanted," Adjin's voice came, and I looked up to see that Tammad had tossed away his swordbelt—and the null was beginning to swing the weapon toward him! Mind-tool or not, I'd run out of time, and whatever I did had to be done *fast!* I gathered the sensation of touching something unbearably hot, pushed it forward, then swung it *around* toward where the null's emotions should have been. There was an agonizingly long wait of seconds, and then—

"Yeow!" the null screamed, flinging away the weapon he'd almost had leveled on the barbarian. Tammad's eyes lit with delight, a growl sounded in his throat, and then he was launching himself at the man he so achingly wanted to reach.

By rights it should have been over with then and there, but I'd forgotten the reason why Secs didn't need to carry weapons. Adjin was still shaking the pain out of his hand when Tammad reached him, but at the last second he turned and lashed out with a kick. The big barbarian grunted and bent over, the impetus of his charge wiped out, and Adjin grinned and put himself into an odd-looking semi-crouch. He wasn't much smaller than Tammad, but it was clear his confidence came from something other than size.

The next couple of minutes made me get to my knees on the bed and clench my fists, but despite the fact that Tammad wasn't doing at all well, I knew I couldn't interfere. Every time it looked like the big barbarian was about to get his hands on the Sec, Adjin would lean away and land a kick, but if I tried helping by touching him again, I knew Tammad would be furious. At that point I wasn't feeling very understanding or reasonable, but I had to admit he would have had cause to be furious. I'd lately been part of a number of confrontations myself, and with one or two of them I would have flayed anyone who tried to interfere for whatever reason. There are some battles you just *have* to fight for yourself, and what Tammad was then engaged in was one of those.

Despite the fact that he was losing. They'd only been

going at it for a few minutes, but the barbarian was already sweating and not just from the exertion. Most of the sweat came from the pain he'd been given, and at first Adjin had really enjoyed giving it. After the first couple of kicks Tammad had learned to shift just a little before the blow landed, and Adjin hadn't liked that. He kept on kicking at him and reaching after that, but he was no longer grinning while he did it.

The punishment went on and on, but if I was upset I would have bet Adjin was frantic. Every time the Sec kicked him now it looked like he expected the Rimilian to go down, but Tammad refused to do it. He staggered under the strength of the blow, his body streaming the sweat of agony, but the kill-look in his light eyes refused to fade and his hands refused to stop reaching for the throat they wanted. Adjin knew that if he faltered even once he was done, but all that kicking must have been very tiring. His white uniform was beginning to darken with his own sweat, but he didn't dare stop to rest.

I was listing again all the reasons I shouldn't interfere, my palms aching from the fingernails dug into them, when the end suddenly came. Adjin, horribly tired but forcing himself to go on, launched another kick, but one that lacked the speed the previous ones had had. Tammad, exultation in his mind, immediately grabbed the foot coming at him, something he'd done once before earlier in the fight. The first time Adjin had shifted his balance and kicked up with the foot he'd been standing on, and Tammad had been thrown back and away, having time to return to his feet but with nothing to show for his efforts.

The second time, however, was another story. Almost automatically Adjin tried using his free foot again, but the strength and speed just weren't there. Tammad knocked the second kick away with his arm while throwing himself forward, and the two of them went down together. Adjin tried desperately to reach Tammad with his hands, but the big barbarian moved behind him and wrapped a wide arm around his throat. Adjin screamed as his body was pulled back in an arc, struggled to free himself and reach the man who held him, but it was too late. An almost soundless snap came, and his screams were ended forever.

After that there were two unmoving bodies on the floor, and I lost no time getting to the one that was still breathing. Tammad's mind was filled with nothing but pain and exhaustion, even the sense of victory buried beneath those two, but I no longer had to worry about distracting him. I knelt on the floor and pulled his head into my lap, then reached out to him with the pain control that was healing. I also took one of his hands to hold, but as far as I know that did nothing to add to my mind's efforts.

It took quite a few minutes, but when I felt his body and mind eased far enough that his own recuperative powers could handle it from then on, I withdrew. I opened my eyes to see a pair of blue eyes gazing up at me, a smile on the face beneath them, the hand I held now holding me as well. It's unbelievably good to open your eyes to something like that, and I couldn't help matching the smile I was getting.

"Have I ever told you what a really beautiful sight you are?" I asked, smoothing aside a lock of his long, blond, still-wet hair. "Especially when you come crashing through a door like that?"

"I seem to recall a time when you felt differently, *wenda*," he answered, his smile changing to a grin. "It was the occasion of your very first banding, and I doubt that you would have aided me as greatly then as you did this day. Also did you aid me in withholding aid after the first of it, and I find myself greatly satisfied to see that at last you have learned the mind and heart of the *l'lenda* who is yours."

"I thought it was about time I did," I said, deciding it would be wise to refrain from adding how close I'd come to doing exactly the opposite. "It was particularly wonderful seeing you arrive like that because I never thought you would. How did you find me?"

"I followed the trail of your thoughts," he said, his grin slipping just a little as he forced himself to sitting. "It was not your mind which I came upon when I was able to seek you, *hama*, it was a—trail of thoughts which showed your passage. I know of no other way to give explanation to one who has not hunted, yet was the matter clear to me and easily taken advantage of. It was a trail of longing which I followed as a hunter, and at the end of it was you—and *that* one."

The gesture he made in the direction of Adjin's body was full of the contempt and disgust he felt, this time both of the emotions tinged with the sense of victory he hadn't been able to feel properly earlier. I was surprised that something like what he'd done with his mind was possible, but that wasn't what kept me from even glancing at the former null. The terror I'd felt every time I looked at or thought about Adjin was gone, more completely than his being dead would account for, despite the fact that emotions like that tend to hang on and haunt you even after the reason for them is removed. I thought about the oddity for a moment, and then suddenly I *knew* why it had happened. My terror had come from the very real possibility that he would kill Tammad, but I hadn't known that. I'd thought it was personal terror I was feeling, but once he'd died the terror had done the same.

Tammad and I spent a few minutes getting ourselves and/or our possessions together, and then we left the room. I followed him through a part of the complex I'd never seen before, one that was apparently underground, the walk taking us past line after line after line of small metal doors stacked one above the other. There was also an endless amount of mechanical equipment I couldn't identify and didn't know the purpose of, but for some reason I didn't like it. If Tammad hadn't had his arm around me I would have put a near-death grip on *him*, and to hell with how helpless-female-like it would have been. There was something about those oblong metal doors that bothered me, and sometimes it feels good to admit just how frightened of something you are.

I would have enjoyed leaving that area as fast as possible, but we walked for a good ten minutes before we came to the end of it. By that time we also came to something else, a group of our own people who had turned from the wall they'd been examining when they'd heard us coming. One of the group was Ashton, and I could have felt the relief in her mind a mile away.

"Tammad—bless you for finding her!" she called as soon as we were near enough, stepping away from the others to meet us part way. "We were all sick with worry, but when you disappeared too, we began feeling some hope. You'd better get her back above to let the others know you rescued her."

"It would be far more accurate to say the rescue was accomplished through the efforts of us both," Tammad answered, his arm briefly tightening around me as he grinned. "I find myself filled with great pride over the doings of my *l'lenda wenda*, and also over that which she *fails* to do."

"I figured out how to reach the mind of a null, but didn't step in when it came to finishing him off," I explained with a shrug in answer to Ashton's questioning look, inwardly very satisfied with the arrangement Tammad and I had come up with. I took care of the mental fighting while he took care of the physical, each of us doing what he or she did best and using it to protect the other. Then Ashton's look changed from questioning to sly, so I thought it best to change the subject.

"How can you people take standing around down here sightseeing?" I demanded, muffling a shiver. "Looking at the null's *body* wasn't as hard to do."

"So you feel it too," Ashton said with something of a smile, gesturing to the others in her party. "So far only two of us have gotten the creepies, but that could be because we know what it is. Have you ever seen this much stasis equipment before?"

"What's stasis equipment doing way down here?" I asked, finding no relief in having the machinery identified. "It's usually set up a lot closer to food distribution points, and why would they need so much of it? Even with the number of people needing to be fed in this place, they must have enough here to hold three times their number for a thousand years."

"This equipment has nothing to do with food," she answered, then hesitated very briefly before adding, "Terry, do you remember saying the male Primes here weren't able to think about what happened to a First Prime when a newcomer defeated him? Well, did it ever occur to *you* to ask why they would train Primes as far as they could, only to put them out of the way when they were finally defeated? It wouldn't make much sense, would it?''

''No, it wou—'' I started, intending to agree, and then I felt a shudder run completely through me. ''Oh, Ashton, you don't mean— They couldn't have—''

''Wiped out the final defeat from their minds, then put them in stasis?'' she said, the faint smile on her face doing a bad job of hiding the sickness she felt. ''That's exactly what they did, we're told, and they've been doing it for many years. If we'd waited much longer to hit them, we would have been badly outnumbered. Our—reluctant—informant told us they were just about to start bringing them all out of it, the first step in their active plan of conquest. Now *we* have to figure out how to do it, and in a way that will hurt them the least. Need a job when we get back to Rimilia?''

I shivered again and didn't answer, just looked for and found the way out of there. No wonder that place was so awful, all those living minds stopped virtually in mid-thought! They were living dead men who would know nothing of the passage of time when they were brought out of it, who would still think they were the best ever made, who would still be spoiling to face challenges. Work with that? I knew I'd rather be back working for Aesnil in Grelana.

It took us a while to trudge up the ramps that led aboveground, but once we made it the peace and quiet were over. The fighting had long since stopped from the initial attack, but bodies were still being cleared away, wounded were being treated, and the resident Primes without ringing heads were making absolute pains of themselves. I called up my curtain to filter out as much of the mental noise as I could, then sent my mind searching for Rissim and Irin. I made contact long before I saw them, which meant they were both grinning by the time they were in view. Irin hugged me while Rissim thanked Tammad with slaps to the back that should have knocked him down, then Rissim hugged me while Irin got up on tiptoe and kissed Tammad's cheek. They'd sent someone to tell Murdock I was all right they said, and then they had to leave to go back to what they'd been doing. We arranged to meet again after things had quieted down a little, and then Tammad and I went searching for a calm corner where we could sit down and talk.

When I looked into the lounge I was hoping it was empty, but the answer turned out to be, no such luck. Instead of being empty the room held quite a few *w'wendaa* guarding a number of prisoners, and as soon as they saw me a cheer went up.

"*Chama*, we knew you could not have been slain!" one of the women said for all of them, coming forward with pleasure in her mind. "These *darayse* are naught, and far from the ability required to best you. We feared only that they had harmed you with unfair means."

"They tried, but happily they didn't make it," I answered, speaking in Centran as I stepped farther into the room because the *w'wendaa* had. Apparently all of our force had been equipped with both languages, and—

"Hey, sweet thing, how about putting in a word for me?" a voice called, startling me into looking around to see Kel-Ten getting to his feet. His gold outfit was dirty and sweat-stained, and a small line of dried blood showed at the corner of his mouth. "After all these hours, I think I'm getting tired of being patient."

"It's all right," I said to the *w'wenda* nearest him who was reaching for her sword, then moved a few steps closer. "I'm sure the First Prime will prove to be no enemy—once the drugs and conditioning are removed from him."

"And there's probably more of it to remove than even *I* thought," he said with a grimace, relief showing in his mind when the *w'wenda* took her hand from her hilt. "I spent hours asking myself why you'd left without me—and then got around to wondering why you'd found it possible to go alone when I hadn't. I didn't know then what sort of mind you really had, but the question was enough to start me thinking. When I faced you across the training room and felt you ordering me to have patience instead of begging me to forgive you, I knew something was going on. I thought starting a riot was the least I could do, especially after you'd gotten them ready for it by shaking them up. We were so far into it we almost got cut down by these people of yours, but they seemed to know it wasn't them we were after."

"They're good at knowing things like that," I agreed with a nod. "When they finally get things straightened out enough to turn you loose, check with one of the technicians before you use a chef to get anything to eat or drink. I know they intend getting rid of the drug programming, but I don't know when they'll have time for it. If they haven't gotten around to it, use someone not in the memory to order for you."

I started to turn away from him, relieved to have gotten through the conversation so easily, but he wasn't through. He put a hand on my arm to stop me, and when I looked up at him he grinned.

"Speaking about the drugs and what they do to you, I—ah—still have something of a problem," he said, the hand on my arm squeezing suggestively. "Since you still owe me for what I did for you, how about the two of us going back to my apartment where you can—see to my problem."

He began to send me the heat in his mind, a heat that had more personal choice than drug-induced need behind it, but I didn't get the chance to throw it back at him the way I wanted to. A thick arm reached over my left shoulder, the hand attached to the arm closing on his throat, and suddenly heat wasn't the main problem on Kel-Ten's mind.

"Should you wish the touching of my woman, you must first face and best *me*," Tammad said, his calm tone widening the eyes of the man he held by the throat. "Such a doing is called offering a challenge, and in no manner will you find me reluctant to answer. Is this what you wish, to offer a challenge?"

It was right then that I discovered how satisfying—and amusing—it can be to have a certain someone take care of certain annoyances for you. Kel-Ten's mind darted to Tammad's, took one good look, then flinched back in a hurry. At that point in time Kel-Ten was slightly stronger than the barbarian, but only because he had trained and practiced so long. He had no trouble recognizing a mind that had the potential of being *much* stronger, and wanted nothing to do with a mind like that—or the sword worn by the body surrounding the mind. When he shook his head, Tammad let him go with a small push, sending him back to sprawl again on the couch where he'd been sitting.

"Outworlders are clearly more than foolish," the *w'wenda* standing to my right said to Kel-Ten, grinning faintly at the way he rubbed at his throat. "Think you our *Chama* is unprotected in matters not concerning the power? Such is the purpose of the *l'lenda* who bands her, to see to her safety at times her *w'wendaa* cannot. To her go the duties of the mind, to him the duty of the sword. To protect one of such importance is a duty fit only for the best of the best, which we have learned this *l'lenda* is. You, too, I think, have now learned the same."

The look Kel-Ten shot Tammad was *not* one of awed respect, but I barely noticed that in the midst of the—pleasure—pride—flattered happiness—that was coming in waves from the man standing beside me. I didn't quite understand what that meant, so once we had left the lounge I decided to find out.

"Have you given up your plans to be *denday* of *dendayy?*" I asked, trying not to dread the answer. "You seemed to be so pleased with what that *w'wenda* said about you, but I thought . . ."

"*Hama*, I have *not* given over my ambitions," he said with a smile, sending me reassurance. "My people now no longer need protection from those who would use them badly, yet is there still the matter of adjustment to consider. They will require guidance and assistance, aid I mean to see they have."

"But the woman spoke of you as nothing but my protector," I said as we moved along the hall, more confused than ever. "If you still have plans to be much more than that, why weren't you insulted?"

"I felt no insult for the reason that I, too, consider the matter of your protection to be greatly important," he said, stopping us where we were so that he could make me look up at him. "Think you there are any about who would joy to see your life held in the hands of one with little or no skill? Such a one is not I even should there be others, but *wenda*—do none in your worlds have *two* tasks of great importance which they see to? Such things are not *easily* done, yet are they possible of accomplishment. Do you feel I would seek to shirk one or the other?"

I shook my head as I leaned against him, holding him around as he held me. Most men, I felt, would have considered being my bodyguard a menial task, especially if they happened to be important in their own right. That Tammad looked at it differently—and more wonderfully—was not that much of a surprise, but hearing him say it only reminded me that I also had something to say.

"*Hamak,* I have to tell you something," I whispered after a moment, really wishing I *didn't* have to. "Help me find some place private where we can talk."

He smoothed my hair as he looked down at me, concern in his mind as well as his eyes, but he didn't argue. It took us a while to find a small lounge that wasn't being used for something else, but once we did we closed the door and sat down on a couch to hold each other around. I didn't know if he could feel the fear in me, but before it turned me speechless I started the story of the child that had been ours. By the time I was through I was crying, my shield closed tight to keep his reactions from me, the reactions I was very much afraid would be hatred and disgust. He held me tight to his chest as he stroked my hair, his silence more painful than what had been done to me in the complex, and then he sighed.

"*Hama,* this tale you tell distresses me greatly," he said, very little life left in his voice. "I had not understood the reason for your own distress over my not having told you of my intentions to reclaim you from your embassy, yet is my understanding now more than clear. A man who wishes the child he has planted retains the *wenda* who carries it. To send her from him, most especially with no other there to band her, is to say he wishes naught of the child. I had not known I had put such agony on you, and nearly do I lack the courage to once more ask your forgiveness."

"*My* forgiveness?" I blurted, raising my head to look at him. "But the child was *yours*, and I never even told you about it! If you'd known you probably would have told me what *you* were doing, and all this grief could have been avoided."

"And yet, I did not then look upon you as I do now," he said, raising one hand to stroke my face. "Then you were beloved yet no more than a *wenda*, and no *l'lenda* has need of sharing his intentions with one such as that. This tragedy was given life in the same manner a child is—by the combined doings of two. Perhaps best would be that we share the burden, and in such a manner lighten it each for the other. You say you have already taken the lives of those responsible for our loss?"

"Some of them," I answered, opening my shield to find that he *was* grieving rather than blaming. "There are others also responsible, and if they survive the attack on their headquarters on Central, I think we ought to pay them a visit."

"*L'lenda wenda*," he said with a faint smile, taking my face in both of his hands. "Indeed are you changed from the woman I knew, changed in a manner I had not thought would please me. No longer do you accuse me of all manner of odd doings, no longer do you seek to disobey me in all things, no longer do you deny the love you feel. And I, I am fully as changed as you, for no longer do I feel your obedience necessary to my happiness, and no longer do I wish to discount what council you give me as foolishness. Much pain did we both need to suffer to accomplish these ends, yet have we finally and in truth accomplished them."

He lowered his head and kissed me then, knowing I wanted him to, but I discovered he'd made more progress in reading emotions than I'd thought. The kiss only continued for a minute or two, and then he raised his head.

"Something continues to disturb you," he said, trying to look at me with his mind as well as his eyes. "I feel the presence of the disturbance, yet am I unable to reach its cause. Will you speak of the matter to me?"

"I don't think I should," I answered, leaning forward to put my cheek against his chest. "That last time I mentioned this problem to you you refused to listen, which made me do some things to force you to go along, which eventually got me spanked. I don't care for the idea of getting spanked again."

"*Hama,* you cannot mean that you continue to feel we must part!" he protested, more confused than angry. "After all we have faced, both together and apart, how are you able to believe such a thing?"

"Do you think the choice is mine?" I asked in turn, raising my head to look at him. "You may be a heartless, overgrown barbarian who spanks the woman foolish enough to love him, but that's a habit that can be broken and there are plenty of men around with worse faults. I don't *want* to believe what I'm feeling, but preferences don't seem to matter."

"I cannot see how such a thing may be," he said with a shake of his head, anger and frustration finally getting a grip on him. "Who is there about capable of taking you from me? Who might there possibly be to lure *me* from *your* side?"

"I think you're sounding a little too interested in that second question," I said, narrowing my eyes at him. "Maybe what I'm being told is that I'll catch you fooling around with another woman, and because of that I'll drop a building on your head."

"Such jealousy does not become you, *hama,*" he said with a grin, really enjoying the way I was feeling. "Each time you imagine me of interest to another, you speak of doing me harm. I, however, in greater generosity, speak only of doing harm to he who might take you from me. Clearly are *l'lendaa* possessed of more generous natures than *wendaa.*"

"Oh, *sure* they are," I said with a very slow nod. "Their natures are so generous, they feel it's their duty to share themselves with every female who walks, staggers or crawls past them. Unfair as it undoubtedly is, people with natures like that do sometimes come to a bad end."

"There is but one end I currently find of interest, *hama sadendra,*" he said, his grin still there as he pulled me down flat on the couch with him. "Try though I might,

I cannot envision any other end ever taking my fancy as does the one I possess. Though duty may call me a thousand times, ever shall I return to the end which is mine."

"*How* many times?" I demanded in a growl, raising my hands to bury my fists in his hair. "If nature doesn't kill you, duty has a damned good second shot at it!"

He laughed aloud then held me still for his kiss, and it wasn't long before I was rushing to get out of the brown uniform. We'd teased each other about jealousy and then made very strenuous love, but that doesn't mean we erased the cloud of the child we'd lost—or forgot the probability that we'd never have the chance to make one to replace it.

The day after the attack was calmer than the previous night had been, and I spent the morning working with some of the community's people trying to get through the conditioning of the female Primes. It was a job very much like pulling out teeth using nothing but fingers; we knew what we wanted to do, but couldn't seem to get a good enough grip to accomplish it.

While I was occupied with frustration, Tammad and a large number of our fighters went to sort out the mess in the smaller building that was a short distance from the main complex. A couple of crash teams had entered it at the same time different ones had entered the main complex, but all they did then was disable every mechanical system in the place except for what was labeled life-support. Most of the personnel in that building had been locked in their apartments or rooms for the night, and were going to be tackled one or two at a time. I would have preferred going along with Tammad, but the stubborn beast decided I couldn't and that was that. With the only fighting likely to occur being physical in nature he did have a point, but point or not I didn't like it.

He and most of the others were back by lunchtime looking very little the worse for wear, so he and I found Rissim and Irin, and we four went back to racking our brains while we ate. Our little group had done the same the night before, but we were coming up with so much nothing you would have thought we were a full committee. I *knew* I would never belong to Tammad but I didn't know *why*, and none of us could come up with a reason for it—or a suggestion as to how it might be avoided.

We had just reached the point of agreeing that what was causing my conviction might very well be that Tammad and I were destined to die of frustration—with Irin and Rissim joining us—when one of the expedition people came to interrupt. Murdock sent his compliments, and asked that I join him for a short while to discuss something important. I couldn't remember ever receiving someone's compliments before and was tempted to return my criticisms along with my agreement, but I was the only one who considered the situation amusing. Irin immediately decided he was about to send me off somewhere again—the hidden reason behind my feeling we hadn't known about before—and promptly stood up with the very clear intention of committing murder. Rissim also stood, mainly with the intention of keeping her from doing anything foolish, but part of him was sharing her urge toward violence if it turned out her guess was right. Tammad made it a threesome when *he* got to his feet, and it wasn't even necessary to touch his mind; the way he stood very straight but loose, as though he might need to draw his sword at any minute, the lack of all expression on his face, the cold, distant look in his eyes . . .

I sighed before I got up, but sighing didn't accomplish anything at all. I still had three grim silences following me as I followed Murdock's messenger, giving me the feeling I was casting a triple shadow.

The room we were led to was in the executive wing, a large, poshly decorated setup meant for party-meetings rather than just meetings, and Murdock turned out not to be alone. Ashton was there and so was Lamdon, and with them was the woman from the group who investigated mental abilities. Our guide led us in then left after closing the door, and Murdock showed one of his wintry smiles.

"I hadn't expected you to have an escort, Terrilian," he said from the chair he sat in, his mind more amused than his expression showed. "I'm somewhat surprised there are no *w'wendaa* as well."

"If it's a *w'wenda* you want, I may soon oblige you,

brother,'' Irin said, stepping forward to stand beside me. ''What is it that you want from her this time?''

''He doesn't necessarily want something from her, Irin,'' Ashton put in from her chair to Murdock's right, obviously trying to soothe her sister. ''You three look like we intend dismantling her to find out where her power comes from. Has any of you any idea how much strength *that* would take?''

''I do,'' I said, trying to keep it light. ''Especially after the meal I just had. I must be fueled for a month, not to speak of against all comers.''

''Why don't all of you sit down,'' Murdock suggested, nodding toward the half circle of empty chairs facing the four already occupied. ''You all know Lamdon and Kaila and they know you, so what need is there for us to act like a group of strangers?''

''At the moment there's *no* need,'' Irin said, not conceding an inch of ground. ''If that happens to change, you'll be the first to know.''

She headed herself to the chair to the left of the one I was taking, but she and I were the only ones who sat. I didn't have to turn around to know Tammad and Rissim had stationed themselves behind my chair, and the small, satisified smile on Irin's face said she knew it, too. Three of the four people sitting opposite us were clearly dying to ask what was going on, but the show was Murdock's and he was more interested in getting on with it.

''Terrilian, I asked you to come here so that you might be told a number of things,'' he said, ''and one of the items should be of interest to Irin as well. I would like to begin by informing you that our strike at Rathmore Hellman and his people was just as successful as our enterprise here. An interim deputy now holds his chair, one of our people, I might add, and very soon there will be places for many of ours in the government. We mean to see that those of our blood are never captured and used again.''

''She doesn't want to go back to Central, and she doesn't want to work in your government,'' Irin said flatly, staring at Murdock. ''What she wants is to stay on Rimilia.''

"A gratifying decision, inasmuch as Rimilia is where she will be most needed," Murdock replied politely, almost distracted enough to be puzzled. "We mean to build a relocation center there, to house those of our nonassociated brothers and sisters who wish to join us, as well as the current residents of crèches. From now on we will train our own blood, *without* the conditioning which makes tools of them."

"And don't forget about the retraining of the residents of this building and its basement hideaway," Ashton said, for a moment sounding bone-deep weary. "I think we'd all better plan on living *very* long lives."

"Each problem will be seen to in its own time," Murdock said, sounding serenely confident. "With the help of the Rimilians themselves, we'll build something worth being a part of. But we also have an additional goal now, and I yield the floor to Kaila so that she may tell you what she so recently told me."

"Our group has done some investigating, questioning, guessing and concluding, and I'm wondering where to start," Kaila said, smiling at me as she shifted in her chair. "I don't know if anyone's told you, Terry, but our community was established on Rimilia because one of us at the time discovered that a number of Rimilians had mind abilities very like our own. Not only were we able to hide on the planet, we were also able to bring in strong new blood to add to ours. At the very beginning males were needed for the high percentage of females born, and when some of our girls got old enough they went out with *l'lendaa* to protect them and looked for men to take back as mates. Quite a lot of them were dark-haired and green-eyed, and that's why those traits are so highly prized among Rimilians even today."

"Indeed," Rissim said, drawing a flash of amusement from Lamdon. "What *l'lenda* would fail to prize a woman with the power, to have in his furs if for naught else."

"There are additional considerations, of course," Tammad said in agreement, "yet would that point alone be sufficient."

"Yes," Kaila said after clearing her throat, knowing

they were teasing her, but also knowing better than to continue on with the subject. "We were rather upset, to say the least, when we learned Rathmore Hellman's group meant to use the planet, but there was nothing we dared do to stop it. It wasn't beyond Rathmore to cause an 'accident' that would decimate the population of the world if he didn't get the cooperation he wanted. Murdock will tell you more about that in a little while, so I'll just skip to what happened with you and your abilities, Terry."

I nodded as I dialed the chair for a glass of wine, wondering if I would like what I was about to hear. I knew what had happened to me better than she did, but she seemed to be looking at the scenes with more information than I had.

"You started out with nothing more in the way of ability than any other Prime, but that soon changed," Kaila said to me, her smile still warm and friendly. "Thanks to Murdock's planning you were allowed to remain awake when you first returned from Rimilia, and his theory—that our people didn't develop in their talents because of being unawakened most of the time—was proven almost immediately. According to your own account you began discovering the possibility of a shield as far back as your assignment on Alderan, which was really the beginning of it."

"A beginning fraught with disturbance for one who knew not what was occurring," Lamdon said, empathy flowing from his mind to mine. "Another might well have retreated from that unknown; your courage does you credit, girl."

"After that you progressed slowly, until the time of your struggle in the resting place of the Sword," Kaila went on, giving me no chance to correct Lamdon. *I* didn't have courage; all I had was stubbornness. "You were given quite a lot of pain because of the storms raging at the time, storms you'd never grown used to because you weren't raised on Rililia."

"You know, I never thought of that," I said slowly, ignoring the glass of wine my chair had produced for me. "If you people live in that area all the time, those storms must make your lives absolute hell. How can any of you stand it?''

''After the first few, the storms never bother us,'' Kaila answered, her voice soft and her eyes alive with the sense of imparting something important. ''Terry, those of us born in the valley develop a shield during our first storm season. The shield is like the one you developed after your battle, the sort you call impenetrable. Those of us who are raised off-planet are—*suggested* out of using the shield until we're adults, and can judge the times to use it without detection. Those who grow up on the planet use it constantly, especially during storm season, and none of us ever develop that light shield you told us about. You proved we're capable of developing it by teaching Len how to form one, but none of us ever do. If Len hadn't had us make him forget about his heavier shield when he knew he'd be working with you, we might have thought you were unique.''

''But—I don't understand,'' I said, shaking my head at her. ''What can shielding have to do with anything? A shield *stops* you from using your abilities.''

''It does more than that,'' she said, dialing her own chair for refreshment. ''You gave us so many of the answers, I'm surprised we took so long. Look, let's start from another side. Do you remember what you said about how you called up your curtain? You said you had to feel a *need* for it, and then it was there. Quite a lot of what you developed came about because of need, and not necessarily to save you from danger or hurt. Once the change had started you simply had to feel a need for something, and if it was possible for you to do, you did it. *Need* is the key for developing talents, not pain but *need.*''

''But that's good news,'' I said, still not quite understanding. ''I'm delighted to hear none of you have to go through what I did, but I still don't understand what any of this has to do with shielding.''

''We think we may have run across a principle similar to that governing speech,'' she said, sipping at her kimla while keeping her eyes on me. ''If a child doesn't learn to talk by a certain age, it never learns. It's possible that the development of a light shield is a necessary step in progressing further with our abilities, and that may be why we're stopped where we are. We never go through the light shield phase, and because of the presence of our heavy shields we rarely feel the *need* for more. Those two factors together, we believe, have kept us from doing what you did."

"Then none of you can move up to where I am?" I asked, reaching for the wine I hadn't touched earlier. I was beginning to feel alone again, and this time *really* didn't want to.

"We won't be sure until we try, but we have cause for hope," she answered, this time joining Lamdon in sending me reassurance. "The fact that Len was able to develop that light shield has turned us ecstatic, because when some of *us* tried we were able to do the same thing. What we'll have to do is force ourselves to give up our heavy shields, then start all over from the beginning using the key you gave us. If we're successful the heavy shields will develop again when we *need* them, and by then they won't be the equivalent of cloth wrapped around our feet in childhood."

Every female in the room must have flinched at that comment, referring to a former practice of one small segment of the style-conscious population of Alderan. For a few years some of the women had been binding the feet of their girl children in an effort to give them "delightfully dainty" feet, having no idea what they were really doing until those children began growing.

"And, of course, we'd like your help when we start the experiments," Kaila said, her sense of optimism strong and real. "Not only did you give us the key we were looking for, but you've also opened our eyes to something we should have seen long ago. Would have seen, too, if we weren't still basing our beliefs on the nonsense put out by those idiots on Central. Terry, would you like to tell me what we of the blood are?"

"Why—we're empaths," I answered, immediately trying to figure out what she was talking about *this* time. "We're a bunch of human beings born with the empathetic ability."

"Something we've always been told and can even

prove,'' she said with a nod, the cup of kimla at her lips doing nothing to hide her amusement. ''Now tell me this: what does healing, and precognition, and telekinesis and—something we haven't even named yet that increases a person's thinking and planning ability—got to do with empathy? You can do all the rest of that, you know. Ashton saw you doing some of it. The balance you told us about yourself.''

''When did I ever increase anyone's thinking and planning ability?'' I demanded, then took a good swallow of the wine I held. With my head spinning the way it was, those were the only two things I could *think* of doing.

''Ashton saw you doing it with our strategy and tactics people,'' Kaila said gently, throttling back her amusement. ''They were having all sorts of problems with details until *you* got there, and then everything began clearing away like magic. Our approach to the complex, the number and size of the transports we needed, who would command where, how the complex residents were to be handled—one thing after another just fell into place, letting us move faster and more efficiently than any of us thought we could. All because you were in a hurry to get the attack going and *needed* it done.''

''Just like you *needed* the attack on the *Chama*'s palace in Vediaster,'' Ashton put in, her own amusement more evident. ''When we were there, I heard someone mention how well their planning had gone with you there. And in case you were about to ask, that block you removed from Leelan was very fine telekinesis. No need to look so surprised. If you think back, I'm sure you'll come across some other instances when you did the same things without knowing it.''

I wasn't surprised; I was stunned, but being stunned didn't stop me from remembering more than one odd incident—the conversations I'd had with Garth, the unexplained insight Dallan kept showing—hell, I could even remember getting answers I needed from my own reflection in a goblet! It was all very unsettling, but Kaila ignored my state of mind as she leaned forward with a smile.

''You've proven to us that all the talents we've been

considering odd residuals are just part of the whole picture,'' she said, and again her voice was gentle but firm with conviction. ''Empathy isn't all there is to it, it's just the *first* thing we can do, the crawling that comes before the ability to walk. Even if it turns out that *we* can't go back and start over, our children and children's children won't have that problem.''

''And also must we investigate more closely the differences between Centran and Rimilian abilities,'' Lamdon put in, looking very pleased. ''We who are part of the community have learned Centran ways, doing naught with that which was given us by our own. Your *memabrak* has been forced to finding his own way about much as were you, *wenda*, with results somewhat different from what has been considered the norm. His efforts were, of course, necessitated by your presence, therefore must we thank you for this as well.''

Tammad's hand came to my shoulder and squeezed gently, a gesture of approval and agreement according to his thoughts. *Everyone* seemed to be looking at me with the same sort of reaction, which was an odd incident all by itself. The reaction I evoked in people wasn't usually approval, and I didn't know how wise I would be getting used to it.

''And now would seem to be the time to point out the reason for all these happenings,'' Murdock said, shifting just a very small amount in his chair. ''A Prime was needed to do the job Rathmore Hellman wanted done, and that's why Terrilian was sent with Tammad to Rimilia. That single decision was meant only to save Rimilia and yet it precipitated events which caused all the rest, Rathmore's downfall included. For many years I've sought the reason for my having had to bring very great pain to my own flesh and blood, and most of that reason was just given you. The final point is that now *we* have the opportunity of righting the wrongs done by those who were our enemy, of establishing a government capable of *feeling* the needs of the people it governs, not simply assuming what we believe those needs should be. For this, also, we have Terrilian to thank, and Irin and Rissim as well, for the sacrifice they made. There was indeed a reason, and now we know it in full."

To say Murdock glowed would not be completely accurate, but his mind was certainly lighter and brighter than I'd ever before seen it. Irin was staring at him in an effort to maintain stubborn anger, but the anger was dissolving too fast for her to keep it together. If everything they'd said turned out to be true, our forced separation would bring benefit to uncounted numbers of people. Since we weren't missing knowing each other entirely, there was a lot of room for forgiveness.

"Well, that seems to settle most of it," I said, standing up as Ashton, Kaila and Lamdon did the same. "Now maybe we can get back to kicking around a problem that isn't quite planetary in scale."

"What problem?" Ashton asked while Tammad came over to put his arm around me. "Come to think of it, you four *have* been spending an awful lot of time with your heads together. For a while Murdock and I were afraid you were planning a revolution of your own."

"We're not really into revolution," I said with a headshake, wondering if Ashton was capable of being serious for longer than fifteen minutes at a stretch. "And what we *have* come up with is so meager, I can't say I think much of that planning-enhancer ability you claim I have. With all the skull-sweat we've put into it, we should have had an answer by now."

"Maybe you four aren't capable of coming up with an answer," Kaila said, her wrinkle-browed expression showing she wasn't trying to be insulting. "Possibly the person you enhance has to have the ability to do the answering to begin with. If it's a technical problem, you may not have that sort of expertise among you."

"In a manner of speaking, our difficulty is precisely that," Tammad put in, his thoughts pleasantly surprised. "The woman is possessed of a conviction, one we have thus far found no basis for, yet is there no doubt within her concerning its veracity. Should we be unable to resolve it, all we have attained will be meaningless for us."

"Then let's get Murdock working on it," Ashton said, immediately turning brisk and efficient. "I've been watching him develop convictions for years, so he's the expert you need."

"What's this?" Murdock asked as we turned to him, Irin and Rissim coming over to join us. "What is it I'm needed for?"

"Murdock, Terry is sure something is going to keep her and Tammad from being together," Irin blurted, looking at her brother anxiously. "She doesn't know what, but the feeling is so strong she can't simply forget about it. What are they going to do?"

"I get nothing of the same myself," Murdock answered with a frown, his stare unfocused, and then he was silent for a moment before asking, "Is that precisely the conviction you have, Terrilian? That you and Tammad will not be together?"

"Just about," I admitted, more disappointed at his lack of immediate help than was rational or reasonable. "Not long ago it came to me that I would never belong to him, and the feeling refuses to go away."

Murdock shook his head helplessly, frustration strong in him, which made my disappointment even stronger. I was just about ready to suggest we simply give up, when suddenly Ashton began laughing. She was so truly and completely amused that all we could do was stare at her, and finally she noticed the silence and shook her head.

"What were you saying about your *'so-called'* talent?" she asked me, still chuckling and enjoying herself. "I don't think I ever got an answer this fast in my entire life, not even after all the experience I've had with Murdock."

"What are you talking about?" Irin asked her in annoyance, starting to get angry. "Terry's life is about to fall apart and you think it's *funny?*"

" 'Interpretation is the key to precognition,' " Ashton answered as though she were quoting, giving her sister a grin. "She said she would never *belong* to him, which is completely Rimilian and absolutely true. The conviction isn't telling her she won't *stay* with him, it's saying she won't *belong* to him. To Rimilian men women are belongings, but I saw myself that Tammad now thinks of her more as a companion adventurer. She'll never be his belonging again, but that doesn't mean they won't belong to each other."

I turned to look up at Tammad in shock, and when he felt in my mind that Ashton was absolutely right he let out a whoop of delight and reached down to lift me off my feet. He danced me around the room for a minute, laughing as hard as I was while I squeezed my arms tight around his neck, and then he stopped so he might kiss me. Together we made it a very long kiss, and when it was finally over we looked at each other.

"My happiness is now complete," he said, still touching my lips with his. "The woman I have desired so long is now forever mine."

"Only because you're also hers," I reminded him with a grin, holding his broad face between my hands. "Now we have all the time we need, and I'm going to use that time to good purpose. Of course, you'll have to do your part if it's to work. It takes two to make children, you know."

His grin widened as his eyes began to shine, and then he kissed me again with a silent vow that he would make all the children in the world if I wanted them.

Beloved barbarian. He did.

DAW